BEHIND THE VEIL

KATHRYN NOLAN

That's What She Said Publishing, Inc.

This book is dedicated to my dog Walter, whose adoption day (December 8th) was right in the middle of Behind the Veil's many drafts. Thank you for distracting me, ripping up half of my writer's notebook, eating my couch and sitting on my laptop when you wanted my attention.

I couldn't have done it without you.

1

HENRY

Oxford, England

"More whiskey, Henry?" Bernard asked, holding up a tumbler of amber liquid.

"Certainly," I replied, gripping the glass to keep my fingers still. Part of me needed the liquor to quiet my rattling nerves.

Part of me worried I'd never keep the whiskey down. Not with what I was about to do.

"Lovely conversation as always," Bernard mused, standing up with his cane to place another log in his fireplace. I was the remaining guest at tonight's dinner party; an event he held every week for a variety of distinguished faculty and visitors. But I was usually the last person to leave, content to share a glass of whiskey with my mentor as the fire died down. "Elizabeth seems able to discuss Plato until we're all blue in the face, although I love a good debate over *The Republic* as much as the next person."

"I agree," I managed, even as my heart leapt in my throat. Bernard Allerton was the most famous librarian in the world. He was remarkably brilliant and possessed a visionary spirit that had done more for the field of antiquities than any other. For the past decade, he had also been my boss and close personal mentor.

And tonight I was here to accuse him of being a thief.

I watched him struggle to lift the log with gnarled fingers and spotted hands. At seventy, Bernard Allerton still commanded the attention of everyone in the room; he had a silver mustache and piercing eyes that never missed a single detail. But his limp had increased this past year, the hunch in his back more pronounced. His cane was an ever-present accessory now. It was hard to believe such a man would ever have the audacity to *age*—yet even I had to admit his spryness was ebbing away.

The effort it took him to lift a single log evoked such a wave of sympathy I almost didn't say the words.

"Maybe next week," he began, slightly out of breath, "I'll invite that new history professor—"

"*Tamerlane* is missing, Bernard," I said.

There was a distinct shake in my voice. Even so, the words hung like a solitary gunshot in the air. He went absolutely still at the fireplace, the log forgotten.

"I'm sorry?" he said. "I didn't quite hear you."

He didn't turn around. A few seconds ticked by as I gathered my courage.

"The library's copy of *Tamerlane and Other Poems* is missing. Gone. Unless you stored it someplace different and forgot to tell me?"

He drummed his fingers on the mantle. "A book can't just *disappear*, Henry. It must be somewhere."

"That's the thing," I continued. "It was supposed to be stored for cleaning for another few months, per the conservation calendar." A calendar that I kept. "But a professor at

Oxford requested a viewing so I went searching for it earlier than scheduled."

It was a crucial misstep on Bernard's part; a vital unraveling of the threads of fate that had me exposing the flaw in his careful crime.

"I don't know how—" he said, sounding frail. He hunched over as though I'd struck him.

"I know you took it."

Regret tightened my throat. I'd practiced those words in the mirror a dozen times this morning, but they still sounded foreign to my ears. Because I *wanted* Bernard to be innocent.

My mentor was curved over the fireplace, looking sickly.

"I know you *stole it.* And I've been watching you. You've taken much more than the *Tamerlane.* You've stolen—"

"Stop talking."

Bernard's tone was sharp as glass.

In slow motion, I watched him pull his spine straighter than I'd seen it in years. He let his cane fall to the ground with a *whack.* Then he turned to me with a look of mocking bemusement. If a herd of zebras had swarmed through the room, I wouldn't have been more surprised, more appalled at the transformation happening before my eyes.

My frail, benevolent mentor appeared to be aging *backward.* And when his narrowed, piercing eyes assessed me, they clearly found me lacking.

He laughed.

My fingers gripped the chair, attempting to tether myself to some kind of reality. "I'm hard-pressed to find the humor here, Bernard."

"For someone so young, you certainly do have poor short-term memory," he said, smiling. He strode confidently through his flat into a back office. He returned with a sheet of crisp, white paper. "I was really hoping I wouldn't have to remind you of this. But you've left me no choice."

I sat forward in my chair. "What are you talking about?"

With one finger—and a taunting arch of his brow—he slid the paper across the gleaming mahogany table until it was right in front of me. "I'm surprised you've forgotten."

I read the words on the page. Fear slithered up my spine.

"This is to confirm that the following work, Tamerlane and Other Poems by Edgar Allen Poe, has been officially withdrawn from the McMasters Library of Oxford as part of a recent de-accession."

Books that had been withdrawn from libraries were free to be sold and bought by the public—a rare book dealer would take this as proof that the manuscript had been purchased legally.

And at the bottom of the sheet, *my* signature: *"Dr. Henry Finch, Special Collections Librarian."*

I looked up at Bernard, who seemed to flutter before my eyes like a bad hologram.

Blink: Bernard the visionary. My mentor. My professional hero.

Blink again: Bernard the criminal. Bernard the *forger*.

A deluge of contradicting memories washed over me. He was the consummate host, and these weekly dinners were like a modern-day salon—a place where philosophy and politics were discussed over glasses of fine wine. It wasn't odd for him to refer to me as his "young successor" at these dinners, confirming what every staff member at the McMasters Library already knew.

But I had thought Bernard Allerton had taken me under his wing for a purpose: to ensure I could take his place as Head Librarian when the time came for him to retire.

And now the truth hit me in the face like a bucket of freezing ice water.

Bernard had taken me under his wing so I could take the fall for him if he needed it. He had made me *complicit* in these crimes.

"I've…I've been watching you," I said, voice shaking harder now. "I have proof. I'll tell the police I didn't sign this."

Bernard shrugged, removing a piece of lint from his cuffs. In the span of three minutes, Bernard now appeared ten years younger. "That's of no concern to me, Henry. I'll tell them that you did."

My mouth was dry. "There are others. I've been inventorying our collection. Pages, sections, whole books are gone now. *You* took them."

Even as I'd prepared to confront my boss this evening, I had doubted myself. I wasn't a detective, I wasn't a police officer—what did I know about gathering evidence? And I'd seen this man cradle rare manuscripts as though they were newborn infants: with the greatest care, with the greatest love. He inspired me to seek greatness every single day, to value rarity above all else.

Had that been fake too?

"And I have similar letters with *your* signature for every single item." He took a deliberate sip of whiskey. When he leaned forward, his next words dripped with condescension. "Don't make the mistake of thinking I'm an amateur, Dr. Finch."

A powerlessness shuddered through my entire body. I hadn't considered anything past my confrontation with Bernard—because deep down, I'd hoped to be either wrong or witness to a tearful confession and a promise to change.

So stupid.

"This is bigger than you," he continued. He stared at me, pinning me to the spot. The air crackled. How could I ever have thought this man was weak and frail? "And I know you have student loan debt from your many advanced degrees. I know how little librarians make when they're first starting out." He shook his head dramatically. "Poor Henry, living far away from his family in England, trying to make some extra money to pay the bills."

Bernard's face was blank, chilling, as he lied.

"What the *fuck* are you talking about?" I croaked.

"I'm reminding you of the story I'll be glad to tell the police, should you do what I believe you are about to do."

"*None* of that is true, and you know it." I reached for my phone, prepared to call the police anyway and give them everything I had on my boss. I expected to see him panic, but my move only seemed to strengthen that bizarre smile.

"Henry, in the ten years we've known each other, have I ever led you astray? Professionally-speaking?" he asked, crossing his ankle over one knee.

"No," I replied, my voice a wispy thread now.

"So, listen to me when I tell you that what you *think* you uncovered is happening throughout our industry in record numbers," he said softly. "We have a very special occupation, Henry, with *very special* access. The works we are responsible for are an expensive commodity."

I leaned forward, matching his tone. "The works we are responsible for belong to the *public* and should be free for anyone to see."

"Five million dollars," he replied.

I shook my head, picked up my phone again.

"Five million dollars is what I expect to receive from the *Tamerlane*. There's a reason why I have four houses in four countries, Henry. The travel, the thrill, the excitement, *all the bloody money*." He was grinning wildly now, practically *vibrat-*

ing. "You have two intriguing options this evening. You can call the police—and I will provide them with all of those signed letters you forged before selling off the library's books." Bernard held up one finger, then a second. "Or you and I can sell this book together."

My mind blazed with thoughts of piles and piles of money. Five million dollars was an amount I couldn't truly comprehend. Not once in my entire career had I ever considered simply *taking* one of the rare manuscripts I was responsible for. It was as if Bernard had suddenly developed the ability to control my mind—showing me images and desires I'd never once entertained.

My thumb hesitated on my phone, lulled by the siren song of millions of dollars.

"Did you really intend on being a librarian your entire life?" he prodded.

But I refused to answer him, even as the growing restlessness I'd felt this past year tugged at his words. A restlessness I hadn't quite known what to do with—this sudden need for adventure was shaped so differently from my other passions. I'd left Philadelphia for England to complete my PhD in Library Science at the University of Oxford working at various libraries throughout Europe before securing the job with Bernard at the McMasters Library. So this recent agitation didn't entirely make sense to me because I'd just spent the past ten years traveling through famous cities and handling some of the rarest manuscripts in the entire world.

"Suit yourself, then," he finally sighed. "It's only truly a crime if you get caught."

I took in the man in front of me—famous in his own right, rich as sin, a celebrated philanthropist. A beloved academic.

That sense of powerlessness reared back, but I shook my head, standing up. Bernard didn't control my mind.

And he *couldn't* control what I was about to do. "I don't care what you say," I said harshly. "I'm going to the police now. And I'm calling Louisa." She was the president of our board. And now I was cursing my own cowardice with not going to her first, cursing the respect I'd carried for Bernard Allerton that had apparently been blinding me for years.

With a smirk, he reached beneath the table, as if pressing something.

His phone rang—a shrill explosion of sound in the hushed room. Someone knocked on his door.

"Enter," he called to the space behind me. Then he answered his phone with a casual, "Good evening, Louisa. We were just talking about you."

Goosebumps broke out over my skin.

Bernard's sharp gaze narrowed past my shoulders. He crooked his finger, and the skin on the back of my neck prickled.

"Oh," he said—and even I could hear the mock sympathy. "I am so sorry to hear that. How absolutely awful." I strained to listen, then stopped when I turned and was confronted with a scowling bodyguard that towered over me.

Since when did Bernard have *bodyguards*?

"Louisa," I said loudly, hoping she could hear me over the phone, "Bernard has taken the—"

He tapped the paper—the forged document that implicated me in the theft of a book so rare only fifty copies existed in the world.

With a growl, I reached forward to grab it.

The guard stopped me.

Bernard wagged his finger like I was a petulant child. Fury, anger, shame, guilt—all of it welled up inside of me, causing my fists to clench and my vision to darken.

But Bernard was smug and safe with the guard looming behind him.

"So, you're saying our intern *just* discovered the *Tamerlane* is missing?" Bernard said. My mind leapt with this new information. I started to back away, toward the door, toward whatever decision I was going to make next. "Louisa, I hate to jump to conclusions, but this kind of theft usually starts with the staff. The *lower* staff."

I was awestruck at how deeply off the rails this confrontation had gone.

In the middle of the room, Bernard Allerton stood like a newly crowned king, surrounded by his many books, a decadent fire roaring behind him.

"Yes, I know," he said soothingly into the phone, "it is horrible when we discover how few people in this world we can *truly* trust."

He arched his brow again and held up the forgery.

And I turned on my heel and ran.

HENRY

*L*ouisa believed I was a liar.

I'd called her as I left Bernard's flat, barely able to form a coherent sentence. She ordered me to meet her at the library. It was past midnight, and the library glowed with an almost eerie light. I was used to the tranquility of its quiet hallways—but without any patrons, the absence of sound felt menacing.

In her office, I found Louisa frantically digging in a top desk drawer. Pens, rubber bands, sticky notes went flying.

I rubbed the back of my neck as I caught my breath, attempted to pull together the threads of my bizarre tale. As she sifted through desk drawers, nodding along, I confessed my first suspicions of Bernard that had begun a month earlier, tracing them all the way to tonight's confrontation at his dinner party: the forged letters, his smug confession. Even as I told the story, it felt like it belonged to another person, another life.

I was a rare book librarian, not a secret agent.

"Sheila discovered that the manuscript was missing late this evening, responding to an email from that professor whom you never answered," she said. "She called me right away."

"I thought it was important to confront Bernard first," I said.

"Yes, and in the time it took you to act out that charade, it's been hours since it went missing. Hours we *needed* to get it back," she snapped.

I leaned against the wall, crossing my arms. "Bernard has been stealing books for some time. It could have been missing for months now."

Louisa stopped searching, throwing her hands in the air with exasperation. "Henry, you and I have known each other for a long time. And that is the single most absurd story I have ever heard."

"But I have notes on his actions and his movements," I protested. "We need to inventory the collection—"

With an exaggerated flourish, she slapped a black-and-white business card down on the desk. She tapped the word *CODEX* with her fingernail, took out her phone, and began to dial the number listed on the back.

"We need to call the police."

"No," she said sharply. "Let me see what these people can do first." She dropped her voice even though we were the only two in the building. "We don't need the media spectacle of a stolen *Tamerlane* right now. Donors would be furious. I've heard excellent things about this company. They specialize in the recovery of stolen manuscripts. Quickly and *quietly*."

I forced myself to take one steady inhale. "Where is Bernard now? If he was innocent, wouldn't he be here?"

"Bernard has been dragged away last-minute for a speaking engagement in Greece. In fact, he was about to call and tell me when I called him about the missing *Tamerlane*."

"He doesn't have a last-minute event," I fumed. "I know his schedule inside and out. Bernard is lying to you."

"And Bernard Allerton has done more for the field of rare books than any man or woman who has come before him."

Louisa wasn't lying. The antiquarian community was small but powerful, and if we had monarchs, then Bernard would be king. Years ago, he had founded this very library's collection of rare and specialty books. He was a professor at Oxford, he gave speeches around the world advocating for the power of libraries, the vitality of stories, and the democratization of library materials. Each year, the Bernard Allerton Research Fellowship was a grant awarded to the most promising scholar in our field—and this man gave tours to schoolchildren and lectures to presidents alike.

"I know you've worked with Bernard for ten years, but I've worked alongside him for twenty. The *thought* that he could steal the *Tamerlane* is so beyond ludicrous there are no words to accurately describe it."

"He also threatened to turn me in to the police. He forged letters with my signature! And did you know he has a bodyguard? With a gun?" I said frantically.

There was a *spark* of indecision in her eyes—but she suppressed it.

"I don't know what happened between the two of you this evening," she hissed, "but there isn't a single universe where Bernard Allerton is a book thief."

❧

"You look like hell."

I squinted up into the fluorescent light to find a sharply dressed man leaning against the door. He had black hair peppered with gray at the sides and a scowl that appeared permanent.

"Excuse me?" I asked. "Who are you?"

The man smoothed down his tie and dropped into the chair across from me. "Abraham Royal. I'm the CEO of Codex."

"You're the company that Louisa hired."

Abraham nodded, tapping his pen against a pad of legal paper. It'd been about ten hours since my conversation with Louisa, and I'd spent most of that time holed up in one of the smaller study rooms at the McMasters Library. Beyond this door was a 350-year-old library with vaulted ceilings and carved sculptures and some of the oldest books in human history.

But this room was claustrophobic, without windows and filled with stale air. My file and notes were spread around me, the table littered with scraps of paper.

"You got here quickly," I said.

"For certain names, I will drop everything." Abraham assessed me cooly. "Louisa tells me you have quite the story to tell."

"She didn't believe me."

"Louisa suspects you," he said simply.

"Of course she suspects me." I pinched the bridge of my nose. Who would she believe? Me, or the most famous, well-respected man in the profession?

"Who are you, anyway?" I asked.

"We're a small team of private detectives," he explained. "All three Codex agents have a law enforcement background. But all three of us are now fairly...disenchanted with law enforcement. Clients like your library hire Codex to track down rare manuscripts without alerting the authorities. Usually." He pressed his lips together into a grim line.

"Without the red tape and bureaucracy of an FBI field office or a police department, Codex agents are pretty nimble. And highly successful."

"I've never heard of you."

"Exactly," he replied.

I turned that information over in my mind, more intrigued with Codex than I cared to admit.

"Do you know what a *codex* is?" I asked.

"I know it's Latin for *book.*"

My foot tapped an anxious rhythm beneath the table. "The *codex* is the style of bookmaking now universally popular in the Western world. It replaced the scroll because it was so compact and you could read it more easily while traveling. In Central America, their codices were printed on fig bark."

The man from Codex was listening to me patiently, but there was an urgency to the way he gripped his pen.

"Sorry," I said. "I'm a little shaken up. The librarian in me wants to give you a lecture on scrolls now."

"It's been a tough night for you," he said softly. "But why don't you start from the beginning, okay?" Abraham flipped open his legal pad to a clean page. "Tell me who *you* think is responsible for the *Tamerlane.*"

The ten hours I'd spent in here—and lack of sleep—were warping my memories. Had I been enjoying an evening of refined academic discussion with Bernard just last night? I scrubbed my hands down my face and hoped that the stranger in front of me was prepared to believe every mystifying word.

"About a month ago, I started to suspect that Bernard Allerton had stolen something from our collection," I began slowly. "A seventeenth-century book of Latin poetry that hadn't been viewed or on display in years. When I asked him about it, he told me it was on loan to the Cardinal Madrid Museum in Spain."

Abraham scribbled quick notes. "And why did that make you skeptical?"

"At first I thought it was missing the proper paperwork. Bernard is known for being meticulous, but an honest mistake wasn't out of the picture, or maybe an intern filed it improperly. So I called the museum."

Abraham's brow lifted.

"It wasn't there."

His pen stopped.

"You're sure of that?"

"I am," I replied.

He *almost* smiled, but then said, "Continue."

"I went right back to him, concerned that the museum had lost our book in transport. Bernard was irritated. Told me he'd facilitated the loan himself and the person I'd spoken to must have been an idiot." I grimaced at the memory of that day—not once in the ten years I'd worked for him had he ever been angry with me.

And he'd been *furious* with me that day.

"What did you do?"

"I believed him." I plucked at the edges of my notebook, uncomfortably guilty.

But Abraham's face was neutral. "Next?" he prodded.

"After that, I kept a careful eye on him. He was keeping some strange hours. Requesting to clean some of the manuscripts himself, even though at this stage in his career he'd usually have someone else do that for him. A few times..." I shifted in my chair, feeling uneasy. "A few times I'd see him with people he swore were interns but I didn't recognize them. And they wouldn't come back again."

"You gathered all of this information yourself?" He glanced at my stacks of scribbled notes with interest.

"It was the only thing that kept me grounded," I admitted.

"Because if you told me a month ago that *Bernard Allerton* was systematically stealing manuscripts from this library I never, ever would have believed you."

"Is that why you didn't report this sooner to the police? To Louisa?" he asked.

I rubbed my jaw. In the last hours, guilt and I had entered into a symbiotic relationship. "You have to understand. I've looked up to this man my entire career. No one garners more respect, more accolades, more admiration than Bernard. To accuse a man like that of doing the unthinkable..." I shook my head. "I didn't fully believe it *myself* until tonight. I thought...I *hoped* I was wrong."

He nodded.

"I know it was stupid of me to wait," I confessed.

"Men like Bernard are experts in manipulation, Henry," he said. "Take it from someone who's spent his entire life chasing people like him."

It didn't make me feel better.

"Well," I continued, "everything came to a head a couple days ago when I discovered two missing things. The first was page seventeen of Isaac Newton's *Mathematical Principles of Natural Philosophy*. We own an extremely rare copy that contains his handwritten notes in the margin. It's usually displayed, flipped open for viewers to see. It was scheduled to be cleaned, and that's when I noticed the missing page. Like it was cut clean off."

Abraham leaned forward. "Go on."

"I didn't say anything for a day, trying to come up with some strategic way to confront Bernard. I was also trying desperately to prove myself wrong, searching our index. Like maybe...maybe this copy had *always* been missing page seventeen."

"I'm guessing that wasn't accurate."

"You would be correct," I sighed. "And then the next day I discovered the missing *Tamerlane*." I fanned my hands out over the scattered pages. "I hoped it would all be this great misunderstanding. Surely the most famous librarian in the world wasn't a..."

"Criminal," he finished.

"Yes," I said softly. I told him the rest of the story—every bizarre bit of it, up to this current moment. To his credit, he stayed expressionless and nonjudgmental, even as I grew more and more furious.

"I know Louisa doesn't believe me," I said at the end. "And I'm not sure if you do. But that's everything."

Abraham was silent, eyes wandering over my notes. "That was very thorough."

"One of the things I do best," I said dryly. "Research."

His eyes narrowed, like he was about to say something, but stayed quiet. So I asked, "Bernard's on the run, right?"

"It's looking like. A man like that can hide out in any number of countries without arousing too much suspicion. Not for long though." He leaned back, crossing one ankle over his leg. "I believe you may have done the one thing both the FBI and Interpol have been trying to do for years."

"What is that?"

"Make Bernard Allerton afraid." His lips twitched in an almost-smile. "I've been hunting your mentor for a long time, Henry. Before I founded Codex, I was an FBI agent, working in their Art Theft department for more than a decade. I always had a gut feeling that Bernard was not the person he appeared to be. To be honest, I pegged Bernard as a criminal mastermind."

The words *Bernard* and *criminal mastermind* couldn't belong in the same sentence. My pulse skipped a rapid beat stomach twisting into more knots. "Then *why* hasn't he been arrested sooner?"

"Same story," he replied. "Bernard was always on a short list of suspects but entirely based on my gut. No hard evidence at the time. *This*, however"—he tapped my notes—"could be evidence."

"Those letters he showed me. I didn't sign them, Abraham. They're forged. Is there a way…"

"Professionals can discredit forgeries," he added, avoiding my eyes as he wrote something down. "Interpol should be able to clear your name once they're analyzed."

All the breath left my body.

"Can I have this?" he asked, indicating my folder.

"Of course." The guilt I felt was being replaced with exhaustion. I wanted to lie facedown on the floor until all of this faded away. "What's next?"

"For you? Sleep." He tapped the pages together and slid them into a briefcase. "I'll call if I need anything."

"And what are you going to do?" I asked.

"Simple," he said, standing up and extending his hand for me to shake. "I'm going to find that damn book."

3

HENRY

I leaned against a column at the back of the library, the glorious greens of Oxford stretching before me. It was early November, and frost dotted the blades while students rushed across the grass to make their classes in time.

Two days had passed since Bernard had fled and I'd confessed my story to the man from Codex. Louisa had instructed me to stay absolutely quiet about the theft to allow Codex the best chance to succeed. Which I'd done, however reluctantly. During the day, I pasted on a fake smile when people asked where Bernard had gone. Even though his excuse sounded flimsy to my ears— *"A sudden speaking engagement cropped up and he had to leave quickly."*—students and staff didn't bat an eye.

Bernard Allerton could come and go as he pleased in this world.

My mind rattled constantly with the information I'd learned in the last forty-eight hours: Bernard had forged my signature to make me complicit in his crimes. Bernard had fled the country. According to Abraham, Bernard had been suspected of being a book thief for a long, long time.

And through it all, my body *thrummed* with a feeling I didn't yet want to address.

I watched two students stroll across the frost-covered green, holding science textbooks to their faces and laughing.

How strange that the world in front of me spun cheerfully forward even as my understanding of it disintegrated.

How strange that I was still convinced that what was happening right before my eyes wasn't *real*.

"Beautiful view."

I turned to find Abraham behind me, dressed in a black pea coat and leather gloves, his scowl firmly in place.

"It never gets old," I admitted. "You're not here to arrest me, are you, Abraham?"

"You should call me Abe. And no, I'm not."

I nodded, still wary. "How can I help you?"

Abe slid his hands back into his pockets. "You did fine work, Henry. Your notes were invaluable these past couple of days—the behavior you noted, the way you tracked Bernard's movements and actions. You have an eye for detective work."

"I'm a librarian."

He held my gaze. "Louisa is reporting the theft of the *Tamerlane* to Interpol as we speak. They're partnering closely with the FBI on this one. I gave her all the evidence you had provided to me. Louisa is also reporting the other thefts you had listed in your notes. The staff are inventorying now, and the extent of his crimes is becoming rather obvious."

My brow furrowed. "You're joking."

"I've never been a man with a sense of humor." He looked down for a moment, as if analyzing each blade of grass. "You'll be called in for questioning, of course. Because of your connection to Bernard, the notes you took, and the forgeries."

"Am I a suspect?" I asked.

"I doubt it," he said. "But you're certainly a person of interest. You should bring a lawyer, just in case."

My neck felt hot. I toed the grass with my shoes, both heartened by Abe's news but also terrified. "So Codex isn't working this case any longer?"

"Louisa canceled our contract. I was unable to work fast enough for your boss. The single lead I was following dried up almost immediately." He stared into the horizon, spine rigid. "On the bright side, Bernard Allerton is likely to become the FBI and Interpol's main suspect."

"I still can't truly believe that."

"You will," he promised. "With time."

His business card appeared between his fingers.

"I was an FBI agent for a long time," he said. "And I watched us fail, continually. The expanse of theft in the world of antiquities is more massive than you'll ever know."

Bernard had alluded as much to me—his woefully naive successor.

"The thefts got bigger, our resources got smaller, and through it all, rare manuscripts and valuable art slipped through our fingers like grains of sand. We were steadily failing. Private detectives don't have legal powers—they can't arrest suspects or bring someone to trial. But we have the unique capability to slip into a situation undercover and gain someone's trust." Abe squinted against the autumn sun. "A book thief will confess to a world of sins when there's trust involved."

Images flew up in my imagination: shadowy figures, cloaked daggers, secrets whispered in the night. I found myself turning fully toward Abe, desperate for him to keep talking about Codex.

But instead he asked, "How do you feel right now?"

"Relieved," I lied.

"Bullshit," he said.

We stood for a minute while I untangled the complicated mess of emotions that had lodged itself in my chest, made more complicated by my response to Codex.

"Angry," I finally said through clenched teeth. "I'm fucking furious with Bernard. With myself. With everything."

"And what else?"

I faced away—*this* was the feeling I hadn't wanted to face. But it was there, steady as my pulse. "I want revenge. I want to catch the bastard myself. Wipe that smug look off his face."

"Good man," he said. I turned and gawked at him, surprised. "Bernard was going to blackmail you. Try to send you to prison for a crime you most definitely didn't commit. Who wouldn't want revenge?"

"True," I said. "But revenge isn't really my style. And I'm mostly angry with myself."

"In my career, I've worked with many victims of fraud, Henry," Abe said. "People who were scammed in pyramid schemes or were conned out of their life savings. It's like talking to a sleepwalker; the way they suddenly awaken to the manipulation. You're not the only one, believe me. But my question to you is: what are you going to do about it?"

"I've done everything I can," I protested. "The evidence has been handed over. I'll go in for questioning, like you said, give them everything I have. I can't go *after* him. This is the end of the road."

Abe flashed a secretive smile. "At Codex, we fit puzzle pieces together, using a combination of research and gut instinct. Sometimes it's thrilling. Sometimes it's boring. You'll sit in a car for six hours, waiting for a suspect to leave their job. Or maybe you'll go undercover to gain someone's trust."

A shiver raced up my spine, a buzz of something wild and unruly.

"Our entire job is to recover a stolen piece of history. Bernard took something you loved." He held the card in front of me, and I took it. "How would it feel to get it back?"

"Are you asking me what I think you're asking me?" I said.

Another tiny smile. "My flight leaves tonight. I'll call you when I get back in the States. For what it's worth, I think you'd make one hell of a private detective."

Abe vanished as quickly as he'd appeared, leaving me alone with my chaotic thoughts. I pictured Bernard, smirking at his table: *It's only a crime if someone gets caught.*

And Abe: *Who wouldn't want revenge?*

If Bernard could be a respected academic *and also* a book thief—who was to say a librarian couldn't become a detective?

4

DELILAH

Three months later
Philadelphia, PA

The art gallery was packed with thieves.

I could *sense* them all around me.

Abe had ordered us to the opening of the Smith Sampson Gallery in Center City—a glitzy event that attracted Philadelphia's wealthiest art patrons and philanthropists. Freya and I stood in the corner of the wide, brightly lit room, clutching glasses of champagne, smiling. And trying to decipher who our target was.

Freya kept tugging on her dress with muttered curses. Her trademark blonde bun was a little less messy than usual—her version of dressed-up.

"One hour," I said, holding up my finger. "One hour and you can put your yoga pants back on."

"Thank God." She pushed her glasses up her nose. "Yoga pants are the uniform of a proper Saturday night."

I took a sip of expensive, bubbly alcohol. And my eyes found Henry Finch, our newest Codex detective, standing near a vivid blue painting in a tailored suit. He was studying the canvas like it held a secret he'd very much like to know. We'd barely worked together these past few months—I knew that he was thirty-five, spoke four languages, was brilliant, and had studied his entire life to be a rare book librarian.

And, according to Abe, Henry's former boss was a notorious book thief.

I watched Henry adjust his glasses as he accidentally caught my eye across the room.

I looked away quickly.

Patrons decked out in pearls and mink coats buzzed around us, chattering, laughing, gossiping. Like moths, attracted to the glittering light of wealth.

A few were talking loudly about the upcoming Copernicus exhibit at The Franklin Museum three weeks away. It was a Philadelphia high society event all right. And we were searching for a thief that had stolen the twenty-third copy of Ray Bradbury's *Fahrenheit 451*. Codex had been hired yesterday to track it down, and Freya had spent all night in online underground markets where the *provenance* of items was of less concern to the potential buyers than their rarity.

"I got pretty cozy with a seller who was *very* excited to share they'd recently come into a first-edition manuscript of a 'famous book about fire.'" Freya used air-quotes with an arch of her brow.

"Clever," I said. "Did they use the code?"

Freya nodded, eyes traveling through the crowd. Henry had moved on to the next painting, which he examined as deliberately as the first. "Didn't we once meet each other at Reichenbach Falls?" she quoted. It was a reference to the famous Sherlock Holmes story where he fakes his own death. "But when I tried to pin him down on meeting him tonight for a buy, he'd only direct me here."

"We'll find him," I promised, body already vibrating with adrenaline. There was nothing I loved more in this world than the hunt. "I bet I could flash him my gun and he'd run off scared as a rabbit."

Freya gave me an approving look. "Are you *carrying* beneath that dress, Delilah Barrett?"

I shrugged, sipped champagne. On instinct, my hands moved to a side-holster that wasn't there—a habit I hadn't lost, even though it'd been two years since I'd left the police force. Instead I forced a smile, discreetly nodded at my leg.

"Thigh holster," I whispered. "I'm never not packing heat."

Freya tapped her temple. "Computer nerd. I'm never not packing heat."

I swallowed a laugh. She might have been Codex's resident hacker and a self-described Quantico washout, but she could still kick ass like an almost-FBI agent. It was why we made such a good team.

I scanned the crowd for anything strange. I recognized a few of Philadelphia's famous rich people—most notably Victoria Whitney, the wealthiest woman in the city. An eccentric heiress, a beloved philanthropist, a lover of all things antique and rare. She was standing in the middle of a group of avid listeners, pontificating about a piece of art like she was Julius Cesar.

"I didn't know Victoria would be here," I said, senses prickling. "I always expect her to show up to these events with a white tiger on a leash."

Freya snorted. "Me too." She lowered her voice even further. "What are we supposed to do with Henry again?"

I let out a frustrated sigh. "I'm on babysitting duty per Abe's express orders. I need to make sure he doesn't do anything stupid."

Henry had been hired on a probationary basis a few

months ago—and while he'd been studying and passing his private detective exam, he'd been helping Freya with research and authenticating manuscripts when we recovered them. He'd been supremely useful in that area, but Abe had suggested he come along tonight, even though it was way too early to let a complete newbie out in the field.

"Yeah, you should probably...go do that." She grabbed another glass of champagne from a passing waiter wearing a bow tie. "Bring this to him. It'll settle his nerves."

I watched Henry's large palm smooth down his tie as he slid his other hand into his pocket. He was chatting amiably with an older couple, and his body language was loose, open. Oddly enough, the former librarian looked *comfortable* in this high-wealth crowd.

"On it." I grabbed Freya's elbow. "Go mingle, listen, try to start conversations about Sherlock Holmes. Our target will bite."

She winked and tossed me a fake salute. "See you in a few. Have fun babysitting the nerd."

"*You're* the nerd."

"Oh, that's *right*." She tapped her temple again before fluttering away. I passed Victoria Whitney as I walked, her chin tilted and brows raised as she lectured. Henry saw me approach and smiled before he caught himself.

"Drink," I said, handing him the glass.

"I'm sorry, am I supposed to acknowledge you?" he whispered. "Doesn't that blow our cover?"

"We don't technically have a cover," I whispered back. "Just...talk to me. Like normal. We're here enjoying whatever the fuck this thing is." I waved my hand at the painting behind him. This time he smiled for real—a slow reveal of full lips and perfect teeth.

"Are you...doing okay? You seem like it." I said, a little envious of his ease. Crowds like this made me itchy.

His shoulder lifted. "I spent the last ten years charming people so they would donate to libraries. I know this world."

I nodded. "And art?"

"I have a minor in art history," he said. "But modern art I know nothing about."

I watched him assess the painting behind me—face open, as if taking in every detail. "You like it, though," I said.

He thought for a minute. "I do."

As if previously choreographed, we started to wander through the rows. Up close, Henry smelled like old books and cedar.

He dropped his head closer to mine. "Should I go up to people and ask them if they're fans of Ray Bradbury?"

I grimaced. "No. That's *very* obvious."

"Then should I go up and ask them if they've ever been to Reichenbach Falls? I feel like I should be doing something and I'm just standing here."

"That's our job," I said quietly. We were rounding the corner—Victoria came into view. I felt that same *prickle* again —like electricity zipping along my scalp. "Yours is to listen. React. Don't draw attention."

"Okay," he sighed. "I'm a little more nervous than I'd care to admit, Delilah."

He had a deep voice that curled around the syllables of my name.

"Don't worry. You hide it well."

He narrowed his eyes at me behind his square glasses— but his lips twitched in amusement.

"So it sounds like I should ask if anyone here has stolen something recently."

"That's the spirit," I replied, looking around him at Victoria. Although the seventy-year-old was diminutive in size, her entire being *screamed* power. Another man was trying to get her attention, and his profile was eerily familiar.

Through the crowd, I spotted Freya staring daggers at the man.

For the tenth time that night, I cursed Abe's insistence I bring Henry along. I knew he needed field training but I also needed Freya by my side. Something was about to happen—I could sense it.

With as much grace as I could muster in stiletto heels, I moved close to Victoria Whitney just as the man reached forward to grasp her elbow.

Henry opened his mouth to speak. My hand landed on his chest as I shook my head imperceptibly. His brow furrowed.

"What's wrong?" he asked, the words like a shout in the hushed room.

Victoria glanced our way, concerned. I managed a weak smile and tried to temper my annoyance.

Freya and I had been field partners for two years at Codex —I'd forgotten how easily we read each other's body language.

As Henry stared at me, I tucked a strand of my short hair behind my ear and tapped it. *Listen,* I mouthed.

"Victoria, how nice to see you this evening," the man said. Just like that, his name came screeching into my brain: *Charles Kearney.* I didn't even have to look at Freya—Codex had had Charles on a short list of potential targets for a year now. He was an oil tycoon with sticky fingers—he kept getting fined by the police for being in possession of stolen art. But every time he blamed the seller, claiming he never knew they'd come into the piece illegally.

"You as well," she said mildly. A crowd was beginning to gather around her again, and it was obvious she was preening on purpose. "How may I help you, Charles?"

"A fine evening," he mused again.

"Yes, yes," she said. Two people jostled into my back, and I tipped forward. Henry grabbed my shoulders, steadying me. This time he didn't speak, and I shook him off, stepping back.

"I haven't seen you in a while. In fact, the last time was at the falls, wasn't it?" Charles asked.

Henry and I both went rigid.

"And which ones would that be, my dear?" Her voice was half-interest, half-threat.

My hands curled into fists at my sides.

"Reichenbach, of course," Kearney said.

I looked down at the ground—listening, running through scenarios. This didn't make *sense*. If Charles had the stolen Bradbury in his possession, why would he assume he was here to meet Victoria Whitney?

There was a long silence—so long I thought Victoria might have wandered off. But when I chanced lifting my head, she was staring at Charles like he was an exotic bird she wanted to kill and mount on her wall.

"We'll talk about Reichenbach another time," she said, turning her smile back toward the audience that was gathering.

Behind her hung a painting with an entirely black background and blood-red shapes in the middle. I noticed for the first time her regal accent—something I suspected she picked up at various boarding schools. "It's all interconnected you see," she began, as if understanding we'd all been waiting for her to speak. "The violence inherent in this work is the same we would see in some of the Northern Renaissance's most famous pieces, although they are centuries apart."

Next to me, a look of recognition moved over Henry's face. He was staring at Victoria with laser focus.

"Take the infamous *Judith Slaying Holofernes*," she continued. "The lines here recall the body of the general, the blood, the sword. There's a dreadful darkness here, even without human subjects."

Impressed, I watched Victoria Whitney raise her arm in explanation while gripping her glass of champagne. She wore sophistication like it was going out of style.

"An homage, perhaps?" Charles suggested, not taking the hint.

"That's certainly what I see," she said.

Charles was nodding as if he'd won a prize. "It's nice to see a painter reference Caravaggio in a piece like this."

A frown slashed across her face. And before she could open her mouth to respond, Henry said, "Not Caravaggio. Gentileschi."

Victoria turned regally. When her eyes landed on Henry's tall form, she examined him like a lioness. "Artemisia Gentileschi?"

Henry nodded respectfully. "The greatest female painter of her time. Her painting of Judith and Holofernes is less celebrated than Caravaggio's. Although I would argue her version is superior."

Charles was petulant, clearly unused to being interrupted. He opened his mouth, but Victoria cut him off.

"Many critics would say she was a far better painter than her male peers," she said to Henry.

"Those critics would be correct," he replied.

I glanced up at Henry—saw him backlit against the lights of the gallery. His suit fit his tremendously tall, broad body like a glove. Henry was black, with dark-brown skin and close-cropped black curls, and when he let loose that charming smile, I *felt* the audience sigh in response.

Victoria the Lioness looked like she'd spotted her next meal.

With one last lingering look at my coworker, she read-dressed her audience, regaling them with a story about Renaissance painters that was probably only half-accurate. Distracted by Henry, I hadn't noticed Charles slink off—until Freya was a blur of movement heading out the front doors.

Shit. We usually handled meetings together, and I wasn't sure how she felt confronting him alone. Maybe if I—

"Hello there."

When I turned, Victoria Whitney was standing right in front of us. Her silver hair was swept in a low bun, and her lightly lined face was alabaster white. The diamonds in her ears could have paid my rent for a year.

When neither Henry nor I responded, she extended her hand, fingers dripping with rings. "Victoria Whitney. I'm sure you've heard of me."

"Delilah," I said quickly, taking her hand before Henry could. I didn't want him to say his last name. "This is Henry."

"Good evening," he said smoothly.

She fluttered her lashes, touched her hair. "You have my attention, Henry," she said. "I didn't expect someone to bring up Artemisia Gentileschi in the middle of a modern art exhibit."

"She's a favorite." He leaned in slightly, as if sharing a secret.

"Mine as well." She straightened the mink around her shoulders. "I loved how she never shied away from the brutality of the act of decapitation. The blood, the fear, the grotequeness..." Her light eyes gleamed.

"She was far better than Caravaggio," he replied.

She regarded first Henry, then me. "I *like* him," she purred.

My mind was racing back and forth like a ping-pong ball.

"I like him too," I finally admitted. Henry was bemused. "What, um...what brings you here this evening?"

The last time Freya and I had gone undercover was months ago—I was rusty.

"I am expected to be here, because it is expected I will purchase one of these pieces of art."

"And will you?" I asked.

"I could purchase each one ten times over," she sighed. "But these bring me no joy. Now if an original Artemisia was hanging here, I'd buy it in a heartbeat."

My scalp prickled again as I raced to put together the pieces: the code, Charles' presence, Victoria's prestige.

"It's a shame then," I ventured, "that every surviving piece of hers is in a museum somewhere, locked up from the private collectors."

She eyed me over her champagne, lifting one delicate brow. "It's the greatest shame, indeed."

She waved at someone behind me and almost made a move to leave.

"I'm a collector as well," Henry said. "Rare manuscripts, antique books. My collection pales in comparison to yours, I'm sure."

Victoria beamed.

And how did Henry know *Victoria Whitney?* I knew Henry was from Philadelphia, but he'd lived in Europe for the past decade.

"You're aware of my collection?" she said, smiling at him from under her lashes.

Henry balked; gave me a beseeching look. "I'm a rare book librarian. Many of us are familiar with you."

The ping-pong ball in my brain had bounced far off course.

"Oh, you're flattering me," she sighed.

"Absolutely not," he said, palm against his chest.

"You can do conservation?" she asked, fingers touching her pearls.

"Yes, ma'am."

"I occasionally hire conservationists to work in my collections room. Maybe I could hire *you* sometime?"

I held my breath.

"Certainly," he said.

Victoria flashed a smile, and I let out a soft exhale. Was Henry getting us access to Victoria Whitney? She'd never been a Codex target but she was filthy rich and had an ego the size of Pennsylvania.

And Charles Kearney had given her the code.

What the *hell* was going on?

"Where have you worked, Henry?" she asked. A few members of her former audience were standing in the sidelines of this conversation.

"Oh, you mean as a librarian?" he asked.

Her eyes narrowed. He rubbed the back of his head, looking almost sheepish. "Let's see... I've worked in New York City at the Central Park Library. I've worked at Trinity College in Dublin. Cardinal Madrid in Spain. I, uh..."

"He freelances now," I filled in. "As a consultant."

I prayed that librarians could be consultants.

"How *lovely*," she sighed. "You probably know my dear friend. Bernard Allerton. Head librarian at the McMasters Library in Oxford for years and years."

"*Bernard?*" He gripped the stem of his glass so hard I worried he'd snap it.

"Yes," she said, taking a step back. A dozen slightly ill-fitting puzzle pieces flew together in my brain. Abe told us Bernard was Henry's former boss at the McMasters Library and currently on the run from the FBI for theft. Over the past three months, Abe had fed us updates from his contact at the

FBI, but they were keeping his name from the papers, hoping to flush him out.

The last we'd heard, Bernard was still missing.

"I'm sorry," he apologized, "I was just surprised you knew him. I never—" Henry coughed, "I never had the privilege of working with him. But I certainly know who he is."

"*Such* a shame you've never met." She fluttered her hands. "Fifteen years ago, when I began collecting antiques, I went right to Bernard and demanded a meeting with him. Wanted to know every valuable item I should collect. The time period, the pieces." She tilted her chin with a Mona Lisa smile. "I saw him every time I went to Europe."

Henry's jaw flexed.

"What a...small world," he said thickly. "You've seen him? Recently?"

Her expression grew guarded. "Oh, I can't remember when last. Months ago, probably."

I wished Freya was here. Something wasn't *right* about this.

"And now I have one of the most coveted private collections in the entire world." She sipped her champagne; flagged down a passing waiter for more. "All of it thanks to that man."

Another passing distraction caught her attention. She moved to my right, about to leave.

"Are you excited for the Copernicus exhibit next month?" I asked, desperate to keep her talking to us. Out of the corner of my eye, I saw Charles, looking rumpled and flustered. No sign of Freya. "The one at the Franklin?"

Victoria paused in her step, looked between the two of us like she was *bursting* to share a secret. But all she finally said was, "Of course. I sit on the board of every single museum in the city. I even helped facilitate the exhibit. Do you know how many first-edition copies of *On the Revolutions of the Heavenly Spheres* there are left in this world, Henry?"

"267," he said without hesitation.

"Not many in private hands, I assume."

"No, ma'am," he said. "There are a handful, but that manuscript is 550 years old."

"Meaning?" Her tone was sharp.

"Meaning..." Henry started. He tilted his head, dropped his voice. "Meaning it would take a highly skilled private collector to get it into their hands."

She was flattered. "Highly skilled *and* richer than God."

He laughed—a husky sound that made him look even more handsome.

"It sounds like you're up to the task, Victoria."

"A lady never tells her secrets, Henry," she replied in an almost-whisper. Her eyes were glittering.

"Delilah and I were planning on attending the exhibit," he continued.

"Yes, well..." She clicked her rings against her glass. "Who knows how it will turn out."

Charles wandered over and tapped Victoria's shoulder sheepishly.

From her answering expression, I guessed Victoria Whitney didn't enjoy being *tapped*.

"Later." She bared her teeth at him and he slunk off. "I'm sorry," she said. "I was supposed to pick an item up from him this evening but I've lost interest. I came into something quite extraordinary recently. Bernard is going to *die* when I tell him."

Everything in the room fell to a muted silence—a precipitating event that usually meant I was about to get a lead. In the police force, before everything happened, my nickname had been *the Bloodhound* for my ability to sniff out a thief. And right now, I was only aware of the sophisticated heiress posing in front of me, framed by the blood-red painting she'd described as filled with a *dreadful darkness*.

Victoria Whitney reeked of lies and deception. The kind of stench that had me yearning for my handcuffs like a missing limb.

I leaned in close, allowing myself one last second of contemplation before I trusted my instincts. The past two years had been a slow, painful process of learning to trust myself again—and every time I took a single step forward, I tumbled two steps backward. But my gut was practically screaming at me.

So I took a deep breath and touched her arm like we were the best of friends. "This might be a bit forward," I said, voice low. "But didn't we once meet you at Reichenbach Falls?"

Victoria held my attention for a long, agonizing minute. She crossed her arms delicately, champagne glass aloft.

And when she grinned, it was full of mischief.

"Henry and Delilah," she murmured. "The two of you just became even more interesting."

"You probably can't tell us about your...new acquisition, can you?" I said this timidly—knowing it was a long-shot. Victoria was essentially a walking ego but she wasn't stupid.

Her expression confirmed this. "No, my dear." She patted my hand. "But I will keep the two of you in mind for the future. For *your* collection, Henry."

I guessed he was probably confused by all of this—and luckily he stayed silent, merely nodding along.

"We would love that."

Victoria beamed at me. Then grabbed my left hand and held it toward her face. "Now, let me ask *you* a forward question."

"Uh...um, okay," I stumbled.

She stared at my left finger. "What's a married woman

doing without her wedding ring? Henry, don't tell me you never bought her one."

I almost dropped my glass.

"What did you say?" he asked.

"A *ring*, darling," she said, speaking to him like he was a child. "Your wife is the most beautiful woman here and she's not even wearing a diamond, let alone the four diamonds that she deserves."

"Delilah and I aren't married," Henry said. He glanced back and forth between us as if waiting for another explanation. And I watched as Victoria's attention began to sharpen, spotting a fake.

"Henry has a...a very dry sense of humor," I stammered. Two years of training with Freya kicked in. I slid over and wrapped my arm around Henry's, laying my cheek against his jacket. "He likes to joke around."

His arm moved—as if to jerk away—and I locked mine tighter. Trapping us together.

"The two of you are just the sweetest." She pressed her hands to her chest. "I'm sorry if I overstepped my bounds, but any hopeless romantic worth their salt can see it."

He was struggling to contain his confusion.

"I guess," I said, shrugging meekly. The ping-pong in my head was back.

But Victoria shook her head in disbelief. "So humble," she *tsked*. "It's glaringly obvious."

"What is?" Henry asked.

She propped her hands on her hips. "That the two of you are *newlyweds*."

5

HENRY

"Oh, wait a moment," Victoria said, holding her talon-like finger up. "Bitzi is coming. You can tell both of us about your wedding. And I want an answer about that ring, Henry."

"Who's Bitzi?" I managed. A woman who looked almost exactly like Victoria came striding through the crowd. Victoria waved—but beneath her breath said, "She's my archnemesis. I *despise* her."

And then she proceeded to greet her nemesis like a long-lost sister she hadn't seen in a decade.

Delilah took the brief reprieve to curve her body into mine, tipping her lips against my ear.

"We're definitely married. Follow my lead, newbie."

She moved away but kept our arms lightly entwined.

It was my first day in the field as a private detective for Codex. And I was already fake married to my coworker.

The past three months had been a whirlwind of chaos and change. After many interviews with Interpol, I was—thankfully—no longer a person of interest in Bernard's case. And like Abe had predicted, the forged letters were discredited almost immediately. I'd resigned from the McMasters Library, much to Louisa's fury and the community's shock. Packed up my flat in Oxford and moved back home to Philadelphia, where Codex was located. Began the process of becoming a private detective—all while spending most of my days *positive* Abe would realize the giant mistake he'd made in hiring a rare book librarian to do the job of a law enforcement officer. I'd mostly been separate, squirreled away doing research for Abe as Freya and Delilah tracked down stolen books.

But deep down I'd wanted this, wanted this taste of the thrilling adrenaline I'd felt the night I confronted Bernard. Wanted to give into that thirst for revenge that was now a constant presence in my thoughts.

And now that I was here, in the field, I realized how little I knew.

"A pleasure to meet you," Delilah said to Bitzi, who barely acknowledged her before turning toward me.

"And who is *this*?" she squealed

"My husband," Delilah blurted, nudging my shoulder. The word *husband* stunned me into silence—and in reality, I was still stunned from Victoria's admission that she knew *Bernard*. I wanted to press *pause* on this entire interaction and beg her for more details.

But instead I took Bitzi's hand and brought it to my lips. "Yes, of course. So nice to meet you. How long have you and Victoria known each other?"

"That's top secret information, Henry," Victoria crooned. "Now I was telling Bitzi the two of you are newlyweds. How long ago did you get married?"

"One month ago," Delilah said, at the exact moment as I said, "Six months."

There was a long beat of awkwardness. Delilah stared up at me with barely concealed irritation.

"Um..." I started.

"Do you not know how long you've been married?" Victoria's words dripped with elegant sarcasm.

"You know librarians," Delilah simpered. "He's always got his head in the clouds."

"I guess..." I started, "it feels like we've been married for ages." I turned to my coworker. Up close, I noted the flecks of sea-green in her blue eyes. "It feels like we've always been married, if I'm being honest."

Her lips parted on a breath.

"So how long has it been?" Victoria's brow arched.

"One month," we said in unison. Thankfully.

"Such a perfect young love," Bitzi said. "I haven't gotten my husband to look at me the way Henry looks at *you,* darling, in ages and ages."

Victoria's knowing smirk spoke volumes about her opinion of Bitzi's husband.

"Now tell us about the big day. Are there pictures?" she asked.

Delilah opened her mouth. Closed it.

"We eloped, actually," I said hurriedly. Delilah squeezed my arm in surprise. "One of those spur of the moment things. We were visiting Trinity Library, wandering through the stacks, and..." I paused, tried to let an imaginary movie play in my mind. I considered my coworker, whom I'd barely spoken to in three months. She had the bearing of a silent film star: tall, lithe, graceful. Delilah had pale-white skin, full red lips, and a mess of raven curls. And she could take down a man twice her size without batting an eye.

How would you propose to a woman like that?

"The sun from the stained-glass windows was illuminating her," I told Bitzi and Victoria. "And we've been together for so long, the only reason we hadn't done it was because we were waiting for the time to be just right. But really, shouldn't the time be when you are madly in love?" I didn't even chance a glance at Delilah—I'd either burst out in nervous laughter or sprint from the room. "So I got down on one knee and asked her to marry me. And when she said *yes*, I suggested we get married that day, right where we were."

Bitzi watched me with an enchanted expression. Victoria plucked at her pearls and seemed sad.

"You must have been so surprised," Bitzi said, clutching at Delilah's arm.

Delilah nodded. "Yes. Very, very surprised. We got married an hour later. Right in the...in the famous place at Trinity Library where everyone gets married. You know the one."

"The Long Room?" I asked.

"Is it a question?" Victoria looked as confused as I felt.

I faked a laugh. "It was The Long Room. The library patrons were our guests. They stood around during our ceremony and tossed, um..." I racked my brain. "Tossed rose petals that someone bought at a corner store."

The back of my neck felt hot and my heart was clamoring so hard I felt almost dizzy. But next to me, Delilah seemed serene. I couldn't tell if I was ruining everything or actually convincing them.

"He's always been a romantic," she said. She tucked herself against my chest just as I happened to turn—causing my lips to brush the soft strands of her hair.

"Yes, I can see that," Victoria said. "And the ring?"

Fuck. I should have been using this time to come up with a plausible reason why Delilah wasn't wearing a ring.

"Oh, it's...um..." I stammered.

"We just haven't found the right one yet. For either of us." Delilah nudged my side, and at the last second, I realized what she wanted.

"I'm not wearing one either." I held up my left hand. "So if you have any good jewelers please send them our way."

"Yes," Victoria said softly. "I just might." She handed us one of the postcards that had been floating around advertising the Copernicus exhibit. "Can you place your phone number there for me, please?"

"Of course," Delilah said, snatching the card from her. "Henry, let's use yours." She gave a subtle nod. So I scribbled down my real phone number for the most famous woman in the city.

As Bitzi bade us farewell, I stared at the postcard, recognizing the famous manuscript on the front. I'd once handled Oxford's copy of *On the Revolutions of the Heavenly Spheres,* and it had been one of the most magnificent books I'd ever seen. Since it was printed in the handpress era, it was riddled with mistakes, overcome with age, and the gilded flowers on each page had permanently lost their sheen. But there was no doubting the feeling it evoked in me—that sense of glorious wonder.

"So, will we see you at this exhibit in a few weeks?" I asked.

"No, that's unlikely," she said. "And, if I can be perfectly honest, I don't suggest going." She reached between us and snatched the card back, depositing it in her purse. "I think you'll find it sorely lacking." She grimaced at something behind us. "As much as I'd love to talk with you two for this entire night, I'm afraid my audience expects me. I'll be calling you, Henry. And I *do* expect you to answer."

And with that, Victoria Whitney disappeared into the crowd.

As soon as she was out of sight, Delilah sprang from my arm like it was on fire.

"I'm sorry, did I hurt you?" I asked.

"No, no," she said nervously. "I'm fine. But we need to go find Freya. And we *really* need to talk to Abe."

"Okay," I said, slipping my hands into my pockets.

Delilah bit her lip. Tapped her foot. "Okay."

She turned and left as quickly as Victoria, like our entire interaction—and sudden marriage—had never even happened.

6

DELILAH

*C*odex was located on the second floor of a 300-year-old carriage house in Old City. The first floor was Marple's Home for Used and Abandoned Books, run by a seventy-five-year-old woman named Bea. She had two great loves in her life: Agatha Christie and men with cute butts, and she let us run amok on the second story without ever saying a word.

It was almost midnight now as Freya, Henry and I wove our way through stacks of dusty books and climbed the rickety spiral staircase to our offices. Abe was sitting behind his desk in a dark suit with a glass of whiskey in his hand, fire roaring behind him. When Abe had started Codex, he hadn't changed much of the second story's historical details—old wood floors, brick walls, fireplaces in every room.

"Returning triumphantly?" he asked.

"Yes, which means I deserve some of that whiskey and to change back into my yoga pants." Freya yawned, placing a wrapped package on the edge of Abe's desk before loping off to the bathroom.

"Is this what I think it is?" he asked.

"It's the Bradbury," I said, sinking into a chair. Henry sat next to me, still looking immaculate. He'd barely said a word as I rattled off our conversation with Victoria to Freya on the ride home.

"Will you verify before I call the library, Henry?" Abe asked.

"Absolutely," he replied. He reached forward, cradled the little book with reverence.

Freya came back out in her usual oversized sweater and black leggings. "So you'll never guess who the seller was." She took Abe's glass of whiskey as he scowled at her. "Charles fucking Kearney."

"Is that so?" Abe drawled.

"It *is* so." She drained the glass and sat next to me. "And I only had to threaten to kick him in the nuts once before he basically threw the book at me."

I reached over, squeezed her shoulder. "You're a bad-ass, Frey," I said.

"By any means necessary," Abe said approvingly. "I shall bring you donuts tomorrow."

"World's Best Boss, ladies and gentlemen," she mock-swooned at him.

"Don't get too excited," he said, but the edges of his mouth tipped into a smile. "Well done."

She shrugged. "And you haven't even heard the craziest part yet."

I turned and made eye contact with Henry for the first time since we'd left the gallery. It'd been so strange and uncomfortable to play at being married with the newbie that we hadn't even debriefed.

"It's about Victoria Whitney. And Bernard. And the Copernicus exhibit." I paused, searching for that same feeling from earlier. It was like attempting to discern navy-colored threads

46

in a black sweater: easy to miss if you didn't know what you were looking for. But Victoria had dropped plenty of clues and subconscious admissions—and I needed to put them all together. "I think she's up to something."

Without a word, Abe slid two more glasses of whiskey over the desk—one for me, one for Henry. "Start from the beginning."

Abe listened with a steely expression as I unraveled the evening's peculiar events: Henry impressing Victoria with his art history knowledge, the code word, her almost-buy with Charles, the strange way she was talking about the Copernicus. The fact that she seemed to know Bernard Allerton very, *very* well.

"And Victoria was vague and a little guarded when I asked her the last time she'd seen him," Henry cut in. "If they're *that* close, she might know that he's in hiding."

Abe leaned all the way forward, hands fisted together. "Tell me what she said again. The very last thing."

"I think you'll find the exhibit sorely lacking," I quoted.

We were all quiet while Abe followed the trail of clues I'd presented.

"I might have something," Henry interrupted. He dropped his elbows to his knees, one hand rubbing his jaw. I knew what this was—had felt it often when I was a police detective. That nagging in your subconscious demanding your attention. "I wasn't lying to Victoria when I told her librarians the world over know of her private collection. I knew of her before even meeting her tonight. She has a reputation for owning some of the rarest manuscripts in the world. Specifically from the handpress era. Like the Copernicus."

Henry's dark eyes landed on mine. "Tonight, she said she first met Bernard many years ago, right?"

"She did," I said.

"Bernard used to talk about this woman he called his Lady Love. She never came to the library, but he'd meet her all over the world. Istanbul, Barcelona, Paris. And she was from the States, so he often spent weeks at a time visiting her here. It stopped, about a year into my working with him. So nine years ago. I never gave it a thought, it was just one more funny quirk about him."

Awareness flooded his features—and a hint of that charming smile. "He always told me she was richer than God. And she was fascinated with the scientists who had discovered the heavens."

Henry pulled one of the postcards we'd been given at the event—the one with the picture of the Copernicus book on it. It was open to a famous drawing of the planets, drifting in orbit around the sun. I returned his smile—a tentative one—and his grew. I knew that feeling well, *chased* that feeling every day here. When the jumbled puzzle pieces of your mind clicked together to make something real.

"I'm thinking something crazy," I ventured.

"I'm listening," Abe said.

"What if..." I took a deep breath. "What if Victoria took this book? Or is planning to take it, setting up a job before the exhibit?"

It was a big leap—but Abe and Freya were already nodding.

"I've certainly always suspected Victoria of dipping her toe in illegal waters," Abe said. "When I was with the FBI, we had a lot of suspects like her—supremely wealthy collectors who had lawyers on retainer and *always* claimed they never knew anything." He stopped, cocked his head. "I agree with you, Delilah. None of this sits right with me."

Freya fiddled with her bun. "This would certainly take the cake for most peculiar case...but I can see it."

The trust Abe and Freya returned to me so easily here always felt like a gift. One that I treasured greatly.

Henry, however, was silent.

"How did you get her to cozy up to you?" Abe asked.

I coughed into my hand. "It's nothing, really."

Freya hummed the opening bars of the "Wedding March" beneath her breath.

"Victoria thought Henry and I were newlyweds, so we went with it. She thinks we eloped one month ago in Ireland beneath a veil of rose petals." My palms were sticky as I dragged them up my thighs.

Abe swirled his drink with expert care. "Interesting approach," he mused. "Especially for your first day in the field."

"I didn't do much," Henry said. "Delilah took the lead. She did a great job on the spot."

"Delilah's quick on her feet," Abe said, giving me a nod of approval.

I nodded back but knew later he'd ask me about Henry's performance, how he kept his head under pressure. It wasn't that he didn't have the ability to charm a target—but he'd floundered when pushed past his comfort zone. If Freya and I could figure out a way to work this potential Victoria case, we'd *nail* it. No awkward training needed—Henry could get out in the field at a later date, for a case that would be a little less conspicuous.

"So what do we do next?" I asked. Abe and Freya mirroring my suspicions had my bloodhound senses turned *way* up. My fingers flexed into my palm. I'd had mandatory Krav Maga self-defense training at the police academy, and when Abe learned I still practiced, he had a bag and a few mats installed in the office. Abe and Freya sparred with me sometimes, but I usually took my frustrations—or excitement—out on that punching bag. My knee was jiggling, and Freya placed a gentle hand to stop it.

Abe tapped his pen hard against the desk. Stared out the window. "Usually, Codex is *hired* when a book is missing," he said to Henry, by way of explanation. "We don't go to a potential client and beg for a job. So I'm not saying we should do this all of the time. And it's certainly a massive risk."

"But we'd have a huge reward," Freya sang.

"Are you suggesting we go to the Franklin Museum and ask them if their Copernicus is missing based on a collective *hunch*?" Henry asked.

"Yes," Abe said. "Does that concern you?"

"It does," Henry said, blowing out a breath. "I'm not trying to step on any toes, and I'm certainly no expert, but what is our hard evidence exactly?"

"None." Abe shrugged. "But Delilah and Freya have fairly good instincts I find are right the majority of the time."

"And when they're wrong?"

Henry cast his gaze toward me. But I didn't have a response for that.

"I don't believe they are," Abe shot back.

"Okay," Henry conceded, after a moment of silence. But he didn't expand.

My fingers flexed at my sides in preparation, attempting to ignore my disappointment that my new coworker seemed reluctant. But Abe was already on the move—standing swiftly, tossing his jacket over his shoulders. "Then I think we should go pay the president of the Franklin Museum a late-night visit."

7

DELILAH

*P*ale moonlight shimmered on the broad steps that led to the very top of the Franklin Museum. The building sat like a coliseum—round columns towered over us as we raced up the stairs. The museum was utterly silent, tomb-like, but Abe insisted that Francisco would be there.

"On a scale of one to *fucking ten*, how would you rate your first day of field work?" Freya asked Henry. To his credit, he wasn't even out of breath, taking long, confident strides that dwarfed my own.

"Fucking ten seems fair," he said. "I suppose I thought there'd be more HR paperwork to fill out before I embarked on this evening's adventure."

Freya shook her head. "Only if you fuck up."

Henry's warm laugh echoed in the quiet of the courtyard. We'd reached the main doors, but Abe was leading us to an unremarkable-looking side door. His phone was at his ear in an instant.

"Francisco," he said. "Fancy a late-night visit from an old friend?"

"How does Abe know him again?" Henry asked, dropping his voice.

"FBI contacts," I replied. "Before he left to start Codex, he'd worked Art Theft for years. He knows everyone in Philly connected to art. And they all seem to owe him *favors*."

Henry slid his hands into the pockets of his jacket. "Interesting."

"What?" I asked.

He adjusted his glasses. "This night is nothing like a typical night in my former life as a librarian, that's all. Just noting the difference."

"In a good way?" I asked.

Our eyes met in the darkness. "Very," he said.

"The only reason a bunch of Codex agents would be storming my castle past midnight would be if I stole something." A short, balding man with tan skin and gold glasses was standing in the unremarkable doorway.

"Well, did you?" Abe asked.

The man huffed out a breath. "Come in. The kettle is on. For God's sake, don't touch anything."

We trailed in after Francisco and down a long hallway lit with glowing lights nestled in the floorboards. Rooms opened up on the left and right—empty exhibits, glass cases standing like guards, looking eerie in the absence of patrons. My detective instincts were intrigued at the shadowy corners, the darkened hiding spots.

Next to me, Freya mimed running her hands over every object until I had to stifle a laugh.

"In here," Francisco said, opening the door marked *Francisco Abila, Executive Director*. "Let me go get the kettle."

Inside the cozy office, Abe perched on the edge of the director's desk while Freya found a small couch. Henry and I both moved for the same chair at the same time—bumping each other clumsily.

"Oh, sorry, do you —"

"No, not at all," he said. "I insist."

"I can stand," I said hastily.

"Delilah," he said, and there was a smile in his voice. "Sit. Please."

I did—but not without wondering how on *earth* Victoria Whitney had assumed Henry Finch and I were newlyweds.

I sat and Henry leaned his back against the wall next to me, which made him appear even taller in the narrow space. All four of us were silent—but Abe's fingers tapped rapidly against the desk.

"I'm not even going to bother with many pleasantries," Francisco said, coming back in with mugs of tea for each of us. It was hot and soothing—but it couldn't quell the spiky adrenaline still coursing through my veins. "I'm assuming you all work for Abe?"

Abe waved his hand at us absent-mindedly. "Freya Evandale. Delilah Barrett. Henry Finch."

Francisco glanced up sharply. "Henry *Finch*? You're the special collections librarian from Oxford, aren't you?"

"I am," Henry replied, surprised. "Or, I was, rather. I work for Codex now. Have we met before?"

"No," Francisco said, "but your name is rather familiar in certain circles, I'm sure you know. Because of Bernard Allerton."

It was unclear what Francisco meant—and I knew enough from Abe to understand that Bernard's current situation wasn't entirely public. But Francisco was already moving on. "And I haven't seen Abraham in years. Has it been more than five?"

"I was still with the FBI, leading a team that recovered a

stolen Gutenberg Bible that had been taken from the museum during a burglary," Abe added.

I looked up at Henry.

"There are only forty-nine surviving copies left. It's extremely rare," Henry explained.

"It was absolutely horrible when it was taken," Francisco said. "And agonizing during the search and recovery. But Abraham got it back. It had been stolen by a trio of thieves who'd broken in through our air conditioning ducts." On cue, we all stared up at the ceiling. "*Which* are now protected against that kind of thing. They'd been able to sell the book to the highest bidder—privately—within fifteen hours."

"Did the bidder know it had been stolen?" Henry asked.

"Yes, he most certainly did," Francisco replied.

I noted Henry's shocked reaction at that. Which was strange, given what I knew had happened to him before he'd come to Codex. But maybe he'd been less aware of theft and fraud than I realized.

"I've heard great things about the upcoming Copernicus exhibit," Abe said, directing our conversation to the potential crisis at hand.

For a split second, Francisco's expression wavered. Then he plastered on a conciliatory smile. "We're truly excited. It's one of the highest honors that's ever been bestowed upon this museum."

"Hit any snags? Any issues with the planning of it?"

"Not at all," Francisco said smoothly. "It's been clear sailing."

Abe tapped his fingers again and held the other man's stare. I could *feel* Abe turning the situation over in his mind, searching for holes. "We've come into some information that I thought you needed to be made aware of immediately, which is why we're visiting you at such an odd hour. It's about the Copernicus exhibit."

"Go on," Francisco said.

"Henry and Delilah were working a case at the Smith Sampson art gallery opening this evening, and they had a very intriguing conversation with Victoria Whitney, your board member."

"I'm well aware of our most famous and beloved board member," Francisco sniffed. "What about her?"

Abe let another silence linger until Francisco fidgeted. "We suspect she might be planning on stealing the Copernicus manuscript before the exhibit in three weeks."

"That's the most preposterous thing I've ever heard." Francisco looked down at the floor. "You mean *the* Victoria Whitney?"

"If you haven't already, you need to find an even better way to secure it," Abe said softly. "Believe me, we know it sounds absurd."

Francisco was still looking away, nostrils flared.

"Francisco," Abe continued, "certainly stranger things have happened in the time that we've known each other. I can have Freya and Delilah consult on your security system if you'd like, make sure there are systems in place to ensure a person like Victoria can't gain special access to it."

"She's president of the board. Of course, she has special access," Francisco replied. "She's had special access this entire time."

His face was turning a sickening green right in front of our eyes. And my heart leapt at the phrase *special access*.

Abe arched an eyebrow at Freya and me. I sat forward, tugged by that pesky voice in my subconscious. With a nod, I mouthed *do it*.

"Of course," Abe began, "this would be an entirely different conversation if the book had already been stolen."

That sentence landed like a grenade in the quiet room.

"Abraham, if the Franklin Museum had been the victim of a theft of that magnitude, don't you think you would be aware of it?" Francisco's voice held a tremor that hadn't been there before.

Abe didn't answer. His body language was sharp but knowing. Francisco's was fearful. I peered up at Henry to see if he was watching—evaluating the many ways the body can expose a lie was good training for a new private detective.

But Henry was watching *me*.

"*If* the museum has been a victim of theft, don't you think Codex would be able to help?"

Francisco sipped his tea angrily. Grumbled beneath his breath. An intense stare-down occurred between the two men —one that I imagined contained years of working history and professional respect.

"You know I'm always right," Abe finally said.

Francisco's cup clattered onto the saucer.

"Our first edition of *On the Revolutions of the Heavenly Spheres* was stolen two weeks ago, the day that it arrived from England."

All the air left my lungs. Next to me, Henry stood up straight, as if primed to run.

Abe, meanwhile, sat still as a statue. "Who's working the case, Francisco?"

"The local police. The FBI. They've been sworn to secrecy so there isn't a media spectacle but they—" He ran a palm over his head. "They can't seem to find it and they're running low on suspects. It's an absolute mess." Unburdened, he sank back in his chair and held his hands up, as if in apology. "Is that what you wanted to hear?"

"Of course not," Abe said. "But if they're not making any headway, let *us* get it back for you. You know we can do it."

Confronted with the enormity of this case—its high-profile nature, the stakes, the *money*—I was hit with the full extent of the risk Abe was taking. But he appeared cool and confident perched on the desk while goosebumps broke out across my skin.

"All of this is a disaster," Francisco said quietly. "The museum that's loaning us the copy is beyond furious. I've had to lie to the press. The board is out of their minds. It'll be my head on the block if this gets out."

Freya slid a concerned look my way. Maybe Victoria had hinted at the missing Copernicus because Francisco had told her—not because she was the thief. My stomach rolled violently at the thought—had we leapt to all the wrong conclusions already?

But Abe forged ahead, unperturbed. "Codex can recover it. You know how high our close rate is. Higher than the FBI."

"Yes, and it will cost me a small fortune," Francisco replied. "Right?"

Abe lifted a shoulder. "You know our prices. Would you rather pay Codex or lose a priceless manuscript for good?"

Francisco pushed himself up from the chair. "Don't patronize me, Abraham. You know which option I would prefer. But I can't just pay you. I need the treasurer to sign off on your exorbitant fee."

"Don't let the treasurer tell Victoria," Freya put in. We all turned to look at her—her head was cocked, giant glasses glowing in the dim light. "If we suspect it's Victoria, it's best if she doesn't know about Codex. That will only impede her trust. From the way she was talking tonight, she clearly thinks what law enforcement has done so far is a joke."

Abe gave her an approving look. "Yes. What she said."

Francisco sighed irritably. "If I employ Codex in the recovery of this manuscript, are you seriously going to entertain the *absurdity* of Victoria Whitney as your suspect?"

"Who we entertain as our suspect is not within the client's responsibility," Abe said. "Absurd or not."

"You go after Victoria and you'll only end up embarrassing yourselves." Francisco's harsh tone had me itching to jump to Abe's defense. But he was still collected, merely shrugging as if going after the most notorious woman in Philadelphia was neither here nor there.

"I'm serious, Abraham."

"As am I, Francisco."

Another stare-down ensued until Francisco finally caved. "Give me until the morning. And I hope I don't have to remind your staff of the intensely confidential nature of this ordeal."

"They won't say a word," Abe promised.

In a fog, I followed everyone back through the dark hallways and out the side door, the spring wind whipping through my curls. I'd felt so confident back at Codex, but now that we faced the possibility of tracking this book down, I was doubting every single thing I believed I knew.

Freya wrapped her arm around my shoulders and gave me a squeeze. "We're a dream team, remember?"

I tried to smile at her but I could tell my worry was in plain sight.

"So...good meeting," she joked. "Guess we've got a new case. Any ideas on how we get into Victoria's good graces?"

Abe ran a hand through his hair, staring out at the skyline of Philadelphia, which glittered brighter than the few stars we could see. When Henry's phone rang, it startled all of us.

"Unknown number," Henry said, staring down at the screen.

"Put it on speaker," Abe instructed.

Henry did, and when he answered an unfamiliar voice responded.

"Good evening. Am I speaking with Henry?"

"You are," he said smoothly. "And you are…"

"Cecilia. I'm Victoria Whitney's personal secretary. She gave me your number this evening and asked me to invite you to attend an art auction with her next week. You and your wife —" There was a muffled sound. "Delilah?"

I took a step back. Abe stared at us both like we'd been dipped in solid gold. He circled his finger in the air, as in *keep going*.

"Um…oh, yes," Henry replied. "Delilah is my wife."

His eyes on mine were apologetic.

"Wonderful. And I didn't quite catch your last name. Henry and Delilah…"

He searched desperately for inspiration. A few seconds ticked by. "Thornhill," he finally said. "Henry and Delilah Thornhill."

An almost *illicit* feeling shivered up my spine at the thought of being a wife. His wife.

"I shall add your name to the list for entry. It's very exclusive, you understand. I will call to confirm later next week. Good evening."

The line went dead—Henry looked like he'd seen a ghost, parading up the museum steps. Freya hummed the "Wedding March" again.

Abe assessed Henry and me with narrowed eyes as if sizing us up. "Looks like we've discovered the way into Victoria Whitney's good graces. Henry and Delilah are getting married."

8

DELILAH

*A*be and I perched on the top of the stairs at the Franklin Museum. My stilettos were in my hand, bare feet on cool concrete. My dress was wrinkled, my makeup smudged, while Abe seemed prepped for a photo shoot even at one in the morning.

He'd asked me to stay back and sent Freya and Henry home.

"I can tell you're angry with me," he said.

"I'm not," I replied, flexing my toes.

He pinned me with a knowing stare until I relented.

"I'm not angry. I'm confused."

"Whether you're confused *or* angry," he continued, "leave it at home on this case, Delilah. We've taken the biggest job in Codex's short history, and I need everyone sharp and unemotional."

When Abe had hired me, I'd been gone from the police department for barely six months. I'd spent half that time recuperating with my fathers—both park rangers who lived four hours away in a nature reserve. Back home, I could slip into who I used to be: the girl who grew up in a rural, small town and understood the forest that surrounded our cabin more intimately than breathing.

But as soon as I'd come back to Philadelphia, I ached to my core. I wanted a badge, a gun, criminals to hunt down without mercy. The world was filled with a universe of wrongs and making them *right* was my life's purpose. Freya was the partner—and friend—I'd always yearned for.

Abe was the kind of boss who garnered your respect within the first five minutes of meeting him. So I knew he was right.

And I was still mad. *And* confused. "Henry's first day in the field was six hours ago."

"And how did he do?"

"He's smart. He knows a ton about the world that Victoria operates in." I remembered the way she'd gazed at him—the way she'd fluttered and purred like a woman on a first date. "He charmed her," I admitted. But *didn't* want to admit that I knew one of the reasons why: my fake husband was devastatingly handsome.

"Then that's our way in, whether he's ready or not," Abe retorted. "Victoria is now fascinated with Henry and Delilah Thornhill, so that's who you will become."

"But he's also never been undercover before. He's...he's awkward, slow to respond. He can't read me, we have no *flow*. No chemistry."

"And Victoria wants to show off the books she's *potentially* stolen to people she perceives as being antiquities experts. That is not you. Or Freya. You have a very specific set of skills, Delilah," he continued. "Henry complements them with the fact that he speaks four languages and knows more about rare manuscripts than anyone else I've ever met."

"He can't be my partner," I said, exasperated.

"Why?"

"Because he's not Freya." Freya and I *fit*. In the middle of an undercover case, she could arch an eyebrow at me and I'd know what she meant. What we needed to do. "There's no trust there. He can't shoot a gun. He doesn't know hand-to-hand combat. He can't watch my back, and he can't protect himself."

"Last time I checked, Delilah Barrett was perfectly capable of protecting herself," he said gently.

I glanced over at him. Abe was smiling—a rare gesture. "I'm not trying to be insubordinate. I'm just concerned." I blew out a breath. "I might have convinced you to go after a case that doesn't exist."

He let a comfortable quiet hang between us—he'd known me long enough to understand when I was processing my thoughts.

"Do you ever think a person's instincts can disappear for good? If they've been wrong—really wrong—in the past?" I asked, finally.

My boss knew which parts of my past I was talking about.

"I don't believe that at all. Our instincts never disappear, regardless of what may have happened. You're still the most brilliant detective I know."

"I'm the office Jezebel, Abe." I could still remember the sickening shame that had invaded my body the first time I saw those words in print. And they weren't a quote from the reporter. Mark had said it. "And I might have led us on a giant wild goose chase," I said grimly.

"For the record, Freya and I are more than willing to beat the living shit out of Mark for calling you that."

"You've made that clear, thank you," I said. But I did smile at him.

"And secondly, your instinct led us to Francisco, who confirmed our suspicions almost immediately." He nudged my shoulder. "*Your* suspicions. And believe it or not, Henry's background knowledge attracted Victoria to the two of you. I'd call that a good partnership."

"You're not nervous about what happened back there?" Because I certainly was.

Abe was silent—staring out at the sea of city lights like a ship's captain, alert for hidden dangers beneath the surface. "I wouldn't have done any of this if I didn't trust both of you to handle it." He stood up, placed a hand on my shoulder. "Now you need to figure out how to trust each other."

9

HENRY

*T*he first time I'd examined a rare manuscript, I'd felt a sense of awe infuse my very bones. I was newly graduated, interning in special collections at the Oxford Library, translating a sixteenth-century German journal that had been recently discovered.

It was small, bound in vellum, the pages dry and almost too fragile to turn. I hadn't grown up in a religious household —my parents worshipped at the altar of academia. But sitting in that room, with the scent of history all around me, I'd felt something akin to grace.

I searched for that feeling now as I carefully removed the bindings that protected the recovered copy of *Fahrenheit 451*. It was the morning after we'd fled to Francisco; the morning after I officially became fake married to my coworker, Delilah. I'd woken up feeling jostled, thoughts scrambled—as if I need to run or jump or scale a tall building. Abe had encouraged all of us to head home, get a good night's sleep—that we'd make a plan as soon as we were back in the office.

But in the space of a few hours, I'd gone from office researcher to undercover agent. It was so beyond the edge of my understanding it was like trying to leap to the moon from the earth. It felt, quite simply, impossible.

So I'd come in early instead, attempting to reconnect with the feelings of awe that had shaped the majority of my life until now.

"Hey."

I looked up to find Delilah, leaning against the doorway. She was dressed neatly in a gray pencil skirt and sleeveless blouse, the streaming dawn light setting flames to her black hair.

"Good morning," I said.

"You're in early."

"I know Abe wanted this done. And I needed some quiet reflection after the night we had."

She crossed her arms. "So I guess we'll be working together on this Copernicus case, huh?"

"It looks like," I replied. "You don't seem too happy about that."

"I'm used to working with Freya," she explained. "We've been partners for two years. And you're..."

"Terrible?"

"No," she said quickly. "Just new. Green. This is going to be high-profile, and we're going to have to be fully undercover as a married couple. We barely know each other, let alone having the kind of trust we need to work this case."

I crossed my arms, mirroring her pose. "Tell me what you mean by that."

"It's the *reading* of the other person, their gestures, their body language. Like you can read their mind. *That's* what I have with Freya. If you and I had been partners for years, this would be fine. But we can't fake that kind of intimacy. It comes with time."

I rubbed the back of my neck. "Delilah, I want to do a good job on this."

"I know you do," she said. Her posture was hard, unyielding.

"And it seems like we'll need to convince Victoria that we're in love." I thought I saw the faintest blush in her pale cheeks. "That means trust, right?"

She nodded. "Trust is the single most important thing. I need to feel like if I fall, you'll catch me." She tilted her palms up, like a plea. "I'm not sure I can get us there in the amount of time that we have. It feels impossible."

"That's interesting," I said. "I had the same feeling when I woke up this morning."

A painfully awkward silence stretched between us.

"So what do we do?" I asked.

"We have our marching orders." Her tone was brisk. "Abe wants us to be fake married, so I guess I better have Freya photoshop a picture of us dancing under rose petals in the middle of Ireland or whatever."

I laughed, surprised—and her lips curved in a cautious smile.

But then the smile quickly disappeared.

"So the auction is in a week," she said. "We should start working together on some things. Get to know each other better so that our undercover roles feel more comfortable and less stilted."

"I can do that," I said. "Speaking of, do you want to see the book I'm working on?"

"Yeah," she brightened. She took a few steps closer. I moved out of the way so she could view it—the wings of the book were splayed open to the title page. Delilah came even closer—it felt like I was trying to get a skittish fawn to eat from my hand.

"Ray Bradbury signed the first fifty copies of *Fahrenheit 451* in 1953 and had them bound in asbestos. A protection against fire." Without touching, I indicated the line of italic text beneath the title: *It is specially bound in Johns-Manville Quinterra, an asbestos material with exceptional resistance to pyrolysis.* "According to the library that reported the theft, there were two things that made number twenty-three especially rare. The nick in the spine. And the fact that he signed it *Ray*. No *Bradbury*."

"I wonder why," Delilah said. Our eyes met and I held her gaze. "Seems like a pretty important thing to forget."

"I guess that's one of the guiding reasons why I do what I do. Inventory mistakes, misprints, all the unique variations that make each book distinguished in its own right. Each error tells a story."

Delilah bent down to examine the signature more closely. When she exhaled, I felt her breath on my fingers. "Maybe he was about to sign his name and a delivery guy came with the biggest, greasiest, cheesiest pizza he'd ever seen."

"Or...he looked out the window. Saw a bluebird and thought about spring."

"I like your idea better," she said. She stood back up and crossed her arms again, revealing edges of muscle in her shoulders. I knew she practiced on the punching bag out front —but I'd never seen her in action. "Do you do that a lot? Come up with stories for each mistake you find?"

I nodded. "Or sometimes I'll imagine the daily life of the people who last touched it. Not private collectors like Victoria. But the original owners."

She tilted her head, and a curl slid across her forehead. She brushed it away with fingernails painted the same shade as her mouth.

"What?" I asked.

"Just thinking something through," she said. She looked back down at the book, and a wave of happiness moved across her face. She positively glowed with it.

"You must really love Ray Bradbury," I said

"I actually don't read much," she admitted. "Does that make you hate me?"

"I am breaking the Librarian's Code by talking to you."

Her eyes brightened—like she wanted to laugh but was holding herself back.

"What made you look at the book that way?"

"Justice. Righting what's wrong. Catching bad guys. It's why I first became a police officer."

I studied her for a second. "But we don't have the power to arrest people as private detectives here at Codex. Isn't the *justice* in the recovery of a book to its rightful owner, regardless of who stole it?"

Her voice was steady. "Abe has an old contact at the FBI Art Theft department. Any evidence that we legally gather that could help their investigations, Abe sends to that contact for them to take action on. And occasionally, if the FBI is stalled on a case, Abe receives crumbs of information that could help us in *our* investigation."

I mulled that over. "Is that why you can do this job? Because suspects are always being arrested in the background, even if you're not doing the arresting?"

"That's exactly why," she said.

"So it doesn't matter that what we recover are vital pieces of our cultural history? All that matters is the bad guy gets punished?" Even as the words left my mouth, Bernard appeared in my mind again, waving my forged signature in the air with that pompous grin. Had I given any thought since that night about the manuscripts he'd taken? Or had I only been focused on punishing him?

"Of course this matters," Delilah said. "This book is important. But all of this—the thefts, the shady black-market websites, the wealthy thieves with connections—is bigger than rare books. When people like Bernard have unlimited amounts of money, they start buying and selling more than just books, Henry."

I hadn't thought of that. Bernard, with his multiple houses and piles of money, could certainly be involved in something even more nefarious than just antiquities. How far did all of this go?

How much had I *missed*?

"Since we've been paired up on this case, what's your goal?" I asked. "What's the end game here?"

"Our orders are to gain Victoria's trust to recover the stolen Copernicus."

"But what's your priority?"

"Depending on what we uncover, legally, the FBI could receive a lot of incidental evidence from us. They could use it to eventually arrest Victoria. She's all but admitted to *us* that she dabbles in this world. *One* incriminating photograph is all it would take."

I took her words in, part of me knowing she was right. But my eyes landed on the Bradbury, and my entire career unfolded before my eyes, tugging at the core of my being. "My priority is the book."

"Just the book?"

Bernard's taunt came back to me: *What you think you've uncovered is happening in record numbers throughout our industry.*

"We'll never stop the stealing," I continued. "The least we can do is get the book back."

She narrowed her eyes at me. "That's what Abe says all the time."

"That's *my* priority."

The front office door crashed open. Freya strode in wearing a Ravenclaw sweatshirt and glasses even bigger than yesterday's. "Good morning, Mr. and Mrs. Thornhill," she smirked.

Delilah propped her hands on her hips and smirked back at Freya. "I get married, and you don't even throw me a bachelorette party? There should be strippers here right now."

Freya snorted. "Let's all picture Abe's expression if he walked into the office and it was filled to the brim with strippers."

Delilah laughed fully—it was husky and very, very contagious.

"Don't you get donuts today?" I asked.

"It's a post-successful-recovery tradition. Although things are a bit different because we need to immediately start on The Case of the Missing Copernicus." She unzipped her laptop bag, taking out a sleek, shiny computer. "I'll start on the online forums, see if anyone's dropping hints about dead astronomers."

Abe walked in with a bag of freshly baked Federal Donuts. The warm, cinnamon-sugar scent wafted through the office.

"Your reward," he said to Freya, laying the bag on her desk.

She squealed, opening the bag and handing a donut to Delilah.

"Cheers, partner." They flashed goofy grins at each other before taking a bite at the same time.

But then Freya's eyes widened. "Henry, I almost forgot." She handed me one—it was still hot from the oven, pieces of sugar crumbling into the palm of my hand. "You're part of the tradition now too."

Delilah gave me a shy smile that I was eager to return. It wasn't that Freya and Delilah had ignored me for the past few months, but we'd mostly been separated during my probationary period. They were often out in the field, trailing suspects or on long stakeouts while I was doing research for Abe or studying for my private detective's exam. This—this silly tradition of donuts and coffee after a successful recovery —felt like my *real* first day at Codex.

"That was some good undercover work on the fly last night," Freya said.

"Thank you." I took a bite. "And this is delicious."

"Welcome to the dream team," Freya said.

"Speaking of teams," Abe said, shuffling a stack of papers on his desk, "Delilah, I want you and Henry to get eyes on Victoria's property tomorrow night."

"But Frey and I usually handle that," Delilah said casually, cutting another donut in half and laying it on Freya's plate.

"I know. But you and Henry are partners on this case so I want you and Henry to go."

His voice indicated there was to be no argument.

But Delilah's head snapped up anyway. "It's easier if she and I do it, though."

Abe's lips pressed into a thin line. Some silent argument was happening between the two of them—and I had an inkling it was about me.

"Henry, how much experience do you have staking out a private residence?" she asked.

"Uh...zero."

"Good thing I'm sending him with my most experienced detective," Abe replied, closing the door to his office.

Freya slid off the desk, opening her laptop. "Delilah, it's fine," she said softly. "It's just different, is all."

Delilah sighed and pulled a pen out of the other woman's hair. "How many of these am I going to find in there today?"

"One billion," Freya shrugged. "This is no Bradbury case. This is the real deal."

"I'm a good student, I promise," I said.

Delilah re-crossed her arms, slowly assessed me from head to toe. "And I'm a tough fucking teacher."

10

___

DELILAH

*V*ictoria Whitney lived in a Tudor-style mansion out in the Main Line, the wealthiest suburb in Philadelphia. According to the plans Freya dug up from the County Clerk's office, it had thirteen bedrooms, fourteen bathrooms, a pool, a sauna, a tennis court and a garden designed as intricately as the Palace of Versailles. It was built of red brick, with charming arches and multiple gables and, of course, the lawn was manicured to perfection.

"Do you see any evil henchman?" Freya's voice crackled through my cell phone.

"Negative," I said. "All the henchman going in and out of Victoria's house look perfectly reasonable."

"Well, *that's* a relief," she said. I glanced at Henry, who was looking out the window but grinning. There was a pause where I imagined Freya back at the Codex offices, typing away on her keyboard. "You two have eyes on the mansion. I'm going to gracefully attempt to ask a bunch of shady book dealers if they've come into any extraordinary merchandise recently."

"Are they responding to the code?" I asked.

Victoria's house was lit with ground spotlights—clearly indicating to any passerby that it was the biggest one on the block. A thick forest of trees wrapped around her property, mimicking the other mansions on this block that were granted privacy through large, extravagant bushes. A few other cars were parked on the street—a lucky break, since we couldn't stand out. But I'd still parked us beneath a giant weeping willow whose branches almost touched the ground.

"Nope," Freya said. "I'm getting the impression that code is used for lower-level deals. Like a Ray Bradbury. For the Copernicus, everyone seems tight-lipped. And I can't figure out if Victoria is one of the people I'm talking to."

"Victoria would pay someone to do this for her," I said. "This is too dirty of a detail."

She hummed. "Well, I hope one of the henchmen walks past with a giant box that says *Fragile: Stolen Books Inside* because we might be on a wild goose chase."

I snorted—but a swell of nerves followed in its wake.

"You go chase. Henry and I will watch for a bit."

"Over and out," she said.

When Henry slid into my car earlier, my eyes had landed on the swell of biceps his soft tee-shirt exposed, the muscles of his forearms, his big, strong fingers. Yesterday I'd watched him handle that book with deliberate intention—fingers caressing each page as if he were memorizing the words through touch.

Switching off Freya's voice had plunged us into quiet, while outside cicadas sang.

"My only knowledge of stakeouts comes from reading thrillers," he said. In the tight space of the car, his rough voice felt too intimate. "Should I have brought fast food?"

"Depending on how long it goes, Freya and I usually bring French fries and tacos along." Admitting that made me miss her, though we'd just spoken. It felt awkward in the front seat with Henry, whose body and cedar scent seemed to invade every inch of my car.

"A wise choice," he said. "What are we looking for exactly?"

I waved at the windshield. "If Victoria recently stole a book with as much media attention as that Copernicus is currently getting, she would probably change up her routine. We want to see who's going in and out of her place, what's changed. We watch, take notes." I held up my notepad. "Being a private detective is about perceiving the clues that exist in the most mundane exchanges. A late-night delivery, a deliberate word choice, a connection of eyes meeting across the room." I heard the scratch of Henry's pencil on his own notebook. "In my experience, both as a police officer *and* a detective, criminals want to get caught. And their subconscious slips up in a bunch of tiny but significant ways."

"When you were a police officer, what did you do?" he asked.

"Burglary," I said automatically. "Theft, that kind of thing."

"You loved it?"

"Yes, I did," I said, throat tight. "Very much."

"Can I ask why you left?"

"Not right now."

I felt his eyes studying me in the dark, but thankfully he didn't pry further. "What else are you teaching me tonight, Delilah?"

I tucked a strand of hair behind my ear—noted two probable neighbors out walking their three dogs. "Our assignment is to go undercover as newlyweds. We need to get our story straight. We need to live and breathe as the Thornhills so that Victoria will trust us with her dark secrets. Or make a mistake and say something she shouldn't."

"Does Abe think if we appear passionately in love Victoria will take us to the book?"

"That's too easy," I admitted, as much for Henry as for myself.

"Then what?"

Our eyes met in the dim light. "We need time with Victoria, to learn her weaknesses. To crack her open. It's like putting together the clues of a book you're conserving. Kind of like you were explaining to me yesterday."

He rubbed his jaw. "That makes sense. Victoria is a rare manuscript with no discernible history. We need to figure her out."

"Because my first guess would be to shelve her in the *Egomaniac Wealthy Heiress* section," I said, "but in this line of work you learn that people are more complex than their labels."

He studied me for a moment. "You must have been an incredible police officer."

I shrugged. "I was pretty good."

"Do you miss it?" he asked. "Actually, never mind. I'm sorry. You told me you didn't want to talk about it."

"It's fine," I rushed to say. "We need to focus, okay?"

"Okay."

It was hard for me to think about the police force without feeling a deluge of wrenching guilt and mortifying shame.

"Anyway," I continued, "we need to help you become a brilliant liar. Undercover work is about immersing yourself in the persona you've created. Which should be easier for you because Henry Thornhill's fake career is technically yours. A lot of the base knowledge is there already."

A black sedan turned down the street, heading our way. "Get down," I commanded, gripping the soft edge of his shirt. We ducked low and waited for it to pass, headlights crawling through the trees surrounding us. Our heads turned toward each other—both whispering as we waited to make sure the coast was clear.

"Delilah?"

"Yeah?" The windows of the car that had passed were tinted, which set my mind whirring.

"You can let go of my shirt now."

I dropped it like it burned. "Sorry."

"It's fine," he said. "Won't we have to get used to doing things like that anyway?"

"Shirt-clutching?" I asked.

"Touching each other."

"Uh, right," I said. "We can sit back up now."

I craned my neck as I did, attempting to get a license plate.

"Something off with that car?" Henry asked.

My senses were waking up. "Maybe," I admitted. "We'll see if it comes back." Lights began to flicker on in various windows of Victoria's house. "Okay, back to training."

"I'm ready," he said.

"Think about the backstories you create for every mistake you find in a book. You'll be doing that for Henry Thornhill. And constantly. You have to get into the mind of this man that doesn't really exist. So that as Victoria asks you questions or digs into your past, you answer right away. Correctly. And, as a rule, if she asks us both something we haven't discussed, I'll answer for us first."

"So, for example, it doesn't appear as if neither one of us knows how long we've been married?"

It was funnier now, absent of that night's tension. So much so that laughter threatened to burst from me.

"I spent half of that conversation wondering if I should have sprinted for the emergency exit and run all the way home." Henry grinned.

That had me laughing for real—but when he caught my gaze, I dropped it just as quickly.

"Focus," I chided softly, a command more for me than him. "Have you given much thought to who Henry Thornhill is?"

"Some," he said. "I don't feel ready for Saturday night though."

I was nodding—even as half of my attention was aimed at the mansion.

"I'm Victoria," I said. "Ready?"

"I don't—"

"How did you and Delilah meet?"

He was frozen, watching me.

"How did you and your lovely wife meet?" I asked again.

He dragged a hand over his mouth, mildly panicked.

"Henry."

He blew out a breath. "How do you come up with ideas this quickly? I've already fucked up, and we're only thirty seconds into the training."

I mentally backed up, tried to recall hours of instruction from the police academy, from Freya. "Okay, I'm sorry. That was the wrong way to start." I went to touch his shirt again but accidentally grazed his biceps. It was hard as granite. "Close your eyes. Let yourself truly imagine Henry Thornhill as a person. All his likes and dislikes, his random memories."

He sat quietly for a minute, and I attempted to wrangle my impatience. But what other choice did I have? Abe had instructed us to partner on this case, and I was nothing if not a loyal foot soldier. But I was anxious to *go*, to hunt down Victoria, to respond to the seductive call of adrenaline that'd been thrumming in my bloodstream for two days.

"Imagine a time you've been madly in love," I continued.

Henry cleared his throat. "What if I've never *been* madly in love?"

I shifted in my seat, happy he couldn't see me. The last time I'd *thought* I'd been in love was Mark, and digging through those memories felt like sticking your hand into the creepy, dark space under your sink: half-convinced it's fine, half-convinced you'll land on a web filled with spiders.

"It's like...um...an obsession. A craving that feels really *good* to give into. A sense of rightness. Completion." I glanced at his profile in the darkness. "Does that help?"

"Yes," he said. "Does it matter that I've never been married?" He opened his eyes now, watched me carefully.

"I've never been married either," I said. "I guess we can talk to Victoria about..." I tapped my fingers on the steering wheel. "I don't know, how we always fight over who does the dishes more?"

A grin tugged at the corner of his mouth. "Right. I should definitely hate how loudly you snore at night."

"I've never gotten along with your parents."

"In-laws," he sighed, shaking his head.

We shared a brief, private smile.

"But," I said, stopping the game, "Henry and Delilah Thornhill eloped. They're...passionate. Impulsive. True romantics. *That's* what Victoria was responding to. Hold that at the center of your persona."

"I'm obsessed with you," Henry said. "I mean, not *real* you. Fake you."

"Exactly. Let's try again, okay?"

He flexed his fingers like he was preparing to fight. "Go."

"How did you and Delilah meet?" I said again.

"An art lecture, about five years ago. It was specifically on the topic of the feminine expression in twelfth-century—"

"Too specific," I cut in. "The more colorful you make the lie, the less believable it is. Plus we need to stay simple."

"You *are* a tough teacher," he muttered.

I arched my brow at him.

"Go," he sighed.

"How did you and Delilah meet?"

"At work. She used to come into the library. We'd talk about her favorite books."

"*Perfect.*"

"Yeah?" he asked, surprised.

"Simple, to the point, not much to explain." I switched back to my Victoria voice. "Why did you decide to become a consultant, dear? You're obviously *extremely* talented."

A low laugh rumbled from his chest. "Feels like I'm sitting next to real Victoria."

"Who would have spotted your lies a mile away by now."

He stared out the window, as if the answer lay tangled in the branches of the tree. "Tick-tock," I said.

"Bureaucracy. Too much red tape, you know?"

I snorted.

"You like that one?" he asked, face bright.

"Yeah, that's good," I conceded. "Just make it one trillion times faster."

The black sedan flew down the block like a speed demon.

"*Shit,*" we said in unison, sliding all the way down. My heart jumped into my throat.

"Same car, second time," I murmured. Two lost drivers who happened to have suspiciously tinted windows maybe? "Let's stay down."

When I turned my face toward Henry, his was close.

"My turn," he whispered. "So Delilah, your husband is a talented librarian. What is it that you do again?"

"Philanthropist," I shot back. "I'm a trust fund baby."

His eyes flared in challenge behind his glasses.

"I came prepared," I said with a sly grin. His eyes dropped

to my mouth for a split second, before headlights sliced across his face.

"*Lower*," I hissed. He dropped as instructed.

"What made you propose to her like that on the spot, Henry?" I said, listening for boot steps heading our way. I wanted to push him to think clearly even in high-stress situations. I was wearing black yoga pants and my running shoes—I was more than ready to bolt if we had to.

"I'd never seen her look more beautiful."

My head whipped toward his before I could stop it. It wasn't really fair that he was a handsome librarian who *also* had a voice that sounded like fucking. Tangled-sheets, sweaty-limbs, headboard-shaking fucking.

"What did you say?"

"Sorry," he said quickly. "Is that too personal?"

"No. Not at all," I said. But I felt slightly out of breath. "We're pretending. That's probably the kind of thing Victoria wants to hear."

"Impulsively romantic, right?"

"Um...yeah," I said, distracted. The air outside had a charged feeling I recognized—quiet before a storm. There was a volley of sharp *cracks:* car doors slamming, the pop of male voices. With a racing pulse, I picked my head up inch by agonizing inch—until I could *just* make out Victoria's mansion. The black sedan had become five black sedans, and a group of giant men with pistols were stepping out and standing in Victoria's driveway with deadly-looking posture.

"What the fuck," I breathed.

"What is it?"

"The evil henchmen have arrived."

One by one, they made their way inside her house—although a handful went toward the perimeter. I understood heightened security for a stolen book but this seemed excessive.

My fingers twitched on the door.

"Delilah," Henry started.

"How fast are you?" I asked, already cracking the door open.

"Pretty fast," he admitted. "I run five miles a day."

I grinned at him—ready for the chase.

"Then you should be able to keep up."

And I bolted toward the henchmen.

11

HENRY

*I*f this was another lesson, I didn't want to fail. So even though I had no idea what Delilah was doing, I sprinted from the car, keeping my head low like she did. She'd show me what to do as long as I watched carefully.

Victoria's few neighbors all had houses hidden behind gigantic trees and pruned bushes. It meant no one was watching us as we ran—except for maybe the armed security guards that had spilled out of those sedans like they were clown cars. Delilah ran for the edge of those trees and I followed. When she crouched behind a large tree trunk, I almost slammed right into her, grasping the sides and digging my heels into the soft earth.

"Are you okay?" she asked, not looking at me.

"Yes but..." I caught my breath. "What are we doing?"

"Reconnaissance." She turned her head—her profile breathtaking in the moonlight that slipped between the branches: full lips, high cheekbones. I wanted to kick myself for saying what I did back in the car, but she'd pushed me to speak on the fly. As I'd stared into her wide blue eyes, the only word that had reverberated through my brain was *beautiful*.

"I just want to get a closer look at who these guys are. They don't look like typical security guards," she said.

I peeked around the edge of the tree. Two large men stood a hundred feet away—their hands were resting securely on the guns holstered at their waists. The sight of their weapons kicked my pulse up faster than when I'd been sprinting. Delilah's arms came carefully to the small of her back. With practiced ease, she unsnapped a handgun from the waistband of her pants. It glinted in the moonlight as she lowered it to her side.

I swallowed hard, attempting to ignore my body's immediate response to her holding a gun. The women I'd dated in the past were all academics—bookworms like me, smart and analytical. Delilah Barrett could force me to my knees in an instant—quite literally. In the lingering moonlight, she looked gorgeous but fatal, like a Bond girl with a weapon.

She leaned out farther, beckoning me to do the same. I placed a hand on the tree trunk, next to her head. My chest brushed lightly against her shoulder blades.

"Maybe Victoria's afraid," I whispered. "Worried having the book makes her a target."

The guards' radios crackled in the silence, and we both startled. One turned and I had a fleeting impression of *big* and *scary* before we slid fully behind the tree. Delilah spun around to face me. Both of my hands bracketed her head as we panted in unison.

Delilah held one finger to her mouth: *quiet.*

I shifted my feet and a twig snapped—the sound like a fucking *firework* in the hushed forest. Her eyes widened with annoyance.

"Sorry," I mouthed.

She didn't reply, but she flicked the safety off on her gun. I felt suspended in time, wished I knew what she was thinking. A strand of her hair brushed the back of my hand.

A minute crawled by. Two. Then three. Hidden behind the tree, we could only stare at each other, forcing me to notice the spray of freckles across her nose, barely visible in the dark. The indentation in her full, lower lip. The proud arch of her eyebrows. I steeled my expression, aiming to keep it neutral.

Her expression was entirely unreadable.

One more minute of utter stillness. She tilted her head to the right.

"Let's go," she whispered.

We crept softly, carefully, beneath the trees, aware of the guards and any sudden movements. The car felt miles away. I watched our feet for twigs and piles of leaves, squinting in the darkness. Every step ached with heavy danger and the threat of being spotted. My muscles shook and sweat had my shirt sticking to my back.

And if I hadn't been staring that intently at the ground, I never would have noticed Delilah's foot about to touch the wire.

12

HENRY

I caught Delilah around the waist and I pulled her hard into my chest one millisecond before her foot touched the wire. She let out a yelp in surprise before I covered her mouth with my palm.

A shout came from the guards to our left. But we were surrounded by enormous, leafy trees on all sides. I prayed we weren't visible.

"I think that's a tripwire," I whispered, lips against her ear.

I held her body steady as she peered down—felt her shock when she recognized it for what it was. We were balanced together, tilting back on the balls of our feet. Were there wires behind us? In front? I took rapid, shallow breaths, and beneath my arm, her body rippled with coiled strength.

A series of branches crashed to our left. Flashlight beams crisscrossed like spider webs nearby.

Delilah lowered her raised foot to the ground—gently. No sound. I let my palm drop from her mouth, but she was still pinned to me.

"*Gun,*" she hissed, wiggling her elbows against my ribs. "Henry, I need my gun."

"Sorry," I hissed back, for what felt like the hundredth time that night. I let her arms go, watched her grip the weapon with both hands—lowered at her side but ready.

The beams of light were *definitely* getting closer.

I yearned for the ability to read her mind, shoot a gun, do *something* other than continue to put us at risk. Every element of Delilah's still, focused posture screamed *hunter* while I was bumbling around like prey.

With incredible balance, she pivoted toward me, avoiding the wire.

"On the count of three," she whispered, "we run."

She held up one finger, and an explosion of sound came from Victoria's house. Sound and a blinding light.

Two. Her second finger went up.

The guards were perilously close.

She didn't even get to three. We took off toward the car in a dead sprint, racing with arms pumping and legs flying over logs and leaves—and then jarring back onto the asphalt.

I tasted fear in my mouth, like old copper pennies.

But there was no denying the feeling concealed beneath the fear: *exhilaration*.

I didn't dare look behind me as we reached the car at the same time, throwing open the doors and jumping inside. Delilah started the car and peeled away, tires squealing, and it wasn't until we were back on the main road before either one of us truly exhaled.

"Please don't ask me a Victoria question right now," I managed.

Her knuckles were white against the steering wheel, but the rest of her was oddly composed, as if already anticipating the next step of the investigation.

"Who were those guys?" she muttered, dialing Freya. As the dial tone rang out, she chanced a whip-fast look at me before putting her eyes back on the road. "Henry, are you okay?"

"I'm absolutely fine," I said, somewhat amazed. "A little confused. Slightly shaken up. But I'm not hurt. Are *you* okay?"

But before she could answer Freya clicked on. "What happened?" she asked.

As Delilah relayed the details of the guards, I fixated on her check-in with Freya—the easy way they communicated. There was a comfort there I admired—they were friends, partners, coworkers—all of it blended together in a way I knew Delilah and I would never get to. At least not for this case.

"Armed guards and trip wires," Freya mused over the phone. "What is going on with our kooky heiress?"

"It could be the Copernicus. It could be something else entirely. We could have stumbled into a hotbed of perfectly legal activity." Delilah bit her lip—looking nervous for all of a second before she stopped herself.

"Maybe the Thornhills could get her talking about it on Saturday," I suggested.

Delilah drummed her fingers on the wheel. "I like that idea."

I hid a smile behind my hand.

"I'll talk to Abe and we'll debrief tomorrow," Freya said. "Get home safe, okay?"

"I'll bring you more donuts tomorrow," Delilah said.

"And that is why I'll love you forever." Freya clicked off and I saw the happiness in Delilah's face recede—only to be replaced with a stilted silence.

"I'm sorry," I said.

"For what?"

"Giving us away back there. Exposing us. I should have been more careful." I had a feeling the sound of that breaking twig was going to haunt my dreams.

Her brow furrowed, but she didn't respond. Finally, I said in my best Victoria voice, "Where did you and Henry go on your first date, my darling?"

She glared at me in disbelief and huffed out a frustrated breath. "Okay, fuck, you got me."

"I'm giving you a hard time," I said. Outside the window, the city's skyscrapers narrowed down to brick rowhomes on cobblestone streets. "Do you want to try again?"

"Yeah," she said. "Hit me."

"Where did you go on your first date?"

"The art museum. Then out for drinks. I knew right away he was my..." She stopped.

"Your what?" I asked.

"Never mind," she stumbled. "Concise. No details. We went to the art museum and out for drinks." She parallel parked in front of my brick rowhome with the dexterity of a native Philadelphian. "You're sure you're okay?" Her voice was soft.

"Better than okay," I promised. "I'll see you in the office tomorrow."

I was halfway to my door when she rolled down her window. "Henry?"

I turned back, crouched down at the car door so I could see her. "Did you forget something?"

"Yes, I mean, kind of," she said. "It's just...thank you. For grabbing me before I stepped on the trip wire. You were paying attention and I wasn't. You had good instincts tonight. And uh..." She glanced down at the steering wheel. "You know everyone does things like that in the field. We can't control what happens to us out there. Twigs snap."

The surprise compliment dragged a smile across my face. "You were right, by the way."

"About what?"

"You are a tough fucking teacher."

That comment earned me a real smile from Delilah—full lips and a dimple in one cheek. "And you're a quick fucking study."

13

DELILAH

*J*t was late when I found Henry in his darkened office, surrounded by piles of open books and handwritten notes. I stood in the doorway for a long time before he realized I was there, so intently was he studying the words.

It'd been three days since we'd staked out Victoria's house. Our debut as a married couple was the next day.

And in those three days, I'd *almost* managed to forget what it had felt like to be pinned against Henry's hard body as my foot balanced over that tripwire. His hand over my mouth, his mouth at my ear, the threat, the adrenaline—it was a memory as erotic as it was romantic. Because Henry had protected me from danger, and I hadn't experienced that in a long time. Watching him now—deep in thought, immersed in language —sent a spark of awareness glowing between my legs.

"You should go home soon. Get some rest," I said—quietly, so as not to startle him. The lamp on his desk cast the only light.

"Delilah," he said, turning to look at me. "I didn't know you were still here."

"Following up on a couple leads Freya found." I shrugged. "None of them panned out. For better or worse, Victoria is still our main target."

He leaned all the way back in his chair, rolling his neck. He'd shed his suit jacket and slipped off his tie, leaving his white shirt unbuttoned at the neck. "Come sit," he said. "I'll show you what I'm working on."

I did, keeping our chairs far apart. "What is that?" It looked like a series of faded mathematical equations and circular drawings.

"This," he said, "is Copernicus's understanding of our solar system. This illustration is seminal in the scientific community because it was the first to posit the theory of a heliocentric universe. The sun in the middle, all the planets orbiting."

I watched his finger trace the orbiting circles—Mars, Saturn, Jupiter, Neptune.

"The first edition of this book was printed using a hand-press in 1543 in Nuremberg. It was extremely controversial. Ptolemy's theory was the prevailing one, that the earth was the center. The Copernicus was so controversial it was placed on the Index of Forbidden Books and pulled from circulation."

"I usually know more about the person who stole the book than the book itself," I confessed. "But I can see why this book would be desired by a private collector."

"And only twenty copies are in private hands, according to the last census. Victoria would be one of a very chosen few."

Henry's fingers continued to trace the planetary orbits with precise accuracy; I was entranced by the circular motion. In the darkened office, there was a surreal intimacy, like we were the ones floating, not the planets.

"This is what you did before you came to Codex? When you worked with Bernard?" I asked.

The look on his face made me immediately regret mentioning that name. But he shook it off. "My job was to understand a rare manuscript at the deepest level—the texture of the pages, the smell, the way the spine curved or broke or fell apart. I'd catalog its owners, its journey from wherever it was discovered, buried in some attic somewhere. I mean..." He sat back, locked his eyes on mine. "This book that we're chasing is 476 years old. It was individually handpressed by a printer in Nuremberg whose name we'll never know. Touched, caressed, disdained, discarded—then cherished and applauded. All of that emotion exists within its pages, like a vibration."

I'd never thought of the book we recovered like that—they were objects to me, meant to be returned to their rightful home. The stolen books were items that balanced the scales of justice, but there was no *emotion* to them.

"It's good that Abe hired you," I admitted. "Codex needed someone like you. You're the right fit."

"I'm really happy to be here," he replied.

I rapped my knuckles against the tabletop.

"We should practice again. For tomorrow," I said.

"Ah, yes. Our debut as the Thornhills. Holy matrimony." He scooped up stray pages and paper and stacked them neatly, leaving the table clean. I admired his mouth—the full, smooth shape of it. Remembered it at my ear and the sensations it had evoked, low in my belly. Even with guards coming. Even with my own gun, cocked and ready—in so many ways, Henry could have had me.

"I'll be Victoria, okay?" I said.

He leaned back in the chair, stretching his long legs out in front of him. The tip of his shoe brushed against mine. "Hit me," he said.

"How long did the two of you even date? I'm sure your families weren't happy about the elopement."

"They weren't," he said. "Which is why we're having a reception in a few months."

"How lovely," I crooned.

"And Delilah and I have been together for five years. To be honest, I think we waited too long."

"What did she *wear* on your wedding day? She couldn't possibly have found something respectable that quickly."

Henry peered down at our feet, a centimeter apart. I nudged him.

"White dress from a thrift store. Red shoes."

"Nice detail," I said, surprised. "Colorful but doesn't sound too much like a lie."

"Plus, you like the color red. The real you," he clarified. He tapped our shoes together again—my heels were scarlet.

"You noticed that?" I asked.

"Details are my job."

I crossed my legs, separating our feet.

"Did she have a veil? Flowers?" I arranged my face in mock horror at the travesty of a wedding with no *flowers*.

Henry's eyes crinkled at the sides. "Yes," he said. I could see him thinking. "She, uh..." He cleared his throat. "I found a small bouquet at a farmer's market next to the library, and two of the librarians made a veil for her on the spot. I can still remember lifting the gauzy fabric and seeing her face. How gorgeous my almost-wife looked."

"Nice save," I said. "You two live in Society Hill?"

"Luxury rowhome. Working elevator. Three-car garage."

My brow lifted. "Fancy."

"My wife is very rich." He smirked. "Haven't you heard?"

"And the cross streets?"

Henry blanked. "Um...Spruce and...12th."

"You don't know where your own home is, Mr. Thornhill?" I placed my chin in my hand.

"Spruce and 12th," he committed.

"What's the street address? I'll send a driver."

"1234 Spruce Street."

I narrowed my eyes—but hid my smile behind my hand. "*1234* Spruce Street?"

"I don't make the rules, Victoria. That's my address." His mouth curved up.

"Don't get cocky."

"I'm more terrified than cocky," he admitted. He scrubbed a hand down his face, and I saw exhaustion etched into the lines around his mouth. "But every morning on my run this week I pretended to be Henry Thornhill. Consultant, unscrupulous collector, newlywed husband."

"Good," I said. "It has to fit you like...like the clothing you're wearing now."

"Have you ever done a high-profile undercover like this?" he asked.

I shook my head. Assessed my partner in the dark. "I'm a little worried too."

"A little?"

I shrugged. "Just a little. I know Krav Maga and carry a gun. When you can punch or shoot your way out of any situation, it helps."

"And where's your weapon now?" he asked. It might have been the late hour, but there was a distinct grate in his voice that hadn't been there before.

"I'm unarmed." I held up my arms, showed him my empty hands. "Does that make you feel safer?"

"Less safe actually," he said. "I like knowing you can save us."

My cheeks warmed.

"Do you feel like Mrs. Thornhill?" he asked.

"I have pictured us arguing over who's doing the grocery shopping this week, yes," I said.

His eyes sparkled. "We're re-doing the master bedroom and choosing paint colors is a nightmare."

"We're *always* redoing our master bedroom," I said with mock exasperation.

"Victoria *thinks* we're madly in love but really...the spark is gone," he sighed.

I bit my lip. Smiled. "We had a good run. I guess you could always be having an affair."

"Cheat on *you*?" he asked.

I had been joking—enjoying a sneaky game in this private moment. "What? You don't think Henry Thornhill is capable?"

"I think cheating on you would make Henry Thornhill an idiot."

That grate in his voice was back, like the sound of teeth scraping against skin. I recrossed my legs, and my silk skirt dragged up my thighs. Henry's eyes stayed glued to mine, but his fingers tightened where they gripped the desk.

"You're absolutely right," I replied. "That would make him an idiot."

The night of the stakeout had shown me there was a hard, muscular body beneath his tailored suits. The feel of his chest pressed to my back as we balanced precariously in the woods had *seared* me. For days, the skin between my shoulder blades had glowed like a brand.

"So no marital discord," he managed. "Victoria will fall in love with our impulsive, whirlwind romance."

"Do you think we had a honeymoon? I forgot all about that."

"A passionate elopement would naturally lead to an exotic honeymoon, don't you think?"

"I don't know," I said. "This is all new territory to me. I've never had a boyfriend in real life do anything passionate for me."

The words spilled out carelessly—a side effect of the late hour, my weariness, the confidential darkness of the solitary lamplight.

This time, Henry's eyes *did* drop to my exposed legs. I felt it, as surely as if he'd smoothed his palm from ankle to thigh. "That makes them idiots as well, Delilah."

"Paris, right?" I rushed to say. "It's the kind of city Victoria would respect. Married in Ireland at the spur of the moment. Then you whisked me to Paris for a weekend in the most expensive hotel in the city. View of the Eiffel Tower. Pricy room service. Champagne."

Twisted bedsheets. My thrift-store wedding dress shoved over my hips. My legs spread. Our fingers entwined.

Henry hadn't even responded, but I was already standing up, seeking distance. "That sounds good. And you should rest," I repeated, my tone sharper than I intended. "We both need to sleep, okay?"

"Yes, ma'am," he replied.

But as I moved around the office, gathering my things, he remained, staring at the pages of the Copernicus with such intimacy I wanted to blush. His fingers, tracing the orbits, the path toward the sun.

Another symptom of becoming a detective I recognized— even at the limits of exhaustion, your brain will continue to search for clues. I didn't want to disturb his process, but he called to me as I was about to leave. When I turned, he was framed in the doorway, hands in his pockets.

"Were you fired from the police department, Delilah?" he asked.

The question knocked me back a step. I contemplated

lying. It wasn't something I necessarily wanted a new partner to know.

I opened my mouth to spin some half-truth—but it sent my nerves jangling.

I trust you, Abe had said. *Now you need to trust each other.*

"Yes," I finally answered. "I was fired. How did you know?" There were still a few articles online with my name in them. The thought of Henry reading them made me vaguely nauseous. "You didn't—"

"Look you up?" he asked. "No, I wouldn't do that. It's your body language when I've asked you about it. Everything says *walls up.*"

"You're becoming a real detective now."

"I'm learning from the best," he replied.

"Why do you even want to know though?" I asked. Stalling for time.

"You said it the other day," he said. "How can we be partners if we don't know anything about each other? Especially since we need to convince our target we're madly in love?"

I was so fucking grateful for the curtains of darkness that surrounded us.

"That's why I thought I'd ask."

"I don't really like talking about it," I said. Every time I believed myself to be over it, a swell of anger or embarrassment would startle me from my dreams, hurtling me right back to the moment my world fell apart.

His posture softened, conceded. "Forget I—"

And for the first time in ages, it made me want to *share.*

"I trusted a man," I said, steeling my tone. "I trusted a man that I shouldn't have. My boss. I was younger than him and—" I hated saying it. "Younger and stupid."

"I doubt very much you've ever been stupid, Delilah."

"Not all of us have advanced degrees," I countered. "Anyway, I was actually just a pawn for him to climb the career ladder. Something to manipulate, move around, do with as he wished. A body to use. Not a person."

Even from across the room, I felt a charged jolt from Henry: anger.

"I'm sorry."

I shrugged, even as my fists curled at my sides. "It's not your fault. And it's ancient history now."

I sensed he wanted to say more so I waited.

"Abe told you why I came here, right?"

I nodded. "Bernard."

"I trusted him too. For ten years. I looked up to that man as much as I looked up to my parents. I modeled my career after his, mirrored his every move, sought his approval constantly. The night I'd walked to his flat to confront him, I'd almost convinced myself I was wrong—even with the evidence staring me right in the face."

I knew this feeling as deeply as any other.

"I think all of us believe we are immune to people's manipulations," I said. "It hurts the ego, realizing that you're the same as everyone else. That a sociopath can come along, charm the shit out of you, and leave you fucked up and confused. Like realizing you're wearing blinders—but you have no memory of ever putting them on."

"*Yes*," he said, taking a step forward. "That's what I've been feeling."

"There's nothing wrong with you," I said. "You're only human."

"And so are you, Delilah Barrett," he replied softly.

The darkness concealed my smile.

I glanced at my phone: 1:27 am. "Not anymore. I am now officially Delilah Thornhill."

He stepped back into his office, lips in a grim line. "Promise not to yell at me when I come home late, wife?"

I shivered again.

Wife.

"I promise," I said. "And get some sleep for real, Henry. It all begins now."

14

HENRY

"*D*elilah?" I said, knocking on her office door. "It's almost time for us to go."

"One second," she called back, voice muffled.

Abe was on the phone with Francisco, and Freya was hunched over her laptop, fingers moving in a flash.

"Okay, Mr. Thornhill," she said, pulling a pencil from her hair and scribbling something down, "if Victoria feels absolutely compelled to do some digging on you, you now have a website."

She turned it around with a look of pride. It was a real website for my fake consultant business—I was a traveling librarian, available for hire.

"You think she'll really dig?"

"If she doesn't, that security team will," Freya said. I hadn't even thought about that—the ease with which your identity could be traced online now. "I've also created fake Facebook profiles for both of you." She scrolled and I blinked in amazement—she must have grabbed photos from our actual pages, but cropped them, added links and posts that made these forged profiles look active when they really weren't. "And finally, Delilah now has a website for her family foundation. I gave her a cool, sexy maiden name." One last click and a website for the Delilah Gatsby Family Foundation appeared, advertising local grant awards for Philadelphia charities.

"Wow," I said, impressed. "I'm happy *you* thought of these things."

"One of my many jobs," she said, clapping me on the shoulder. "*Oh,* and I almost forgot the best part for tonight."

She walked over to a wall safe and spun the lock. Reached in and pulled out two black velvet boxes. "You can tell Victoria you found the right jeweler, finally."

It took me a moment to comprehend what she was giving me. I snapped the box open—inside sat a delicate gold band with a cluster of diamonds.

Delilah's wedding ring.

"Congratulations," she teased.

I was about to put a gold ring on the left finger of an undercover partner I barely knew.

Freya walked into Abe's office, which left me entirely alone when Delilah stepped out in a floor-length ivory gown.

This entire week had become a personal study in self-denial. Which was technically good, since before Codex I'd made an entire career of studying; deciphering information, taking every detail apart, assembling it back together. I'd once spent two days cataloging every unique imperfection in a manuscript's gilded edges. I knew *study*—the way Delilah's instincts pointed her toward corruption, my instincts pointed me to obsess over any beautiful piece of history that captivated my attention.

Delilah was not a piece of history. She was no object, no book to be labeled and shelved. But from our first night in the field until now, I was painstakingly aware of my fascination with my partner. I studied that fascination, understood it to be wrong and complicated, unprofessional and potentially dangerous.

Focus was the priority while undercover, I knew that much to be true.

So as Delilah strode toward me, I didn't notice the silk of her gown and the way it clung to her hips. I didn't regard the contrast of her raven hair and the white diamonds that dangled from her ears. Her blood-red lips were of no concern to me—and the distinct way my body had begun responding to the sight of my coworker was something to be ignored.

"If Henry wasn't fake married to you, *I'd* marry you," Freya said, then wolf-whistled from behind me. Delilah laughed. I'd been rendered speechless—which was troubling, given the case we were about to embark upon.

"No one will be marrying anyone this evening," Abe said drily. He assessed us with an almost-smirk. "You two clean up nicely."

"This old thing?" Delilah smoothed her hands down the silk, and I remembered the flash of muscled thigh I'd caught a glimpse of last night. Her demure smile, the *very* beginnings of her trust. I wanted to know more about this older man who had pushed her around like a chess piece. Delilah Barrett didn't appear to be easily moved, and yet the pain of that experience had been evident in her voice.

Freya grabbed both of our wrists. Delilah wore a thin silver bracelet, I wore a gold watch. Both contained tiny hidden cameras.

"I doubt you'll catch any illegal theft happening out in the open at this auction," Freya said, "but don't be afraid to snap away. Who knows what we'll be able to use."

"Freya and I dug around on the license plate number Delilah got from the black sedan at Victoria's house," Abe said. He crossed his arms. "Private security company called

Dresden I've never heard of before. But they seem to work specifically with the mega-wealthy—"

"—and the mega-shady," Freya interjected. "It's a red flag for sure."

"Listen for codes. Keep yourself open and available to Victoria," Abe instructed. "Remember: you're not just two lovely married people she wants to be friends with. You operate in her world of theft. Convince her of that. And Dorran's taking you guys in the limo tonight."

"Who's he?" I asked.

"Old contact from the FBI," Abe said. "An actual reformed getaway driver. Changed his ways after two different stints in prison. But he'll still take the odd job to help me out. Cool under pressure, asks no questions. He'll be escorting you for this entire case."

"And what did Francisco want?" Delilah asked. "Checking in?"

"No progress from the FBI. Nothing local. The Copernicus is still missing, and Francisco says every member of his board is having, quote, 'a tiny, daily aneurysm.'"

"And Victoria?" Delilah asked.

Abe gave a wry smile. "According to Francisco, Victoria is *beside herself* with horror."

"What day is the exhibit again?" I asked, all of us aware of the beating countdown.

"Seventeen more days."

Delilah's hands fluttered at her sides—whether from nerves or adrenaline, I wasn't sure.

"Henry?" Abe asked. "You're good?"

"Yes, sir," I said. "I'm ready."

His nod was curt.

Delilah touched my arm.

"Let's go," she said.

As we walked down the spiral staircase, I kept my eyes trained on the top of her head. Not on her backless dress and the miles of pale skin it revealed. Not on the wings of her shoulder blades or the enticing curve of her lower back. And it wasn't until we were firmly seated in the back of the limousine that I rediscovered the ability to speak to her.

"It all begins now," I said, repeating her words from last night.

She steeled her expression, straightened her spine. I was watching a transformation, a focusing of her body.

"I'm counting on you, Henry," she said, finally letting her blue eyes land on mine. "We're partners now."

I tugged on my cuff links. "I'm ready to be Henry Thornhill." With a nervousness I couldn't place, I reached into my pocket and took out the boxes. "We can't forget the missing piece." I removed Delilah's ring from the box. It was whisper-light, the diamonds dazzling in the city lights streaming in through the windows.

Without thinking, I held out my hand, and she placed her fingers on my palm—a barely-there caress. I didn't look at her —couldn't—as I slid the ring all the way down her finger. She yanked her hand back just as quickly, and when I took out my own gold band, she didn't return the gesture.

For such a small object, it had an unfamiliar heaviness. Delilah was staring at it.

"Delilah," I said.

"Yes?"

We were only a block away from the art auction where we were to be Victoria Whitney's esteemed guests. Dancing white lights heralded the entrance of the marble building, and I spotted couples in furs strolling toward the front.

Once a year, the Shane-Arbor Auction House hosted a private event for their most illustrious patrons; a night catered only for them with items only available for their view. You did not need to be a well-known antiquities collector to garner an invitation. You did, however, need to be extraordinarily wealthy.

"I wanted to ask you about touching," I said. "We'll need to, to make our marriage seem realistic."

"You're right," she said. "I forgot to talk to you about that." Delilah was seated on the seat across from me in the limo, legs crossed, hands folded neatly in her lap. "Do you want to come closer?"

"Of course," I said. When the car came to a stop, I slid next to her, thigh-to-thigh. If Victoria saw us now, she'd guess we were heading toward a swift, awkward divorce. "I don't want to make you feel uncomfortable. Or..." I thought about our conversation last night. "Or used."

"I appreciate that," she said, and there was a tiny curve to her mouth. "And I think you should touch me in any way that makes our marriage appear realistic. Like you said."

We stared at each other as I reached forward and encircled her wrist with my thumb and index finger. I was searching for any signs of distrust, but her eyes were watchful. Curious.

With delicate care, I turned her hand over and slid my fingers between hers. I was now holding hands with Delilah.

"Like this?" I asked.

Her fingers squeezed back. "That's okay."

I untangled us, laid my palm on her knee. A casual, friendly gesture. The strength of her thigh beneath my hand was obvious. "And here?"

"That's okay too." Her voice had a huskiness now that hadn't existed back at the office.

I reached for the curve of her shoulder, hand splaying on her bare skin. My thumb slipped beneath the strap of her dress. "And this feels okay?"

"Yes." She was staring at my mouth.

I was barely aware of the limo pulling up to the curb and the sounds of the world outside attempting to distract me from the sensation of my palm gliding down the camber of Delilah's spine. Resting, ever-so-lightly, on the small of her back.

"This too?"

"That's good." She sounded out of breath.

I was too, if I was honest.

"We're at your location," our limo driver called from the front.

Delilah blinked, as if waking from a trance. She slid a foot away from me. "Let's go." She opened the doors, beckoning me to follow.

The Shane-Arbor Auction House was housed in an old ballet studio from the late nineteenth century—brilliant chandeliers bathed the room with resplendent light. The ceiling arched high above us, and the room contained twelve rows of chairs, fanned out in front of a mahogany podium. A stern auctioneer assessed the audience—wearing an austere black turtleneck, and an even more austere expression.

Delilah grabbed two glasses of wine from a passing waiter and handed me one.

"Do you see Victoria?" I asked. She nodded, lips on her glass. Her hand touched my chest, right over my heart. I wondered if she could feel the rapid rhythm her shy touch evoked. "This is okay, right?" Her palm slid down my chest—barely six inches—but the sensation elicited a primal response.

That and the glint of the ring on her finger.

"Oh my, look at these *beautiful* newlyweds."

Delilah and I sprang apart, but then I saw it was Victoria. Her steel-gray eyes danced with mirth. Another mink coat hung from her shoulders and diamonds dripped from her throat. I had a split second to snap into my role. Even after a week of practice, staring at Victoria Whitney again—live and in the flesh—had me desperately grasping at my persona as if it was brand-new.

Henry Thornhill. Rare book consultant. Married to Delilah. Procurer of stolen antiques.

You have never worked with Bernard. You do not know that Bernard is underground.

You are wildly, passionately, impulsively in love.

My fake wife tucked herself against my side. I almost wrapped my arm around her waist but stopped myself. We hadn't discussed touching that area of her body.

"Ms. Whitney," I said, extending my hand. "How lovely to see you again. And thank you for tonight's invitation."

She placed her hand in mine primly. Instead of shaking it, I brought it to my lips.

"Such manners in this one," she cooed.

Delilah swallowed. "Sure," she managed. I saw her body refocus—like a fuzzy picture snapping into frame. Then she smiled warmly, shoulders dropping in relaxation. "Henry has always been a charmer."

"I can see that." Victoria's fingers dazzled with rings that shone as brightly as her white hair. "And you're very welcome, Mr. Thornhill. Bitzi and I had such a wonderful time with the two of you. And I know that we share some common interests."

She flashed us a calculating expression as she tapped her glass with her nails.

"It appears that we do," Delilah said, referring to the code. Victoria's smile appeared brighter than the chandeliers above our heads—but there was an obvious greed there too.

"Good," she said, dropping her voice. "I do like having friends who enjoy visiting Reichenbach this time of year."

I interlaced our hands, noting that Victoria was tracking our movements.

"Rings!" She clapped her hands together and forced Delilah's hand into her own. "Oh, you finally found the ones you wanted."

"It was meeting you that did it," I said.

I hadn't thought to ask Freya if the diamonds were real—Victoria's discerning scrutiny could probably spot a fake jewel from a mile away.

"Our meeting must have been fate. And this ring is extraordinary," she crooned. "Four diamonds, Henry? You must love her *very* much."

"Yeah, um, y-yes." I coughed awkwardly.

Victoria lifted a manicured brow.

The Thornhills are passionate, romantic, impulsive. Delilah's guidance was an alluring reminder in my subconscious. What I'd admitted to her in the dark quiet of her car had been painfully true: I'd never been in love before. In many ways, this aspect of my new job was more unchartered than being a detective.

The words Delilah had used to describe her understanding of love had been *obsession.*

Craving.

I sank back into the memory of the limo ride and my tentative movements. If I wasn't restrained—if I was truly married to this woman standing in front of me—where would I have put my hands?

Where would I have let my fingers wander? My mouth, my tongue?

"There aren't enough diamonds in the world for my love," I said.

I gently removed Delilah's hand from Victoria's grasp, rubbed her ring finger back and forth with my thumb. In this moment, Delilah was mine.

Obsession. Craving.

"I can see why you snatched him up," Victoria murmured to Delilah, who gave a shaky laugh.

"Did you end up buying anything from the art gallery the other night?" Delilah asked.

"Oh, some silly thing." Victoria waved her hand. "My real interest is in a sixteenth-century Book of Hours they're auctioning off tonight. And maybe some letters from Paul Gauguin."

I didn't even have to feign astonishment. "You'll be fighting with some big spenders for that, I'm sure."

Victoria leaned closer. "I have an iron will, Mr. Thornhill. It's never difficult for me to acquire the things that I want."

"I'd love to take you up on your invitation to view your private collection," I said. "It would be a professional honor."

Victoria gave a throaty laugh. "We barely know each other, and you're already trying to see my *privates*?"

I coughed into my champagne, but Delilah grinned. "I bet you were a heartbreaker back in the day. And still a heart-breaker now."

"I did have a bit of a reputation." Victoria glanced between the two of us but didn't elaborate. And I noticed she didn't *really* extend her invitation to her private collection again. "How did you two lovebirds meet?"

I opened my mouth to say *The art museum, then out to a bar for a drink*. But that was our first date. Right?

"Henry's work," Delilah demurred. "When he worked at the Central Park Library about five years ago. I was always embarking on some serious research project for the foundation, so I just *had* to have his help whenever I was in New York City."

Her words jarred my memory.

"Every time she came in, I noticed her," I said, slipping my hands into my pockets. "It's hard not to."

I contemplated Delilah's profile, framed in the golden light of the auction house. A capricious tendril of hair lay against her cheek. And even though we hadn't discussed it, I brushed it behind her ear.

"We'd talk about our favorite authors, the most beautiful passages in literature. I always knew I'd fall for a well-read man," Delilah purred.

Victoria beamed and clutched her wine glass, enthralled. "You must have known." Victoria laid a hand on Delilah's arm. "Didn't you?"

"Know what?" she asked.

"That he was your *soul mate*, of course, darling," Victoria replied. "Was it love at first sight?"

But Delilah was saved from answering by the appearance of a hulking, military-looking man dressed in all black.

One of the guards from the other night.

Fear gripped me. Had we been identified as we ran through the woods, jumping over logs and narrowly avoiding tripwires?

"Oh, Sven," Victoria said airily. "What is it?"

He said something low in her ear, and she shook her head dismissively.

"It's about to begin," she said. "Come join me, lovebirds. Sven's gotten us seats toward the front."

Victoria led us through a crowd of people desperate to get her attention, just like the other night. Items were beginning to roll out onto the stage, and the auctioneer was tapping her gavel against her palm with a vicious impatience. The room was a hive of wealth and gossip.

And as soon as we sat, Victoria clapped her hands together again. "Henry, I'm assuming a rare book librarian speaks French."

"You assume correctly."

She placed a catalog into my hands. "Read this for me."

"Um...I mean, sure," I said. Delilah's thigh pressed into mine. As she read over my shoulder, an earthy, lavender scent floated up from her hair. I breathed in—pictured a field of wildflowers, Delilah in the sun.

Flipping the book open, I searched for the Gauguin letters and attempted to focus on the sea of French sentences.

Inhaled—thought of Delilah's soft skin beneath this dress.

Exhaled—and caught Sven glaring at me.

15

DELILAH

"*T*ell me what this says," Victoria commanded. She tapped the catalog across Henry's lap, opened to display the Gauguin letters.

He read it softly to himself, cleared his throat, and began to speak. Henry's deep voice curled around the heavy French vowels in a seamless accent—the sound of it was like a bite of decadent dessert. I fluttered my eyes closed, let his voice slip through me. Whatever he was reading sounded as scholarly as it did *filthy*.

Would a husband like Henry do that for his wife? Whisper dirty words in her ear in four different languages?

He adjusted his glasses after he finished. "To be quite honest, this appears to be a letter regarding the dissolution of their marriage."

"*Divorce?*" Victoria asked. "I thought it was a love letter."

"There is passion here. But anger, not love." He handed the booklet back to her. He was dressed in a light tan suit, collar open, no tie. The triangle of dark brown skin exposed there was tempting; his throat, his pulse.

Victoria was shaking her head, earrings dangling. "No, no. That won't do. I can't have that in my home."

She began flipping through the booklet with Henry, asking his opinion on different items up for auction, which he gave willingly. So I zeroed in on Sven, Victoria's terrifyingly large bodyguard, who'd been glaring at Henry and me like bugs he was looking forward to stepping on.

He *couldn't* have seen us the night of the stakeout. If he had, and recognized us, Henry and I would be on the ground right now.

But still. His glare felt like a sunburn and it sent my mind spiraling toward possibilities.

"We have a few moments alone." Henry's mouth was at my ear like it had been on the night in the woods. "Victoria went to see Bitzi."

I cast my eyes over—saw Victoria and Bitzi laughing uproariously.

"You can see how much they hate each other. It's obvious," Henry said.

His hand landed on my knee. I could feel the tip of every finger. "Are you okay, though?"

"I'm good," I whispered. We locked eyes. "You?"

He nodded. "You gave more colorful detail about how we met than we discussed."

"Just...reading the moment." I kept my tone light but inwardly cursed myself. Getting swept up, pushing the boundaries—*that's* how Mark had manipulated me. Convincing me to tap into unprofessional passions that were better kept locked away.

Henry's thumb caressed the side of my knee. And up, just once. And just barely.

"She probably thinks you're whispering sweet nothings into my ear. But we're clearly arguing over those paint choices for our kitchen renovation," I joked, reorienting my thoughts.

"Of course," he agreed. "Do fake Henry and Delilah have fake kids? A fake dog? That's something else we can bicker about."

Victoria was moving back through the crowd—watching us with a swooning expression.

"I've asked you to mow the lawn three times this week, and you still haven't."

His laughter against my ear was a low rumble. I felt my cheeks flush. I *liked* making Henry laugh—it was a sound as joyful as it was sexy.

"What are you two giggling about?" Victoria admonished with a teasing smile.

"A funny memory," Henry said.

I let out a big breath—*this was for the case.* The easy affection. The flirting.

This wasn't the same as Mark.

"The auction's about to begin," Victoria beamed. "Do you have your bid paddles ready?"

Henry and I waved ours obediently as the lights dimmed. Like a switch being thrown, my bloodhound senses reared up. Maybe it was Victoria's nearness. Maybe it was the presence of antiques and rare books being paraded around without adequate security. As a cop, there was a literal—and metaphorical—armor that helped me move through a space like this. Handcuffs and a badge could do a lot of damage. As a private detective, my vocation was to examine body language and look for clues in discreet nods, to move between worlds seamlessly without alerting others to my presence.

This room felt filled with secret handshakes and shadowy back hallways. Auction houses like the Shane-Arbor staked their reputation on verifying the authenticity and provenance of their items. And yet in the past two years, Codex had tracked down stolen books right to their doorstep. Which meant if Victoria hadn't stolen the Copernicus—if all of this was one giant, colossal fuck-up on my part—the *real* thief could be in this room.

I accidentally locked eyes with Sven. He attempted his most menacing look, but I refused to turn away.

"Don't you *love* a good auction? The thrill, the chase, the *fight*." Victoria's voice cut into my thoughts. "I love every single minute. It reminds me of a hunt."

I knew what that felt like.

"I completely agree," I said, leaning past Henry so she could hear me. My shoulder brushed his chest; his mouth was disturbingly close to my hair. "And I'm going to guess that you're a fierce huntress."

She pursed her lips primly.

The first item—an eighteenth-century sword from Germany—was rolled out and placed onto a table with a scarlet velvet tablecloth. The audience seemed to ripple with appreciation. The auctioneer picked up her microphone.

And then I was adrift in a sea of white bid paddles flying up and down like the wings of diving birds. The auctioneer rattled off numbers, gesturing enthusiastically, dollar amounts going up $10,000 at a time.

"$55,000—do I hear $55,000? Thank you to the gentleman to my left. And now I see—oh yes, thank you. Can I see $75,000?"

The wealth and privilege in the room astounded me, antiques being auctioned off like cattle. Victoria was sharp-eyed, assessing each item with a vicious arch of her brow. When the Book of Hours was brought to the front of the stage, carefully laid on a velvet cloth, I leaned over and said, "Good luck, Victoria."

"I don't need luck, dear," she said. "I have money."

"We shall start the bidding at $75,000," the auctioneer called out.

I inhaled sharply, watched her tighten her fingers on her bid paddle. It flew up before the auctioneer could even pause. Victoria matched every competing bid, dollar for dollar, with an expression that was as icy as a snowstorm. It was evident in her body language she knew of her spotlight—knew it and thrived with the attention.

And at the end, Victoria Whitney was the final bidder at $250,000, an amount she dropped as easily as one might drop a penny on the ground and ignore it.

"Well done, Victoria," Henry said.

She gave a secret smile, but her cheeks were flushed. "You must come with me when I collect it," she said. "Give me your professional opinion?"

"Gladly."

The final items went quickly in a blur of paddles and exorbitant bids. Less than an hour later and we were striding into the back of the Auction House with Victoria and Sven. He carried a large box that looked minuscule in his beefy hands.

Three assistants greeted Victoria like she was royalty before retrieving a glass case and lifting out a small book encased in cloth.

"Henry, care to look?" she asked.

I watched my partner step forward and examine the 500-year-old manuscript. He didn't touch, merely took it all in with a look of grateful appreciation. I'd seen his laser focus in action several times now, the ability to notice and appreciate and consider. It imbued his words with a different type of honesty.

"These books were used by peasants in Europe," he said. "They prayed with them on the hour. It would have sat in a place of honor in their home. For many, it would have been their only book. Treasured, cared for with devotion. Passed down through generations."

"It's quite pretty," Victoria said.

His jaw flexed.

"Yes," he said. "Pretty."

"It should appraise well by the time I sell it in a couple of years."

Sven lifted the glass case and opened the side. The assistants placed the book gently inside before he closed it. "It's essentially a portable museum case," Victoria said. "Temperature and light-controlled."

A red flag unfurled in my brain.

"Can I see?" I asked. I dipped down before she answered. It was a simple glass box with a handle. But the implications were more complicated than that. I wanted to take a picture with my bracelet, but they were all staring at the book. I didn't dare look at Henry, but I stored the information away for a later debrief. If Victoria had the resources to both *store* an item like the Copernicus but also *transport* it—what was stopping her from already selling it?

An assistant broached the topic of payment, but she waved it away and directed him to call her accountant. "I don't have time to prattle on about meddlesome details. Bring us champagne. I want us to be taken to more items in the back."

Henry stood next to me, posture loose, hands in his pockets. I slipped my hand around his arm, studying him with an expression I hoped conveyed *madly in love.*

"Hey there, beautiful," he whispered. His grin was crooked, charming.

Dangerous.

"The, um, items in the back?" another assistant asked. "I'm

not sure which ones you're referring to. This is what you purchased."

"Young man," she said sharply. "Bring Alistair to me. Now."

"Um...yes—"

"Bring him."

Victoria turned to us and let out a girlish giggle. "To young love."

We clinked glasses—my blood fizzed like the alcohol. Part of it was Henry's scent and the muscle beneath my hand.

Part of it was something else entirely.

The gentleman named Alistair walked into the small room, ushered the harried assistant out with an exasperated expression, and flashed a knowing smile at Victoria.

"Ms. Whitney," he said. They air-kissed like old friends. Henry had gone still, muscles rigid with tension. "I'm sorry for the poor service. Gregory is new."

"It's not a worry," she said with a facial expression that read *fire him immediately*. "Did you see what I won?"

"An excellent choice," Alistair praised. He peered at Henry and me as if finally noticing the two other people in the room. For a split second, I thought Henry might bolt—I could *feel* his body pulling toward the door.

"Alistair Chance"—Victoria waved at us—"Henry and Delilah Thornhill. My new wonderful friends. They're collectors themselves."

"A pleasure," he replied, shaking our hands. "Victoria is our best patron."

"Because I give you all of my money, Alistair," she sniffed. She wrapped her mink more firmly around her shoulders. Stared at Henry and me as if deciphering a challenging puzzle. "Henry and Delilah have visited Reichenbach Falls. Isn't that right, you two?"

"Absolutely," I said with as much confidence as I could muster. Because hearing the code spoken so openly sent a shockwave through me.

Alistair appeared surprised, but then steeled his features. "How lovely."

"Is there anything else you'd like to show me at this time?" she asked softly.

Now it was Alistair's turn to stare at us—an assessment that found us lacking. "Perhaps later. After you've bid farewell to your guests."

I expected Victoria to exert her will, to demand to see whatever it was she was referring to. Was it the Copernicus? Or another book entirely? But instead she merely nodded her understanding.

"I see," she said. "Come, you two. We will drink our celebratory champagne before I'm called back to Alistair." I couldn't get a read on the way they said goodbye to each other—anger? Distrust? Concession?

We followed Victoria back down the gleaming hallway, out into the auction room with the chairs and the chandeliers. I felt desperate for Abe and Freya's presence, if only to verify that we'd heard a staff member at Philadelphia's most respected auction house allude that he could show Victoria Whitney stolen goods.

When she turned back to us, Victoria again appeared calm, ice-like. Triumphant.

"You know," she started, "my dear friend Bernard used to say that human beings had a special capacity to go after that which they admired the most. A compulsion that we *must* give in to." Her eyes glittered. "We crave to own things that are beautiful. Things that no one else can have."

Henry's nostrils flared at the mention of Bernard.

"Henry and I certainly agree," I jumped in. I smoothed my palm down his back—an attempt to focus his attention.

She smiled at that. "There are levels in this world. You understand."

"Of course," I said. "Alistair seems like a wonderful... contact." I chose that word carefully.

"He is." She glanced around the room, waved like the queen at a few other patrons. It was a strange sensation, being the center of Victoria's persistent scrutiny. Because *she* was the center of everyone else's.

"Private collecting," she said, turning toward Henry. "When did you begin, Mr. Thornhill?"

I needed Henry to play the game with her. He adjusted his glasses, glanced around the room like Victoria had done. He appeared to be verifying that no one could hear us.

"Like Bernard," he began slowly, "I have a very special occupation. With a very special access. It seemed only natural to begin our own collection. There are so many different ways one can come into a rare manuscript. If you're smart, you can find them."

"I'm incredibly smart." She tilted her chin.

"I can see that," Henry agreed. He leaned in as if sharing a joke. "I once read an article about you in the newspaper. Your collection contains many scientific works. Any reason why?"

"I'm always being called for interviews, you can't even imagine," she said, looking pained. I painted my face with mock sympathy. "My mother had a mind for science and math, which was interesting since my father was the oil man. But it was her finance skills that grew his money so rapidly. Her head was *filled* with figures."

I felt a bizarre twisting in my gut at the mention of Victoria's mother.

"I never took to it myself, but it felt right to honor her

memory with scientific texts. The ideas of our greatest thinkers are housed right in my mansion." She preened, looking positively delighted. "It's a source of power, I'm sure you know. To own something others want. To own the theories that have shaped our very understanding of the universe."

I watched my fake husband. His thumb swept across the nape of my neck. "The more you seek that kind of power, the more you desire it." Another drag of his thumb, setting off nerve endings I never knew existed. "I'm certainly the kind of man who has the kind of capacity Bernard referred to. I crave things that are beautiful."

His thumb left my neck. Replaced by his entire hand, spreading between my shoulder blades. I arched into it a little —shamelessly wanting his hand to caress every inch of my back.

But he didn't.

"It's why I love to visit the falls," she said.

Henry didn't respond, but he did raise his glass toward hers with a wink. It was a charming move, and she tipped her head flirtatiously.

"The Philadelphia Natural History Museum is hosting their annual gala a week from today. Come be guests at my table. I have two empty seats with your names on them."

"We'd *love to*," I said, even as my heart dropped. The clock was ticking on the Copernicus, and seven days away felt like forever. I could already see Abe's disappointed face. "Unless you'd like us to visit your collection sometime this week? We're free tomorrow."

It was a desperate toss out. And Victoria knew it immediately.

"I don't just invite *anyone* to see my collection, Delilah." Her tone was sharp.

"Oh, I know, I thought...Henry might be able to look at..." I turned to him, eyes pleading. "I thought you wanted him to view it. And we're available this entire week. Pardon my eagerness."

Her face didn't appear to pardon anything.

"There are levels in this world," she repeated. "Levels you will care to respect."

"Of course." I stepped back, hand on my chest. "Of course, I'm so sorry."

"My wife knows that viewing your private collection is a professional dream I've had for a number of years," Henry said smoothly. His hand between my shoulder blades traced down my spine. "We apologize for the inference. It was pure excitement. And love for me on her part." His lips grazed the top of my hair down to my temple in a soft, impossibly tender kiss.

Victoria thawed the *tiniest* of amounts. But still—her body language remained guarded as Sven appeared like clockwork to mutter something in her ear. "I must leave you two now. My assistant will call you."

She left us without her usual effusive goodbye.

"*Fuck*," I muttered.

I needed to punch the shit out of something.

16

HENRY

*D*elilah struck the punching bag with a sharp *slap*.

"That's my girl," Freya cheered. She was behind the bag, holding it steady as Delilah attacked it with a fierce precision. "Float like a butterfly, am I right?"

Slap slap. Delilah was nimble grace on her feet, bouncing lightly, fists at her face. "Don't move. I don't want to accidentally punch you, Frey."

She shrugged and winced as Delilah hit the bag with a vicious *whack*. "I can take it. Last time you and I sparred, I think I won."

"Bullshit," Delilah teased.

"Last time I believe *I* won," Abe said. He was leaning against his desk with his legs crossed in front of him. The fireplace was lit, and Freya's table was a mess of papers, highlighters, computer screens blinking rapidly. "Our new hire doesn't know self-defense. At least, I'm assuming. Is that correct, Henry?"

Every head swiveled my way. Delilah and I had left the auction, and as soon as we arrived, she'd stripped off her dress and returned in a sports bra and yoga pants. And proceeded to spar with the bag like it had committed a personal offense against her.

"Um...no," I said. "Not really a reason to engage in self-defense while earning your PhD in Library Science."

"You should teach him," Abe said to Delilah. We locked eyes. Delilah was panting lightly, sweat misting on the muscles of her lean abdomen. Her eyeliner was smudged, but her lips were still blood red.

I had a fleeting vision of her kicking me to the ground, foot landing on my chest. The way she'd smirk down at me, as if she knew the domination was the kind of punishment I'd beg for.

Twice now I'd told her she was beautiful—and both times it was the goddamn truth. Not an element of our fake fairytale, but bone-deep honesty. Maybe having Delilah Barrett force me to my knees in submission wasn't a smart idea. Part of me wanted to take it—let her use my body however she saw fit.

Part of me wanted to make *her* beg.

Which meant *all of this* was a bad idea.

"This is a great idea, actually," Abe continued.

"I'm a quick study, remember?" I managed to say.

Delilah looked me up and down in a perfect mimic of my fantasy. Blood rushed to my cock. "And I'm still a tough fucking teacher."

"What she's trying to say," Freya cut in, "is that she'll kill you."

Delilah pulled Freya in for a hug.

"Ew, you're all sweaty," Freya squealed. "Keep punching."

"Punch and talk," Abe corrected. "We need a game plan for what's happening next."

I let out a long exhale, grateful for the high-pressure distraction from Delilah. I shrugged out of my jacket and scrubbed my hand down my face.

This evening's coursing adrenaline vanished by the end of Abe's next sentence.

"We have seventeen days until the exhibit. The gala Victoria invited you to is in seven. That leaves us, honestly, less than ten days after that to convince Victoria to show you the Copernicus."

"*If* she has the Copernicus," Delilah said. "Who knows? The contact she introduced us to tonight, Alistair, knew the code word. And had potentially more pull than Victoria in whatever..."

"What?" Abe prodded.

"Whatever this world is. This...system of buying and selling stolen books that we operate in. Tonight, it felt like we were witnessing something structured. An illegal auction hidden inside a legal one."

"When I was at the FBI, I always had a theory there was one person at the top of this pyramid," Abe said. "One person pulling the strings. I always thought it was Bernard Allerton."

I grimaced. If I hadn't been at that auction house as an undercover Codex agent, it could have been a regular Saturday night for me. Back at Oxford, Bernard and I frequented auctions together—often with the library's donors.

Had I really been that naive?

"I think I know Alistair," I admitted. All three heads whipped toward me again. "That man. He didn't recognize me, but I told Abe one of the suspicious behaviors I was tracking with Bernard was the bringing on of interns or assistants that I wouldn't see again. They'd be at the library for 'special projects,' and Bernard had the kind of sway that meant no one would double check who they really were. Alistair, he... I think he was one of them."

"Recently?" Abe said. "Like you saw him the month before Bernard fled?"

I shook my head, trying to remember. "Years ago. Maybe five. It's a unique name, which is why I remember it. He may even have introduced him as someone who worked for an auction house. But either way, *that* man was given access to whatever he wanted at our library."

"That was allowed?" Freya asked.

"It was allowed because Bernard allowed it." I crossed my arms, feeling uneasy. I'd recycled Bernard's words tonight and it had left behind a sick feeling. *I have a very special occupation. With special access.*

"We have to get into that house," Abe said.

"What about her psycho killer guards though?" Freya asked. "Plus, Henry and Delilah said she might be able to transport rare manuscripts. Victoria has a mansion in Santa Barbara. A penthouse in New York City. And an apartment in Paris. If she stole the Copernicus, she could have moved it or sold it already."

Now it looked like Abe wanted to punch something.

"If I could convince her to let me see her private collection..." I started.

"I agree," Freya said. "The psycho guards are a complication, but getting *in* to that Main Line mansion of hers would be a big help."

"But then what?" Delilah asked.

"We'll cross that bridge when we get to it," Abe said firmly.

Delilah and I exchanged a look behind Abe's back.

"Let me see if I can put you in Victoria's path before the gala next week," Freya said, dropping the punching bag. "The more face time with her, the better."

"And I'll go convince Francisco that we're making progress," Abe sighed.

Both of them began picking up their things, packing bags,

extinguishing the fireplace. Delilah and I, however, seemed rooted to our respective spots.

"I should make it clear though," Abe said, standing in the doorway to leave. "We are making progress, even if it doesn't feel that way. You two did good work tonight."

"Thanks, boss," Delilah said.

"Thank you, sir," I nodded.

The door closed but she still vibrated with energy, running a hand through her wild curls.

"Do you want *me* to hold the bag?" I offered.

She chewed on her lip, then shrugged casually. "Sure. Keep it still, okay?"

I walked over, gripped the bag tightly. She flexed her fingers, cracked her knuckles.

Whack whack whack.

"You told me that partners know how to read each other," I said. She propped her hands on her hips, panting. "I'm going to go out on a limb and guess you're...angry."

She executed another series of jabs. "I'm not angry. I'm just stressed out about the case."

She shook out her fingers, rolling her neck.

Avoiding my eyes.

"Delilah."

Another series of jabs had the bag shaking against my hands. But I let her go, hoping she'd reach out and grab the olive branch I was offering her.

"I sounded desperate tonight with Victoria," she finally admitted. "You had her in the palm of your hand, and I made us look like idiots."

"That's not true," I countered. "You were right to ask. She basically left an opening for you to do it."

"No, she didn't." She danced back on her toes. "I came off

as overeager, and she admonished me like I was a disobedient child."

"Hey," I said softly. She didn't stop. "Delilah, look at me."

She stepped back, wiped her brow. Raised her blue eyes toward mine. I almost said *you're beautiful* but I stopped myself this time.

"We're under a lot of pressure. I feel it. Freya and Abe feel it. You heard what he said—we did a great job."

"I'm supposed to be training *you,* Henry," she said. "Showing you how to gain a target's trust, which is a very delicate push and pull. I wasn't delicate. I pushed too hard."

"You also told me that you can't always control the environment when you're undercover," I argued. "You just... stepped on a twig. Now we're even."

"Even?" She tilted her head with an *almost*-smile.

"You've seen me fuck up in the field about seventy times," I said. Her lips twitched at the ends. "I've seen you fuck up *barely* once. It hardly seems fair."

She sank back onto the edge of Freya's table, pulling on a tee-shirt. "I don't know what the fuck this case is, Henry. And I hate that."

"I understand," I said.

She studied me for a long time, as if she was about to make a hard choice. "Henry. Do you know where Bernard is?"

My brow furrowed—and then I realized what she was accusing me of.

"You can't be fucking serious, Delilah."

She raised her hands in concession. "The other night, what you said about Bernard, his relationship as your mentor. I told you I know what it's like to be taken advantage of. It can make you do things you wouldn't normally do."

"Like conceal the whereabouts of a known criminal?"

She didn't look away. "I've been in your shoes," she said with a gentleness I didn't expect.

"I've spoken to the FBI and Interpol multiple times. Given them every piece of evidence I have. Delilah, he was going to *frame* me."

"I know he was," she replied. "And you wouldn't be the first person to still believe someone like that was innocent."

This is *bigger than you, Henry*. Bernard's taunt hadn't left me—in fact, those words reared up whenever I needed reminding of my guilt.

All the anger left my body as I sat down wearily next to her on the desk. "Tonight, I witnessed what we believe is confirmation that one of Philadelphia's most distinguished auction houses sells stolen antiques. I met a man from my past who could have easily walked out of the McMasters Library with anything he wanted—that's how flimsy our security system truly was." I scrubbed a hand down my face with a heavy sigh. "A few weeks ago, I was holding out hope for Bernard. Now the only thing I understand is that I must be a special kind of fool to have been blind to all of this my entire career."

Delilah placed her hand on my back. "You know why I had to ask you, right?"

I turned to look at her. "I do."

Her blue eyes softened. "You have a lot of integrity, Henry. And you're no fool." She paused, seemed to consider her words. "And you really did charm Victoria tonight. This role fits you. And you saved me *again*. Jumping in like that when I was flailing...it helped. You reversed some of the damage."

I didn't think it smart to admit that the words had been Henry Thornhill but the actions had been unabashedly mine. Stroking the smooth skin of her back, pressing my lips to her temple. My partner was in distress, and my first instinct was to *soothe*.

"No thanks necessary," I replied. "I'm being taught by the best."

Delilah turned away from me, like she was hiding a blush. "I didn't teach you French or how to get a wealthy heiress to become enchanted with you. Or how to look impossibly handsome in a suit."

"You think I look handsome in a suit?" I teased, almost unbearably pleased with her honesty.

"Victoria does," she corrected. But she was still blushing— a deep pink was spreading up her throat.

"You make a very convincing fake wife, Delilah," I said.

"And you're a very convincing fake husband," she replied. "And we haven't even finished fighting over the fact that you forgot to take the garbage out again."

I laughed—and she revealed a big, silly smile I hadn't seen before.

"Everything that happened tonight," I said, "you felt comfortable with? The touching? The...words?"

"Of course," she said firmly. "We're undercover. It's like being an actor in a movie. I know you're playing a role."

"Yeah," I said. "That's it exactly."

In the quiet of the empty office, my words came out sounding forced. There was a space—a momentary pause— where I thought Delilah was going to say something. But our phones chirped with a text from Freya.

Victoria is being honored tomorrow by the Bristol Foundation as Philanthropist of the Year. VIP event. Very fancy. Rooftop. Bust out your cocktail attire.

17

DELILAH

"*I* love the city skyline this time of night," Henry said, strolling up to me with a glass of wine.

The look of Henry Finch in a light gray suit—I was learning—caused a visceral reaction best ignored. Instead, I placed my elbows on the bar and watched the pink-orange rays of light glimmer through the skyscrapers. "Even though it's still spring, it reminds me of long summer days as a kid. The way your days felt like forever."

I watched the audience milling around us for a moment, searching for Victoria. But she was nowhere to be seen as of yet. I exhaled, tasted the crisp white wine on my tongue. Turned my body toward my fake husband, debonair in the coral twilight.

"You're from Philly, aren't you?" I asked.

He nodded, smiled. "It was an added bonus when Abe offered me the job. My parents live by Rittenhouse Square right over...*there*." He pointed in the direction of the famous park. "They're both tenured professors at Penn."

"A genius family. Makes sense, Mr. Librarian."

"We read constantly," he said, staring down into his glass. "During meals. While cooking meals. On the weekends and every night. Every spare moment when I wasn't sleeping. My parents had me arguing philosophical theory with them by middle school."

I narrowed my eyes at him. "Really, though?"

His smile was almost sheepish. "Not *well*. But I tried." He glanced back toward the park, slipping one hand into his pocket. "I actually have younger twin siblings. Joelle and Jeremiah. They co-own an organic coffee shop out in West Philly that also functions as a studio space for artists."

My eyebrows shot up.

"They're not brainy, like my parents and I. But they *did* force us to look up from our books. Dragged us to concerts or movies or anything fun and outrageous. I always wanted to be more like them."

"Like how?" I asked.

"Charismatic," he replied.

Behind us, a trio of finely dressed women was staring at Henry and pointing. Two of them giggled while one blushed.

"I don't think that's a problem for you, husband." The endearment slipped out so easily I wouldn't have noticed if not for Henry's expression: something possessive or maybe *primal* curled his lips.

"Did you miss them in England?" I asked.

"Every single day," he said. "Although traveling through Europe, living in England, hopping on a train whenever I wanted and picking a destination...it was every dream come true." His eyes darkened. "Or I thought it was my dream." I waited, let him chase whatever thought he was struggling with. "I think Codex is that dream now."

"You think so?"

He shrugged, glanced at me sideways. "I guess it depends on how everything turns out."

Philadelphia was a panorama of reflective metal buildings that glowed with the fire of the setting sun. Two rivers, bridges, New Jersey in the distance, the brick row homes and cobblestone streets and whimsical alleys. My heart was divided evenly between my love for the wild and overgrown forest I grew up in—and this city that shone all around us.

Henry and I stood and watched the sun dip—close, but not touching. Without Victoria's scrutiny, he stayed back a respectful distance. I wished for her arrival, if only for the professional excuse to reach down, slide my fingers through his.

"Abe's serious about self-defense training tomorrow, isn't he?" he asked.

"Just a couple basics," I promised. "Nothing to be afraid of." I studied my fingernails and faked a sigh. "Besides getting your ass kicked, of course."

"No warning needed," he grinned. "I've been afraid of you since we met, Delilah."

"Who, me?" I widened my eyes. "You're joking."

His dark eyes were teasing behind his glasses, body curving toward mine. "You know I'm not—"

"And what, pray tell, are you two doing here?"

Henry and I were both half-laughing when we turned and practically *knocked over* Francisco Abila, the head of the Franklin Museum.

"Sir," I said immediately, straightening my spine. I was acutely aware of my tiny black cocktail dress, the ridiculously high stilettos Freya had convinced me to wear. "What are *you* doing here?"

Francisco appeared haggard around the eyes and permanently aged from when we'd seen him a little over a week ago.

"*I* am here as a guest of Victoria Whitney, my board president. And you still haven't answered my original question. I would like to know why Codex agents are having a date night while I am paying you for an extremely high-profile job."

My cheeks burned but I kept my chin lifted. "Codex agents are undercover." I dropped my voice as low as I was capable. "Your board president knows us as the Thornhills, and I'll trust you not to blow it."

Francisco looked ready to snap. "Abraham has had you continue pursuing Victoria even with my very legitimate doubts?"

"Yes, he has," I said.

"While the police and the FBI are combing this city for hundreds of suspects, you're still on this ridiculous quest to go after a woman who garners *this* kind of community reputation?" He indicated the hundreds of people surrounding us, here to celebrate a woman who gave away so much money she was being *awarded*.

His words poked at the tender edges of my worst fears— that I'd led Codex on a wild goose chase for nothing; that this case would amount to nothing more than a heap of misread clues and misunderstandings.

But instead I said, "*You* pay the contract. We find the book. This isn't up for discussion."

"And after *I* pay the contract and *you* don't find the book, Codex's reputation will be ruined. Permanently."

Francisco stormed off and I took a shaky breath.

My worst fears were forever intertwined with Mark and the firing. Abe always trusted my gut instincts, even though he knew what had happened at the police department. That trust had been epically vital to me when I joined Codex—it was the life preserver I needed to pull myself out of self-doubt.

"He's right," I admitted, feeling queasy.

"Delilah," Henry warned.

"You know he is."

"Victoria Whitney has admitted to us on two separate occasions that she knowingly purchases stolen goods."

"She has *not* admitted to having stolen one of the rarest books in the world from a museum weeks before its exhibit," I argued. "She might buy a stolen Bradbury but is Victoria Whitney into thefts that are this high-profile?"

I set my wine down, placed a hand on my jumpy stomach. The audience began to ripple with awareness and applause—it was Victoria, looking glamorous in a red gown, taking the short steps to the stage. Cameras *popped* and flashed, capturing the heiress in her classic proud pose. Behind her, a presentation kicked up: photos of children, books, classrooms, and happy, smiling teachers. It was all for *Victoria*. She was beaming with a sweetness I'd never witnessed in her before.

The tip of Henry's finger landed beneath my chin. He slowly tilted my head up, until I was focused on him.

"After I confronted Bernard, I ran to our board president, Louisa," Henry said. "I told her about the theft. I told her that Bernard was planning on framing me with forged letters. I told her a *very large* guard with a *very large* gun had appeared in Bernard's flat to threaten me." His finger left my chin and I wished it hadn't. "Louisa told me it was absurd. Sure, she'd known Bernard for twenty years. But she and I had also had a close professional relationship the entire time I'd worked there. Guards, guns, forgeries, thefts... Of course it was shocking. It'd be like...like if someone appeared right now and told you the Easter Bunny was real. I was shocked as hell, furious, scared, confused. But Bernard's reputation carried so much weight, Louisa thought I'd made up the story on the spot."

He waved behind us—at the high-society event where once again Victoria was the star. "People will go to great lengths to ignore what is right in front of them. Denial is a powerful currency. *You* told me that."

I let out another breath—less shaky.

"I believe Victoria Whitney is a criminal hiding in plain sight. And I believe *you*, Delilah."

18

DELILAH

I believe you.

"Ladies and gentlemen," a voice was saying, "it is my sincere honor to introduce you to our Philanthropist of the Year. A woman whose generosity has changed the lives of so many here in our great city. A woman who truly needs no real introduction: Victoria Whitney." The crowd erupted in cheers and applause, but I was still staring up at Henry, absorbing his words.

"Thank you," I said as the crowd continued to cheer.

"You don't have to thank me. And we should probably watch Victoria," he said softly.

"Oh, right." I turned around awkwardly, Henry moving behind me. Victoria was staring out at the audience with a serene, happy expression.

"Are we officially the Thornhills now?" he asked. His lips brushed my ear.

"Uh...yes," I nodded, pretending to clap enthusiastically for the book thief on the stage. "Back to holy matrimony."

I heard his low chuckle. Then his palms landed on my bare shoulders. Squeezed. Just a husband and wife, enjoying a

VIP cocktail event together. I could feel his body heat but didn't dare lean back. Those strong fingers stroked down my arm to my elbow. Down my elbow to my wrists and all the way back up again.

"Is this okay?" he whispered. Another teasing stroke.

"Yes," I managed, swallowing the moan that threatened to escape.

One lingering caress and Henry had me practically purring in a room filled with hundreds of people. Francisco, Victoria, the Copernicus, the case...all of it faded away as his thumbs smoothed around my shoulders. I'd never experienced such an automatic reaction to physical touch before. The mere *suggestion* of Henry's breath near my skin brought forth an urgent desire.

"Good evening," Victoria said in her clipped, boarding school accent. "It is truly an honor to be here this evening with all of you, receiving an award I already know I will treasure for the rest of my days." The presentation clicked by. There were photos of her reading books to children in classrooms, gifting giant checks to worthy charities. "I am known for being a lot of things in the city of Philadelphia. But not many people know that I am a bookworm, through and through. Literature was held in the highest esteem in my family, and it was expected that my siblings and I would understand and appreciate the greatest authors of our time. Later, as I grew older, this esteem grew to include art, history, music. It's why I dedicated myself to building my private collection." She smiled angelically. "I cannot bear to part with something as beautiful as a book."

There was a ripple of appreciation in the audience. Henry's expression was completely unreadable.

"It's why literacy programs are vital in this city. Reading gives us worlds we never thought we could reach for. Literature can take us to the moon or send us to the core of the Earth. Literature turns us into dragons and sea monsters, princesses and peasants. Books are the key to everything, I believe. So when the Bristol Foundation comes calling for donations for libraries, they don't have to ask me twice. It's more than my responsibility. It's a privilege."

She gazed out into the audience like she was delivering the State of the Union. "They were not aware I would be doing this, but tonight, in front of all of you, I'm committing to another five million dollars in funding for libraries and literacy programs in our great city over the next five years."

More camera flashes *popped* as the audience cheered their appreciation. The Foundation's director was on the verge of grateful tears.

To the far left of the crowd, Francisco clapped as if his life depended on it.

Then stopped to shoot daggers my way.

I didn't balk from his anger—even as Victoria's speech made my skin itch. Was this really the same woman who had so casually admitted to us she knowingly broke the law? In my years as a police officer, my moral compass had developed a rigid sense of *right* and *wrong*—and there was no room for a thief who donated money to charity.

The director presented Victoria with an award, who placed a hand to her chest in a show of modesty. More cheering, more applause, and she was descending the steps back into the crowd. She was immediately mobbed.

"Let's go sit," Henry said. He placed his hand on my lower back, guiding me to two open bar stools. Heat lamps warmed the spring air, and golden twinkle lights were strung overhead. We perched on the stools—and I searched the crowd desperately for Victoria.

"You're sitting very far away for someone who's supposed

to be madly in love with me," Henry said. I turned back to him, distracted. He was leaning against the stool, legs spread in front of him. Suit jacket unbuttoned, relaxed smile on his face. I suddenly felt like the blushing women I'd caught spying on him.

"I guess you're right," I mumbled.

My fake husband reached forward beneath my bare legs and gripped the ledge of the stool. Both of us looked down. His arm was a single inch from brushing the backs of my legs. He pulled me over until our knees touched. "That's better."

Victoria was moving through the crowd, but I wasn't sure if she'd spotted us. My hands were in my lap. Henry took one, turned it over. Traced his fingers down the palm to the inside of my wrist.

"Just in case Victoria's watching," he said hoarsely. His index finger moved in precise circles right over my pulse point.

"Of course."

"Delilah," he murmured. "You still seem a little out of it."

"I'm a little nervous about Victoria. I don't want her to think we're stalking her, especially after what I said to her last night."

"Which is why we don't address her unless she comes to us, right?" He was repeating the plan we'd worked on with Freya this afternoon.

I nodded, straightened my posture. "I became a police officer to punish people like her," I said. "In the scales of the universe, she's wrong. But here she is doing something that's right. It's making me feel...a little off."

"Off?"

I bit my lip. "Okay. I feel like my head's about to explode."

He rubbed his jaw, looking out over the skyline. The stroking of his thumb was inciting an answering pulse between my legs. Only my hand blocked that thumb from stroking the bare skin of my inner thigh. I recrossed my legs—taunting and teasing something I absolutely *knew* I shouldn't. The motion disrupted the placement of his hand. And when I resettled, his palm landed on my thigh, two of the fingers slipping beneath the edge of my dress.

Now who was disrupting the scales of the universe?

"Do you remember what Victoria said to us last night? About human beings giving in to our base craving to own things that no one else can have?"

"I do."

Henry's eyes flicked down to the juncture of my thighs, where his fingers gripped me hard. Like he was stopping his hand from gliding beneath my dress. "I've seen Bernard give hundreds of lectures in our time working together. And if he said that once, he said it a hundred times."

"He *told* students that?"

"No, he told them the exact opposite. 'As humans, we must always stifle the compulsion to hoard beautiful things just for ourselves. Libraries and museums exist to let the world in, to expose the world to that which is truly magnificent,'" he quoted.

"What a fucking liar." I shook my head.

"That's it, though," he continued. "I don't think he was lying. I think Bernard actually believes in that concept. I became a librarian for those exact reasons. I became a librarian for the exact reasons *Victoria* mentioned. Because I believe books are magic. And everyone should have access to that magic. I'm starting to believe that Bernard exists between these two worlds fairly easily. Victoria does too."

I shook my head—even as I was forced to confront the potential evidence right in front of me. "Good. Evil." I held out my hands to indicate the two choices. "Victoria and Bernard go in the *evil* category. They broke the rules. They're *breaking* the rules."

Henry stared at me until I felt a flush work its way up my neck. His palm gripped my thigh tighter, and I was tempted— so fucking tempted—to spread my legs for him on this damn stool. Allow that desperate, urgent desire to crest beneath fingers that kept coaxing me toward sin.

Because I was a rule breaker too. I'd done it once, with Mark—I'd broken the rules as surely as Victoria and Bernard.

"I made a series of unforgivable mistakes in the month leading up to Bernard going missing. I doubted my instincts. Didn't believe what I saw. And instead of going to the police, I thought confronting Bernard would make him..." He chuckled derisively. "I thought I could get him to confess to me and change his ways. That's how naive I was, Delilah. Where does that place me? Good? Evil?"

"You feel guilty about that?" I asked, because I didn't really know the answer to his question. He leaned away from me, removing his hand from my leg. I almost snatched it back.

"Constantly," he confessed.

"Bernard is a criminal mastermind. You just got in his way. He was going to end up underground whether you confronted him or not."

"Or he could have been arrested that night if I'd made a different choice." His jaw tightened, a deep line etched between his brows. "But I genuinely believed I was doing the right thing."

Tentatively, I reached for his hand. Brushed his skin in what I hoped was a soothing gesture.

"I understand why you did what you did," I said and meant it. "I believe you."

The echoed statement hung between us in the perfumed

air. We stared down at our joined hands—I caressed his palm, entwining our fingers together.

If Victoria saw us now, what would she see—tenderness... affection...*trust*?

"We have to stop meeting like this."

As if I'd called her into being, Victoria Whitney appeared by our side.

Henry and I didn't even have to feign surprise—I'd been so wrapped up in the moment I'd forgotten myself again.

"It's the woman of the hour," Henry exclaimed. He stood and she let him take her hand, kiss her ring like she was the fucking Queen of England. I kept my expression bashful.

"Congratulations," I said. "What an extraordinary accomplishment."

"Thank you, Delilah." She pursed her lips together. "What are you doing here?"

"Francisco invited us," I said hurriedly. I waved to where he was still standing, chatting with a group of donors. To his credit, he waved back with a smile of feigned delight. "Henry and Francisco know each other through the same professional circles."

"Must be fate," she said. "I can't seem to shake the two of you."

For a terrifying second, I thought we'd blown our cover. I half-expected Sven to come charging through the crowd. But instead she tilted her head, weighing last night's awkward social faux pas.

"We've been supporters of the Bristol Foundation for years," Henry said. "When Francisco told us you were being honored tonight, we called our accountant to arrange a gift in your name."

Victoria arched her brow. "Is that so?"

Henry leaned down to whisper in her ear. The lines of his suit jacket clung to his broad shoulders.

She cast her eyes to mine, impressed. "That's quite a sum, dear."

We hadn't rehearsed this but Henry winked at me. It was fabricated affection that evoked a real blush.

Victoria noticed.

"When you control your family's foundation, you can give as much as you'd like, whenever you'd like," I offered. "We've enjoyed spending time with you recently and we believe in the work that you're doing. We wanted to show you that."

"It's a lovely gift," she conceded. "And I *am* doing amazing work. I swear, this city is more obsessed with the hats that I wear than the fact that I'm the single most generous person in it."

"A travesty," Henry said, shaking his head. "We do hope to still see you at the Gala next week?"

"Of course," she said. "I expect to see *you* in a tuxedo."

"I think that can be arranged."

I hid my giant sigh of relief by looking up into the sky, inadvertently pulling Victoria's attention along with me. "It's a pity we can't see any constellations here," she said.

"Back home, I could see the Milky Way every night," I said. Henry stilled behind me.

"I thought you grew up in the city, dear?" Victoria asked. *Shit.* Had we discussed where we were from? Or was Victoria making an assumption?

"Delilah's not a city kid like me," Henry replied, linking our pinkie fingers together. He squeezed once before letting go.

"I've lived here for a long, long time," I explained. "But I grew up way out in western Pennsylvania. Coal country.

Nothing but trees and skies so dark you can't see your hand in front of your face."

"It must be stunning."

"It is," I said, feeling a pang of homesickness slide through me. My dads had let me stay with them for the months after I'd been fired; let me do nothing but hike through the woods and wonder if I'd ever trust my instincts again. They hadn't judged me for what happened—but it seemed to make them worry more. Which was why I hadn't said a word to them about Victoria or her armed guards.

And I definitely hadn't told them about Henry.

"You must be busy with the Copernicus exhibit," I ventured.

That secret smile appeared on her face again. "Not in the ways that you would imagine. Quite the fuss is being made over it though. It's exhausting." She lifted one shoulder elegantly. "I do so enjoy the heavens. Imagine, a man like Copernicus, positing a theory thought to be strange and blasphemous. When in actuality, he understood what others did not."

"Why the stars?" Henry asked. "Did your mother love them as well?"

"You remembered," she smiled. "She did love stargazing when we were children. Thought it was important for us to have a sense of awe about this world. Something my father didn't care a lick about."

Victoria peered up through the twinkle lights, searching a pale darkness where barely any stars were visible. "I cannot buy them."

"What?" he asked. He glanced over at me.

"The stars." She waved her arms at the sky. "The vast, infinite universe cannot be purchased by Victoria Whitney. And so I'll always desire it. Isn't that how it goes? We always want what we can't have."

I craned my neck, mind scrabbling to come up with our next conversational entry-point. She was going to lose interest, but I had no conceivable ideas on how to ask her if she had stolen the Copernicus without *actually asking her*.

"Ms. Whitney, I hope you don't mind my interruption. But there's a supporter who'd love to meet you." I heard Victoria and Henry turn, and an oddly familiar voice greet her.

"Commissioner Davis, ma'am. It's a pleasure. The police department wanted to be here to show our support for the funding you've given through the Foundation. Makes our job a lot easier, I'll tell you that."

I hadn't heard that smarmy fucking voice in more than two years. In fact, I'd done everything in my power to forget it. From the sound of it, he'd jumped four ranks in that time.

I wondered how many other people he'd used to get there.

In the mediation I'd been forced to sit through before the department had fired me, the only thing he'd claimed was that every single aspect of our romantic relationship was a fabric of my overactive imagination.

"I don't want to make this about age or gender," he said, avoiding my murderous gaze, *"but this isn't the first time a young female detective has latched herself to a superior officer. It does happen."*

Anger blazed so fast and so hot I forgot for a full minute that Victoria Whitney believed I was a philanthropist with a massive trust fund who'd never shot a gun in her life.

"Delilah?" Henry asked. "Are you okay?" His body was shielding me from view while Victoria talked. We needed to get out of here before Mark recognized me and destroyed all of our progress with Victoria.

"We need to—" I started to say.

"Is that Delilah I see?"

The conversation around us quieted. I gave Henry a pleading look that I trusted he understood: *get us out of here.*

We turned and I faced the man I'd never wanted to see again. He seemed older, as if his multiple promotions had aged him rapidly.

"Hello," I said. My mind raced through a thousand lies and possibilities.

Victoria was watching me quizzically.

And Mark's answering smile was as smug as the day he fired me.

19

HENRY

"*I*s that Delilah I see?" The older white man had been introduced as Mark Davis, the Police Commissioner. But he was staring at Delilah like a meal he very much wanted to eat.

But I blinked and his expression disappeared.

I instinctively slid my arm around Delilah's waist and pulled her into my side.

She was trembling.

And whoever the hell he was, he'd just blown her cover.

"Delilah, do you and the Police Commissioner know each other?" Victoria asked. She was staring between the two of them like they were puzzle pieces that didn't fit together. "What a small world."

"Ancient history," she said weakly. "And I'm Delilah Thornhill now." She put a special emphasis on *Thornhill*.

Her words triggered a memory—the two of us talking in my office late at night. *I once trusted a man I shouldn't have. But it's ancient history now.* Was this man the reason Delilah had been fired?

"We used to work together," Mark said to Victoria. "Although I don't know who you are?"

He reached his hand out as if to shake mine.

"Henry Thornhill," I said firmly, ignoring the gesture. "Delilah's husband."

Mark's lips thinned as he dropped his hand. He glared down at Delilah's left hand. "I see."

"Weren't we all talking about *me* a moment ago?" Victoria cut in.

The Commissioner took the hint.

"As I was saying," he said, dragging his eyes away from Delilah, "we wanted to thank you for your good work and service. You've done so much for the city of Philadelphia."

"Yes, thank you for acknowledging that," Victoria said primly. "I'm quite sure you have as well, Commissioner Davis. I so admire the police department."

"It's a great job," Mark agreed. "Serving the community. Doing what's right. Don't you agree, Delilah?"

I smoothed my palm up the curve of her spine and desperately searched for a way out of this situation. Victoria *could not know* that Delilah was a former police officer.

"Sure," she said curtly but didn't elaborate.

"You know I read about you in the paper the other day," Victoria said. "An article about the new rules and regulations you've been implementing in the city department. Sounds like you stepped into quite a mess when you were first appointed."

"Corruption," he said, raising his wine glass as if giving a toast. "Corruption is everywhere, Ms. Whitney. Before I was appointed, we had officers abusing taxpayer dollars for personal expenses. Romantic relationships between superior officers and subordinates." He shook his head. "It was a mess I was all too happy to clean up."

Delilah's trembling intensified.

"It is *startling* the lengths that people will go these days to break the law," Victoria said. "There are so few people these days you can truly trust."

My head snapped up at that—half of me was concerned my partner was about to faint. The other half was wrenched back to the night I'd confronted Bernard. The calm, even way he'd spoken to Louisa over the phone: *It's horrible when we discover how few people in this world we can truly trust.*

Victoria Whitney was shaking her head along with Mark, as if devastated at the thought. I was struck at the similarities between her and my former boss: their serene confidence, a *certainty* that the rules did not apply to them.

"Henry," Delilah whispered. I plunged back into the present, where Delilah was looking at me with wide blue eyes. I shrugged out of my jacket and placed it over her shoulders, rubbing her arms up and down.

"You look freezing," I said, cupping her face. "Are you alright?" My thumb moved across her cheek. Whether the gesture was real or fake, I couldn't be sure. But seeing Delilah Barrett weak-kneed was evoking a sweep of unfamiliar feelings. I wanted to wrap her in my arms and take her someplace safe, far away from here.

"When did the two of you work together again?" Victoria said. She was staring at Delilah. Mark was staring at Delilah.

But Delilah was looking up at me.

And fainted right to the ground.

20

HENRY

*E*verything seemed to happen in slow motion. There was a gasp from Victoria. Delilah's head lolled to the side. Her knees buckled and she pitched backward to the ground.

I might have said her name. She might have said mine. The only thing that was real was my driving motivation to catch my partner before she fell. And I did—one hand beneath her shoulder blades, one at the back of her head—a mere inch before she hit the floor.

"Delilah, oh my God," I whispered.

Someone was bringing us a glass of water. Victoria was demanding people get back, give her space. I laid her down gently, with as much care as humanly possible. I brushed the hair from her forehead—then she fluttered her eyes open. I was kneeling next to her, our faces a foot apart. She moved her lips but I couldn't hear.

"Tell me you're okay. Do you need a doctor?"

"*Faking,*" she whispered—so quiet at first I didn't entirely catch it. Her mouth hovered at my ear—and the heightened tension of the moment couldn't prevent my body's reaction to her pretty mouth on my skin. "I'm faking. You need to get us out of here."

I brought her palm to my lips. Kissed it as I let out a very real sigh of relief. "She's okay," I called to Victoria. Mark was nowhere to be seen. "She has low blood sugar sometimes. She just needs a moment."

"Of course, my dear," Victoria said, hand to her chest. She strode over with a glass of ice water as I helped Delilah gingerly sit up.

Delilah winced, took the glass. "Thank you," she said. "I'm feeling embarrassed."

"Don't be," Victoria admonished. "You think I haven't fainted from exhaustion before? As women, we push ourselves too hard. *All* of the time." She laid a hand on Delilah's shoulder almost tenderly. "People think having a trust fund isn't stressful. But you and I both know how hard it can be."

My fake wife deserved an Oscar nomination for her ability to keep her face neutral.

"You're right," she murmured.

"You need your rest. And for your handsome husband to take care of you."

Delilah nodded. I took her hand, helped her stand up. "I'll be well by the gala, I promise."

Victoria squeezed us both—looking at us proudly. "Oh, I can't wait. Now take your beautiful wife home, Henry. I have to get back to being the center of attention."

"Yes, ma'am," I said, extraordinarily grateful when she finally left us to mingle back into the audience. Under the pretense of comforting my wife, I pulled Delilah into my chest, my lips on her temple.

"You're brilliant."

"I know," she whispered.

"We'll leave and try to avoid Mark. I haven't seen him. I think he's —"

"Do you need medical help Officer Barrett?"

Commissioner Davis had sidled back, expression filled with an abundance of fake sympathy.

"We were leaving," Delilah said, subtly looking through the crowd. We were both aware of Victoria potentially watching us.

"I have to say, I'm utterly shocked to see you. What's it been, two years? And you're married to boot." He shot his eyes up toward mine. I was at least six inches taller than him. Delilah walked on unsteady legs to his side. My brow furrowed, concerned. Her fingertips flew to her forehead, as if she was light-headed.

"Delilah?" I took a step toward her.

"I'm only going to say this once," she said to Mark, tone dripping with a quiet fury. "If you ever talk to me again, I will kick you in the dick so hard you won't be able to stand upright for weeks." Absent Victoria's presence, Delilah dropped the act—straightened her spine, the muscles in her arms rippling with restraint. "If you ever talk to my *husband* again, I'll lodge this stiletto heel into your goddamn face."

He didn't say a word as she brushed a strand of her hair back down. With immaculate grace, she walked back to my side and took my hand. "Shall we, darling?"

"I didn't say this conversation was over," Mark snapped, but there was a desperation that hadn't been there a moment ago. His arm shot out like a snake toward her. Before I could form a rational thought, I caught his wrist. Stepped between Delilah and the Commissioner.

"My wife was clear," I said. "You and I both know what she's capable of. I suggest you heed her warning."

Mark wrenched his wrist away, shaking out his fingers like

a sullen toddler. He didn't say another word, just fixed his tie with a sniff and left.

We watched him for a minute. I tracked Victoria's movements through the audience—she was laughing gaily with Bitzi Peterson and posing for pictures with her award. I doubted she'd noticed our altercation.

"Let's go get your coat," I said, exhaling through the flare of anger, the surge of possession. I led her toward the coat room. It was one story down on the top floor inside the building. We wove our way through the crowd, a few people flashing concerned looks at Delilah. I opened the door, got her inside. The coat-room attendant was missing so I walked into the tiny space, searching the hangers.

Delilah stood next to me, arms crossed, teeth snagging her bottom lip.

"Who was that man?" I asked her softly. "Your old boss when you were a police detective?"

"He was Lieutenant Davis then," she replied. "And yes. He was my direct supervisor. And my boyfriend."

That stopped me in my tracks.

I turned, listening.

"He was also the man who fired me."

21

DELILAH

*T*he coat room felt stifling with Henry in it.

He was too tall, too strong, too devastatingly handsome. My feigned faint had been a literal trust fall—but he'd caught me as if I weighed nothing; laid me on the ground like I was the person he cherished the most.

The moment *could* have belonged to Mark—who had become even more of an asshole in the two years since we'd seen each other last. And a tiny part of me would always have the pure joy of threatening to stiletto Mark's fucking face.

But that memory was honestly insignificant compared to opening my eyes to Henry's lips, hovering inches from my own. To hear his husky voice when he kissed my temple and declared me *brilliant*.

And I'd always treasure the memory of Henry stepping between Mark and me in a clear act of protection.

Not that I needed the help—I surely did not. I just liked knowing I could have it.

Henry reached for the door after my pronouncement, closing it with a soft *click*. "Do you want to tell me what happened?"

"Not really," I admitted. "It's a shitty story. But I think we should tell each other things like this. If we're going to keep being partners."

"I think so too," he said. His eyes held a kindness I desperately needed.

"Two years ago, I thought I had fallen in love with my supervisor," I began. "Mark Davis, the man out there. He was older than me by two decades and very..." *Charming* wasn't the right word. Not now that I knew Henry. "Convincing. He was very convincing. As you can probably guess, it was forbidden for a supervisor to date his subordinate in the police force."

"You're not really a rule breaker, Delilah."

"No, I am not," I agreed. I rubbed my fingers along my collarbone, and Henry tracked the movement. "We snuck around, dating each other, for about a month. This is where the young, foolish, and stupid part comes in."

He grimaced. "I told you the other night that you're none of those things."

"Falling for that man was very foolish," I said quietly. "It cost me a career I'd worked a long time for. And a good deal of other things. But I got very swept up in the idea of our love. Star-crossed lovers kept apart by their jobs. The moment his mask fell away, I couldn't believe I didn't notice how evil he was before. I'm sure you felt something similar when you finally saw Bernard for who he was. And now, being here with you and seeing Mark tonight, I feel *embarrassed* to have lost my job for that fuckwit."

Henry's lips twitched at the ends. "He was, perhaps, one of the biggest fuckwits I've ever met."

"I tend to agree." We shared a private smile. "He was the one who actually fired me from my job. And obviously he did not get into any trouble and has been getting promoted ever since." I let out a long sigh, leaning back against the wall for support.

"You know," he said, "I would actually really enjoy seeing you stiletto his face."

"And I would do it if I wasn't so exhausted from having a trust fund," I said, quoting Victoria.

His laughter was sexy and full-throated. The catharsis, the adrenaline, the relief of sharing even the tiniest pieces of this story with my partner—emotions were weaving through my body like the first warm breeze after a frigid winter. There was a release, a blossoming, a thawing. I smiled at Henry and it felt *marvelous*.

"There it is."

"What?" I asked.

"Your real smile," he said. "You look like that when you talk to Freya. You even smile like that at Abe."

"I've known them for a long time," I said. "Codex is my second family."

He rubbed his jaw, eyes crinkling at the sides. "You haven't smiled like that for me. Except when you're Delilah Thornhill."

We were both quiet for a moment—I noticed, again, the tight space. The closed door.

"I don't want to steal the source of that smile, but what happened the day you were fired?"

I blew out a noisy breath, the memory forcing its way in like it always did. I'd paid extra special care to my hair that morning, added a dash of lipstick, a spritz of perfume. The day was supposed to be monumental—and I wanted to feel beautiful.

What we have here, Ms. Barrett, is a very serious violation of our personnel policies. And an extremely serious violation of trust.

"Can I tell you that part another time? It's…hard for me to tell it."

"Of course you can," he said.

"I want to end this night on a high note, where Victoria confirmed our invitation to the gala. And I almost kicked an asshole in the dick."

"Abe told me this job would have moments of tedious boredom," he mused. "So far he has been wrong." With a flourish, he held out my jacket, nodded down at it. "Your coat, Mrs. Thornhill." I walked over, turned around. "I'm neglecting my husbandly duties. Victoria instructed me to take you home to bed."

I was grateful that Henry couldn't see the effect those words had. *Bed*. Such a mundane word and yet I hadn't shared a bed with anyone since Mark. These past two years at Codex had passed in a blur of closing cases with Abe and stakeouts-and-tacos with Freya. I wanted to hunt down stolen books and trust my instincts again.

Take you home to bed.

"For all their faults, arguing over trash day and who didn't load the dishwasher, I think Henry Thornhill would take very good care of a wife who just fainted from exhaustion," I said.

The heat of his chest warmed my back. I slid one arm into the right sleeve, then the left.

"Yes, I think he would." His deep voice set off goosebumps.

I knew how he would take care—bringing me tea, wrapping me in blankets, stroking my hair as I fell asleep. Our bed would be deliciously warm with the softest sheets, such a glorious contrast to the sensation of his hard body.

A husband like Henry would know how to wrap his arms around my waist in the morning; know how to wake me with his lips along my ear, my throat, my shoulders. A husband like Henry would know how to slip his talented fingers between my legs and bring me to a slow, lazy, decadent orgasm as dawn's rays broke through our window curtains.

Henry's breath caressed the nape of my neck. "Before we go," he said, "I need you to know that I fully understand what you're capable of. I know you don't need my protection."

His mouth lingered on my hair. A few tendrils of hair had caught beneath the coat collar. His fingers dipped beneath, freeing them, stroking the back of my neck.

"I liked that you stepped in for me," I murmured. "Thank you."

For one perfect moment, we stood there, not touching, just breathing in unison. When I finally turned around, Henry was *right there*. There was no one watching us—no case to work, no fake identity. I didn't really need to step into his body heat, lay my hands on his chest, and brush my lips to his cheek. The scent of his skin, the play of muscle beneath his shirt, the muted sigh, low in his throat—it was a full body sensory experience.

I pressed my lips firmly now. A proper cheek kiss. "And thank you for catching me when I fell."

"You knew I would," he said, and there was no question about it. I *had* known he would. His large hand cupped my face, fingers sliding into my hair with a poetic devotion. I pulled back an inch, but that hand held me still, trapped my mouth close to his.

"I did know." I beamed at him again, and his answering grin felt like a new beginning.

"If there are people fucking in here again, I swear to God —" A harried assistant stormed into the small room, forcing us apart. "Um...oh. Wait, *were* you—"

"We were just leaving," Henry said curtly. "My wife and I had a splendid evening. Please give our regards to Ms. Whitney if you see her."

As soon as he and I made it back outside to the busy city streets, the spell between us had been broken. Dorran and his limo were waiting for us, idling at the curb. Once inside, it was hard for me to meet Henry's eyes—so I looked out the window instead. Avoiding the temptation I suddenly had to crawl across those seats and settle on Henry's lap.

"I'll, uh, call Abe," I managed. "Give him the rundown on tonight."

"Oh good," he said. "We're still on for tomorrow? Kicking my ass, so to speak?"

"Bright and early."

We rode the rest of the way to Henry's home in silence—and I distracted myself by counting every row home we passed. I didn't need to make any more passionate mistakes this evening. When we arrived, he gave me a brief nod of goodbye.

"Good night, wife," he said.

"Good night, husband," I replied. I couldn't begin to decipher his expression—but he held my eyes before slamming the door. As we drove off, I allowed myself a single glance out the back window, not surprised in the least that Henry Finch cut a striking figure beneath the glow of a streetlamp.

And that he was watching me too.

22

HENRY

*D*elilah was the embodiment of agile strength.

She was blasting music and hadn't heard me come in—didn't notice me discretely watching her in skilled motion. Her stance was relaxed, left leg back, hands at her face as she jabbed at the bag. In the last week, I'd grown accustomed to Delilah in cocktail dresses and floor-length gowns. But there was something so intimate about her face, scrubbed of makeup, her loose tank top with a faded Temple University logo. Her bare feet and toenails painted chipped pink. It felt like I was seeing Delilah-on-a-Saturday-morning; the girlfriend I'd drag out of bed for brunch—then back to it for sleepy weekend sex.

She struck the bag so hard it rocked back.

All the blood in my body rushed south.

Something had changed between Delilah and me in that coat closet last night—a vital aspect had shifted. I'd been given a gift that I'd worked hard to earn. However small, I intended to hold on tight.

After a series of fast jabs, she spun around and finally saw me.

Her smile was astonishing.

"Hey," she said, panting. "I didn't hear you come in."

"Didn't want to scare you," I said. "Have you taken out all of your aggression on that thing?"

She studied the punching bag, hands on hips. "I was planning on taking my aggression out on you, actually."

She was joking—and so I laughed.

But she didn't have to know what her sweet kiss had cost me—the effort not to haul her up against the nearest wall had probably taken years off of my life. Years and a bit of my sanity. The soft tendrils of her hair beneath my fingers had been as captivating as the gilded edges of a book. I'd had to stop myself from leaning in and *smelling* her.

And her lips on my cheek had been a seduction that kept me awake all night. Over and over, I'd reached between my legs to palm my cock, if only to quiet the persistent ache. I imagined those lips on my throat, on my chest. Wanted her beneath me—writhing as I pinned her down, scraping her fingernails down my back. Knew that if I ever got that woman into my bed, I wouldn't stop making her come until she begged. But every time I let my fingers stroke, I stopped. Because it felt wrong in all the right ways to fuck my hand and fantasize about my beautiful coworker.

"Where do you want me?" I tossed my gym bag on the closest desk. Abe and Freya would be joining us in an hour, but until then it was only us.

"Take your shoes off and come over here," she said. "I rolled out our old mats in case you fall."

"Pretty big assumption that I'll fall, right?"

"Pretty big assumption you think I won't take you down." She smirked. She indicated I should hold my hands out, so I did, letting her wrap my hands in protective tape.

"Tell me what you know about self-defense," she said.

"Literally nothing."

"Okay, newbie. I can't speak for other private detective agencies, because I've only ever worked here, but Abe's always valued having his agents be able to protect themselves."

"Do you really think we'll ever be in a situation where we need it though?" I countered. "Everything we've done so far has been safe."

"Except for the trip wire. And we're currently tailing a woman who employs trigger-happy armed guards." She was suddenly very serious. "I have a license to carry a concealed weapon, but at the end of the day, we're not the police. We're not FBI agents. It makes us very *nimble*. But it also leaves us exposed."

I rubbed the back of my neck. "You know, when I took the private detective exam, I never expected a situation like this."

"That's why we're practicing. You're my partner, Henry. *I* want to protect you."

"And I want to protect you," I said softly.

"Good." She crossed her arms, tilted her chin. "In the FBI, Abe had training in Krav Maga, which is a form of self-defense first developed for the Israeli army. But a lot of officers in the FBI and the police force receive training in it because it's so efficient."

"So Abe has the training. You have the training. And Freya..."

"Underwent some basic training at Quantico before she left," she said. "That's why we're here."

I flexed my fingers in the tape. Shrugged. "Okay then. Show me what you got, Barrett."

"It would have been really fucking cool if you'd said that and I executed some complicated roundhouse kick."

I liked this goofier Delilah.

"But it's not fancy. It's just very, very effective."

She walked over to me and I caught a whiff of lavender. Without makeup, her blue eyes were even prettier. "Is it okay if I touch you?"

"Of course," I said, watching her drop down and grab my left ankle. "Okay, back up a foot." She steadied my right leg. Stood and grabbed my wrists, bringing my hands six inches from my face. "Picture holding a basketball." Delilah mirrored the movement until I got it. She admired her handiwork.

"You look like a badass," she said.

For a few minutes, she showed me basic punches: a jab, a cross. Made me watch as she demonstrated the lightness of her back foot, the way it punched her body forward, the strike of her fist. She strapped black pads to her hands and said, "Hit me."

"Delilah," I said. "I have my PhD in library science. I've never hit anything in my life."

"Last night, with Mark, he went to grab me and you caught his wrist. You anticipated his movement, used force with precision. I was impressed," she said.

"Don't patronize me." I took a step back, shaking out my arms. Plus that had been different—that response had been fueled by one thing only: the desire to protect my partner.

She was shaking her head.

"I'm not patronizing you," she said. "Come on. Hit." She assessed me for a second. "Picture Bernard."

"Seriously?"

"*Yes,* seriously," she urged. "Give me everything you've got. You know I can take it."

My nostrils flared, wondering if *punching* was a good way to channel the pent-up sexual energy that had been thrumming in my veins. But I'd been given a directive.

Same as Victoria, Bernard had received countless awards for his philanthropy and work in our field. I'd sat through many a dinner applauding Bernard's esteemed accomplishments, in awe that of every single librarian who'd ever angled to work with him, he'd chosen me.

My young successor he'd always say. Like Victoria, moving gracefully between the worlds of good and evil. Because the extraordinarily wealthy could.

I hit the pad.

Delilah shook her hand out dramatically. "I wouldn't want to be Bernard right now. But keep your back leg loose and twist at your hip more." She demonstrated again—*jab-jab*. "Hit me."

I struck back in a mimic of her fast movements. "*Nice*," she cheered. "Now keep going."

Her eyes were shining with good humor.

"You're not fucking with me?"

"Nope. And I didn't tell you to stop, Dr. Finch."

A growl rose in my chest. I wanted Delilah to command me to my knees. So I let it out through my fists—striking, stopping, striking again. She paused every few minutes to give me feedback. But it felt *good*.

"Cathartic, right?" she said, slightly out of breath. I was panting, sweat slicking my back. I ran every single day, but this was a different kind of physicality. "Were you imagining every single person who'd ever returned an overdue library book?"

"How did you know?"

She handed me the pads. Strapped on thin gloves. "Now we'll switch. Get 'em up, Henry."

I lifted, eyed her perfect form. The intensity with which she glared at my hands.

"Who are you picturing?" I asked softly, already knowing the answer.

"I didn't like seeing him last night." Her fist landed so hard I rocked back a step.

"You good?"

"Yeah," I said, stretching my neck. "Don't hold back."

She whaled on the pads for a full minute before she bounced back, chest heaving.

"Cathartic, right?" I repeated.

Her mouth curved.

"Were you a natural when you first learned at the academy?" I asked.

"I picked it up pretty quickly, yeah," she said. "Not that I didn't fall on my ass constantly. I was nervous too. I wanted to be an officer so badly that I tried *really* hard to be the best every step of the way. Looking back on it, I think one of the reasons that Mark chose me was my over-eagerness. My desire to please my superior officers. I was an easy target."

There was another minute of precise jabs. My palms were starting to sting, even through the pads.

"But I was always a physical kid," she continued. "I grew up in Glensbury State Park, up north. Both of my dads were rangers there, and we lived on a property inside the park. Just our cabin and the woods, basically. From the time we woke up, until the time we went to bed, my siblings and I tore through the forest like hellions. Running, jumping, climbing, building..." She beamed at the memory, watching me with bright eyes. I liked seeing her distance herself from the distraction of Mark.

"How many siblings?" I asked. She punched a few times, but it lacked the heat of earlier.

"One sister, one brother. We were all adopted one year apart. Max is five years older than me. Elizabeth is two years younger. My dads wanted their children to grow up in kid-paradise, basically."

"I was a city kid," I said. "We had two trees on our block. I rode the subway to school. The idea that you can *climb* a tree is bizarre to me."

"You should go sometime," she said. "Up to Glensbury. It's beautiful."

"Maybe you could teach me how to climb a tree?"

"Yeah," she smiled. "Yeah, maybe.

"I'd like that," I said. Our arms were loose at our sides—I was immersed in the details of Delilah's private life. They felt like rare jewels. I wanted more.

"Okay." She clapped her hands together. "Enough chit-chat. I'm here to kick your ass, remember?"

"Oh, I remember," I drawled.

Her cheeks flushed pink. "That's the basic strike move. If you and I are out in the field, being attacked, you'll focus on the weak spots of their body." She reached up—then stopped. She ran her fingers through her hair and huffed out a breath. "It feels a little...weird to touch you when we're not pretending to be married."

I wondered if we were ever going to talk about the coat closet; the five minutes of stolen affection. It was just my cheek —and it was only a moment—but it had cracked me wide open.

"Do you want to pretend now?" I asked.

Her lips parted, blue eyes dilating. "I don't...actually, it's fine. We're sparring. It's not weird, right?"

"No, it's not." It wasn't weird at all. In fact, part of me wished it was weirder.

"Let's get back to it. Your goal is to strike at their vulnerable places." She touched my forehead. "Their eyes. Their nose." Her hand landed on my jaw. "Their jaw." She gripped my throat. "Their throat."

"Got it," I said hoarsely.

"And, uh..." She glanced between my legs. "Well, you know about that part."

In my fantasy, Delilah squeezed my throat, dragged her palm down my chest, over my stomach, down to a cock that had been achingly hard this entire time. I'd be entirely at her bidding, eager to serve.

"Right," was all that I managed to say.

"Come close, right in front of me."

I took a big step, crowding into her space.

"A common attack would be someone reaching for your wrists. Trying to pull you into their body to subdue you. So go ahead and make a move toward my wrists."

I did, completely unaware of what would happen next. Which was Delilah yanking my body forward as she used my body weight to lean back on her leg with the grace of a ballet dancer. Her right leg extended straight up into the air—foot stopping six inches from my face.

"Got ya," she teased, then let me go.

Those few seconds had been a blur of admiration for her dexterity combined with the sight of her long, muscled leg hovering in the air. An urge to lean forward and kiss her ankle gripped me like a kind of madness.

"You're so fast."

"I've had a lot of practice." She shrugged, like it was an ordinary feat. "Now we'll do it slow motion." She nodded at me to go. I grabbed her wrists again.

"It's about using your attacker's body weight against them," she said, our eyes locked together. "As you lean forward to grab me, I'm leaning backwards, bringing your face closer to my body."

"You want my face on your body?" I asked.

"I'm bringing you into my knee, basically." She pulled, hard, and as my head lowered, she shot her leg up and out again, this time balancing her foot on my shoulder. "This is one way to do it."

She wobbled and I grabbed her foot to steady her. My hand wrapped around her ankle.

"You okay?"

She seemed a little dazed. She dropped all the way back. "Yep." Bouncing on her toes, she wiggled her shoulders. "Try and grab me again."

I did—three more times, each time adding another layer of sexual torture. It was the force of her yanking me into her body, as if she craved me like a drug. The scent of her lavender shampoo and her full lips curving into a smirk because she *liked* besting me.

And God help me, it was her leg. Every time she kicked up, all I saw was the flexing muscle of her inner thigh, the curve of her hamstrings, the *barest* swell of her ass exposed by her tiny running shorts. Delilah's legs were becoming an erotic film I was forced to watch, over and over. A fourth time. A fifth time.

On the sixth time, she wobbled hard—and instead of her ankle, I grabbed the inside of her leg by mistake, a clumsy meeting of limbs and fingers. Her cheeks blazed red, and we were both panting like marathon runners.

"Still a tough fucking teacher, Barrett," I said, wincing as I dodged a jab. "How am I doing?"

"It's too early to tell." She *tsked*.

"Liar," I scoffed. "I'm a natural."

"You're something all right."

I made a tepid move to grab her, and she danced out of my grip. "You're getting tired, husband."

"Never," I said. "You're my wife. You know I never get tired."

"You and I both know that's *not* true."

I shook my head. "If only Victoria was here to see this real-life marital banter."

I made another attempt for her wrists, grabbing them harder than I intended. For a single second, we were locked together, poised for action. She was struggling not to laugh. I was struggling not to lean in and kiss her.

Instead, I moved—jerking her into me with all of my strength. But I'd underestimated the skill of my partner. I pulled, she pulled—and at the exact moment I thought our faces *might* collide, her leg shot out with the force of a high-speed train and kicked me square in the chest.

"Don't even try," she panted. She was balanced on her back leg like a crane, but her ankle was shaking. Eyes locked, both grinning, I made a move for her back leg—with purely comical intent. But she gasped out a *"fuck,"* grasped my tee-shirt with both hands, and tumbled both of us to the ground.

23

DELILAH

*H*enry and I landed on the mat with a shared groan. I experienced the unsettling sensation of falling backward—and then the incredible paradise of his body landing on mine.

His hands hit the mat on either side of my head, controlling his body weight. For a delicious, delirious thirty seconds, we stared at each other like lovers. He'd taken off his glasses to practice—without the added barrier, his dark brown eyes burned with lust. The knowledge of it felt like a fist tightening in my low belly—my body was eagerly attuned to the call-and-response of his need. My legs were spread, his hips cradled between my thighs like he'd always belonged there.

His cock was an unyielding pressure against my sex. His smoky-cedar scent enveloped me. His full lips, this close, confirmed a thought I'd been secretly coveting the past few days.

Henry's mouth would wreck me.

I heaved in a breath, knew I should shove him off before I made the exact same mistake I had with Mark: allow my passions to cloud my judgment. But these thirty seconds beat between us like a rapid heartbeat, mimicking the blood roaring in my ears. My hips tilted up of their own volition, seeking completion.

"I guess this means…I won?" he said.

"Or maybe it's all a trick? To lure you into a false sense of complacency?" I taunted.

His jaw tightened. My arms were still thrown back—what if he reached forward, interlaced our fingers? What if I let my fake husband pin me down, slake his sexual need on my willing body?

"This doesn't feel like part of the official training manual, Delilah." His rough voice caressed every syllable of my name.

I shivered, contemplated my next move.

"You don't know what you're talking about, newbie." I levered myself up onto my elbows, bringing our faces dangerously close. I could kiss him right now. Thread my fingers into his curls and crush my mouth to his. He'd tear my shorts in two, shred the barrier of my underwear.

"I'm pretty sure I know my wife," he whispered, *almost* dipping his mouth down. I could see him considering it: the stakes, the consequences, the fallout. It was in this brief moment of mental distraction that I wrenched my hips up, twisted my left leg up and over.

Flipped Henry Finch onto his back.

I was straddling his waist, seated firmly on a cock that had grown even harder in the space of a single second. He looked surprised, then delighted, then *hot*. His hands stayed on the mat, fingers digging in.

I raised my arms overhead like a boxing champion. "Delilah Barrett for the win!"

He laughed, the vibrations echoing up my thighs. In the

flip, his tee-shirt had ridden up a half-inch, exposing a sliver of ridged abs. I stood up as quickly as I could—before I planted my palms on his chest and ground myself against him. It would have been so fucking easy, so fucking *good*. At the *height* of sneaking around with Mark—stealing kisses in the hallway or making out in elevators—I hadn't felt as achingly turned on as I did in this single moment.

"I told you," Henry said, bouncing up and off the mat. My neck craned to maintain eye contact as he regained his height. "I'm just a librarian. I have no skills."

"That's not true and you know it," I said lightly. "You're incredibly skilled."

"Not compared to you."

"Different skills," I clarified. I threw a few, silly shadow boxes his way and he ducked, laughing.

"They are markedly different." We were both still grinning —I hadn't felt this light-hearted in a long time. "And I do have talents you're not aware of, wife."

I smirked at that, attempted to ignore the rush of heat his words sent through me. "Cocky husband."

My fists lashed out again, but this time, he caught my wrist. Tugged. I fell against his chest easily. One arm tightened around my waist, trapping me, while his hand gripped my face. Eyes wide, lips open—I could only stare up at him in absolute adoration.

"What...what are you doing?" I panted. Henry was dropping his mouth low...then lower.

"Delilah," he whispered, and I could *hear* his restraint. We weren't kissing—not even close—but if I'd pushed up on my tiptoes our lips would have connected. And I wanted to—*I wanted to*. He was too warm, too sexy, too hard, too charming. And this ghosting of Henry's mouth, inches from my own, felt *magnificent*.

"Maybe this is all a trick," he said, repeating my taunt back to me, "to lure you into a false sense of complacency."

His eyes sparkled with humor.

"I see the student has become the teacher," I said airily.

"Except I don't want to stop these lessons." He pinned me with a look overflowing with honesty.

Codex's office door creaked open, and Henry let me go, clearing his throat and waving to our coworkers. Freya was yawning, bun messier than usual, eyes bleary behind her glasses. Abe was immaculate in his suit.

"I'll make an educated guess that Delilah won," he mused, flipping on lights and beckoning us to follow him into his office. We did, obedient as schoolchildren. Freya yawned again and leaned into me for a hug.

"Mark was there last night," I said, giving her a big squeeze.

She reared back, brow furrowed. "Do you need someone to help hide his body?"

"Delilah threatened to put her stiletto in his face," Henry said.

Abe arched his eyebrows at me. "*Not* with Victoria around, I'm assuming?"

"Please, I'm a professional."

Freya snorted, reaching into her bag. "You deserve this gift I brought you even more." It was a greasy breakfast sandwich from my favorite food cart. My stomach growled at the smell.

"You're an angel," I said. "Victoria confirmed our invite to the gala," I said, relaying the details from the night before: Francisco's anger, Victoria's revealing comments, Mark, my faint.

Behind Abe, Freya had hung a whiteboard on the exposed brick wall, where she was keeping track of the various online personas she kept active online. Her notes were scattered, filled with underlines and exclamation points and a short-list of suspects that also could have taken the Copernicus.

In the middle of the board was our countdown.

Days Until Copernicus Exhibit: 13

Freya was listening enthusiastically, biting her nails like I was telling a ghost story. Abe sat impassive, expression neutral.

"Francisco called me this morning," he said when I finished, drumming his fingers on the desk. "He wanted to convey his disappointment in the two of you last night."

I rolled my eyes.

"At which I repeated what Delilah said to him, only with a few extra choice words."

"You're not worried you'll piss him off? That he'll drop our contract?" Henry asked.

"Francisco and I have known each other for a long time," Abe explained. "I understand what he's going through. But I reminded him that we have a higher case close rate than the FBI's Art Theft department and he'd be advised to let us work the way we work."

My eyes fell back on the countdown. *13 days.*

"He also wanted to let me know that the FBI have brought in a suspect."

"Wait, what?" I asked, leaning forward.

"Obviously, they won't give Francisco the name. But since you were just mingling with Victoria last night, I think it's safe to assume it's not her."

"What does this mean?" Henry asked.

Abe cast his eyes over at me. "Either the FBI has the right suspect, and we've been chasing the wrong one. Or vice-versa. We won't know unless the person is formally charged."

"But the book's not back yet?" I said.

Abe shook his head. "No manuscript anywhere. It cannot

be found." He paused. "Doesn't necessarily mean they have the wrong suspect though."

"At the end of the day though, that's what we want, right?" Henry said. "We want the book back. Who cares who finds it?"

Abe and Freya shared a bemused look at my expense. Henry had barely been here three months and yet he was more comfortable with the gray area Codex operated in than I was.

"The book is the most important," Abe said. "Always."

"And at least the FBI can actually arrest them," I grumbled, knowing I was picking at an old argument that wasn't going to go anywhere. It would have been hard—but not impossible—to find my way into another police unit. But the experience had left such a nasty taste in my mouth I had hoped becoming a private detective would quench my thirst for chasing down bad guys—but without the bullshit of an office environment, the pesky red tape and bureaucracy. And in so many ways it did, especially after two years of it.

But my job was no longer to arrest, handcuff, charge, or jail. That was not within Codex's purview.

"Unless they have the wrong person," Abe shot back. "Last time I checked, we were chasing down a strong lead."

His faith in me felt like too much pressure, especially in light of what he'd told us.

What if it was all a bad instinct—Mark all over again?

"I think we're chasing the right lead too, but all this trust-building is taking time," Freya interjected. "Not that the two of you aren't doing a great job," she added. "But time is not our friend here. You two need to get into her private collection. Like immediately."

Anxiety gripped my nerves—the detective in me wanted to run to Victoria's house, barge in, and find that book. *If* it was there.

But I glanced at Henry—the strength in his forearms, the curve of his biceps. And I wanted to be back on that mat with him.

"Which is why I have *another* present. This one's for you, Henry." She waggled her eyebrows at him as she went into our secure storage area, coming back with a small package wrapped in newspaper.

"A book for the librarian," she said with a mock bow. "I was up all night working on this." Freya took out her laptop, typed furiously for a minute, then turned her screen around. "There was a big theft at the Fordham Rare Manuscript Library in Los Angeles last week," she said. "Thieves broke into the library, stealing twelve rare books in the seven minutes they had before the cops responded to the security alarm." She nodded at the package. "Open it."

Henry did—a big, sexy grin spreading across his face when he saw what it was. I leaned over to see, cheek brushing his shoulder.

"*A Room of One's Own?*" I read.

"Virginia Woolf's famous feminist essay on women and writing," he said. He opened the cover slowly, whistled beneath his breath when he saw the cover page. "Signed?"

"In her signature purple ink and everything," Freya said. She adjusted her glasses, shoved up the sleeves of her sweater. "The owner over at Pickwick Rare Books on Front Street is my personal fucking hero. That and Abe, who authorized quite a bit of cash for us to buy this. I basically spread a rumor in the online forums last night that one of the books stolen from LA made its way to Philly. According to what's been reported in the papers, some of the stolen books were by Virginia Woolf. But they haven't printed the titles yet. If she's heard even an inkling of what's happened, the name will pique her interest."

"She'll think we have the strings to pull to gain access to something so notorious," I said.

"What did she say to you guys the other night? About the different levels?"

I nodded. "We bring her a high-profile gift. Maybe she invites Henry and Delilah Thornhill to see her collection as a thank you."

"She thinks it puts us on her level," Henry said. "Potentially."

Freya tapped her temple. "Office nerd saves the day again."

I tore my breakfast sandwich in half, placed it in her lap. "You deserve this more than me."

"The gala is in five days," Abe said evenly. "If this works, she needs to invite you to her home within a week of the gala. And that book has to be there. Or we miss whatever sliver of a window we had."

"Last time I checked, we were chasing down the right lead," I repeated, the words flying out in a nervous jumble.

"I believe that," Abe said. "I truly do." He knocked his knuckles against the whiteboard behind him—square in the middle of the 13. "We just can't forget this. The clock is ticking."

I couldn't look at Henry. I hadn't expected trusting my partner to lead me to this temptation. Twenty minutes ago, I'd been straddling him on a mat as the precious hours we had to find this book slipped away.

"Pull out all the stops on Saturday night," Abe ordered. "You need to get her eating from the palm of your hand. The more you stroke her ego, the more information Victoria Whitney will cough up."

"If she thought the two of you were madly in love before, wait till she sees you at the gala," Freya added. "Dial everything way the fuck up. You're two wealthy private collectors

179

who are desperate to worship her. And you have a love that rivals Romeo and Juliet."

"But don't die at the end. I'd like to make that perfectly clear." Abe considered the three of us, as if sizing up our potential. "Let's get back to work."

24

DELILAH

Freya and I sat on the curb at a taco stand on South Street, watching the late-night revelers stream by. My muscles ached from self-defense training with Henry and the mounting tension of the day. Avoiding my blossoming feelings for my fake husband—and the impending pressure of Saturday night—had me rigid with nerves. And Freya, with all the awareness of both my friend *and* partner, had steered me here as soon as we'd locked up for what she called "taco therapy."

"I can't eat another," I warned, licking salsa from my fingers.

"Oh, but you *can*," she said, handing me another taco with a triumphant grin. "I have twenty more behind me, so don't worry about holding back."

I rolled my eyes—watched an insanely cute couple on a date walk past us on the sidewalk. I imagined Henry doing that with another woman and felt such a sharp pinch of jealousy I almost dropped my food.

"Hey, I got us tickets to the flower show next month," she said, cutting into my jealous reverie.

"You *didn't*," I cheered. "Thank you."

In the years that I'd lived away from my lush, verdant home, I'd filled my Philly row home with an abundance of greenery, even tending to a rooftop garden that Freya loved to visit. I liked feeling like my house was endlessly in blossom; roots, leaves, and dirt were the textures of my childhood. A few times a year, I dragged Freya to flower shows—the only caveat being she was allowed to name every new plant after a wizard in Harry Potter.

"It'll be a nice treat after this fucking *bonkers* case." Freya handed me another cup of salsa. "A celebration for all of your hard work."

"I've got to get the book back first," I sighed.

"I'm pretty sure you will though." She winked.

We ate in companionable silence for a minute, content to people-watch as the city unfolded around us. "So," she said, nudging our shoulders together, "how was seeing Mark last night?"

I sighed again, but it came out more like a growl. "He was smarmy as fuck, as usual. There to schmooze Victoria for some bullshit reason, but really I could tell he was networking."

"Looking for his next set of victims," Freya concluded.

"He's disgusting," I said softly. She studied me for a minute before placing another taco on my plate. "I wish I didn't..."

She didn't interrupt, let me trail off.

"I wish I didn't relive the day he fired me so many times."

"If my supposed 'boyfriend' fired me from my fucking job so he could get a promotion, I'd relive it every day."

I turned toward her. "I don't see you ever making a mistake like that, though. You're so...self-assured."

Freya snorted. "Well, thank you for that compliment, but believe me, I make mistakes left and right, *especially* when it comes to matters of the heart." She dipped a tortilla chip in guacamole, chewed it thoughtfully. "Because I'm human, just like you."

"I hate making mistakes." I propped my chin on my hand.

"I know, doll," she said. "We all do."

Mistakes like Mark poked at my black-and-white world-view, and I didn't like it. Where did Henry's actions with Bernard fall? Where did Victoria and her charitable giving fit in?

If Henry had touched his lips to mine today—like I'd desperately wanted him to—I would have kissed him back, without regret. I knew that kissing coworkers *always* made things complicated. But I still would have done it, willingly.

"Can I talk to you about something serious?" Freya asked.

When our eyes met, I knew all hope was lost. If Victoria believed Henry and I were madly in love, then surely Freya could see our smoldering attraction to each other.

"Of course," I hedged.

"You seeing Mark got me curious to see how Philadelphia's Slimiest Police Commissioner was doing."

"Oh," I said, simultaneously relieved and *more* nervous.

"I found a website," she said. "It was launched last week. Do you remember another police officer named Margaret Pierce?"

"Yeah, I worked with her," I said, brow furrowing. "Same station, but different units. She was in Narcotics."

"She's claiming that Mark did to her what he also did to you, about a year after you were fired. And she says three other women have come to her, claiming the same thing. It looks like they all either worked in your unit or with him in previous units. But it's the same pattern, Del. Lure women in, use them, fire them, use it for political gain."

I'd been a bright-eyed new recruit when I realized the full

extent of the corruption in my unit. Misuse of funds, romantic relationships, tax dollars being wasted. But I'd been there for a job—to catch bad guys. It was my dream, and it was far too easy for me to exist in that dream, ignoring everything else around me. When the local papers started to report on our unit, I ignored it, believing I was doing the right thing.

Until the local papers were reporting on me, of course.

"I found the mayor's speech when he appointed Mark to his position," Freya continued. "*Cleaning up corruption* was the golden reputation he'd reportedly garnered over the past two years. Climbed that ladder right on up, using women like you as stepping-stones."

"*Such* a fucking bastard," I said, nostrils flaring.

"I know," she said. "Would you want to tell her about your story?"

My anger shriveled up—along with my courage. How come chasing down suspects in dark alleys didn't make me feel afraid but this did?

"I don't know." Freya's expression was open, kind. "I mean, it sounds like they have some other testimonies if they're building a case against him?"

"They do. Might be nice to add your voice to it, is all."

I held myself by the elbows. "Do you think I'd end up back in the papers again?"

"Possibly," Freya said. "Unless you chose to remain anonymous."

I swallowed around a suffocating tightness in my throat. "No," I said clearly. "I don't want to do it. It's been two years, and I sincerely hope last night was the final time I ever see him."

"I hope so too," Freya said. "And I think your decision is the right one for you."

I laid my head on her shoulder. "Thank you for telling me.

I'm happy someone's going after him. Margaret's a tough cookie."

"Just as tough as you," she said.

She handed me another taco, and we sat like that, side-by-side, as South Street swelled with bar patrons and tourists. And I found myself thinking not about Mark—not at all.

I was still thinking about Henry.

25

HENRY

*T*he Philadelphia Natural History Museum had a long red carpet extending down the sidewalk, as though this was the Oscars. White rose petals dotted the carpet, crushed beneath the expensive shoes of the museum's patrons. Strains of string music wafted out from the open doors.

"This is always what I pictured prom night to be," Delilah said. "I never went."

"Really?" I asked. I kept my eyes trained on the velvet carpet, beckoning us inside. Delilah wore a floor-length black gown with a slit high on her thigh. The long sleeves were sheer with beaded petals.

She was, quite possibly, the most beautiful woman I had ever seen.

Five days had passed since I'd had the pleasure of Delilah's lithe body pinned beneath mine on that mat. After our wake-up call with Abe and Freya, we both stayed friendly, but professional—I sensed her desire to keep things cool. A desire I felt as well.

And every single night she appeared to me in dreams that

burned like a fever—bodies naked and slick on that floor, my hips thrusting between her spread legs in a rhythm that drove us both mad. Even in my dreams, she'd flip me, ride me, sinuous and strong. She'd squeal as I'd drag her by the waist up the length of my body, positioning her right over my mouth.

Was it so wrong to want to worship the muscles of her inner thighs, the ones she'd flashed at me over and over in our self-defense training? If I used my teeth, would she laugh? If I used my lips, would she moan?

But now we were here—Henry and Delilah Thornhill. And our romantic directive, per Freya, was to *turn everything way the fuck up.*

"My little town was too small," Delilah said, rocketing me back to the present. "We didn't have enough kids in my graduating class to have dances."

"I should have brought you a corsage." I chanced my first real look at her—she was smiling.

"Maybe next time." She was staring up at the museum like a giant puzzle she was trying to put together with only her mind.

"Nerves?" I asked my partner.

"Yes," she said honestly. "A whole fuck-ton of nerves."

I glanced at my watch, surprised, as always, to find a wedding band on my finger. "We should probably go in."

"Okay."

"I'm going to hold your hand. Is that all right?" But before I could move, she entwined our fingers together. Gave my hand a good squeeze. Her eyes focused, spine straightened. I hid my own smile—I loved watching her transform every time we went undercover.

Delilah strode along the carpet like it'd been rolled out specifically for her, the long train of her gown dragging rose petals as I walked alongside her. The museum's main hall was draped in silver and gold—the ceiling hung with glass sculptures of the nine planets. In the center, an impressive chandelier was designed to look like the sun, bursting with rays.

The infamous drawings in the Copernicus manuscript floated through my memory—the celestial shapes, the deliberate paths of orbit around the brightest star. Fifty tables were covered in shiny flecks of metal and flickering candles. A large dance floor dominated the middle of the room where the string quartet played.

"This is better than prom, I promise," I said low against her ear.

A tuxedoed gentleman found our names on a list. "With Ms. Whitney?" he asked, clearly surprised. "Please, come this way."

Banners hung from the walls displaying the event sponsors—Victoria was the presenting donor. We meandered through a crowd decked out in diamonds until we reached the most central table, located right beneath the sun-chandelier. Victoria was standing, surrounded by guests, draped in a white gown and a fox fur.

"My new favorite couple," she crooned, clapping her hands together. She shooed away her other guests like flies from a plate of food. When she air-kissed Delilah, she paused to squeeze her wrist. "And how are you feeling my dear? Did your husband take care of you after the other night?"

"Of course he did," she promised, laying a hand gently on Victoria's shoulder. "There's a reason why I married him literally on the spot."

I stood back, smoothing down the black vest of my tuxedo. When Victoria presented her hand to me, I kissed her ring as usual.

"We brought you a gift," I said, indicating the finely-wrapped book I held in my hand. "Is there somewhere private we can give it to you or is right here fine?"

She tilted her head. "Right here is fine. No one would dare do anything to me here, Mr. Thornhill." I nodded, presented the book into her waiting hands.

She made an approving sound, unwrapping the packaging with manicured fingers dripping with rings. The cover of *A Room of One's Own* revealed itself, looking out of place in a room overflowing with such grandiose decadence.

I suppressed an urge to snatch it back.

"First edition. Signed by the author. We thought it would make a nice addition to your private collection."

A look of recognition flitted across her face—in the wake of the Los Angeles theft, there'd been a brief renewed interest in Virginia Woolf's literary legacy. I guessed Victoria Whitney was the kind of woman who had the papers read to her every morning as she sipped her espresso.

"Virginia is one of my favorites," she said. "How did you know?"

We hadn't, so I culled my knowledge as quickly as I could.

"A pioneer, a feminist, a woman who understood the crucial role of her independence," I hedged. "There are some parallels to what you've done in your life."

Victoria brightened, leaning in conspiratorially. "She was quite lonely, you know. Her writing brought her a kind of divine madness."

My gut twisted. Bernard had said the same thing once.

"Yes," I agreed. "Yes, I believe it did."

She reached forward, touched first my arm, and then Delilah's. "What a thoughtful gift." She held up a single finger, and Sven appeared seemingly out of nowhere. "Prepare this for safe transport." He took it without further instruction—I thought again about that portable case and all of its nefarious possibilities. She held up a second finger and cocktails arrived.

"To Virginia," she toasted. "And new friends. That book must have cost you a pretty penny."

"Not in the traditional sense," Delilah said. Victoria's gaze sharpened. "We took a little trip to Los Angeles."

The recognition on her face returned—but this time it was filled with greed. "How interesting. And how were the falls this time of year?"

Delilah's secretive smile was more real than feigned. "Quite lovely. And certainly a little more *notorious* than Henry and I usually like. But we thought you would appreciate this more than most, given the impressiveness of your collection."

Victoria sniffed—as if receiving gifts of stolen books was an everyday affair. "Yes, well, you would be correct."

I stretched my arm behind the back of Delilah's chair, stroking my thumb across the back of her neck.

"We hoped we could trust you with a gift like this," I ventured.

"Trust, my dear Henry, is the most valuable social currency in the world," Victoria said. "I've lived a very bold life. Bold and a little reckless at times. But life is short, and coloring outside the lines makes things so much more interesting. Don't you agree?"

Coloring outside the lines was an interesting way to say *break the law.* But we nodded loyally, which seemed to please her. The opening notes of "Round Midnight" drifted through the crowd and it made Victoria sigh. "This song always makes me think of Bernard."

Goosebumps broke out across the nape of Delilah's neck. I stroked my thumb in circles, attempting to soothe her even as those words put me on the same high alert.

"Victoria," Delilah said, leaning in close, "did you and Bernard *date*?"

Victoria's coquettish giggle proved Delilah's instincts—and my memory—correct. "Oh, *years* ago. Nine to be exact."

Just as I'd remembered. One year into working with Bernard and he'd returned from a vacation sullen and weary, with no further explanation. He didn't speak about his "Lady Love" after that.

"And it wasn't *that* much of a thing, darling," Victoria mused. "Merely a whirlwind few years. I've had many suitors in my life."

"Why am I not surprised?" Delilah tilted her head with a teasing smile, causing her hair to slide through my fingers. "I told you when we met that I figured you for a heart-breaker. Have you ever been engaged? Married?"

Victoria gave us a sly look over her martini. "Engaged five times. I've never been married."

"Who was your favorite fiancé?" Delilah asked. She placed her hand on my thigh, squeezing.

"Reginald," she said immediately. "He owned exotic animals. Taught me how to tame a lion once."

A few men—all dressed in top hats and carrying canes—were moving through the crowd with their eyes set on Victoria. "It appears as if you have a few *new* suitors coming for you now," I murmured.

She touched her hair discreetly. "I always do." She glanced toward the open dance floor, where couples were beginning to sway to the music. "When was the last time the two of you danced? Was it your *elopement*?"

"Last night in our kitchen, actually," I said.

Delilah dipped her head, as if to hide a blush. Victoria practically squealed.

Three men arrived at Victoria's chair at the exact same

time, and she examined them with a critical eye. She selected the one to the farthest right. As he held out his hand to escort her, she turned to us. "You lovebirds should join us on the ballroom floor."

"Of course," Delilah and I said in unison. Victoria waltzed off, and I held out my hand toward my partner. "Shall we, wife?"

"I don't really know how to dance," she admitted, color in her cheeks.

"But you can subdue an attacker with a throat punch?"

"Well, that's easy," she said, looking around my shoulder at the dance floor. I leaned down to her ear, brushing the hair away. "All we have to do is sway together. I'll take the lead."

Hands clasped, I walked us to the dance floor, where Victoria and her chosen date were in the center. I half-expected a spotlight to descend upon them. We found a spot close to the edge; I placed my palm low on Delilah's back, clasped her hand to my chest. My head lowered until we were cheek-to-cheek. The music swelled around us—I kept her snug against me, moving us in time to the bass player's notes.

"I thought Henry and Delilah Thornhill fought over household errands. Not slow-danced in their kitchen," she said.

"Abe and Freya said *romantic*," I mock-chided. "And actually, I think a couple slow-dancing in their kitchen together would be, well...lovely. Don't you?"

"I do," she said in an almost-whisper. "What kind of couple do you think would do something like that?"

I rested my lips against Delilah's hair. "Maybe a couple so swept up in their love they need to touch each other constantly. Breathe each other in. Feel connected through movement."

"Maybe..." she started, "maybe they love the home they

created together. I can see the Thornhills dancing together at the end of a long day. As a form of comfort. Romantic comfort."

"It sounds like our fake marriage is quite happy," I said. Delilah was dancing easily with me, our bodies attuned to the steps although we'd never practiced. "Perhaps we do it every night."

She hummed a little—a sound of bliss. "Even though I can't dance?"

"I'd keep teaching you," I promised. "And really, it would only be an excuse to hold you."

She squeezed my hand tighter.

"We probably did dance the night we eloped," she said so softly I almost missed it. "A little drunk, still in our wedding clothes, feet bare in our hotel room."

My lips grazed her temple, the shell of her ear. "Then what happened, wife?"

"I think we both know what happened."

Across the floor, Victoria wiggled her fingers at me. I wiggled mine back. I twirled Delilah in a circle, her skirts billowing around her heels glamorously. She looked surprised, then delighted.

I tugged a laughing Delilah back into my chest. "Where does a librarian learn how to dance?" she said.

I twirled her again, and she hammed it up a little this time.

"Now who's a quick study?" I grinned. The tip of my nose brushed along her jaw. "My grandparents lived in a care facility for years with dementia. They didn't always recognize each other, though they loved to share a dance during the facility dance lessons. I used to take my siblings, Joelle and Jeremiah, with me every Saturday for dance lessons there. It was completely silly, completely happy, and entirely heartbreaking, all at the same time."

"They'd still dance with each other though?" Delilah asked.

We were barely swaying now.

"Yes, they did, quite happily too." I smiled at the memory. "They passed away one month apart. I was in high school and I remember my mom taking her first sabbatical after they died. She'd never even taken a vacation day before."

"What did you do together when she wasn't working?"

"Read books. Went to the park. Checked out novels at the library. It wasn't anything particularly spectacular. The ordinariness of that time is what made it so memorable for me."

"Oh," she began, "oh, I love that story, Henry. Your grandparents must have loved each other very much."

"They were devoted to each other," I replied.

Our feet moved back and forth, our bodies pushed together as one as I stared into Delilah's eyes. This was all part of the game, all part of my job—seducing her, seducing the crowd into believing our love was real. At least, that was the lie I told myself when I brushed my lips against her cheek.

"How come no one ever taught *you* how to dance?" I asked.

"I haven't dated anyone who ever wanted to dance with me."

She was tilting her neck, and I was entranced with the column of her throat—the line of her collarbone, the pale flesh disappearing beneath the beads. I wanted to caress her fluttering pulse point but held off. The minute my lips touched such an intimate place on Delilah's body, I was going to permanently lose any remnants of this charade.

There'd be no more pretending between us.

"I don't have a ton of experience with passion or romance." Delilah beheld our joined hands, the diamonds of her ring twinkling. "I wasn't sure I'd do a good job undercover because of it."

"Because you couldn't fake being married?"

"No." Our lips hovered an inch apart. "I wasn't sure I could fake being in love."

I'd worried about this too. And yet even at our most awkward, our partnership had held the shape of something comfortable; a natural texture that made becoming the Thornhills easier and easier for me.

"You do a pretty decent job of bluffing though. Victoria totally believes you're madly in love with me." She was attempting to tease, but I remembered how she'd described her relationship with Mark: *I wasn't a person to him. I was a body to be used.*

Delilah's gown *swished* across the floor as we danced closer and closer to the string quartet. The opening melody of Etta James's "At Last" swirled around us, serving only to loosen my tongue.

"It's not hard to pretend when you're the most beautiful woman in this entire room, Delilah." My teeth lightly scraped at the skin below her ear.

"Henry," she said.

I'd gone too far.

"*Henry.*" Her tone was sharp, entire body stiffening in a single second. I scanned the crowd for Victoria—*goddammit.* I'd been so wrapped up in Delilah I'd forgotten to pay attention to our suspect.

And she was striding from the dance floor, Sven in tow. Heading for a back part of the room with an *Employees Only: Authorized Area* sign hanging across it.

"Follow my lead." Delilah was half-dragging me across the dance floor as my mind scrambled to catch up. Our staged slow dance had left me dazed. But my partner was on the move, two steps ahead, racing toward two burly security guards who were standing in front of the *Authorized Area* sign.

She stopped and I almost ran into her. "Excuse me," she said to Burly Guard #1. "I need your help. Immediately." Her tone was haughty. She gestured for them to stand close to her, and as they moved her index finger pointed at the briefly exposed hallway.

"Some kind of problem?" #1 asked.

"A man, a *gentleman* over there?" They glared off into the distance—and I slipped into the darkness, aware of the other guests, their possible attention. "It's the one in the dark-blue suit."

"Half the crowd is wearing dark-blue suits," #2 sighed. "Ma'am."

Delilah gave her best Victoria impression, crossing her arms and pursing her lips. "Yes, well, can you please go over and tend to them? I've been trying to get a drink for the past hour, and their behavior is upsetting. It's out of control."

As if on cue, two men by the bar began laughing uproariously.

Both guards sighed extravagantly, one of them squawking into a radio. "Yeah, wait right here."

I was flat against the wall, hidden by shadows. Delilah watched them lumber off for all of a second before dashing backward into the hallway, backing right into my chest.

"*Fuck,*" she wheezed.

"It's just me." I grabbed her shoulders. "What's the plan?"

"Where on earth did she *go*?" she muttered. "And it's not like Sven's easy to miss." The carpeted hallway was pitch-black and filled with doors. No windows.

"Delilah? The plan?" We were slipping down the hallway like sharply dressed cat burglars. The raucous sounds of the museum gala faded away the farther we walked.

"No plan, just action," she whispered.

The hallway ended, curving to the right. There were

muffled voices. A louder one—Victoria's. Behind us stretched the long, lonely hallway and a sea of closed doors.

In front of us: Victoria and Sven.

We were totally exposed if she came around that corner.

"And *what's* the delay?" Victoria's tone was abrupt. There was an answering silence, like she was on the phone.

"Unacceptable. I'll do nothing of the sort. I have 300 people coming tomorrow and I would *never* cancel. We'll move it after the party."

"Ma'am." That was Sven. Delilah and I were squashed together, pushed to the wall. "You have to be reasonable."

I heard Delilah whisper, "You're about to die, buddy."

Whatever Victoria said next was unintelligible, but her harsh tone was clear. A cell phone went off, and I thought my heart was going to explode.

"Take that call," she snapped. "I need to get back to my guests. I've been gone too long."

Footsteps. Fucking *footsteps* terrifyingly close to where we were standing. Coming closer and closer. As I stood frozen, Delilah was reaching for the closest doorknob. She turned it. It opened.

And she yanked me inside.

26

DELILAH

*M*y first recognizable thought was: *total darkness*.

A second earlier I'd twisted the closest doorknob and prayed like hell it was open. It'd been a long time since I'd chased a suspect down a shadowy hallway without a second thought. And those times I'd had handcuffs and a warrant. I didn't even have a weapon on me tonight— Abe had been nervous about museum metal detectors going off.

And now my palms were on the closet door—my back to Henry's chest—his hands boxing me in. The only sounds were our labored, panicked breathing. I found the doorknob, engaged the lock.

My ear went to the wood. I heard footsteps, striding away.

"I think she's gone," I whispered.

When I turned my head, our mouths almost connected.

Henry's words came back to me: *You're the most beautiful woman in this room, Delilah.*

"Of course she's fucking *concerned*. She expected a job to get done." Sven's voice barked right outside our door.

Henry wrapped one arm around my waist.

"Not tomorrow," Sven growled.

Henry and I were breathing in perfect sync.

There was a horrible, piercing *crack* against our door. My head snapped back.

"I've got you," Henry whispered.

"What did I just say?" Sven's voice was dangerously low. "And I'm not *afraid* of her."

A bizarre laugh threatened to force its way from my chest.

And then I heard the most wondrous sound in the world: Sven also walking away.

Henry and I collapsed against the door in relief.

But his arms stayed wrapped around me. And pressed to my ass was a cock as hard as steel.

"I think the coast is clear," I managed to whisper. "We should probably go now."

"We should." The reluctance in my partner's voice was its own aphrodisiac. Henry reached in front of me, covering my hand with his on the doorknob. "We should definitely go."

Whatever space I'd landed us in was pitch fucking black and soundless, set adrift from our brightly colored reality.

"Unless," I said, voice trembling, "we're the kind of fake married couple who sneaks away to fuck in a closet at a gala."

He didn't say a *word*. But a hoarse growl came from his throat as he shifted his hips against me.

And the slight brush of friction was enough to make us both gasp.

But I turned the doorknob, even as my baser instincts screamed for me to *stay*. Cracked the door open an inch.

"Why the hell would they be back here? There's nothing except conference rooms and utility closets. Tell Jim he's a fucking idiot. They're still in the audience."

"*Shit*," I hissed, clicking the door shut as quietly as I could at the last second. I spun around and Henry landed hard against me, flattening my back to the door. "It's the guards from the front."

"And all I know is if Karen fucking finds out, we're all *fucking fired*. So open all these doors and search each room, assholes."

Sounds of collective grumbling floated past the door. But no one pulled it open.

Yet.

Henry and I were face-to-face in the dark, every inch of our bodies together, like our slow dance. The difference being that no one could see us here—we were cloaked in a kind of fog, far from the viewing eyes of Victoria and the guests.

Far from the viewing eyes of Freya and Abe.

We were trapped in a place beyond space or time, beyond consequences or responsibilities. A secret place of bodies and limbs, hushed breath and lips.

"If they find us," I whispered, "we can still tell them we'd snuck away to have newlywed sex."

I could *just* make out the edges of Henry's shy smile.

"What's newlywed sex?"

His palm was suddenly on the back of my calf—I could feel the heat of it even through the gauzy layers.

"We recently eloped, right?" I said, breathless. "Newlyweds can't keep their hands off each other. At least that's what I've heard."

His hand danced up the back of my knee now, my thigh—there was the whisper of shifting fabric. He hooked my right leg high around his waist, the silk layers sliding away to reveal my bare skin. The tips of his fingers almost reached the swell of my ass.

And the flimsiest scrap of material separated my pussy from the hard ridge of his cock.

Henry's index finger traced a path from my collarbone, to

my throat, to my chin. Tilted my face all the way up. "We should get our stories straight, wife. In case we have to make this look real." His hips flexed—a purposeful movement—and my clit was treated to a sweet, grinding pressure. My mouth popped open. "Don't you think?"

Outside the door, far to the left, came the sound of doors opening, slamming; a repetitive *"not here"* as they searched the unauthorized area we'd snuck into.

"It's not nice to seduce your fake wife at a gala," I whispered.

Henry grasped my wrists, pinned them above my head with one hand. "Who said your fake husband was *nice*?"

I liked this fantasy—too fucking much. My internal walls wouldn't stop clenching, begging to be filled. He rolled his hips, ghosting his lips along my hairline, at the base of my neck.

"I think..." I said, mind clouded, "if we get caught, we could say..." His mouth found the curve of my throat. He kissed me there, dragging his lips slowly, *fucking slowly*, until they reached my jaw. "We do this kind of thing all the time."

"I fuck you in public?"

Our bodies were writhing together in silent, erotic motion against the door. The sounds of the guards growing closer were practically nonexistent. What *was* real were the sensations already building low in my belly—the consequence of Henry's skilled movements. Every grind was a delicious burn *right* where I needed it. It'd been so fucking long since a man had known how to touch me. But here I was, legs spread against a door as Henry worked my body into a quiet frenzy.

"Maybe it's our kink," I gasped. "The Thornhills are into public sex."

He pressed our foreheads together like he was in physical

pain. Pinned me harder against the door, tightened his hold on my wrists.

"Delilah." It was part growl, part plea. My eyes fluttered closed as pleasure tightened in my core. I was breathing heavily, struggling not to moan. The pressure of his grinding cock felt *incredible*. I let myself tumble back into our fantasy—imagined being dragged into coat closets all across the city by *this* man and fucked senseless against any available surface.

"Look at me, beautiful." My eyes popped open.

Henry stilled and I almost screamed. The sounds of boot steps filled the hallway, the dull chatter of the guards. I couldn't even tell anymore if they were close.

"If I don't kiss you right now, I'm going to lose my *fucking* mind."

My resolve was crumbling like a fine dust. Somewhere, I recognized the distant sound of my moral compass being smashed to bits again; somewhere in my mind existed the anxiety of this case, the stakes, the pressure, the fear. But I'd been hurtling toward this desire since Henry had slid my fake wedding ring down my finger. I fantasized about his lips, had hot, furtive dreams about the feel of his tongue, had traced the outline of my own mouth as I'd daydreamed about this *very* moment.

"I want to kiss you too," I said, honesty blazing through me, as real as my arousal.

He dropped my wrists so he could spear his fingers into my curls, holding me still. "Say that again."

"Please kiss me," I begged.

He grazed his lips against mine in an unhurried discovery. A tasting, like I was a fine wine he wanted to sip and savor; soft, gentle kisses, an exploration. A dance. The sweetness of this first kiss was unexpectedly poignant—it felt like a gift. In the midst of our forbidden fantasy, Henry was kissing *me*—not his fake wife. I sighed into the kiss, wistful; smiled against his mouth as I touched his face, finally experienced the sensation of his hair beneath my fingers.

"You taste like ripe peaches on a summer's day," he whispered. The poetry of it startled me—I was floating on a sensual, simmering cloud. I opened my mouth to answer but he claimed it again. He was charged heat and white-hot electricity, and when he licked his tongue along the seam of my lips, I let him in, let him take possession of me the way my body craved.

And then everything changed.

He took my mouth in a bruising, brutal kiss that didn't hide how badly he'd needed this. We barely came up for air as our lips met again and again. There was no hesitation between us. He took and I gave. I gave—and he drank me in with every swipe of his tongue. The walls *trembled*, the ground shook, our breath was hot, panting, harsh.

I clutched at the lapels of his jacket and shamelessly ground against him. Teeth scraped along my jaw as my right knee was pushed all the way to the door, peeling me open.

"We need to talk about touching again," Henry rasped. His entire hand cupped my sex, with just lace as the barrier. A gratified groan shook loose from my fake husband. "Is this okay?"

"*Yes*," I whispered.

His index finger slid across my clit, still covered in lace. "And this, wife?"

Oh God, this couldn't be happening.

I couldn't even speak—could only nod. When his finger slipped beneath and touched that tight bundle of nerves, I would have screamed if not for his other hand covering my mouth. I was a wild horse, refusing to be tamed—the tighter his hand gripped, the harder he trapped me with his body, the more eager I became.

But he held my eyes, continuing to seek my approval even as I realized this submission was what I desired. Henry caressed my clit with the same reverence I'd seen him exhibit while handling a rare manuscript—like whatever was beneath his fingers was the single most important thing in his universe. Within seconds I was racing toward orgasm, my entire body shaking, eyes locked on Henry's. He covered my mouth with his, swallowing my cries through a series of breathless, intoxicating kisses.

"Please don't stop," I whimpered, shuddering, shivering.

My pussy clenched, seeking *more,* and Henry read my mind. His fingers slicked between my folds, dipping into my center. Henry finger-fucked with an ease I didn't think possible, our mouths connected, his hips still thrusting between my legs, mimicking the work of his fingers. It was the single most passionate moment of my life—to be consumed like this, brought to a fast, blinding orgasm in the dark by the sexiest man I'd ever met. He massaged my inner walls, let his palm nudge my clit, and I burst into a thousand rays of light; I was the sun, arcing across the sky, I was waves of undulating pleasure.

And Henry knew what I needed—keeping his fingers working as I rode out a flurry of after-shocks, he pulled me tightly into his chest, let me scream softly against his jacket, let me writhe and pant as he kissed my hair, kissed my cheek. Cherished every inch of me.

"Delilah," he whispered at my temple, "I think we just had newlywed sex."

27

HENRY

*D*elilah stared at me with so much astonishment I felt my chest physically *tighten*. She'd tasted like ripe peaches and ridden my hand like a goddess. In the span of a few minutes, our red-hot fantasy had transformed into a reality I hadn't realized I craved so very badly.

Would I ever be able to forget the sight of her, coming apart around my fingers?

Could I live without my lips on hers, every moment of the day?

With a grin, I smoothed down her sex-ravaged hair and felt another jolt of tenderness. Arcs of light were spilling across the floor—flashlights. The sound of the hallway guards stormed back into our room almost violently. I stared at the door behind Delilah—and I could feel the spell breaking, a hair-line fracture splintering in our game.

Any second now, we were going to get pulled from this secret place—and then what?

"I need to feel you," Delilah sighed. Her fingers flew to my belt, making quick work of the material there.

"Delilah, we can't—"

My zipper came down. The door in the room immediately next to ours was yanked open—the squeal of it like a chainsaw.

"We haven't checked this one yet, have we?" The guards were *literally* right outside the fucking door, and the only thing I knew was the incredible sensation of her hand, cupping the length of me.

Even in this impossible situation, I was so fucking hard it hurt. And when she pulsed her fingers *up*, I exhaled a raw, grateful groan that echoed in the quiet space. Adrenaline and lust made a potent combination, singing in my veins, tempting me toward all kinds of filthy things I couldn't do.

Like drag Delilah to the ground and fuck her right here, skirt flipped up and stilettos digging into my shoulders.

"Hold on, the doorknob's a little stuck." The stranger's voice sliced through our dark room, knob shaking and turning.

A recognition of *danger* pierced me. I pulled her to my chest, spun us around so my back faced the guards. Their flashlights illuminated the extremely small storage space we'd been hiding in.

The spell broke.

Delilah was *vibrating*. I fixed my zipper, straightened my tuxedo jacket, and turned to the guards with a faux sheepish grin. We were panting, hair mussed, clothing wrinkled.

We'd certainly gotten our story straight.

"Newlyweds," I said with a chuckle. "Are we in trouble?"

It was the two men from before—and they looked both pissed and bemused.

"We'll see ourselves back to the table," Delilah stuttered. She made a move to leave, taking my hand, when one of the guards snagged her by the elbow.

Whatever look she gave stunned him for a moment.

"Delilah," I cautioned.

She blinked and transformed back into her undercover role.

But she still yanked her arm away.

"Not gonna happen," the guy said. "Head of security needs to speak with you. *Now*."

Delilah and I exchanged a panicked look. The sheer magnitude of what happened between us felt life-altering. And now we were being led back into the gala, keeping to the sides, so the guards could escort us to their boss. Delilah was chanting a steady stream of *"fuck fuck fuck,"* and I was scanning the crowd for Victoria.

She wasn't there. Although Sven was.

There was movement in the far corner of the room—a flash of Victoria's white hair. I felt Delilah catch it too—she straightened from head to toe. Push-pulled me in front of her as we sidled through the crowd.

"I'm going after Victoria," she murmured. "Cover for me."

Before I could say a word - Delilah *dashed* toward her, stopping to scoop a martini up from a passing waiter.

"Was that your *wife* running away from us?" Guard #2 snarled. He moved to go after her.

"She'll cause a scene, you know," I said—the first idea that flew into my head. "Screaming, plates crashing, the whole ordeal. She just saw a friend, that's all. I don't want her to ruin the gala because of your actions."

"You're still in fucking trouble."

"I know," I said, feigning sheepishness. "Take me away."

I turned around and Delilah was gone—racing into the *Medieval and Byzantine Era* wing of the museum. I saw her black hair, the long train of her beaded gown.

And then I was being led away by the guards to some uncertain punishment.

28

DELILAH

*T*ailing Victoria Whitney through a wing of Medieval architecture had an intense cooling effect on my nerves. I couldn't think about Henry, or the storage space, or whatever erotic magnificence had transpired between us.

I only saw our target.

She'd already willingly accepted a book we told her had been stolen *last week*—and had barely batted an eyelash. If Abe believed Bernard Allerton had been instigating large-scale manuscript theft for twenty years—and she'd known Bernard for half of that time—who was to say Victoria wasn't more heavily involved?

I followed her through a hallway filled with battle axes and swords forged from steel. It evoked memories of brutality and violent history, plagues and famine—and Victoria was strolling through it like a springtime rose garden. She wove discreetly through the Christian art and Byzantine architecture, and for one terrifying second, I thought I'd lost her.

I turned down a hallway into the cloisters.

There she was.

Cloisters were the courtyards in the center of medieval monasteries, carved in stone and filled with fountains and gardens. The museum had one from the thirteenth century, and the sculptures seemed to contain the peaceful spirit of the monks who once strolled here in the sunshine.

They were eerily quiet, with no visitors except Victoria. She sat in front of a trickling fountain. Alone. There was something about the slump of her shoulders that I recognized.

Victoria Whitney—Philadelphia royalty, wealthy heiress, media darling—was crying.

I approached her like a hunter with a skittish animal—feet soft, voice low. "Are you alright?"

She was sitting on the bench and staring at the fountain with tears on her cheeks. I thought she hadn't heard me, so I sat down next to her, smoothing the long train of my gown off to the right.

"Victoria?"

"Oh, sweet girl," she said, patting my hand. "How did you find me here?"

"This is Henry's favorite section of the museum. He loves to stare at the medieval stained-glass windows."

"Well, your husband is a man that truly appreciates the weight of history." Her smile was watery. I reached into my clutch and found a packet of tissues.

"You and your gifts," she said, taking one gratefully.

"These are neither rare nor signed."

"And yet it's still greatly appreciated."

We sat in silence for a minute. The trickling sounds of the fountain was a balm to my jangling nerves.

"Sometimes being in the presence of great love sends me to hysterics."

"I'm sorry?" I asked.

"You and Henry."

"Oh...oh, Victoria," I started, surprised at her honesty.

And equally surprised at the sympathy that rose in me.

"There is nothing you need to apologize for. It's a compliment, trust me. I know at dinner I was making light of my many engagements. But I've had quite the rollercoaster in my life when it comes to love."

I went to lay a hand on her shoulder—but pulled away at the last second.

"Henry's your great love, isn't he?"

Her blue eyes pierced mine like an arrow.

"Yes, he is," I said without even a pause. I crossed my legs, smoothed down my dress, aware that my limbs were still shaking.

"I've had several great loves in my life, not just my various fiancés. Some of them were even married to other women at the time. A mistake on their part."

"How dare they?" I agreed with a sly smile.

"Well, that's what I've always said." Victoria let out a long, dramatic sigh. "I've never lacked for passion, Delilah. Never lacked for midnight proposals, hasty engagements, romantic declarations. But a love that withstands challenge..."

She sniffed, wiping her nose elegantly. "Although, between us girls, perhaps I'd tire of one man for the rest of my days." Her brows raised. "I can't imagine you ever growing tired of Henry."

The only romantic passion I'd ever experienced had been with a man whose only goal was to toss me away like yesterday's garbage. Yet every time Henry and I ended up in a confined space, I experienced an intensity I never knew existed. His cock beneath my fingers had been gloriously hard, deliciously thick—skin like velvet as I'd explored with my hand. Henry Finch in a tuxedo was too dangerous a temptation—it amplified both his handsomeness but also his brilliance.

What if the guards hadn't come?

What if Henry had twisted his fingers in my hair and brought me to my knees? I already knew I would have dropped to the ground eagerly.

If this startling *hunger* invading my senses was what being with Henry Finch was like all the time, how could you *ever* grow tired of it?

"I'll take your dazed expression for a *no*." She seemed amused.

Heat flared in my cheeks. "We're very much in love."

"That's quite obvious, dear," she smiled. "Everyone in the room can see your love is real. Don't let it go, whatever you do."

Victoria reached forward, grasping my hand.

The most remarkable feeling was blossoming in my chest —I couldn't keep track of who I was. I was Delilah *Barrett,* not Delilah *Thornhill.* And this criminal sitting in front of me had almost certainly stolen a rare book I was being paid to get back.

But I squeezed her hand.

"The gossip columns love to trash me over my many engagements." Her voice dripped with disdain. "They like to make me out to be some batty old lady that collects fiancés like baseball cards. But I love *love*."

"Even though it makes you sad?"

Victoria turned away from me, jaw tightening. "Yes, well. It comes in waves sometimes. The yearning for love, the regret over the past. Seeing the two of you on that dance floor reminded me of a party, just like this one, years ago. I was with Bernard Allerton, actually."

The hair raised on the back of my neck.

"I can't believe your Henry never met him. Not at a conference, anything like that?"

"No." My mouth was dry. "Although he's certainly seen him give speeches before. He really looks up to Bernard, considers him to be a true scholar."

Even now that he fully understood the landscape of Bernard's betrayal, there was a part of Henry that *still* looked up to his mentor.

Weeks after Mark had fired me, I'd sat at the kitchen table with my dads, crying into a large mug of peppermint tea. Not because I'd been fired, but because we'd broken up. It took months before I felt my true self return to my body—and I welcomed the anger over the sadness.

"Bernard Allerton is a pioneer. A true revolutionary in his field." Victoria was watching the fountain—but I was watching Victoria.

"When...when will you see him again?" I asked, tone light.

Her fingers fidgeted in her lap. "Unclear, really." She avoided my eyes for the first time in the conversation. "Did you mean what you said back there, about the provenance of the Virginia?"

"We did. Did it make you nervous?" I asked. "I will gladly take it back."

Her fingers stilled.

"No, it did not. Not everything on this earth belongs in a museum or a library, Delilah. I *appreciate* rarity on a deep level, deep in my soul. It brings me immense joy to own a piece of history." She gave her watery eyes one last swipe. "Oh, you must think I'm an evil person."

"Not at all," I said. The words were only a partial lie. "You don't think Henry is—"

"Don't you say another word. Your husband is a scholar.

And he knows rarity when he sees it. It was a lovely gift and I shall treasure it."

The trickling water sounds washed over us—cloisters still seeped in silence. I twirled my fake wedding ring. "Was that man you were dancing with a new suitor?"

"That man is an idiot," she said. "And that was only for show. Love, love like the kind you have with Henry, is as rare as Virginia's signature on that book."

You taste like ripe peaches on a summer's day.

"Henry is certainly very...captivating."

"That's the perfect word for that husband of yours."

I pulled the rings from my hand, let them shine in my palm.

"When you're not looking, Henry stares at you like you're the only star in his sky."

Our eyes met—a fist was closing around my throat. After Mark, I'd promised myself I'd never break the rules again. Even though I was no longer on the police force, I knew where the lines of *good* and *bad* were drawn.

But I'd stepped right over that line with Henry—gladly. Because I was positive Abe wouldn't approve of his undercover agents dating each other, and yet every cell in my body recognized that Henry was *different*.

Could that be possible? Could you make the same mistake again and have it be no mistake at all?

"How you *blush* when I mention him," Victoria said, wrenching me back to the present moment.

A few other patrons were finally wandering back through the cloisters, speaking in soft whispers. The room demanded their awed respect; the act of devotion clung to the air like the green vines that wrapped around the stones.

"How often do you and Henry visit Reichenbach Falls?"

"Just when we see something that catches our eye." *Should*

I push her here? Or pull? I wanted Henry by my side—our partnership was starting to feel as familiar as what I had with Freya.

How was I going to get access to her collection?

From the corner of my eye, I saw Henry's tall, broad form approaching with the guards. He moved through the cloisters with a masculine grace.

When I widened my eyes at him, he winked.

"Mr. Thornhill," Victoria said, surprised. "I trust you're not in trouble? These are my guests, you see."

"Uh, yes, ma'am." The guard coughed. "We were unaware until Mr. Thornhill told us."

"What are you in trouble for?" she asked. "Did you steal something?" Her eyes glittered with teasing humor.

"The guards caught us in one of the utility closets," I said, touching my hair shyly. "Indisposed, if you will."

Victoria merely waved her hand and the guards lumbered away.

"You two keep getting more and more interesting, don't you?"

29

HENRY

"Thank you," I said to Victoria, reaching out my hand to lift Delilah from the stone bench. "We were enjoying ourselves a little *too* much."

"Young love," she mused. A knowing look passed between her and my partner.

"I trust you and my lovely wife are enjoying the gala?"

Victoria fluffed her hair. "Girl talk. You are certainly the brains, Henry. But your wife has a fierce heart."

That was certainly true.

"Although Delilah told me you were off enjoying the stained-glass windows. *Not* in trouble with the law."

I slid my hands into my pockets, shrugged. "We were a little embarrassed," I admitted, leaning in. "I do come and sit in front of those stained-glass windows, though."

That wasn't a lie—they were one of my favorite exhibits in the city. Watching the sun filter through each unique pane of glass brought me a quiet joy; the hands that had crafted that glass in the tenth century, still present through their artistry. It was enough to leave me speechless.

"Your penchant for rarity is to be admired, Henry."

I intertwined my fingers with Delilah's. "I've always been drawn to the singularly beautiful."

"Is that why you became a rare book librarian?" Victoria asked.

I'd been asked this question hundreds of times in my career—but I couldn't answer it the way I used to.

"For the same reason you collect antiques. The power."

Her eyes flashed steel. "Power?"

"I feel powerful knowing I'm the only person allowed to care for a manuscript so old it has to be handled with extreme care. Sometimes I'm the first person to turn the pages of a book in hundreds of years. All that history, at *my* control, well, it makes me feel like a king."

"I know that feeling," she said softly. "It's like an addiction."

Bernard. I felt a mental tug, deep in my memory. But what?

"It truly is," I replied.

Victoria adjusted the fur around her shoulders. "I see Bitzi, waving me down like a lunatic. I hate to leave you."

Our time with her was drawing to a close, and we'd secured nothing. Time seemed to stretch between us in the hushed cloisters. I wondered if taking this job was pure idiocy —Abe was convinced I had the skill set of a detective.

But maybe this entire case was just me, proving him wrong; seducing my colleague and distracting us from our mission.

"Perhaps you and Delilah would like to come to a little gathering I'm hosting tomorrow evening."

Delilah and I were too stunned to speak.

"Uh...I mean, of course," Delilah said brightly. "Is it a dinner?"

"A party for 300 people," she sniffed. "A small thing."

I have 300 people coming tomorrow. I can't move it.

"Black tie, of course. Everyone who's important in this city will be there." Victoria arched a brow. "I believe you two should be there too. I might even find time to show you my collection."

I wondered if Henry Thornhill was the kind of man who did cartwheels through a medieval cloister.

"It would be a true honor," Delilah said. Her arm slid around my waist, mine wrapped around her shoulder.

"Yes, well, that's very true." Victoria smoothed a strand of hair back into her low bun. "Thank you again for the tissues, my dear."

"Any time," Delilah whispered.

Victoria tapped the stone with a manicured nail. "What kind of secrets do you think exist in these stones, Henry?"

"Hundreds of years' worth, I'm sure," I replied. "But we all have them."

"Of course," she said. "Secrets are what make life interesting."

30

HENRY

"*Y*eah, okay," Delilah was saying into her cell phone, as discreetly as possible. "Yes." She was nodding, teeth snagging her bottom lip. "You heard correctly." Her midnight-blue eyes shot to mine, and those lips curved into a beaming smile. "We'd love that. Okay, bye."

Delilah and I were standing outside of the Philadelphia Natural History Museum, having slipped out before either Victoria or the guards could notice our absence. She'd whipped out her phone immediately to call Abe and Freya, striding down the sidewalk and far from prying eyes.

"Freya and Abe were already out, grabbing late takeout, so Abe is sending Dorran and the limo home. They're coming by to get us instead. They'll be here in five minutes."

"What did they say?" I asked.

Her smile grew even brighter. "They were fucking *thrilled*." Delilah stepped into my space, the tips of our shoes touching. "We did what we were supposed to, Henry. We're going to Victoria Whitney's *mansion*. She's going to show us her *collection*."

Her joy was contagious. "There were definitely several

points in the evening where I truly believed we'd fucked everything up."

"Me too." She bounced on her toes, shoulders doing a happy shimmy. "Good job, partner. You really convinced her at the end."

I rubbed my jaw. "I'm not so sure. *Your wife has a fierce heart*," I repeated. Delilah glowed like a lantern as I said it. "I think you won her over."

"We both did it." Her eyes searched mine. "We were a great team tonight, Henry."

My hips, pinning Delilah to the door. My cock, grinding against her wet heat. Her pussy, clenching around my fingers as she climbed and climbed—

"I agree," I said, pushing the words past the growl in my throat. "What is this...this feeling I have right now? Feels like I could run a marathon. Or jump off that building over there and fly." The caffeine of a hundred coffees hummed beneath my skin.

"Adrenaline." Her chin lifted knowingly. "And success. Now you know why we do it."

"This feeling right here," I said softly. "It's like being the *most* alive I've ever felt."

"Careful. It's addictive," she said, repeating my words to Victoria. "You'll start to crave it."

"Is that so?" I asked. The question came out rougher than I'd wanted. Her full lips parted. "What did the two of you talk about in the cloisters?"

"You go first," she shot back. "What happened when you got in trouble?"

"You mean when I took a bullet for you, basically?"

She shrugged flirtatiously. I wanted to kiss her again—right here, out in the open.

"The head of security read me the riot act. He wanted to

know why on earth I'd attempt a *nocturnal dalliance* in an unauthorized area."

"He didn't say *nocturnal dalliance*."

"Oh, he did. And I had to sit there and take it without my fake wife by my side."

Delilah was trying not to laugh. "What did you say?"

Maybe this is our kink. We like to fuck in public.

"I said getting caught was kind of the point." I tried—and failed—to keep my words as jaunty as our body language.

"Oh," she said. The knowledge that Delilah and I were both thinking about what had transpired in the closet had my cock hardening—again.

"What did the two of you talk about?" I asked again. She shivered as a cool breeze sifted through her hair. I removed my tuxedo jacket and reached around, tucking her inside of it.

"Seeing our...love...made her sad. Made her regret that she'd never managed to find the kind of relationship that you and I so clearly have."

"She thinks it's that obvious?" I asked. I tugged the jacket closed, moved my hands down her arms to warm her.

"Can Victoria see us?" Delilah asked.

I stopped. "No, she can't. I thought you seemed cold. Real cold, not fake."

Her eyes softened, body relaxed. She leaned into my touch, so I kept rubbing her arms.

"Victoria said that when you stare at me, it's like I'm the only star in your sky."

My hands roamed down her back, drawing her into my chest. She tilted her cheek into my palm. How had I not noticed before how perfectly our bodies fit together? No wonder Victoria believed we were truly in love. If you showed me a picture of Delilah and me right now—the simple ardor between us—I would have said the same thing.

"The only star in my sky?"

She nodded.

"I'd say Victoria would be right," I said hoarsely.

Delilah was completely mesmerized. "Abe and Freya are probably going to be here in a minute."

I blew out a frustrated breath, took a big step back. Shoved my hands into my pockets to resist further temptation to touch my partner.

"Are we going to talk about what happened?" she asked. And didn't have to clarify.

And what was I going to say to my coworker? That it wasn't *adrenaline* I was craving.

It was her.

But a car was squealing up to the curb, windows rolled down. Delilah pasted a big smile on her face then turned, casting a look back up to the museum one last time.

We slid into Abe's car and peeled away.

31

DELILAH

*A*be and Freya had picked up something spicy and salty smelling that had me faint with hunger within seconds.

"Gimme," I said, tapping Freya on the shoulder. She passed me a white take-out container and her chopsticks with a silly smile.

"For you, Mrs. Thornhill."

She handed a similar container to Henry. "And for you."

The scent of pad thai that wafted up was maybe the best thing I'd ever smelled in my fucking life.

"Details," Abe said. "All of them." He looked up into the rearview mirror as he slowed to a stop at a red light. "And well done, you two," he said softly.

Henry and I shared a happy look. I was still draped in his coat, and when I turned my nose into the collar, I remembered the best smell was actually Henry Finch.

"Here's what we got," I said, twirling a noodle around my chopstick. "Henry and I gave her the book, and she didn't bat an eye at how high-profile it was. Sven is her shadow and carries that portable transport case with him everywhere they go. And we trailed Victoria into an authorized area at the gala and overheard her yelling at someone on the phone."

"She was instructing them to move something after her party. She sounded furious," Henry added.

"The exhibit is a little over a week away," Freya said. "Which means that book is officially *hot*. If she was smart, she would have already moved it."

I stared out the window at the red brick row homes of Old City, flickering with gas lanterns. "I think Victoria is smart. She just has a big ego."

"I'll give Francisco an update," Abe said. "Not that he'll be happy. He told me the FBI has brought in their second and third suspects."

My blood ran cold. "So they're working on *three*?"

"Yes."

The car was silent as we made a series of turns. Henry leaned his shoulder against mine.

"But no book," Abe said.

I exhaled.

"Francisco said the FBI wants to run the story in the papers the day after the party. They don't want to keep it under wraps any longer. They think the public could help, like maybe some unwitting buyer has it and didn't realize it'd been stolen."

"Fuck," I said. "That's not good for us either. It'll spook whoever has it."

"Sounds like our deadline is tomorrow night regardless," Freya said. "And there has been absolutely nothing online about this that I can find. Whoever has the Copernicus isn't talking about it, at least not in the communities we have access to."

She turned around in the front seat. "She definitely said she'd show you her collection?"

"Her exact words were 'if I have the time,'" Henry replied.

Freya chewed her lip, raked a hand through her hair. "Okay."

Abe was driving so intently I thought the steering wheel was going to snap beneath his fingers. "We'll chat plans tomorrow after we've all had a good night's rest."

We pulled to a stop in front of Henry's historic, three-story row home. I noticed it had the perfect stoop. "I really like your house, Henry."

He winked at me in the darkness. "It's literally filled with books. Wall to wall novels."

I could picture him there, cozy in front of some fireplace, reading a book with that same look of awe I'd seen on his face countless times. I went to slip out of his jacket, but he shook his head. "I'll get it from you tomorrow."

"Oh, okay," I said awkwardly.

His deep voice reverberated through every nerve ending in my body. "Thank you for the ride. And the dinner. I'll see you all tomorrow for our big day." He was speaking to everyone but staring at me. We hadn't gotten a chance to *really* talk about what had happened—and now it felt like he was sending me some kind of message.

"Good night," I said. I watched him stride into his elegant home. Pictured him tugging loose his bowtie; slowly working open each button on his white shirt, pulling back the covers on a bed that would be perfectly warm and smell like books.

"How's Henry doing with this case?" Abe asked.

"Good," I said, trying not to sound nervous. "Actually, to be honest, he's doing even better than I'd anticipated. He's natural with a target like Victoria. A little awkward in the beginning, but he's learning how to pivot quickly, think on his feet."

"I suspected as much," Abe said. "I think he's going to make a really great detective."

"I do miss you," I said, reaching up to touch Freya's shoulder.

"I miss you too," she said. "And I've had to be stuck in the office with this grumpy asshole the whole time."

"And yet I've brought you donuts every single day this week," Abe mused. "Depending on how this case goes, we'll have to talk logistics of all three of you in the field. It'll be a new thing for us. Delilah, at this point, would you be opposed to partnering with Henry on future cases?"

I'd just experienced the most passionate moments of my life with Henry in a utility closet. My mind was either hyper-focused on Victoria—or attempting to rationalize my intense attraction to my coworker. I hadn't *once* allowed myself to think past the recovery. When I'd have to spend every day at Codex, partnering closely with a man who'd brought me to orgasm and then tenderly kissed my hair.

This isn't the first time a young female detective has latched herself to a superior officer. Mark had been so fucking *smug* when he said it. And I'd felt like a love-sick idiot, even though our one-month fling had been very, very real.

I placed a palm on my stomach, attempting to sort out my damaged gut instinct. When I remembered seeing Mark, there was a churning feeling; anxiety, nerves, regret.

I unfolded the memory of Henry brushing his lips sweetly against mine and felt only a tremulous excitement.

"Delilah?"

"Sorry," I said. "Of course. He and I are developing a decent working relationship. Although my number one is always Freya."

"You deserve more noodles for that," she said, handing me another box.

"Who knows," Abe said, "maybe the whole marriage undercover act will work for something in the future. We should keep those rings, Freya. Just in case."

"Right-o." She mock-saluted. "Don't retire the lovely Mrs. Thornhill yet, Del. You might need her for the future."

"Sounds good," I said automatically. Thinking about Henry, as handsome as I'd ever seen him, telling me I was the most beautiful woman in the room. How could I spend the next few cases being fake married to a man that made me feel something so *real*?

"What do you think is going to happen tomorrow?" I asked, more for myself than anyone else.

Abe was silent. And when he didn't answer, Freya reached back and squeezed my hand. "We get the damn book back."

32

HENRY

*T*hat night I dreamed of the heavens.

In my dream, I held the Copernicus. The ancient manuscript had intricate gold flowers woven through the pages. Their leaves grew around a universe sparkling with planets, orbiting a fiery sun. I had the strangest sensation that the pages were *speaking* to me, calling to me through the gilded edges.

Bernard appeared—briefly, muttering something about *passageways*. And when I woke—startled at 6:00 am, alarm blaring—my first thought was *revenge*.

My second—and more captivating thought—was about Delilah.

And by the time I made it to Codex, an incessant *pulse* was the only sound in my ears. Nerves, anxiety, adrenaline—the metronome was the same. A driving charge that compelled me up the spiral staircase, shoving the office door open with more force than was necessary.

The *bang* had everyone swiveling toward me. But I only had eyes for the blue-eyed woman with tape-wrapped hands, holding a punching bag mid-swing.

"Now that Henry's here, we need to talk final plan." Abe beckoned us into his office with one single finger. Freya scooped up her laptop, seven notebooks, scrap paper, and a handful of pens—looking more serious than usual.

Delilah picked up her notebook and pulled on her faded Temple University sweatshirt, biting her lip as we stared at each other.

"Hey," she said, almost shy.

We hadn't spoken about the closet, and I needed her to know that it hadn't been only a sexy game to me.

I peered into Abe's office, made sure they were thoroughly distracted. I reached for a pen in my suit jacket and grabbed the notebook from Delilah's hands. *I missed you last night,* I scribbled. Turned it around so she could read it.

She tucked a strand of hair behind her ear like I'd asked her to the school dance. Her answering smile was a revelation. My fake wife took the pen—brushing our fingers together as she did so—and wrote, *I missed you too.*

"Are my field agents coming or am I having a meeting with myself?"

"Yeah, yeah," Delilah called back. "We're coming."

I followed her into the office. The screen behind Abe's head displayed a gigantic photo of *Sven*, of all people. Freya was perched on the edge of Abe's desk, knee jiggling.

"Are we making a plan for tonight?" Delilah said, immediately composed.

Freya and Abe exchanged a look before he scrubbed a hand down his face. "Freya dug into Dresden, the company Victoria has hired to provide her private security. I'm assuming they'll be there at the party tonight."

"Absolutely." Delilah nodded. "She's completely exposed. It's the smart thing for her to do."

Freya clicked through a few images on her laptop—they

popped up on the screen. Headlines about Dresden, a mug shot of Sven.

"I've been going over this case in my head all night." Abe scowled. Cracked his knuckles. Glared out the window. "I believe I have backed us into a corner that none of you are going to like. Getting into her house is good. Having her show you her collection is even better. You'll have your hidden cameras and can take pictures of anything you see out in the open. But I think we all need to admit that the likelihood Victoria Whitney shows you this book is very, very slim."

I'd been so focused on *getting* to her house I hadn't even considered this next part. Mostly because I figured Abe would have a plan.

"Then there's the new information Freya found last night."

"Dresden has made headlines recently for hiring trigger-happy maniacs." She tilted her head at the face behind her. "Like Sven. Last year they were being paid by that singer, Winona Shine, as bodyguards while she was on tour. They shot into a crowd they thought was getting restless, injuring four people."

"Jesus," Delilah muttered. "And they're still getting work?"

Freya shrugged. "They're for the non-discerning customer that operates in the shadier edges of our society. I have no idea how Victoria came into contact with them, except that several of her wealthy peers have used them in the past."

"Keeping up with the Joneses," Abe said dryly. "If you're going to hire private security, you want to make sure they're the best. These guys, in a certain circle, are considered the best."

"Sven appears to be a bit of a psychopath," Freya said, "but as long as you avoid him tonight, I think you should be...okay."

The worry lines around Abe's mouth were concerning. "What are you trying to say?" I urged.

"Tonight, our best guess is that Victoria Whitney has orchestrated some kind of buy or transport for this book," Abe said. "And she has 300 people at her house. Her security team will be strapped with weapons and eager to please their very rich client."

Delilah appeared unperturbed. "I'll carry my weapon if it makes you feel better."

"Not in a dress and not with her guards watching everyone as they come through the door. Delilah Thornhill would not need to carry and conceal a handgun."

Delilah sat back, fists clenching. "So say Henry and I are able to find the manuscript."

"Highly unlikely," Abe cautioned. The worry lines deepened.

"Just *if*," she clarified. "If by some stroke of luck, Victoria says 'hey you wanna see something neat?' and it's this goddamn book...you want us to leave it?"

Abe leaned across the desk with a grave expression. "If she shows you this book, take as many pictures as you can. Do *not* give yourself away as Codex agents. Leave the party immediately and call the police to report sighting stolen property."

"But that means we'll forfeit our contract," Delilah argued. "And even if the cops get a warrant quickly, she could send the book out a back door with Sven. We could lose it."

"We could lose it either way," Abe said. "One way doesn't involve my employees getting shot by a psychopath."

Delilah blew out an angry breath.

"Delilah," Abe said firmly. "What's the most important thing? Always."

I remembered having this debate with her -- how firmly she wanted Victoria to be punished.

"The manuscript."

"Actually, it's your safety," he said, brow arched. "But yes, a very *close* second is the manuscript. I know you hate it. Fuck, *I* hate it. I've been up all night going over our options and I'm at a complete loss. We haven't even *touched* transporting a 500-year-old manuscript out of a party. It's not something you can wrap in a cocktail napkin and place in your purse."

Freya was scrolling through pictures on her laptop, replacing the ones of Sven with interior shots of Victoria's mansion. "At least if you get confirmation, I think it's likely cops could come before she moved it."

But Abe sounded less confident. "Henry, what are you thinking about?"

Delilah caught my eye. "I'll admit, her violent guards are less than ideal. But it feels like a lot of work to let the book go."

The words tumbled out in a blaze of honesty—I couldn't stop thinking about Bernard, fleeing into the night. Victoria, getting away with a crime because of her wealth and prestige.

When did my priorities start shifting?

"We're not letting it go," Abe said. "We're ensuring it gets recovered regardless. That's our job." He pinned Delilah with a steady look. "We are not the police."

A cavernous room appeared on the screen—high ceilings, crystal chandeliers, scarlet carpet running the length of it. It smacked of high society and ostentatious wealth, with gold filigree and nineteenth-century portraits of royalty.

Passageways. There was that tug again—the memory of Bernard, taunting me in my dream. What *was* it?

Delilah shifted in her chair. "What do you think, Frey?"

Freya glanced up from her laptop, sliding her glasses up her nose. "We're bumping up against a deadline we have no control over," she said. "If we had another week, two weeks, I think you and Henry would have been able to build up the kind of trust you'd need to get her to show you that manuscript. I mean, in some way, the way she acts around you, I believe she *wants* to. Henry is a renowned expert she wants to impress, and she's *clearly* obsessed with him. I believe we would have had a real shot of her showing it to you if we had more time. But we don't. We have this party and a team of armed maniacs potentially guarding it. It's too risky."

An understanding look passed between Delilah and Freya —and Delilah sank backward in her chair, shoulders slumped. I'd never seen her look defeated and I found I didn't like it. It made me want to drop to my knees, tell her everything was going to be okay. The desire to comfort her was sudden and overwhelming.

"Okay," she said to Freya. "I hear you." She turned to Abe. "And I understand."

"Do you though?" he pushed.

"Yes, I do. And I would never put my partner at risk."

Even in this office, surrounded by our coworkers, the look in her eyes revealed her faith in me, in us. The knowledge of that had my heart bruising against my ribcage.

But now that we'd finally gotten there—to this point of *real* trust—we were charging ahead into a situation with our hands tied.

"Is that Victoria's house?" I asked, directing our conversation to the pictures on the screen. Every time I looked at that room, I felt that mental pinch.

"It is," Freya said. "Victoria had this house designed in the Tudor style—this is the great room. And it's not even the biggest or nicest room in that house. But I'm guessing it's the one she uses for parties so I wanted you to see what you'd be stepping into."

There was a wall of curved doors off to the right-hand side. They were painted in gold. "Do you know where those lead?"

Freya clicked through more pictures. "These are from a profile the paper did on her home a few years ago. So I'm not sure exactly where they go." There was a picture of a massive library with four fireplaces and bookcases so high they required a ladder. Victoria was leaning against the case with her arms crossed and a secretive smile. Freya clicked: a professional-looking kitchen. A courtyard garden. An indoor swimming pool. A long, carpeted hallway.

The memory suddenly sparked to life: Four, maybe five years ago. Bernard and I preparing to give a tour of the McMasters Library special collections. I was handling a first edition of *The Hound of the Baskervilles,* which happened to be one of Bernard's favorite books. The students were in training to be librarians—Bernard was a true celebrity for them. And he was watching me examine the manuscript with a careful eye.

As I placed the book gently on a soft piece of velvet, his expression took on a wistful gleam.

"I once knew a woman, Henry. A lifetime ago now. And she loved books so much she built secret hallways to hide her favorites."

Secret hallways.

"Are you okay, Henry?" Freya asked. "You look like you're chewing on something juicy."

I was okay—and I didn't know if this random memory that had been bugging me was *juicy* or not. But it wouldn't leave me alone.

Delilah's spine was still curved forward, mouth set in a flat line. My partner would know what to do with this information —would know how to follow the scent to the end.

"I'm fine," I said, tucking the memory away to share with Delilah when we were finally alone. "Just a little nervous about tonight."

"I think we all are," Freya said. "I'll be on the walkie with the two of you on the ride out there, giving you any updates we might have. Abe and I will be ready to talk to the police *if* you get eyes on the book or any other suspicious activity. And Dorran will be poised for a quick getaway, should it be needed."

Abe and Freya kept talking about tonight as if a literal gunfight was an inevitably. My eyes strayed to Delilah, her calm presence. The strength I knew she possessed, the power. *I'd never do anything to put my partner at risk.* I tried to imagine the man I'd been three months earlier—my days of silence and ancient pages; my nights of elegant dinner conversation and European streets.

There was no point in even making a comparison.

Abe pinched the bridge of his nose, exhausted. "How do we all feel about this?"

"Guilty," Delilah said. "I feel like I rushed us into this mess, and now we're at the end of our rope before the extraction has even been attempted."

"Don't," Abe said. "We've certainly gotten ourselves into stranger situations. Tonight will be...interesting. You'll read the room. Play off of Victoria's vulnerabilities. See where it gets you." He studied the both of us. "And you'll get home safely."

We both nodded.

Freya attempted a cheery smile. "Now let's eat our feelings and get you two dressed up for a fancy party."

a n hour before Dorran was set to arrive, Freya walked into the tiny office that we shared and closed the door behind her.

"I brought you a present," she said. "Also, what are you doing?"

She placed a small package, wrapped in tissue paper, near the black heels I was planning on wearing. She grabbed my shoulders and spun me toward her.

"My eyeliner," I said. "And I love presents."

Freya shook her head, plopped me into the closest chair. "Let me do it for you. It's smudged all over the place."

"That's because my hands are a little shaky," I said.

She made a humming sound beneath her breath and gripped the pencil. "Well, it's a big night. Lots of nerves. Look up for me." I did, enjoying the gentle comfort that came from having your friend do your makeup for you. "You'll be fine, though, for the record. You and Henry will attack whatever problems might arise tonight."

"That's true," I said, wondering which problems she was

referring to. There was a current tie for *how will we recover this book* and *am I developing feelings for Henry*?

Both were the reason for my smudged eyeliner.

"I've never seen Abe admit failure like that," she said, voice quiet.

"Me neither," I said. "Will you be mad at me if I don't get the book back?"

"Absolutely not," she promised. "I'll be mad at you if you go in there, metaphorical guns blazing, and get hurt." She stepped back to admire her handiwork. "You're not a police officer anymore."

"Abe already gave me this lecture." I crossed my arms, sullen as a teenager.

"And I've been your partner, and your *friend,* for two years now. I know your style." Her smile was mischievous. "Delilah Barrett doesn't like to fail. But you might have to on this one. Also it's not really failing. We've taken cases before where we never recovered the book. Sometimes they stay stolen for good."

"When did you get so wise?" I said, eyes narrowed in mock seriousness.

Freya gave a big shrug. "Who the hell knows? But you should open your present though."

I removed the tissue paper cautiously, not wanting to destroy its pristine prettiness. Inside was a wide, black lace garter belt.

"Lingerie?"

"Even better," she said, green eyes bright with laughter. "Just because Abe says no guns, doesn't mean I can't sneak you in a few weapons." She slid a few things from her back pocket —zip ties, duct tape. "I made this last night. Each part of the lace overlay has a tiny hook sewn into it so you can do *this.*"

The zip ties hooked in, dangling carefully. She took the

duct tape, folded it in two. Curled it up and nestled it through the remaining hooks. Then she held it up for me to admire. It looked like a very small, very delicate lace toolbelt.

"I feel like Xena, Warrior Princess," I exclaimed, taking it from her.

"That was my plan."

"I might not be able to carry a gun, but I can still incapacitate Sven." I bit my lip. "Probably."

"Maybe you should avoid Sven," she said lightly. "But incapacitate the others for sure. At Quantico, they convinced us that zip ties and duct tape were all you ever truly needed."

"Bind the wrists and shut 'em up," I said, giving her a toothy grin. "I fucking love it."

"Not that you'll need it," she said somberly. But she gave me a wink. She grabbed my dress—a white, goddess-like gown with floaty, gauzy layers that came right to the ground. It was strapless, baring my back and shoulders, and whisper-soft as I stepped into it. And I couldn't help but allow myself one luxurious minute of fantasizing about wearing this on a *real* date with Henry.

"How's your mobility in this?" Freya asked. I held still while she zipped me up.

"It's fine." I flexed my arms, did a few fast jabs.

"Show off." She rolled her eyes. "But you look gorgeous. Victoria will be fooled, yet again."

I pulled out a pocket mirror—checked my hair, my red lipstick. Admired Freya's dexterous skill with an eyeliner pencil. "I'm already counting down the minutes until we get to partner again."

"Henry that bad of a partner, huh?" she replied in an odd voice.

I turned around to make a joke in response—but her mouth was set in a grim line, brows knit together. My pulse tripled. Freya may have dropped out of Quantico, but she had a gut instinct that rivaled mine and the keenest ability to sense the innate truth.

"You know strange things can happen when you go undercover," she continued. "Our instructors at Quantico used to tell us horror stories in class."

"Like what kinds of things?" I kept my tone easy.

"Moving back and forth between these different realities. These distinct personalities. Some of the agents we knew went deep for months and years, balancing two versions of themselves. It's kind of easy to lose yourself."

Like last night, giving in to the fantasy of being dragged into a closet at a gala for newlywed sex. Or having an emotional conversation with Victoria Whitney—not as a target, but merely an interesting woman who wanted to connect with me over her many heartbreaks.

"You know, I remember having this conversation with my dads, right after I moved back home." The memory was crystal-clear: their two border collies were asleep at our feet as we sat on the large veranda that faced the forest. It was so quiet you could hear the waterfalls. "I told them being with Mark felt like being an undercover operative. Wearing a new identity that was *definitely* not my own."

"I think that makes total sense," she said. Her expression was compassionate, but I knew Freya wouldn't let me off the hook. And I almost said it—almost voiced this persistent feeling I'd been having that everything I'd done with Henry had been the *opposite* of fake.

But I took the coward's way out—again. "Why are you telling me this?"

"For the same reason I gave you *this*," she said, holding up the tiny lace garter. "I wouldn't send my partner into a dangerous situation without the tools she needed to stay safe.

A partner *or* a friend." Freya dropped her voice. "Codex is a team of four. Small office, intimate situations. Not much room to hide your feelings if you had any."

And the look she gave me indicated she knew what those feelings might be.

"I hear you," I said simply. Even though I had no idea what all of this meant or what the fuck I was going to do. "I'm listening."

Freya's eyes searched mine. "You're sure?"

I nodded. Took the garter. "Thank you. For everything." I gave her a hug that she returned in full. She smelled—as usual—like Earl Grey and sugar cookies. "Do you want to go practice punching in your dress? I'll hold the bag for you."

"Let's do it," I said, needing the focus. Needing the release.

"And I meant what I said about tonight," she said. "Stay focused. And stay *safe*."

34

HENRY

*A*be was sitting at his office desk, chair turned around to face the city lights. He had a glass of bourbon at his side, tie undone, shirt sleeves rolled up.

I'd never seen him look so informal.

"You wanted to see me, sir?" I asked, knocking lightly.

"Yes, please come in," he said, slowly turning around. The limo was set to arrive any minute. "Dorran will be here soon?"

I slipped my hands into my pockets. "Yes, sir."

I closed the door behind me—and caught a quick, alluring sight of Delilah laughing with Freya, backlit by the orange rays of the setting sun. She glowed and shimmered—looking at ease, hopeful—and I felt my yearning reach an entirely new level. "Is this about how many times I've compromised our success with my inexperience on this case?"

Abe was briefly startled. Then said, "No. Not at all. You've done stellar work, Henry."

He indicated that I should sit. "I know in the past I've mentioned my contact at the FBI's Art Theft department. Whenever Codex agents happen upon illegal activity during our legal work, I send the information over to him. I'm not sure how exactly he currently uses it, but the former law enforcement officer in me couldn't have my agents walk by something illegal and not at least take a fucking picture of it."

"Do the clients know?" I asked. Delilah had told me as much the other day—the interesting gray area Codex and the FBI operated in together.

"Sometimes," Abe said, "although it's rarely their concern. You'd be surprised at how many of our clients merely want the item back, regardless of punishment."

"Delilah hates that part," I added.

"Delilah is a very just person," Abe agreed. "But she's starting to bend a little."

And I was too—although every day at Codex was nudging me closer to vengeful than I'd anticipated.

"According to my contact, late last night, a bureau agent working with an Interpol field office believed they spotted Bernard in Greece."

"What?" I asked, leaning forward. "They're sure?"

"They're not even remotely sure," he said. "The photos were blurry, inconclusive. It could have been another person entirely. Bernard fled quickly that night, but in many ways, I believe he'd been planning for this inevitability for a long time. The fact that he'd compiled those letters, incriminating you, tells me he had a back-up plan. I believe he is well-prepared to be underground for a while." Abe swirled his bourbon. "I thought you should know."

"Did Delilah tell you she asked me if I knew where he was?"

He rubbed his jaw. "She's smart. Smarter than me, that's for sure."

"Did you think I knew where he was?" I asked. "Does *everyone* here think I was helping Bernard?"

"I never thought that," Abe explained. He sipped his drink,

eyeing me over the glass. "I *did* think you thought he was innocent."

"That's not untrue," I admitted. "I know he's guilty now. I just never wanted to *believe* it."

He rubbed his eyes, glanced down the street for our limo. He sighed raggedly. "I think I fucked everything up, taking this job." I went completely still at this uncharacteristic confession. Almost two whole minutes clicked by before my boss spoke again. "This job was too risky, and not once did I see a clear path to success. But it would have been our highest profile case yet with the largest payout and I..."

"You what?" I asked.

Abe crunched ice between his teeth. "I guess I'm still a little *pissed* that the McMasters Library didn't hire me to go after Bernard and the *Tamerlane*. I can be...unnecessarily prideful. And I hoped that Codex would be able to recover the dozens of stolen manuscripts he'd sold throughout the years more quickly than the FBI *or* Interpol. And more successfully." Abe swirled liquor around his glass—we both watched the splash of liquid. "I started Codex as a way to remove myself from the innate competitiveness of the FBI. The backbiting and politics and internal drama that did nothing to improve our success and everything to diminish it. Now I can't help but feel like I'm back in it, taking a job we can't possibly close just to prove to myself we could do it."

"If Francisco hadn't told us that the FBI hadn't been successful in their recovery efforts, would you have been as interested?" I asked.

His eyes flashed with humor. "Smart man."

I was silent.

"I started Codex because I felt like we lost a lot of things— manuscripts, antiques, rare art—because of slow-moving, bureaucratic bullshit. It's why I think it's important that you're here, Henry. To remind us of the cost beyond one person stealing from another."

"Is that the whole reason why you started it?"

Abe shook his head. "Three years ago, I was leading a small team focused on the northeast region. A lot of rare books were being stolen in this DC, New York, Philly corridor. It was incredibly high-pressure, high-stakes. And two of my employees were dating each other."

It felt like there was no air in the room all of a sudden.

"That wasn't allowed, I'm guessing?" I asked.

"It was frowned on, but not technically in violation. I didn't have a real recourse to prevent it from happening. But their relationship grew volatile. Emotional. They dragged their arguments into the office, and I spent long hours mediating. The toxicity of their relationship bled into every other aspect of our unit." He grimaced, as if the memory still had a visceral effect.

"Did you fire them?" I asked.

"I was starting the process of firing them both during the week we were set to raid a house in Queens. We didn't anticipate the owners having a lot of firepower. Turns out, they did." He gulped the rest of his drink. "One of them was shot in the leg and spent two weeks in the hospital and another four in physical therapy. Because we were all *distracted*."

"I don't you think you can—"

"We were distracted." Abe's tone was firm.

"Right."

And how often this week had Delilah and I almost fucked up because we were distracted? I squeezed the bridge of my nose. At night, on the job, the consequences of indulging in our little fantasy felt sexy and daring.

This just felt shitty. And what was I doing—kissing her in

closets and writing her notes and telling her she was beautiful in a million different ways?

"You can ask Delilah how that romantic distraction feels," he continued, "although her situation was incredibly different. She was manipulated by a sociopath. But when she first started here, she appreciated that we were a team of honest professionals. A team that trusts each other."

"I appreciate that too," I said thickly. My hands drifted to my vest pocket, where I'd tucked away the surprise I was bringing my partner. It felt silly now—and wildly unprofessional.

Was I the same as Mark, pulling this talented, amazing woman away from her dreams?

"Anyway," he continued, "I'd already had the concept for Codex floating around for some time. I had a few friends who were private detectives, and they found their jobs to be rather freeing. And I was tired of losing the books, tired of the infighting and the stress."

"You told me when we first met that you'd been chasing Bernard for a long time."

His eyes were like steel. "I have."

"But Bernard isn't our purview. The book is. Right?"

Abe narrowed his eyes—gave a grim smile. "You're exactly right." He poured another finger of liquor into his glass. "I'm the kind of person that often needs to hear my own advice, Henry. You should know that, if we're to continue working together."

"I understand the desire though," I said. "I'm a rare book librarian. The return of a book like the Copernicus *should* be my priority. But..."

Abe waited.

"I want to personally put Bernard in prison."

"Me too," he said, swallowing his drink. "Being a human being is very complicated, I'm afraid."

There was a honk from outside. "Dorran's here to pick you up. Are you ready?"

I nodded.

"Promise me you'll stay safe."

"I promise," I lied.

35

DELILAH

A white stretch limo sat idling at the curb outside of the Codex offices—looking extremely out of place in this historic part of the city. And so did we. Henry and I were standing in our fanciest clothes, facing Abe and Freya.

"Camera," she said, tilting my wrist. I was wearing the silver band with the secret lens.

"Camera," she said again, grabbing Henry's watch. We both nodded. "Abe and I are both programmed into your speed dial in case you need us. But if something *really* gets tricky, call 911. And call the cops if you get actual eyes on the book. I'll be online, monitoring any chatter. If, for whatever reason, Abe and I pick up on information you need to know, or would be helpful, I'll text you." Freya glanced at Abe.

"See what you see and then get out of there," Abe said softly. "Those are your orders. Delilah?"

Abe knew I needed to be told twice. I gave him a very serious nod. "I understand."

My boss was sending his detectives into a high-risk recovery situation already assuming we'd fail.

I didn't fucking like it.

Dorran beeped his horn—his classic greeting. Abe nodded curtly and strode back inside.

Freya gave me a hug. "Good luck," she whispered. And she startled Henry by doing the same. He looked at me over the top of her messy bun—bemused and then grateful.

"Dream team," she said, pointing between the two of us. "Now go get 'em."

She walked back inside, leaving Henry and me completely alone for the first time since last night. Henry was in a cream linen suit and a white shirt, unbuttoned at his throat. It exposed a tempting swatch of dark brown skin. His eyes studied the whimsical layers of my skirt, the cinched waist, my bare collarbone, the rounded curve of my shoulders. I felt exposed, analyzed, handled with supreme care.

"You look exquisite." His voice was intoxicating.

"The same can be said of you," I said.

Henry opened the door, and I slid into the limo we'd been riding in together for weeks now. Every time it felt massively extravagant with only two people inside. He sat across from me, straightened his glasses, hooked his cufflinks. We were finally alone, in as private a space as we were going to get for the rest of the night, and instead of blurting out the jumble of confused emotions he was making me feel, I could only think of Freya's careful warning.

Henry seemed to be experiencing something similarly frustrating—his brow was furrowed, fingers in fists at his sides. He kept beginning to say something and then stopping. But when he finally managed to speak, he expressed something else entirely.

"I might have an alternative plan for tonight," he said. "What did you think about what Abe said back there?"

"You mean our *orders*?" I corrected.

Behind his glasses, his eyes crinkled at the sides. "Delilah," he said. And in his voice, I heard the intensity of our stolen moments.

I relented. "I don't like them. I feel fucking disappointed. Angry."

Henry leaned forward. "I had this memory when Freya was showing us the pictures of Victoria's house. It might be nothing, I don't know, but I can't stop thinking about it."

The hair on my arms stood up.

"Tell me," I said.

"It was something offhand that Bernard said once. That he once knew a woman who loved books so much she built secret hallways to hide her favorites."

"Wait, what?" I asked, all of my senses sparking to life.

"Secret hallways. To hide her favorites," he repeated.

"You think that's Victoria?"

Henry shrugged. "I think there's a reason my subconscious won't let it go."

"If Victoria has secret passageways in her house, how would we get to them?" My mind was already leaping ahead, puzzling out this new information.

"I have no fucking idea," he said gravely. But I laughed anyway—the sound tugging the ends of his lips up into a grin.

"I'm serious." He was still smiling. "I have no idea. I don't know if we'll know until we get there. And it might mean nothing. And he could have been talking about any other woman. Truly. But this memory's been trying to get my attention for days now, Delilah. Doesn't that usually mean something?"

"Chasing a lead," I murmured. "It can be the best feeling in the world if you know what it means. Or the most frustrating." I tilted my head. "You're a real detective now, Henry Finch."

He was still grinning at me, and my heart beat so fast I felt out of breath, almost dizzy.

"You didn't say anything to Abe and Freya though?"

He leaned back in the seat. "You're my partner. I wanted you to know. Not them. And I don't think Abe would have told us to do anything about it."

Warmth blossomed in my chest. How far we'd come from bumbling around art galleries and moving through this case like strangers.

"It could mean absolutely nothing," my partner repeated.

"Or it could mean everything," I said.

I bit my lip, glanced toward the black privacy window that separated us from Dorran. The thought of this—the hint of *success* for this case—made me feel *reckless.*

"You know, I have a secret too," I whispered. I flashed him a flirtatious smile.

His eyebrow arched, amused. "I don't believe you."

"Well, I'd show it to you, but it's under my dress," I said.

How easily—and quickly—I forgot myself around Henry.

A predatory gleam came into his eyes. I pursed my lips, his look making me feel coquettish.

We were only *looking* at each other.

And it was just one more time.

And just in here.

"Why don't you show me?" he asked. Although we both knew it was a demand.

I crossed my legs beneath the layers—his eyes landed at the juncture between my thighs. I was sitting in the limo with a man who knew intimately the feel of my sex, clenching in orgasm.

Small office, intimate situations, Freya had cautioned.

If Henry and I didn't pursue whatever *this* might be—

would it always be like this? Tempting and teasing each other when we were supposed to be professionals?

If we *did* pursue it—could we ever be truly professional again?

"Delilah," he said, shattering my concerns. "Show me your secret."

I reached down obediently. Clasped the floaty ends of my skirt between my fingers. Slid the material along my ankle and halfway up my calf.

"Slower," he growled. His posture screamed *dominance* in a way I'd never seen before. The closet had been pitch-black, silent—hurried. Beneath that finely tailored suit, what kind of man would Henry Finch truly be like in bed?

Our eyes were locked together, frozen in a kind of battle I didn't truly want to win.

In the end, I let the gauzy material glide up every inch of my legs with the laziest tempo I could manage. And Henry tracked every single inch of bared skin. When I finally, *finally* reached the garter belt, I thought he was going to tear the seat clean in half.

"Zip ties," I said. "Duct tape." My dress was pulled all the way to my hip. "In case we get into a tough situation and I have to tie up Sven."

"I see." His eyes blazed with hunger. "Seems we've both come prepared."

The limo came to—what felt like—a screeching halt. I turned my head toward the window—and my jaw dropped at the sight of Victoria Whitney's mansion rearing up in front of me. It appeared somehow larger and more grandiose than the last time we'd seen it.

"We're here," I said, dazed from the scrape of Henry's voice. Dazed at the evening we were about to have.

He looked like a sleepwalker just coming to. I swung the door open, sinking my stilettos into the wet, manicured grass.

My knees were trembling.

Henry appeared behind me, palm at my low back.

"I'm sorry," he started to say at my ear. "I got a little—"

"I'm not the least bit sorry," I said.

So much *yearning* filled his expression I had to turn away before I leapt into his arms and suggested we drive off into the sunset together. But we were on the job now.

Focus. Stay safe.

"I brought you something."

That yearning was back—this time in Henry's voice. And when I turned around, he was holding a whimsical-looking corsage of pale pink roses.

"Oh," I said, momentarily startled.

"You'd said you never went to prom and I thought you would like this. Even though this isn't prom and we have a very serious job to do." Indecision flashed across his face—and I knew, intimately, what he must have been feeling.

"I love it," I said. "It's perfect."

The slow smile that spread across his face was charming as hell. And it was just for me.

"Can I see your wrist?"

I held it out dutifully, aware of couples around us starting to descend from their limousines, dressed in their finery. This appeared perfectly appropriate—we were two newlyweds, enjoying an evening together, adorned with pink flowers. He clasped my hand gently, turning it over. Slipped the flowers over my fingers, down to my wrist. His thumb caressed circles at my pulse point, and my fingers responded, trapping his forearm. Holding him to me. We stared at each other, content to breathe in this moment.

"There," he said. "You look even more exquisite now."

I took hold of Henry's lapels and pressed my lips to his cheek again—right out in the open, for all to see. Inhaled the smell of his skin for one decadent second before stepping back and letting go. Because we didn't have many of these moments left.

Dorran knocked on the passenger side window, trying to get our attention.

Any more moments of sheer honesty between Henry and me would have to wait.

Victoria's Tudor mansion glowed brightly in front of us, lit up with guests and laughter. Couples were stepping out of similar limousines, dressed to the absolute nines. Notes of classical music floated toward us on the breeze.

I ducked my head down to Dorran in the driver's seat. "Thank you," I said. "You know where to wait for us?"

"I do," he said. "Just call. I'll be ready at any moment." I nodded at him as he drove off.

Lifting his elbow, Henry said, "Are you ready, wife?"

"As ready as I'll ever be, husband."

We both smiled at that—a recognition, a stirring, an acceptance of the job in front of us. The house rose up like a wave of red bricks. And silhouetted in the grandiose doorway was Victoria, dressed in a tapered gold gown, greeting guests like a resplendent bride at her wedding.

Although a myriad of sharply dressed couples vied for her attention, she only had eyes for us.

"Well, if it isn't Mr. and Mrs. Thornhill," she exclaimed. "I've been waiting for you to arrive. You both look ravishing."

Sven flanked her, staring down each guest with a snarl. I ignored him like he was a misbehaving dog.

"Not as ravishing as you, Victoria," Henry said smoothly. "What an honor to be here in your magnificent home."

"I do hope you enjoy the inside," she crooned, aware of the

many eyes on her. "Once I've finished greeting everyone, I must snag the both of you right away. I have something to show you that will knock your socks off."

It could truly be anything: a favorite painting, an old book, an interesting architectural detail.

But my breath caught at the possibility—and Victoria heard it. She squeezed my hand brightly.

"I love your enthusiasm, Delilah."

"I'm so looking forward to what you're going to show us," I said—and didn't even have to fake the sincerity of that statement.

"Good. Go get yourself a drink before I find you." The doors behind her opened into the great room—a fire roared in the fireplace, over which antique swords were displayed. A black bear rug dominated the space, mouth open and teeth snarling.

"It's no Reichenbach Falls," she said quietly—so quietly I thought I'd imagined it. "But I believe you'll still be enthralled. Welcome to the most magnificent mansion in all of Philadelphia."

36

HENRY

A towering display of glasses bubbled with a champagne waterfall between trees draped in wispy fabric. Four crystal chandeliers dangled from a white ceiling engraved with flowers—dotted with tiny twinkle-light stars. The small stage held a string quartet. Glamorous-looking waitstaff flitted about with trays of finger food.

"I can't believe this," Delilah said, staring up at the ceiling and through the crowd. "This is..."

"Incredible," I finished.

She squeezed my hand, and I held it, linking our fingers together. In all honesty, my fake wife was the incredible one— a statuesque beauty in a stunning white gown, her blue eyes brighter than I'd ever seen them before. The shape of her thighs appeared in my mind—the illicit black lace, the scalloped fabric, the flexing muscle. It was everything Delilah embodied: danger and desire; delicate lace and precise strength.

And I wanted to take it off with my teeth.

"Let's get a drink and pretend to be impressed with these portraits," Delilah said. She picked up two glasses from a passing waiter and led us to a wall of heavy-looking, gilded paintings.

"I don't think I have to pretend," I remarked. Before us hung a four-foot-tall portrait of our target, lit with glowing lights. Victoria appeared to be twenty years younger in it but still distinguished. "You don't want to call *too* much attention to yourself," I said. "Just a little something to let your guests know whose house you're in."

Delilah was grinning. "I'd love it even more if she'd had herself painted *as* royalty." She indicated the five portraits of European royalty hanging to her left. "Why do you think she has these?"

"It was certainly common for Tudor homes to showcase the royal family. She's probably aiming for authenticity."

"And who is this?" She was gazing up at a man dressed in white fur, holding a blue scepter.

Christian VII of Denmark, read the inscription.

"King of Denmark," I said. "I remember him because he reportedly used to ask to be tied down and flogged."

Delilah arched a graceful brow. "Interesting."

The shape of two more bodyguards appeared at separate corners of the room. And then Victoria—making her way through the crowd toward us. I tugged Delilah close.

"You see the guards?"

"I can take 'em," she said without a trace of humor.

"I don't doubt it," I agreed. "And our target is coming."

"*There* you are," Victoria exclaimed. "Come, come. We have collections to see. Oh, and you remember Sven, right?" We nodded at the man Freya had described as a "psychopath." "And this is his brother, Hans." A second guard appeared at Victoria's shoulder. "They're here temporarily for some interesting projects I'm working on."

Delilah's body was tense as we followed Victoria through

the crowd, stopping every few feet to greet guests and receive their effusive compliments. The great room opened into a hallway with blood-red carpets and mahogany walls. Each cozy room opened into another, like Russian nesting dolls, until I was almost dizzy with it.

"I had this house built in 1995, and it took absolute *ages*. It's not easy to find contractors who will commit to a full Tudor revival." We passed an expansive library that had my fingers itching to pull on the spines and flip through the pages.

"And you know, there were issues along the way. The papers made it out to be like some kind of Winchester house, stairwells leading to nowhere, that kind of thing. But it was nothing of the sort. Many of these pieces were flown in exclusively from Europe." Victoria nodded at me, tapping her fingers along a wall of paintings as we passed. "Henry, I knew you would appreciate my attention to authenticity. We can't live our lives with fakes, you know."

"Certainly not," I said, passing what might have been an original Monet.

"And this," Victoria said, "is my private collections room. Try not to swoon, Henry."

With a nod from her, Sven pushed open a heavy-looking door into a cavernous room. It felt like an actual museum: glass cases and soft lighting and displays of books, crumbling vases, an old shield and an ancient map.

The gravity of this moment was only surpassed by its surrealism. After weeks of lying to Victoria Whitney to gain her trust, we were standing in her room of antiques. And probably mere feet away from a stolen book worth millions of dollars.

But the quiet intensity of this room also sent a bolt of longing through me; for those early days in libraries before I was made brutally aware of this shady underbelly. My eyes caught the shape of books I hadn't seen in quite some time—a sense of wonder infused my limbs, even as the stakes of this case tightened around us like a vise.

"This is...a professional honor," I managed to say.

"My husband's idea of Disneyland," Delilah said. I could tell she was assessing the room, taking in the displays.

What if the Copernicus was *here*? Somewhere in this room?

The next case displayed a single sheet of paper. I moved toward it with a shocking, painful recognition, every fine detail about this case converging into this one moment. Bernard and Victoria's whirlwind romance might have ended years ago, but the reason they still saw each other now was for something else entirely.

"Is this what I think it is?" The hard edge of my voice echoed in the quiet room. I could feel Delilah turning to me, responding to my tone.

"Oh, is that my Newton?" Victoria inquired, as nonchalantly as one might ask to pass the salt.

"Page seventeen," I said, muscles beginning to tremble. "How specific."

It was the page I'd told Abe I'd discovered to be missing from the McMasters Library six months ago. Newton's handwritten notes were in the margins.

Fucking page seventeen.

"Yes, well, Bernard thought I would enjoy it. Notice the pencil markings."

I'd analyzed and indexed those markings myself, years earlier, working alongside Bernard.

"May I ask how he came upon just the single page?"

Victoria stiffened, patting at the jewels around her neck. "I think everyone in this room is aware of where he got it."

"It's lovely," Delilah said, placing a hand on my back. We

were the Thornhills, we bought stolen books and missing pages and pilfered antiques. Henry Thornhill shouldn't have had to ask. "Henry's a massive Newton fan."

"It's why I'm so stunned that Bernard"—I paused, flashed her my most winning smile— "was able to find this for you."

"Was it a gift?" Delilah asked, in a slightly teasing tone.

Victoria touched her hair. "Why, yes, yes it was."

Delilah's finger was on her silver bracelet. *Take pictures.* In my shock, I'd forgotten the reason we were here, but Victoria was watching me like a hawk. A pleasant hawk, but I still felt a bit like prey.

Sven and Hans cleared their throats, and Victoria shot them a withering look. "My guards are reminding me it's not *ideal* for us to be down here so long. Come along, I need to show you my newest acquisition."

Delilah threw me a look of apprehension mixed with curiosity. There was an orange door Victoria pushed open, beckoning us with a crook of her finger. Delilah reached down and linked our fingers together. My ears roared with the sound of my own heartbeat.

It couldn't be this easy—could it? Victoria, yanking away a velvet cloth like a magician's assistant, revealing what we'd been searching for?

A light illuminated a glass case, which shone in the middle of the room. I noted the temperature controls on the side of the walls, the special lighting.

This was the room of an archivist.

Victoria giggled shyly, beckoning us closer. A low grunt from behind me indicated that Sven and Hans were steps away. I hitched up my sleeve, uncovering my watch.

"I told you I like to own works by geniuses," Victoria said to me. "Which is why I purchased Shakespeare's *First Folio*."

My pulse jolted painfully. My stomach dropped. There, in

the glass case, was William Shakespeare's *First Folio*, a compilation of his plays printed in 1623. It was one of the rarest books in the entire world.

And it wasn't the fucking Copernicus.

I forgot to be enamored—forget to be awed by the sheer magnitude of the text, the history, the greatness. Delilah was squeezing my hand like her life depended on it. I brought her wrist to my lips, kissed her there.

"I'll take your silence for surprise," Victoria mused.

"That would be accurate," Delilah murmured.

"Henry? Any thoughts on this purchase?" She'd emphasized the word *purchase.*

Despair knifed through me. "There are 750 copies of this book left in the entire world," I said robotically. "I've never seen one in person."

Which was a lie—I'd worked on it with a team of conservationists years ago at Oxford. It had been one of the biggest professional accomplishments of my entire life. But I couldn't dredge up that feeling in the wake of such bitter disappointment. "Where did you buy it from?"

A letter of authenticity was framed near the book.

"The Antiquarian Book Festival in New York City one month ago," she said proudly. "I was the highest bidder—by a long shot, of course."

I had a distant memory of reading about the purchase in the paper—I hadn't known at the time the way Victoria Whitney would intersect my life.

"A smart purchase. It will bode well for you in the future." I had no idea if I even sounded sincere. "If you need advice on conserving it, I'd be happy to provide a consult. Pro bono, of course."

"That's very kind of you," Victoria said. "And let me tell you. I've had to hire these men to protect me these past few weeks." She leaned in and said with absolutely no irony, "Thieves are everywhere. A lot of people would do a *lot* of bad things to get their hands on this book."

Exhaustion weighed heavily on my shoulders. Deep down, I'd imagined us as victorious this evening, against all odds—even in the face of Abe's fear we'd never find the Copernicus. Every other outcome felt impossible with her by my side.

"You can't trust people these days." Delilah shook her head. Real sadness was etched into her voice. But she placed her hand on the case anyway. "Knowing you is a privilege, Victoria."

"Thank you," I remembered to add. "What an honor."

"You're very welcome." Victoria lay a bejeweled hand on both of our arms. "If we weren't in the middle of my party, I'd show you so much more of my collection. But I've been looking forward to showing this to an expert like yourself for weeks now."

Delilah wrapped her arms around my waist, and I settled my lips into her hair—and whether this moment of comfort was real or feigned, I honestly could not say. But it was reassuring to inhale her scent.

"Getting to know you has been such a treat. You should be proud of the life you've built together," Victoria said a little wistfully.

"You'll find it too," Delilah said in a low voice. A sea of complex emotions moved across Victoria's face, some reference to their cloisters conversation I wasn't privy to. But I was having a difficult time empathizing with the heiress in front of me. Even without the Copernicus, Victoria was still a thief. A thief that also got to own a *First Folio*.

"Hans and Sven are giving me stern looks," Victoria said playfully. "Let's go before I ignore my other guests for longer than is polite."

We followed both men—and I noticed for the first time the guns holstered at their hips. The journey back to the party, through the confusing maze of Tudor-style rooms, felt even more surreal the second time. We passed through the library again and back out to the party.

"My hostess duties await. Do find me later?" Before we could respond, Victoria fluttered her fingers and moved seamlessly back into her adoring crowd.

I wondered if that was the last time we would see Victoria Whitney. It was wholly anticlimactic.

"Fancy a drink?" Delilah said. "Or ten?"

I smiled grimly. "Let's go find a quiet corner in the great room where no one can hear us." We walked past the library again, and my mind blazed with Bernard's voice: *she built secret hallways to hide her favorites.*

"What?" Delilah asked. "Do you see someone in there?"

"No." I shook my head. "Drinks, then we talk."

But as we moved through the crowd, that *nagging* sensation wouldn't go away. Even as Delilah grabbed two drinks and yanked us toward a corner with less of a crowd. She clinked our glasses together with a morbid look.

Secret hallways.

"Wait." I grabbed her wrist, stilling her. "We might need those fast reflexes of yours."

"For what? We're going home. I took pictures of most of the items in her collection. If any stick—"

"Page seventeen. Bernard stole that from the McMasters Library."

A waiter strolled past, and Delilah plopped her drink on his tray, pulling me even farther into the corner. She made a show of snuggling into my chest, bringing our faces close. "Bernard's still selling things to her."

"He was," I said. "First, that photo is incriminating

evidence, so that alone is a good enough reason for us to have been here tonight. But second"—I dipped my mouth to her ear—"I still think she has it."

Copernicus? she mouthed.

I nodded.

Delilah let out an angry exhale. "Victoria's a thief but she's not *our* thief. It's not that we didn't get eyes on it. She never had it to begin with. Whatever 'gut instinct' I had about her was absolutely, positively wrong." She was already shutting down on me. I could see it. "She admitted she'd hired the security for the *Folio*. The 'new acquisition' she was mysteriously referring to the night we met her was the *Folio*, not the Copernicus. And I have no idea why she was being so dismissive about the Copernicus exhibit, but technically she *does* know it's been stolen."

"Victoria told us her guards were hired for the *Folio*," I said, tugging her even closer. "But we overheard her at the gala. Demanding something to be moved. *Tonight.* That *Folio* didn't look like it was being prepped to be moved, did it?"

"I think I sent this entire agency on a wild goose chase based on a few strange coincidences and a bunch of assumptions," Delilah argued. Defeat carved lines around her mouth. "What did Francisco say that night? Oh, our reputation would be ruined."

"Delilah."

She glowered at the ground. I tilted her chin up, brushed her hair from her forehead. "I had plenty of evidence that Bernard was committing crimes and I didn't do anything about it, because I didn't trust myself. People like Bernard, people like *Victoria*, move through this world with an audacity that boggles my mind. They believe they are *owed* anything they desire, just because they want it. They're like schoolyard bullies, taking someone else's toys because they can."

"I thought you believed Bernard and Victoria were passionate about antiques."

"I believe that they are," I continued. "But I also believe they get a sick satisfaction from knowing things have been stolen. If Victoria can buy a *First Folio*, she can legally buy a third edition of *On the Revolution of Heavenly Spheres* the next time it comes up for auction at Christie's. But she *chose* to take a first edition from a museum exhibit because she could."

That got her attention.

"Tell me about those senses," I said gently. "The deception you sensed the night we met her. It was strong enough to lead us *here*."

She held my gaze. "They've been blaring like a fucking foghorn."

I knew it.

A familiar gleam came into Delilah's eyes—a charge, a thrill, the hunter I'd follow anywhere. And it made me so happy to see I kissed her cheek.

Her fingers went up to the spot. "What was that for?" Her lips curved up.

"I hate seeing you look defeated," I said simply.

"Well, I hate seeing you look defeated too," she said. "When I saw the look on your face when Victoria was prattling on about that Shakespeare book, I wanted to kick Sven and Hans on your behalf."

"You're a true romantic, Delilah Barrett."

The responding hopefulness and humor in her eyes almost had me blurting the words that had existed on the tip of my tongue from the moment we'd stepped into the limo: *what happens between us after tonight?*

"I still think—" She blew out a breath, like she was mulling something over. "I still think the smartest thing to do is to go home. Send those pictures off right away."

"Do you really think that?"

Her fingers gripped my lapels so tightly I feared they would rip in two. The effort it was taking for her to restrain herself was obvious.

"What's Codex's priority?" I said.

"Our safety," she said, repeating Abe's words with little conviction. I waited until she said, "The book. Always the book."

"And I think it's here."

Delilah chewed on her lip. I watched her scan the audience, analyze the crowd. Behind us, guards were posted everywhere.

"So what do you want to do, partner?"

"I might have a plan," I said. "But it might also get us fired."

37

DELILAH

*E*very bone in my body was vibrating like a tuning fork. My instincts screamed *it's here*—even as I wanted to give up, go home, and crawl into bed.

But Henry knew me now, knew that if I'd caught the scent of wrongdoing, I'd need to chase it down.

"Fired, huh?" I said. I pulled out my cell phone, contemplated dialing Abe. I knew what he'd say—even if we knew where the book was, Victoria could still move it, hide it, bury it. "I've never gone against Abe's express orders before."

Henry was watching me with calm eyes. "We're partners. We can't go it alone. The decision has to be made together."

"Abe will fire us. And then murder us."

He was quiet, allowing me time to turn everything over in my mind, examine it for weak points. And there were a *lot* of weak points. "What's this mysterious plan?"

He slipped his hands into his pockets, glanced behind him back at the library. "What if Victoria *is* hiding it in a secret hallway?"

"Like Bernard had mentioned?"

"If you loved books, you might ask your contractors to build you something private off of the library."

I wrinkled my nose, thinking. Victoria had babbled on about the newspapers accusing her of building the Winchester house which I knew was famous for its secret doors and hidden, mysterious rooms.

"Keep going," I said.

"We find the hallway, search for the book. If we find it..." He trailed off. "Maybe the hallway leads to a back entrance, and we sneak away, without getting caught."

"That plan doesn't take into account guards, security cameras, alarms, or that Victoria probably has some kind of torture chamber for friends of hers who try and steal her books."

His lips quirked up. "Not too shoddy for my first one, though."

What if we took *all* of these risks—and the book was nowhere to be found?

What if we took *none* of these risks—and I found out later we'd had a chance and blown it?

My phone vibrated—Abe calling.

I stared at Henry. Trusting him fully.

I hit "ignore."

"We can at least try," I said, hope filling my chest.

I wanted to do what Henry had done—kiss his cheek. Kiss his mouth. Be bold and reckless in the face of a night that could go wrong in a million different ways.

"We'll start in the library?" he asked.

I nodded and took his hand. I tried to convey relaxed and easy smile as we made our way through the crowd—just a newly married couple enjoying this gorgeous mansion. The library was unguarded and magnificent—row after row of bookshelves as tall as the high ceilings, spilling over with books. A rolling ladder sat near a gilded fireplace and bay windows that opened out into the forest.

"This is the—"

"Ms. Whitney doesn't allow guests in here."

A guard stood, arms crossed and eyebrows raised. *Goddammit.* In a stroke of pure luck, I peered back into the great room and locked eyes with the woman in question.

"Victoria *told* us to go in here. We were in her private collection a few minutes ago."

"Does it look like I give a shit?"

My fists clenched at my sides. Victoria was cocking her head at me quizzically. I shrugged at her, pointed at the guard. With an imperious glare, she tapped Sven and said something that caused our guard's radio to crackle a few seconds later.

He brought the radio to his ear with pure malice. I affected the same haughty air, as if his very presence was offensive to me.

"Fine," he barked.

"Why, thank you," I trilled.

"Victoria really does trust us," Henry said softly, running his fingers along the first shelf of books.

I ignored the oddest feeling of guilt at that. Backed myself into the shelf and grabbed Henry by his jacket. Kept my eyes trained on his as I pulled him into my body.

"Mrs. Thornhill," he whispered with a grin.

"We're just two newlyweds, sneaking away to make out in a library."

"Good cover."

"The guard is definitely still there," I whispered. "His back is to me, but I'm going to bet he's watching us from the corner of his eye."

Henry nodded, thinking. "Let's stroll around casually and check for hidden doors."

Hands entwined, we pretended to admire every inch of the library—the rolling ladder, those bay windows. The room was gigantic. I sat on the couches, felt casually beneath the cushions for a lever or a button. Henry plucked at the edges of shelves and dipped his head into the fireplace when the guard wasn't looking. My fingers landed on Tolstoy, Austen, Whitman, Joyce. I wondered if Victoria actually devoured these classics or if she simply enjoyed the look of them.

At the farthest corner of the room, Henry stood with a look of absolute concentration on his face. I recognized that look.

"Tell me what you remember about that day," I prodded.

His eyes were roaming the shelves. "We were about to give a tour to some students. Librarians. I was cleaning a —"

Henry stopped.

There was a loud crash of laughter from the hallway, groups of people gleefully walking by. I had a feeling we wouldn't be alone in this library for much longer.

"What is it about this one that has you captivated?" I asked, starting to press my fingers to books, shelves—searching for a key or a latch, trying to follow his lead.

"The time period is wrong." Henry seemed distracted—stepping back like the shelf was a painting he was admiring. He rubbed his jaw—my eyes shot to the back of the guard. "Ellison, Kerouac, Rand, Ginsberg, Capote... All the books in this section are contemporary. 1950s and later."

He stepped over to the adjoining shelf, then the next one. "This shelf is mid-nineteenth century. This is current, 2000s on up."

He strode back to the original shelf.

"Henry, what is it?" I whispered, urgent.

He reached up—but didn't touch—the spine of a red book. I peered at its title: *The Hound of the Baskervilles*.

"Doyle wrote this in the early 1900s, fifty years before the rest of these. Her shelves are organized by time period."

"Okay," I said slowly.

"That day, with Bernard, I had this book in my hands."

My instincts started roaring at me, loud as a jet engine. I had no idea what this really meant, only that I was sure the guard was going to turn around any fucking second.

"Maybe it means something," Henry was saying. "Maybe we need to—"

Without a second thought, I hooked my finger in the top of the book. Pulled it toward me.

The wall of books immediately next to Henry popped open—a secret fucking door—revealing a dark hallway.

And another guard.

38

DELILAH

*T*he guard was as startled as we were.

His eyes widened, radio heading toward his mouth—but I pushed past Henry and kneed the guard in the groin. He bent over in surprise and pain, and I hit both of his ears, hard.

"What the fuck?" he sputtered.

I punched him in the nose.

Henry pulled the secret door shut behind him, plunging us into darkness. Low lights glowed at the corners—giving me just enough vision to use the guard's bodyweight to shove him to the ground.

"*Sit*," I hissed at Henry, using my stiletto between the guard's shoulder blades like a knife. Henry dropped his knees on top of the guard, effectively immobilizing him. I hoisted the guard's beefy arms behind him, slapping his wrists together. My muscles burned at the memory of doing this on countless suspects over the years—but I hadn't done it in a long time, and the awkward angle had me wincing.

"Wait...*wait a fucking minute*," the guard tried to yell.

"Relax, I'm not going to hurt you again," I said. I reached

beneath my dress and yanked the zip-tie from my belt. Henry watched me, awed. Once the guard's wrists were bound, I grabbed the duct tape, pressing the heel of my stiletto into the back of his head. "But you do need to shut the fuck up."

"Who the hell—"

I slapped the silver tape over his mouth. He wiggled like a fish beneath Henry's weight.

"Come on," I said, pulling a stunned Henry to his feet. I unclipped the guy's pistol from his holster with nimble fingers. I dropped the magazine, checked the rounds, disarmed the safety.

Cocked it.

And turned to find Henry Finch staring at me with blazing lust. We were both breathing heavily.

"I don't need saving," I said, chin lifted.

"I know you don't," he said hoarsely. "And *saving* isn't what I want to do to you right now."

The guard's radio crackled sharply: "What the hell just happened?"

I swore beneath my breath at my own idiocy. Grabbed the radio and went to smash it between my heels.

"Wait."

Henry stilled my movements. The guard was still wiggling and grunting as Henry dropped down and held down the *talk* button on the radio.

"Caught 'em," Henry said, affecting a rougher tone. "It's fine."

I grinned at his genius. The radio crackled something nondescript back—a sigh and then "whatever." They'd still get suspicious, but it could buy us an extra, precious ten minutes we could use.

"Let's go," I said, taking Henry's hand.

We turned the corner and fully took in this strange, secret hallway.

"You were right," I said, allowing one second for me to beam at my partner with pride. He returned my smile.

"I was. But also...where the fuck *are* we?"

Ahead of us stretched emerald green carpet. The walls were an intricately patterned red wallpaper, Tudor-period. Yellow doors appeared sporadically as we walked carefully through the confined space.

"What should we do?" he asked.

"Start pulling on doors, see what's inside." I reached for one, which opened up into a narrow, winding staircase. Henry and I exchanged a glance. Keeping the gun close, I kept Henry behind me as we crept up the creaking steps, backs to the wall. I half expected another guard to pop out. On the walls hung more portraits of European royalty. The stairs stopped, suddenly, leading to a tiny alcove with giant windows.

"It's like a...a widow's walk," I breathed, taking in the impressive landscape that stretched beyond the bare windows. We could see a few other mansions, dotted in the woods, the floodlights of Victoria's party, the cars that stretched for a decent mile down the street. Valet drivers were racing up and down between the vehicles. Henry searched the room, which was almost bare, and I tapped on walls and pulled on pieces of furniture, wondering if there'd be more secret latches.

"Anything?" I asked.

Henry shook his head. Down the winding staircase we went, back into the creepy hallway. I could hear sounds of the party through the walls as we tugged on more yellow doors—all locked.

"Goddammit," I muttered.

"Wait," he whispered, "this one opens." He slipped inside before I could caution him.

Another staircase. This one so intensely vertical we couldn't see past the first curve in the wall.

"Should we take them?"

Henry let out a sharp breath. "Yeah, let's go."

We were winded by the tenth step.

"What is this, fucking Everest?" I huffed.

Henry's lips twitched. The walls were wooden, ancient-looking, with porthole-style windows. We kept ascending, the stairs winding as though we were inside a lighthouse. A creepy claustrophobia started to invade my senses, a disorientation that made my skin clammy.

The top of the stairs appeared out of nowhere—so quickly I bumped into it.

"What the hell is this?" I asked.

It was another fucking door.

With a shrug, I opened it.

And fell right into the open night sky.

39

DELILAH

I was free-falling.

But only for a second.

Henry had my hand in a vise-like grip, tethering me with an impressive strength.

"*Oh my God*," I cried. My left hand and left leg were dangling over manicured grass and landscaped flowers, four stories down.

"Delilah." Henry's voice was calm. Steady. "I've got you."

I closed my eyes. My throat closed, my muscles shook. I was going to be sick all over my dress.

"Delilah, I need you to trust me, beautiful." Ever-so-gently, Henry was tugging me in. My right leg was slipping from its hold on the narrow strip of landing. "Keep your eyes closed."

I complied, not needing to see that view again. I could feel the breeze, the night air—and absolutely nothing else. No wall, no rope, no roof, just a tumble right to the ground below.

Another hand closed around my waist, arm banding tightly. There was a sharp yank.

Both of my feet landed on solid ground.

My body slammed into Henry's solid, broad chest immediately. I was dimly aware of the door being clicked shut. Then Henry's big hand, smoothing down my hair. I was shivering, freezing—but slowly, so slowly, melting against my partner. My fingers clutched at his shirt, gripped his ribcage, caressed up his spine. I laid my cheek right above his heart, which was beating faster than my own.

"Let's never do that again, wife," he said softly.

"Thank you," I stuttered. "I'm terrified of heights."

"Anyone would be terrified of falling out of a door that leads to nowhere."

"What on earth could she use that for?"

Henry still had me cradled against his chest—it reminded me of our moment in the closet, my body still clenching with pleasure, mouth closing around the fabric of his jacket to quiet my screams.

"On the bright side, if we find the Copernicus, we could toss it out this door and pray it lands on a soft bush."

A delirious giggle escaped my lips. I kissed his jaw, his throat, that patch of skin left open by his shirt. The adrenaline and the fear were turning me into the woman Mark had accused me of being—easily swept away by her passions, her inner desires.

As if that was a bad thing. As if being a woman in love with her life was somehow *wrong*.

"We have to keep going," Henry said, ghosting his lips at my temple. "But don't take that to mean I don't want to stay here like this."

I stepped back, tucked my hair behind my ear. Grabbed the gun that had clattered to the floor at my almost-fall. "Let's go."

We both refocused, although Henry kept my hand in his, steadying me down the steep stairs. Back in the main hallway, confusion threatened to swamp my instincts. It was so dark, and every inch looked exactly the same: the yellow doors, the wallpaper, the carpet.

"I'm starting to get the creeps," I whispered. "How about you?"

Henry tried another door—arching a brow at me when it clicked. He creaked the door open a half-inch.

Then slammed it with a horrified expression.

"Oh my God, she does have a torture chamber," I said.

"*Kitchen*," he mouthed. Bent over to whisper, "I think this is another entry point to the kitchen. I saw people, trays, ovens."

"Did they see you?"

We both froze, listening for the sound of waitstaff yelling about secret-passageway-intruders. There was an unbearable crawling of time—but nothing.

We exhaled, backs against the wall, heads tilted up.

"For the record," I said, "I still think this is a brilliant plan."

"For the record," Henry replied, "I still think you are brilliant."

Our smiles were shy.

"Do you think we're heading east?" I asked, attempting to orient us in this claustrophobic hellhole.

Henry stared over my shoulder, breath tickling my ear. "I don't think so."

I sighed, frustrated, anxious, moving quickly toward my gut instinct. We took a hard left, then another. Two rights into hallways that appeared to be exactly the same. "Do you think it could be—"

We walked right into Victoria fucking Whitney.

40

HENRY

*D*elilah gasped and I slapped my palm over her mouth, yanking her back against my body.

"Well, that's what I'm saying, darling," Victoria lectured, "you must get your portrait done with James." In a quieter tone: "You know he removes the wrinkles, right?"

Bitzi Peterson and Victoria Whitney stared directly into our faces, a mere six inches from us—but they saw nothing.

"It's a spy painting," I whispered into Delilah's ear. "Wealthy people used them to watch their guests or spy on their servants. It works like a two-way mirror. We can see her, but she can only see the painting."

I'd guessed that Victoria had them—it fit her flair for drama and "historical accuracy" —and we'd stumbled right into it. I could feel tension vibrating in Delilah's muscles...but her breathing slowed. I lifted my hand from her mouth but kept my arm wrapped around her waist.

"Can she hear us?" Delilah mouthed, right at my ear. I nodded, placing a finger to my lips. Against my arm, her muscles were coiled, ready to strike. Just moments earlier, she'd moved with deadly accuracy, toppling that guard with ease. She'd looked like a warrior goddess in stilettos, holding her gun cocked, her red lips curved with determination.

"You've been spending a lot of time with that new couple," Bitzi said. "The handsome one?"

Victoria was smug. "Henry and Delilah Thornhill, yes. They're quite the treasure."

"He is *unbelievably* handsome," Bitzi said, shaking her head.

"They're very much in love," Victoria said, eyes dreamy. "I believe they'll serve us well in the future. They're fans of the falls, as you know."

Delilah went ramrod straight. Behind the two of them, the party was in full swing.

Bitzi dropped her tone. "Have you heard from him recently?"

She didn't say who the *him* was—but I had a guess. They shared a knowing a look—and then were interrupted by Sven lumbering over, looking pissed as hell.

Fuck. How many minutes had it been since Delilah incapacitated that guard? We'd been wandering around these hallways with no sense of time.

"Ms. Whitney?" he asked. "We, uh...we have a problem."

Victoria glared at him. "Interesting, since I pay you an exorbitant fee to have *no problems*." She cocked her head and Bitzi fled the scene.

"The two people you let into the library? They're missing."

Victoria stroked her martini glass with one manicured talon. "Well, where could they possibly be?"

Sven leaned in as Delilah and I inhaled as one.

"Do they know about the library?"

Understanding flooded Victoria's features. "They're not... I mean, they couldn't *possibly*..." And then she straightened up. "George should be manning the entrance, so if they did figure it out, he'd have them trussed up like pigs by now," she said, tone icy.

Sven gave a tight nod and left.

For a single moment, unaware she was being watched, Victoria placed an adorned hand at her throat. Her fingers were trembling, just slightly. Compassion—or maybe *sympathy?*—twisted through my veins. But before I had time to analyze it, Delilah was already yanking me down the hallway, and we were running. We took a right, then another right, the walls seemingly closing in as they grew darker, the wallpaper a mocking red.

And the walls became *books.*

All the way down the damn hallway—built-in bookshelves from floor-to-ceiling, spilling over with them.

"Oh my God," I whispered. Bernard had been right. Victoria *had* built a second library into these hallways. Her favorites. There were children's books here, contemporary novels, spy thrillers mixed in with antique-looking classics. They weren't arranged perfectly like the previous library but placed haphazardly, with no discernible organization.

On one of the walls hung a black-and-white photo of a young woman who looked a lot like Victoria. She was reading to a group of small children. The inscription on the frame said *Celeste Whitney.*

Victoria's mother. The woman whose head was filled with figures.

Delilah stared at me with wide blue eyes, fingers on the shelves. Her head tilted back, way back, to take it all in. The ceiling was painted like the Sistine Chapel, but instead of angels and gilded clouds...it was the universe.

And in the center: a blazing sun.

For a moment, I forgot my adrenaline, forgot my fear and could only bask in Victoria's beloved novels. A true book lover like me. How could two people be drawn to the same passion —but embrace that passion from two different sides of the moral compass?

The silence was shattered by the harsh sizzle of another radio. We froze like wild deer, trapped in car headlights. Static sounds crackled—to the front? Or behind us?

"Nothing here, though," came a deeper voice at the very end. "I think Sven's losing it."

Delilah's arm shot out, pushing me behind her. She grasped the gun, holding it low in front of her.

"No one's come for it. We're all set for the transport tonight. We gotta get these—"

I watched Delilah turn the corner and surprise yet another bodyguard. Bigger than Sven, he was just startled enough to reach for his gun two seconds slower than she did.

With steady arms, she held the gun up to his face.

"Hey there," she said.

From his hip, the radio crackled with voices.

"She's got a—" the guard started. He shut up when Delilah cocked the weapon and pointed it right at his crotch. He raised his arms with a sheepish expression.

The radio voices were shouting now, and the hallway filled with a red, flashing light.

But Delilah was cool and collected.

"What's this?" she asked. For the first time, I noticed he was standing in front of a door with a small keypad.

The guard just smirked at her.

In a blur of movement, Delilah had the point of her stiletto pressing at his dick, gun back at his face.

"What's this?" she said again.

"I think you know what it is," he said through gritted teeth.

"On your knees," she said, indicating with the gun.

He dropped heavily, and I watched miles of Delilah's gorgeous legs appear as she slid down her lace garter.

She placed the fabric into my hand. "You zip-tie while I try my hardest not to shoot him in the dick."

"Ah, come on, lady," the guard protested.

But Delilah merely arched a brow. I unhooked a tie and bound his wrists—in what was probably the most surreal moment of my professional career. The flashing lights had sped up, and I didn't miss the tightness around her mouth.

She was as worried as I was.

"Keypad numbers," she barked. "What are they?"

"1 2 3 fuck you," he said.

And then he was doubled over, wheezing in pain—because Delilah had kicked him square in the groin. She yanked his head back and lowered her face an inch from his.

"Keypad numbers," she repeated, like she was asking for directions to the bus.

"1...5...4...3" he gritted, face contorted in pain.

She nodded at me.

I punched in the code, my pulse racing so fast I felt lightheaded. Any second now I expected another fifty guards to stream out from behind the walls and drag us off to Victoria's secret dungeon.

Distantly, I swore I heard footsteps. My chest was heaving, lights flashing, walls closing in...

Click.

I opened the door and stepped into a small, dark room. I could tell it was temperature controlled, light-controlled—all the makings of the rooms I'd spent my career in.

Very old things would be kept in here: ancient tomes and scrolls and maps with markings that said *here be dragons.*

Delilah joined me a second later, having duct taped the guard. "Do you see the—"

She stopped, struck completely silent.

Time screeched to a shuddering halt—one *snap* and the world paused in its orbit. The room was draped in utter stillness; pale, smooth walls hushed the sounds of the messy havoc right outside the door. My heart slowed, my lungs gasped for air, my mind rushed to contemplate the sight in front of me.

There, in the middle of the room, backlit by gentle light, was a book encased in glass. Together, we stepped forward until the tips of our feet touched the stand.

It was small—smaller than I imagined, bound in vellum with gold lettering: *De revolutionibus orbium coelestium, Nicolaus Copernicus.*

On the Revolution of the Heavenly Spheres.

"You were right, Delilah," I whispered.

The realization that we'd found the book felt like standing in front of a gale-force wind. I completely forgot to breathe. My fingers ghosted over the glass case, itching to touch something that had become a legend in my mind. Astonishment flooded my nervous system, sent chills racing up and down my spine.

"Henry."

I brought Delilah's hand to my mouth, kissed the center of her palm as we turned to stare at each other. The one thing we had desperately searched for was *here*, right in front of our eyes, and as the lights flashed and the guards ran toward us, there was nothing I wanted more than to kiss Delilah Barrett until the end of time.

"Delilah." My voice was a rough scrape.

I want to kiss you.

I want to fuck you.

I want to...

Her eyes closed, throat working. "I...I..."

"Tell me." I kissed her palm again, her fingers brushing my mouth.

"I...see Victoria's portable case, the one from the other night," she managed. "Can we put the book in there?" She turned toward the door. "Um...very quickly?"

Adrenaline ripped through me. "Right, of course."

I shook my head, moved to the case. The glass was heavy as I lifted and I flinched, expecting another alarm.

"There's probably a silent one," Delilah said.

I nodded, picking up the portable glass case with the handle. My fingers moved quickly along the edges, searching for an opening.

The front panel slid open.

I blew out a grateful breath.

The Copernicus was secured to a mount which removed pressure from the spine, allowing it to keep its shape. I lifted the mount as Delilah held the door open.

"In my jacket pocket, there's a tube of mounting glue," I said. "Can you grab it?"

Her hand slid inside the fabric and retrieved it.

"The glass bottom," I indicated. Holding the mount was making me fucking nervous. I was holding my breath, afraid to breathe on it. "Glue it."

"Did you have this in your pocket the entire night?" she whispered as she spread glue over the bottom.

"A man has to have his secrets," I whispered back.

I slid the mount inside and secured the bottom to the glue. I remembered doing this with Bernard for an exhibition, my second day on the job.

"Will it hold?" Delilah asked.

I let it go gently, like a grenade with a hair-trigger pin. Closed the door of the case. Nodded tightly. "It'll get us back to Codex."

"We have to run now," she said. "As fast as we can."

"What if they catch us?" I asked.

"Keep fucking running."

"Do you know where the exit is?"

"Not at all. My plan was to run until we reached the end of the hallway and pray there's a door. We just have to make it to the woods, okay?"

"Carrying a 500-year-old book in our hands."

Gun cocked, she winked at me and pushed open the door. With the exception of the flashing lights, the hallway was silent. Delilah waved me forward as she raced ahead of me. The case made running awkward and slow—and by the frantic look on Delilah's face, I wasn't going fast enough.

There were footsteps, echoing in the passageway. Gruff voices and squawking radios and I could sense people near us.

"*Faster, faster,*" she chanted, stumbling through the near dark.

Fear coated my tongue, choked my throat. Each turn seemed to take us deeper into this labyrinth of a house.

We were trapped.

Hopelessly lost.

Victoria's maze of secret hallways was infinite.

41

DELILAH

I understood only one directive: keep Henry safe. As we fled through the hallways, my mind couldn't even comprehend that we had a book in our hands. We were trapped in a maze of hallways that was never-ending, seemingly growing narrower, darker. More confusing. But I needed to stay *focused* if I was going to get us out of here without Sven the Psycho catching us.

The hallway ended—abruptly. A midnight-blue door that pulled open in one smooth, clean motion.

"I've *got it*," I whispered over my shoulder, grinning at Henry.

Starlight flooded my eyes. The night air was startling in its crispness—so different from the old, stuffy air of the hallways. It was so exhilarating I almost didn't see the guard, posted right outside.

I turned and was bringing my arm up with the gun when the guard kicked it from my hand.

And then Henry's fist—sailing through the air, cracking him square on the nose.

"Mother*fucker*," the guy wailed.

Henry punched him again.

I scooped up my gun in the commotion and yanked Henry's arm before we got stuck in a fight.

"Run run run run," I chanted, racing across the green vastness of Victoria's lawn, the white river of the Milky Way shimmering over our heads. The forest appeared at the edges of her luxurious pool—the same one Henry and I had run through not two weeks ago.

The one with the trip wires.

I whipped out my cell and dialed *3* for Dorran, barking the word *"now"* into the phone. There was the *puff* of a silencer, and a bullet whizzed into the grass at our feet.

With all of my weight, I pulled Henry behind the first tree, shielding him with my body, gun aimed at the ground.

I chanced a glance—saw three of the guards pointing at the woods, yelling into radios.

"Delilah," Henry gasped. "As much as I appreciate literature, I'd prefer if we didn't die over this book."

"I agree with you," I said, peeking around the trunk. "They're only trying to scare us. I don't think Victoria wants a shootout in her backyard during her party."

"I don't think she wants her Copernicus to be stolen either," he said grimly.

"There's tripwires that way."

"I remember," he replied.

Headlights beamed off of his face. Dorran, at the far edges of the mansion. The flashlights and raised voices were getting closer.

There was no more time.

"We're running to the limo alongside the house. Not through the woods. People might see us through the windows, but that's fine—the guards won't shoot us in front of guests. Drop to the ground and cover your head if you need to." He was panting, glasses askew, lugging around a heavy glass case as we ran for our lives. "I'll protect you."

He barely nodded his understanding before we were a blur of limbs, racing toward the safety of the limo. Shouts for real now—we were definitely being chased.

To the right of me—a wall of trees.

To the left—the red brick of Victoria's mansion.

In front—the small glowing rectangle of the limo's doors, swung wide open.

I was running so fast that I hit the side of the car with a *bang*. Grabbed Henry's arm and hauled him first into the limo. Sven was a hundred yards away, glaring at me like I was a bug he was extremely excited to step on.

He was reaching into his holster, but my gun was up in a flash, stopping him in his tracks. His lips curled in a snarl.

"She'll come after you," Sven taunted.

"I'd like to see her try," I said. Slid into the limo, slammed the door, and Dorran peeled away so fast I flew backward on the seat.

Henry and I could only stare at each other, wide-eyed and panting.

"Am I dreaming," I gasped, "or is that the fucking book?"

I couldn't contain my grin—even as my body rippled with tension.

"That's it," he said. "Or it's at least highly likely."

He placed it on the floor in the far corner, nestled snugly. When he did, I noticed that his knuckles were split open and bleeding.

"Henry, you're hurt," I said, springing to his side of the limo. He was already shedding his jacket and rolling up his shirt sleeves. He examined his broken skin with mild curiosity. I knew it was just the adrenaline, masking the pain. "Also, that wasn't a bad hit. You knocked him right out."

"I thought he was going to hurt you," he said simply.

The intensity that passed through our shared gaze had my knees weak. I busied myself with the first aid kit Freya had been smart enough to stash in here. With his other hand, Henry slipped out his phone.

"This will sting," I said, but he didn't wince.

"You were right about the book," he said softly.

"And you were right about the hallways."

His slow, charming grin was contagious. Victory rushed through me, making me feel light-headed and hopeful. Dazzlingly with sheer joy. Laughter gripped me—bubbling up like a fountain. When Henry started laughing too, tears rolled from my eyes, all the weeks of tension and fear and nerves fleeing through the sound.

"Is Abe really going to murder us?" he asked, still laughing.

"We went against his orders. But we got the book back. I'd say it's fifty-fifty." I wiped my eyes.

He dialed Abe, put him on speakerphone.

"We made this choice together, as partners," I reminded him. "I'd do anything for you, Henry."

The words slipped out as Abe picked up. "There better be an explanation for why my undercover agents are just now responding to my countless messages," Abe said. "And *we were shot dead* is only a partial excuse."

"We have the Copernicus," I said.

Abe didn't say a word.

"I'm not fucking with you, I promise. Call Francisco."

Another long pause.

"Did the guards come after you?" he finally asked.

"A little," I hedged. "Nothing a little hand-to-hand combat and a gun couldn't solve."

"And where did you get the gun?"

Henry and I locked eyes over the phone. "I took it."

"All limbs accounted for?"

This was Abe's grumpy way of confirming we were safe.

"Yes," I promised.

"I'll see you at the office."

And he hung up.

42

HENRY

*D*elilah was patching me up like an expert, bandaging every cut on my knuckles. It didn't hurt —not at all—not with the most adrenaline I'd ever experienced pumping through my bloodstream. My muscles were shaking, nerves screaming—if the limo had broken down and she instructed me to run all the way back to the office, I would have.

Her head bent over, my hand splayed open on her thigh. Every time she inhaled, the curve of her breasts pressed against the top of her dress. The tips of her fingers, stroking along my skin, sent shivers of awareness up my spine.

"He sounded mad," I said.

"There's nothing we can do about it now," she said. On instinct, I brushed a strand of hair from her forehead. "I think he's mostly happy. No damage was actually done. The book's back. We'll get paid. Abe will be *very* happy about that." Delilah held up my hand. "Good as new."

But she didn't move from my seat. Her cheeks were flushed, pupils dilated. I wondered if she felt it too—that unbelievable urge to tear something in half. The sight of her joy, her throaty laughter, had my heart spiraling. I wanted *making Delilah laugh* to become my next vocation.

My palm landed back on her thigh. The gold of my wedding ring stood stark against the pale satin of her dress.

"There's only one thing I'm sad about," I admitted.

"What's that?"

We were hurtling back toward Codex—the reality of the case, the reality of being coworkers. How much time did we have left in this limo? Thirty minutes? Forty?

I intended to make the most of them.

"As soon as we get back, I won't be your fake husband anymore." I reached beneath the gauzy layers of her skirt, smoothed my hand from her ankle, up her knee, along her inner thigh. We watched my hand together—out in the open, not in some dark closet. "Which means I won't be able to touch you like this."

My fingers reached the lacy garter belt. I slipped two fingers beneath it, caressing the soft skin. Delilah's lips parted on a shaky breath.

Then her legs parted.

"Every night that we've played this game," I said, stroking higher, "I've gone home and been jealous of Henry Thornhill."

"Wh-why?" she asked.

My hand slid so high it was hidden by layers of her skirt, bunched at the waist. I traced the outline of her underwear, which was already wet.

"Because he got to strip this dress from your body and enjoy every single inch of your nakedness." I slipped inside, growling like an animal when my fingers touched slick, hot flesh. My thumb found her clit, teased it with light circles. "He got to tie you to the bed you shared. Fuck you for days."

"*Henry,*" she whispered.

She tilted her hips up, knee sliding off the side of the seat to spread herself farther for me. My thumb caressed harder and her lids grew heavy.

"Can't a husband fuck his wife in the back of a limo?" she asked.

My arm shot out, wrapped around her waist. Dragged her onto my lap and wrenched her knees wide.

I watched her nipples grow into hard, tight peaks through her dress. I slid my hands up her hips, her rib cage, her stomach—palming her breasts as she ground herself against me. My breath was coming hot, furious, *frustrated*. I thrust my hips up—just once—and her head fell back with a sigh.

"Do you feel that, beautiful?" I said, ghosting my lips along her jaw, her ear. I gripped her ass beneath her dress, dragged her against my straining erection. "It doesn't matter how much pressure we were under on this case. I was hard for you the entire *fucking* time."

That seemed to snap something inside of her. Her mouth landed on mine in a kiss that shook my body, stole my breath. Her fingers were opening my belt as I bit her lower lip, groaning when she released my cock. Our foreheads came together, breath shuddering, as her hand slicked up, gripped the head. I tangled my fingers in her short curls. Twisted and trapped her. Pulled her head back until we could stare at each other with swollen lips.

"You want me to fuck you in this limo, Delilah?" My voice was a taunt. Hers was a sob. "You want me to make our fantasies real?"

"Yes," she said, panting but firm. "Please, for the love of God, take me right here."

Adrenaline, nerves, fear—I wanted to fuck her like this. Wanted to unleash every predatory instinct she elicited in me.

But even if it was only this one night, only this one moment, I already knew there'd be consequences. I softened my voice.

"Are you sure?"

Delilah kissed me again with sublime passion; a luscious press of her lips against mine. Her mouth opened the way she was opening for me—her tongue, her breath, her fingers in my hair. The fantasy slid away, revealing the full force of my feelings for this woman, a woman whose lips moving against mine brought me a pleasure I'd never experienced before.

I knew full well what the consequences of these moments would be.

"More than anything," she whispered.

Walls down, heart open, grinning with flushed cheeks— the warrior goddess in front of me had never been more perfect, more alive, more *real*.

"I brought a condom in my purse." She reached for it with one hand, eyes never leaving mine.

I had her on her back in a second. In the next, I'd reached beneath her skirt and torn her underwear clear from her body. I let myself enjoy one indulgent second of Delilah's naked, glistening pussy—the dark thatch of hair, the flexing muscles of her inner thighs.

Then I grabbed the condom from her shaking fingers.

"You had this the entire time?" I growled.

"A woman has to have her secrets," she taunted.

I grabbed her hips, yanked her down the seat. Her head fell back, knees pushed wide. She watched me sheath myself with hungry eyes. I dropped my hips against her sex, sliding my cock along her clit.

"How soundproof do you think that window is?" I whispered at her ear, stopping to bite the side of it.

She shuddered, grabbed my ass. "It's not soundproof at all."

"Good thing you've already shown me you know how to stay quiet."

My cock was right where we both wanted it. Her pussy was wet and so hot I almost lost it right there. "Once I'm inside you, I won't be able to control myself."

It was a warning as much for her as it was for me. And like that day she'd taught me how to fight, she propped herself up on her elbows and gave me a dangerous smile.

"You think I can't handle it, newbie?"

With a barely contained groan, I reached beneath her body, lifted up her hips. And pushed inside her inch by delicious inch. She muffled a moan against my throat, grasping my hair. I let her adjust to the size of me, went slowly, carefully, until I bottomed out inside of her.

We were sharing one ragged breath, finally joined together; Delilah was wet and tight and hot and as I gave a tiny, experimental thrust, she raked her nails down my chest. Closed her teeth around my jaw.

"Harder, newbie."

Delilah fell back onto the seat, and I pressed a hand over her mouth as I punched my hips forward the way she'd asked. There was no point in going slowly now—Delilah and I were well past that, driven mad by lust and adrenaline.

Her hands ripped beneath my shirt, fingernails clawing up the muscles of my back. She was moaning softly beneath my hand, brilliant eyes trained on mine, and I was analyzing every single response to my movements.

Even a quick fuck in a limo should be transcendent for the powerful woman I had beneath me. I surged forward, tilted my hips slightly, and her eyelids fluttered.

I wanted us closer, glued together, so I replaced my palm with my mouth. Kissed her hungrily, messily—teeth, tongue, and my cock fucking her with deliberate speed. Our cries of pleasure were muted only by the intensity of our kiss. She sucked my fingers between her lips, bit at me, cut her nails into my ribcage.

Our hands collided as I thrust us forward across the seat, so I wrenched them up and over her head. The position brought us nose-to-nose—and let me grind my pelvis against her clit every time I fucked into her. We were kissing each other with intertwined fingers and slick, grinding bodies. Delilah met me thrust for thrust, every nerve in my body screaming for *more more more*.

And then I was flying—off the side of the seat and onto the bottom of the limo, landing hard on my back.

Delilah had bested me yet again.

Just like in my fantasies, she straddled my cock and rode me with a fury. I gripped her hips and pistoned her savagely, up and down, reaching up and placing my hand over her lips again to keep her quiet. But the sounds that escaped were passionate, real, and so fucking *raw* a voice in the back of my head whispered a warning I didn't want to heed. Not that what we were doing was wrong—unprofessional and complicated and breaking the rules.

No—the warning was shouting that every shared kiss, every caress, every touch was *right*.

I sat up, rolling my hips and dragging a sound from her throat she hadn't made before. "Did you really think you were going to win this fight?" I teased, kissing my way up her neck as she fucked me.

"You like it," she gasped, mouth sliding into a smile.

I twisted her around, slapped her palms on the seat in front of her, and pushed up to my knees. Flipped up her gauzy skirt and slid back inside her with a ferocity I didn't know I possessed. She had to drop her mouth to the seat and scream.

I gripped her hair, twisted the tendrils, and fucked Delilah so deep I lost any remaining scraps of my self-control. I only existed to give Delilah the pleasure she deserved—and even as I was balancing on the precipice of orgasm, nothing else mattered except *Delilah*. I curved my chest over her back, hovered my lips at her ear.

"Feel how much I want you, Delilah," I said. My fingers slid against her clit, and she whimpered. "I have meant every single word I've said to you as your husband. *Every single word*. All of it is true."

She was shaking so much I worried she might fall over. I was hitting some angle inside of her that had her delirious, muttering nonsense words. My thumb worked her clit in purposeful circles until her internal walls clenched so hard that I closed my mouth around her shoulder to bite.

With my last remaining seconds of control, I took her mouth in a ravishing kiss as she orgasmed. I climaxed at the exact same time, our bodies chasing the same pleasure, the same heights. My mind went entirely blank, vision dark; I was crushing pressure and ecstatic release and then perfect stillness.

Delilah's head fell back against my shoulder, and she let out that same adorable laugh from earlier. I kissed her on the cheek.

"I actually think," she said, still breathless, "*that* was newlywed sex."

I gave an open-mouthed chuckle against her shoulder blade. "That sex was for a woman who trusted her instincts. And led us right where we needed to be."

She turned around and wrapped her entire body around mine—clinging to me on the floor of this limo. From the speed we were going, I sensed we were close to the quiet, historic streets of Old City.

Our time was almost up.

"That sex was for a man who is stronger and smarter than his past," she whispered.

And I let her see how honest I was being when I said, "So are you."

Delilah kissed my temple, clung to me tighter. How had this happened? This outpouring of emotion, the tender way she clung to me. But it was the same after the closet—a moment I imagined would be deviously filthy had ended *sweetly*.

"You know, I think we both won," she finally said, giving me a small smile.

"I think you're right."

The limo slowed down. Her eyes were a storm of emotions that probably mirrored my own. Because I was turned on by our shared fantasy—but utterly captivated by the feelings that existed beneath.

The limo stopped, engine idling. My eyes cast toward the corner, where I'd secured the glass case protecting our bounty. Part of me knew Abe might be angry with us—but what could honestly go wrong? We'd had a successful recovery, against odds that were heavily stacked against us. I felt *happy*, indulgent, ready to take on the world with the woman sitting next to me.

I hadn't felt this way since before Bernard had ruined everything.

I held Delilah's hand to my mouth, kissed it.

"Are you ready?" I asked.

"Yes," she replied, eyes bright. "I think I am."

43

DELILAH

*F*reya was a blur of limbs when Henry and I walked through the doors at Codex. As Henry left to place the Copernicus in our secure storage room, she leapt into my arms and squealed.

"I knew you could do it," she whispered. She was dressed head-to-toe in the Harry Potter flannel pajamas she kept in her desk drawer just for nights like this. I felt a sharp pang when I recalled our conversation from earlier:

Strange things can happen when you go undercover.

Like having adrenaline-fueled sex on the floor of a limo with a man who made you feel as filthy as he did cherished?

I meant every single word. His honest confession had soared me to climax as intensely as the raw and passionate fucking I'd just received. His perfect cock, his dirty mouth, his throaty, ragged groans—the deep, glorious angle, the bruises, the scrapes, the *screaming.*

Followed by Henry's fervent, whispered praise; his sweet and beautiful vulnerability.

As I stood there with Freya clutching me tightly, the awareness of what Henry and I had done fully sunk in. And if I'd somehow believed I could keep my feelings for him locked away, I now knew that to be a fool's errand.

"I want to see the book," Abe said tightly. He avoided looking at me but appeared exhausted and *almost* rumpled in his suit.

"Okay," I said, exchanging a brow lift with Freya.

I'd picked up on his *I'm pissed* signals over the phone, but I was distracted by sheer lust. Now, anger was obvious in the way he stalked across the office toward the book.

"Cameras, please," Freya said, miming grabby hands.

"Right," I said, snapping off my bracelet. "Listen, Henry has the background on this, but I think we actually got a picture of a stolen text besides the Copernicus. A page from an Isaac Newton manuscript. Plus, I got photos of the Copernicus in its case."

Freya shoved a lock of hair from her forehead. "Incredible. Francisco directed us to send everything to the FBI agents they've been working with. It looks like our kooky heiress might *actually* get in trouble. She can't claim innocence when the book came from the museum where she's president of the board."

"I wonder how she got it," I mused. "She must have hired someone, right?"

"I'm sure. Victoria's got contacts for days."

I tried to tamp down the peculiar sensation that rose in me at the thought of Victoria being led away in handcuffs, serving real time in prison. I'd never become so intimately involved in a suspect's life as a police officer—there wasn't time and it wasn't appropriate. This—this deep dive into Victoria's vulnerabilities to gain her trust—had me feeling itchy.

"Do you think she realizes that Henry and Delilah Thornhill swindled her yet?"

I thought of watching her through the concealed portrait

window, the way her fingers had trembled when she thought no one was looking.

"Yes, I think she does," I admitted.

Freya eyed me for a second. "Empathy is a complicating emotion when you're undercover. It's very, very normal to feel confused."

I gave her a grateful side-hug but still felt unsettled. We followed Abe into the storage room and watched Henry carefully place the portable glass case into our larger, temperature-controlled safe. Without a word, he stepped back so Abe could drop down to his heels and examine it.

"You'll do an analysis? I've already called Francisco."

Henry beamed at him like an eager student. "Absolutely. I can confirm authenticity."

But his smile faltered when he finally had time to read Abe's obvious displeasure. Henry dared a glance in my direction, but I shook my head discreetly.

"I'd like to speak to both of you in my office now."

"And me?" Freya asked brightly.

"Go home."

Her face fell. *Call me*, she mouthed, before grabbing her things to go.

Henry and I stepped into Abe's office like bad kids about to be reprimanded by the principal. Abe closed the door, cleared his throat briskly. Leaned against his desk with legs crossed in front of him.

"What were your orders this evening?"

So this was how it was going to be.

"Abe, we just returned a book worth five million dollars—"

"What were your orders this evening?"

I let out a long exhale. Disobeying orders wasn't my forte, but I wouldn't have done it if I hadn't been convinced it was the right thing to do. "Case the property. Take pictures. Do not identify ourselves as Codex agents. Do not put ourselves at risk. Call the police."

"And what did you do instead?"

I crossed my arms. "Henry and I, *as partners*, made the call to go after it. Henry had recalled this memory, from Bernard, that led us to these secret hallways. And I had this *feeling* it was there the entire time. We both worried that if we didn't take quick action the book would have been lost forever."

I tilted my chin—keenly aware that, as a former police officer and now private detective—I was arguing that a flimsy memory and a *feeling* was the reason why I disobeyed express orders.

Abe knew it too. He glared at me until I shifted noisily in my chair.

"I run Codex like a tight ship because I've seen firsthand what happens when a small team doesn't respect one another, doesn't respect each other's *safety*. Disregards professional boundaries or goes off-script. Of course I'm thrilled and..." Abe's throat worked. "And *proud* that you recovered the Copernicus."

My chest pinched at his rare show of emotion.

"But I was also worried." Abe smoothed his tie down, avoiding our eyes. "Very fucking worried."

I deflated like a popped beach ball. "Oh, Abe."

"Your plan only seems flawless now because the recovery was successful. But if it *hadn't been*, or either of you had gotten hurt in the process, you would understand how reckless it was." Abe leaned forward—and this next part was directed at me. "The rules are different for private detectives, Delilah. We're not FBI or police anymore. If we do the things we used to, it's illegal. And even if you and I struggle with that, it's the goddamn truth."

"I know why you're mad," I pleaded. "But the *book is back*."

"Yes," he said. "The book we were paid to find by one of the most high-profile museums in the country, in the highest profile exhibit this year."

"Not finding it could have ruined Codex's reputation. Francisco threatened as much," I argued.

"You and Henry getting into a gunfight in the middle of Victoria Whitney's party could have ruined our reputation. And almost did."

I felt, rather than saw, Henry slump in his seat.

"Do the two of you want to continue working at Codex?"

We both said *"of course"* immediately.

"Good," Abe continued. "Because I'd very much like the two of you to stay. But believe me when I say that if you do anything to betray my trust again, I will fire you."

It felt like a bucket of ice water had been dumped on my head.

Abe scrubbed a hand down his face. "I'm going home. I need you both to go home. And I need to think about how we're all going to keep working together in the future."

This time I did look at Henry. "But you just said we're not fired."

"You're not," he replied wearily. "But this was a big violation of trust, Delilah. We're all going to need time."

Abe scooped up his jacket, escorting us out of his office. We all flipped off the lights robotically, creaking down the stairs in total silence. My heart was lodged in my throat—I was torn between sullen anger at Abe and paralyzing guilt.

Outside, Abe hailed a cab with his jacket over his shoulder.

"Listen," he said, opening the door as a taxi pulled up, "it should go without saying that I'm indescribably pleased that the two of you are safe. Don't ever put me in that situation again."

44

HENRY

*T*he streets of Old City were still and silent as a graveyard. Delilah and I stood on cobblestones packed with dirt that told a million stories. Horse-drawn carriages had bounced down these streets through open-air markets. The brick row homes surrounding us were hushed—but 250 years ago this would have been a bustling block, embroiled in the American Revolution.

The night had turned on a dime—from sweet victory and passionate limo-sex, to Abe's anger and disappointment.

We stood beneath the golden circle of a streetlamp, defeat carved into our shoulders.

"Well, I guess someone should file our divorce papers," Delilah said, breaking the silence. Her expression was unsure, wary.

"I'll have my lawyer draw something up."

Delilah ducked her head, but I caught her full grin.

Hope sprang from the curve of those lips.

I took her hand in mine, gently slipped off her fake wedding rings. Removed my gold band, flexing my newly bare fingers.

Then I closed them in her palm. Tapped back into that sense of power and control I'd felt back at Victoria's mansion, harnessing it into words that were pure and unfiltered. Delilah and I had the ability to turn the page, start fresh with a new chapter. Whatever happened next, I knew that my honesty was the only way forward.

"Can I tell you what I'm noticing?" I asked, like I was back at the McMasters Library, talking to a group of students.

She nodded. I was still holding her closed fist.

"I really love this job," I said. "And Abe being angry at us makes me feel like shit."

"Same here. Like total and complete shit."

I turned over my feelings in my mind. "I still...I still feel proud of what we did, though."

"Same here," she echoed. "Very proud. And so *happy*."

My thumb stroked over her knuckles. "Delilah, I thought what we did in that limo might get our sexual attraction to each other out of our systems. Some kind of release that would leave things between us friendly, but professional."

She took a step closer to me.

"I can see now that even entertaining that thought for a second makes me the world's biggest idiot."

"I thought the same thing," she admitted, looking almost shy. She took another step. Her feet slid between mine, hands on my chest.

"Can I be brutally honest with you right now?" I asked, voice rough.

"Please."

"I want you to come home with me."

Delilah placed a hand on her stomach—a gesture I now recognized. "When I was with Mark, I felt slowly roped into our relationship, like I was a rabbit being lured into a snare.

We'd meet up after work for drinks or dinner, and I'd feel bad the entire time. Weird and uncomfortable. I thought it was my body telling me it was wrong for us to break the rules, that after we both left the police force, it would feel better. But it was my body telling me it was being used."

Delilah gave me a long, lingering kiss. When she stepped back, her eyes were clear and sure. And then a huge smile spread across her face.

"What is your body saying now?"

"It's telling me to go home with you," she said.

The kiss I gave her was harder but no less sweet. Delilah gripped my lapels and let me kiss her breathless.

"I want to be clear," I said. I took the rings from her palm and dropped them weightlessly into my pocket. "I'm taking home Delilah *Barrett* tonight, not Delilah *Thornhill*. No more games, no more fantasies. I want *you*."

"No more husband," she said, head tilted.

I cupped her cheek and she kissed my palm.

"Like a date," I said.

An intense emotion shuddered across her face. I wondered if Abe's words were in the background of her mind the way they were for me—*if you betray my trust again, I will fire you.*

His coworkers dating behind his back would assuredly betray his trust, especially after what he'd experienced at the FBI.

Except I couldn't seem to want another way forward other than taking Delilah Barrett home with me. I was as sure of this as anything I'd ever felt in my entire life. She still hadn't answered me—but I wasn't trying to take her home under false pretenses, some lie to make her feel comfortable. Not after what had happened in her past.

"I'd like you to know my intentions, Delilah," I said softly.

"I'm not taking you home to fuck you. Although whatever you need, I'll give it to you."

Her pupils dilated, her body swayed into mine.

"I'm taking you home to spend more time with you. Talk, eat, cook, nap...whatever we want."

"Yes," she said simply. Boldly. "I'd like that very much."

45

HENRY

*D*elilah Barrett was standing in my living room, craning her neck to take in the sheer number of books in my house.

I was attempting to make my house as comfortable as humanly possible. Like most row homes in Rittenhouse Square, I had an old brick fireplace with a mantle, low ceilings, built-in bookshelves. An oversize couch dominated the space, with books and blankets strewn across it. As I stacked wood and flipped the kettle on, Delilah peered at the novels spilling over from every flat surface.

"Why am I not surprised that Henry Finch lives in a house filled with books?" she said, smiling over her shoulder. "How do you organize them?"

"The Dewey Decimal System."

"Really?"

"No," I chuckled. I grabbed two giant mugs. "They're arranged however they'd like to be arranged. At home, I'm less librarian, more avid reader."

Delilah picked up a worn copy of *Bel Canto* by Ann Patchett, flipped through the pages. Her expression shifted from mild curiosity to real interest.

"Do you want that book?" I asked, leaning against the entry to my kitchen. I liked watching her examine the intimate corners of my home—even after our night of running and jumping and limo-sex, she was exquisite in her gown—a statuesque beauty surrounded by dusty bookshelves.

"I was never a big reader, you know," she said. But she kept flipping.

"It's about a hostage situation and an opera singer."

She clutched it to her chest like a beloved stuffed animal.

"Take it," I said.

"I'll borrow it," she clarified.

"Books are meant to be given away. It needs a new owner."

The fire kicked up, and as I watched the water boil in the kettle, I noticed her limp.

"Sit," I said, pointing at the couch. She sank into the cushions with a grimace. I knelt in front of her, shifted all those gauzy layers until I found her feet, which were red and swollen against the straps of her stilettos.

"Side effects of doing this job," she shrugged.

But when I touched her ankle, she winced again.

"How often do you let people take care of you, Delilah Barrett?" I unhooked the leather strap on her right foot. Gently worked it open and away from her skin.

"Not often," she replied. "My dads always said I was the most self-sufficient child they'd ever met. From ten years old, I was taking care of myself. Not because they weren't there. But just..."

"Because you wanted to?" I held her foot steady, slid the shoe off in what I hoped was the least painful way possible. Our eyes stayed locked together—she didn't wince. I kissed her ankle, the top of her foot. Pressed my thumb into the ball and she let out an actual purr.

"I didn't need much as a kid," she said. "The woods, a good game of capture the flag with my siblings. Going on hikes with my dads."

I wanted to ask her how she'd become a police officer, but I was carefully removing her left shoe—and when her arches touched my hardwood floor, she wiggled her toes and let out a luxurious sigh. She might have been exquisite in that gown, but I knew what she needed next.

"Wait right here," I said, pressing a mug of tea into her hands. As I walked upstairs to my room, Delilah was cozying up on the couch, hands in front of the flames. She seemed content, relaxed. A minute later, I'd tossed on gray sweatpants and a white undershirt.

"I come bearing gifts," I said.

She held up a Penn sweatshirt that was five times her size. "Pajamas?"

I shrugged, rubbed the back of my head.

"Everything I ever wanted," she said. She kissed me on the cheek and turned around. "Will you unzip me?"

"Of course," I murmured. I kept my touch light and friendly as her dress peeled away from her skin. She stepped out of it like Botticelli's Venus, ascending from the shell—all pale white skin, glowing with firelight. I wanted to press my mouth to her shoulder blades, kiss her bare back. But though the moment was erotic, it felt more emotionally intimate than sexual. Still facing the fire, Delilah dropped the sweatshirt over her head.

It came to her knees. She rolled the sleeves up four times until it almost uncovered her fingers.

"How do I look?"

Delilah turned—bare legs, the curve of her breasts visible

through the fabric, hair mussed. Seeing her in my clothing caused a possessive feeling to stir low in my belly. It was arousal, but also a feeling of deep, protective yearning.

"Very elegant."

She ran a hand through her hair, messing it up even more. Then she sank back down on the couch with her tea.

I pulled her feet into my lap. "How are your feet, Warrior Princess?"

"Freya calls me Xena sometimes." She grinned cheekily, sliding up the sweatshirt to show me she was still wearing the garter belt. I swallowed a growl and pushed my thumb hard into her foot, massaging first one, then the other.

Delilah let out a heavy, gratified sigh and sank back onto the pillows. "They feel a lot better now. That was a lot of sprinting through hallways in four-inch heels."

I bent my head over, kissed the top of each knee. "You're a beautiful bad-ass."

"You're a very handsome bad-ass," she replied.

The fire *popped* and hissed. She watched me over the rim of her mug. Beneath my fingers, her muscles relaxed. I caressed her ankle, rubbed the knots in her calf muscles. She made that purring sound again.

"Would you do this for me every night?"

She appeared to be teasing, but I said "Absolutely," and meant it.

"Delilah?"

"Mmmm," she hummed.

"Would you tell me the rest of your Mark story?"

She nodded, watching the flames for a minute as I kissed every single one of her toes.

"The unit I was assigned to that year, the burglary unit, was full of corruption. The leadership had been crooked for years. Mark was a sergeant, but it was obvious to anyone that knew him he was nothing but ambition. I think, if you asked him now, he's probably vying for the mayoral seat. But at the time he wanted nothing more than to be the Police Commissioner."

"Was it harder working in such a corrupt office?"

She blew out a breath. "I barely noticed. I mean—" She grimaced here. "I did notice. Misuse of funds, romantic relationships, nepotism... The office was crawling with it. But I was a new officer and was given my own cases, which I worked dutifully. I followed leads, tracked down suspects, arrested them. I felt secure, happy, *eager* to do a good job."

I remembered what she'd admitted the other night—that her obvious eagerness might have been the reason Mark had gone after her.

"There was always this political talk about 'cleaning up our unit' but never any action behind the words." She shrugged, sipped her tea. "I kept my head down and did the job I was honored to do."

I encircled her ankle with my fingers. "I've been there before," I confessed.

That seemed to bring her a measure of relief. "Mark and I began our relationship about a year into my post there."

I tried—and failed—to keep an irrational sense of jealousy at bay.

"It lasted about a month. First meetings that became friendly, flirtatious. Emails that were not appropriate. Text messages. He was older than me and had a charm that worked on a lot of people in that office. I felt special that he singled me out for his private affections." Her jaw clenched, and I wanted to kiss away the tension there.

"Bernard used to call me his 'young successor', especially in front of an audience, or people that I was impressed with," I said. "I think now it was a way to guarantee my trust, endear me to him. It was one of the reasons why I didn't want to believe he was a thief."

"It's how they soften you up." Her smile was grim.

"Yes, it is."

She seemed plagued by something, eyes mournful. I kissed her toes again, her ankles, the first few inches of her calves. Worship was my intention. I did that, over and over, until a smile ghosted across her face.

"Mark is...was...a slimy egomaniac and I knew it. Deep down, I knew it. But he was already drawing me in, and every time he noticed me pulling away, he'd amp up the romantic gestures. Weekend trips, romantic getaways, gifts."

I kept massaging her feet, hoping the relaxation would make her feel safe.

"And all of this was happening against this backdrop of corruption in our unit. There were articles being written up about some of my colleagues in Philly's local papers. My fathers were very concerned that I'd landed in hot water. But I was 'in love' and didn't care."

"Were you really in love?" I asked.

"No, not at all." She watched my fingers wrap around her ankles. "Not even a little bit. Which makes this next part so awful."

I was silent, watching her collect her thoughts. "Our relationship was very much against the rules. I knew, if we got caught, especially with how prominently our office was being investigated, there'd be hell to pay. Mark wanted us to come clean and both quit on the same day so that we could be together."

My stomach clenched at what I knew came next in her story.

"The night before Mark asked me to..." Delilah swallowed. "To delete our emails and texts to each other. As a sign of trust. So that if they found out about our relationship, the evidence couldn't be used against us."

The look that crossed her face destroyed me. I reached across the couch, wrapped my arms around her waist, and dragged her into my lap. She came willingly—but not without a bemused arch of her brow.

"You were too far away," I said.

I settled her against my chest, stroking her back. She felt cozy in my sweatshirt, bare legs tucked beneath her.

"So I deleted them. Every last one of them."

I kissed her hair.

"I went to work the next day with my resignation letter. When I came in, Mark was there and I just...I just *beamed* at him like an idiot. He was with our HR rep, and the look he gave me was disgusted. Almost *afraid*. Although he was playing it up for the rep in the room." She pulled at my shirt, twisting it between her fingers. "Mark, as my supervisor, had the very hard task of firing me. And in front of that rep, he said it was because I had pursued him romantically against his wishes. He even had the emails from me to prove it. Emails that he hadn't returned, of course."

My hands tightened into fists. I relaxed them, held her close instead.

"He said to the rep, 'I don't want to make this about age or gender, but this isn't the first time a young female detective has latched herself to a superior officer. It does happen.'"

"I wish you'd stilettoed his face *and* broke his dick that night we saw him," I murmured into her hair.

"There's still time," she said. "Anyway, that was Mark's plan all along. The first step was finding a willing victim and orchestrating a relationship. The second was to smear me through the press, which he did."

"What do you mean?"

"There were articles about me, opinion pieces. Every asshole on talk radio on the local stations proclaimed me the Jezebel of police officers, attempting to seduce my boss to get promoted—a nickname that *Mark* gave me in one of the interviews. I became the symbol of corruption in that unit, even though with the exception of Mark, my record was spotless and my case close rate was impeccable. All of this was happening while I was up north, with my dads. One of the beautiful things about growing up out there is that internet is hard to come by, and the local one-sheet printed in that town was more concerned about the bear population than anything occurring in the 'big city.' All of it hit me hard the first two weeks, but then I fled to the wilderness, basically."

"What did your dads say?" I asked.

"Well, they didn't say *I told you so,* which made me love them even more. They were furious on my behalf and they let me cry a lot and stare out the window. After a few days of that, they put me to work."

Delilah actually smiled at that memory.

"Tell me more," I urged.

"I was a tag-along ranger with them for two months," she continued. "No running down criminals. No paperwork or bureaucracy. It was a simple job, but hard work. The kind that knocks you out at night so you sleep—makes it hard to lay awake thinking about the mistakes you've made."

"Ah," I said, "that's a very specific kind of insomnia I'm familiar with."

Delilah slid her fingers through my hair.

"What work did you do with your dads?" I asked.

"Checking in campers, cleaning up trails, filing licenses." She tilted her head. "I saved a baby bear from a trash can."

"You didn't," I teased.

"I *did*," she promised. "It's not uncommon. They get

trapped in them all the time. The mama was up in the trees, watching us as I held the can and my dads shimmied her out."

"Did she bite you?"

"Oh, no." She grinned. "She was terrified. That day..." She trailed off for a second. "That day was a real turning point for me."

The fire crackled and roared, bathing us in a comforting heat.

"The week I came back to Philadelphia, I allowed myself five minutes a day to read news about Mark, half-expecting it all to have blown over. It wasn't. His next steps were painting the entire experience as his dedication to *taking out the trash*."

My jaw tightened with anger.

"They promoted him after he rode the coattails of my dismissal. He's been getting promoted ever since." Delilah sat back so she could look at me. "I didn't fight it, Henry, and I could have. I didn't hire a lawyer. I didn't call him a liar or find proof of our completely legitimate relationship. I was too stunned to attack. I just..." She held her palms out. "Sat there."

"You know what I did the night I discovered Bernard," I said. "Sometimes our mind can't leap to the right connections in the middle of our world tearing itself in two."

"That is true," she murmured. "Although Freya was telling me about this case..."

"What case?"

"It's nothing." She shook her head. "Abe and Freya were pretty vital to this whole process too, as much as that day with the bear. When I was interviewing at Codex, I brought up Mark, put it all out there. I mean, any basic Google search would have told him, and I wanted my potential employer to hear my side of the story." A smile ghosted over her lips. "I'll always remember Abe telling me that he'd known Mark for years, they often showed up at the same political functions together when Abe was with the FBI."

I was already smiling. "What did he say?"

"That anyone with half a brain could tell that man was a pathological liar."

My smile expanded—so did hers. "He said I didn't have to explain myself at all. It's why Abe and Freya, it's why *Codex* has meant so much to me. When I first started at Codex, I was all fucked up. Doubting myself left and right. But with every case, I feel better. And *tonight?* Tonight it felt so *good* to be fucking *right*. It's the best I've felt in a long, long time."

"Even with Abe being this angry?" I asked.

She chewed her lip. "I know why he's angry. And I do feel bad about that. You can probably already tell that Abe is the kind of boss who deserves loyalty and respect. But we made the right decision, Henry. No one can convince me otherwise."

I pressed our foreheads together until our breathing synced up: inhale, exhale. "I agree with you. And I want you to know how sorry I am that Mark used you like that." The words felt paltry on my tongue, but her eyes softened and glowed with light.

"It's nice to feel like I'm not...broken, somehow."

"Nothing about you is broken, Delilah." My voice was an urgent plea.

She traced the outline of my cheeks, my jaw, with just her fingertips.

"You know, I would stiletto Bernard in the face too if you wanted," she said. "Free of charge." She raised her fists to her face in a flash.

"Slow down, Xena." I kissed both hands. "Not necessary. Tonight made me believe for the first time in months that justice is coming his way. Maybe Mark's too."

"I hope so," she said. "And I can take Bernard."

"I don't doubt it."

She wrapped her arms around my neck and settled herself more firmly onto my lap. I squeezed her ankles, smoothed my hands up to her knees, over her thighs, beneath the sweatshirt. Gripped her slim hips.

Her eyelids drooped as she leaned in to kiss me.

"Delilah," I said against her mouth, "you're exhausted."

"I know," she said, frustrated. "But you're too sexy for your own good, newbie."

I stood straight up, holding her tight around my waist. "You should talk." I nipped her jaw. "And we both need sleep."

When I'd wanted to take Delilah to bed, I hadn't entirely pictured us *actually* going to bed. But after weeks of sleepless nights and the sudden evaporation of adrenaline from my bloodstream, I felt like a zombie. My warm, soft bed—with Delilah beneath the covers—was suddenly something I craved more than my next breath. I carried her up the stairs like that, and by the time I made it to my bedroom, she was already dozing softly against my neck.

With control, I lowered her into my bed—like I expected, my body reacted strongly to the sight of her there, nestled between my covers. But all of it could wait until the morning.

I reached behind me, pulled off my tee-shirt, and slipped beneath the covers. I wrapped myself around Delilah's body and inhaled the scent of wildflowers in her hair.

"We got the book back, Henry," she said drowsily. "Not bad for your first job in the field, huh?"

There was a long silence—and then we were both laughing again, delirious from lack of sleep and waning adrenaline.

"Yeah," I chuckled, kissing the back of her neck. "It was okay, I guess."

A warning beat a steady drum in the back of my mind —*what are you going to do about all of this tomorrow?*

But it was drowned out by the comforting hum of city noise, the soft caress of covers, the perfect fit of Delilah's body in mine.

"We got the book back," I repeated.

46

DELILAH

I woke up to a wall of solid muscle, to strong arms holding me like a cherished object as I slept.

Henry.

My eyelids fluttered open. The sun was rising over the skyline, shimmers of light beginning to invade Henry's dark bedroom. I had no idea of the exact time and found I didn't care. I'd slept so deeply last night my only memory was Henry pulling the covers around us both. The sleepy end of our conversation. And then nothing.

Unburdening myself to him had brought me a relief I felt in my chest—a dancing lightness. I was used to feeling embarrassed—that awful shame—as I told the story. But I knew what Henry had experienced with Bernard, knew that he'd understand the way I'd been manipulated, blindly led from one mistake to the next. He wouldn't judge me.

And he didn't.

Instead, he fed me tea and massaged my feet and the words spilled from me easily. There was no fear in sharing a part of my past with this man I'd come to trust so fully. Only strength and a real acceptance; an understanding that I could only get better from here.

In fact, the only feeling I could realistically tap into as my body awoke from its slumber was lust.

Henry's naked chest was at my back—I could feel the heat of his skin through the sweatshirt I wore. During the night, he'd kept the lower halves of our bodies a respectful distance apart. I shifted myself back six inches or so and was rewarded with his cock, pressed against my ass. A cock that was hard and thick, even at this early hour.

I gripped the pillow and allowed myself to indulge in the memory of Henry fucking me like a wild animal on the floor of that limo; the way his cock had stretched and filled me so deliciously; the nerve endings that sprang to life beneath his skilled thrusts. Before I could stop, I gave a circular grind against his lap and moaned softly.

My eyes popped open, afraid I'd woken him.

And I had—because in the next second, Henry's arm around my waist was tucking me snugly against him. His fingers sifted the hair from my ear as he kissed me.

"Good morning, Warrior Princess," he said, voice raspy with sleep. "Did you sleep well?"

And then he thrust his cock between my ass cheeks. It was not a movement with sleepy, early-morning intentions. It had *purpose*.

"Ye—yes," I sighed. He did it again, holding my hips steady as he rolled against me. I pushed back shamelessly, and he scraped his teeth down my neck. "How about...how about...you?"

"I was dreaming about you."

He continued to roll his hips as his palm slipped beneath the sweatshirt and traveled up my stomach. Henry cupped one of my breasts, and we both made a raw, guttural sound.

My nipple pebbled against his skin; his thumb teased it, over and over.

"What about?" I panted. I was working my ass against his cock as firmly as he was dry-fucking it—half my mouth pressed into the pillow.

"Fucking you with my mouth."

"*Yes*," I whispered.

Henry pinched my nipple lightly, and I almost tore the pillow in half.

"In my dream, I ate your pussy for hours on end." His cock was sliding in and out through my ass cheeks—and even separated by barriers of fabric, it was igniting sparks of pleasure *everywhere*. "I couldn't get enough of your taste."

Henry stopped his ministrations, and I pleaded for him to continue. But he was only pausing to shove me onto my back. He sat back on his knees in front of me—nothing but sweatpants and the incredible outline of his cock through the thin material. His chest was lean muscle, stomach strong, brown skin and dark hair. His shoulders seemed even broader like this, arms roped with strength.

"Take that off," he commanded, eyes as predatory as I'd ever seen them.

I did, even as my fingers trembled, then lay back against the warm, soft sheets in nothing but my underwear.

Henry's eyes closed for a second, like he was in physical pain. When they opened, his expression was primal, body vibrating. I could see the effort it was taking for him to restrain himself.

I was getting off on it. I was getting off on the fact that I'd pushed this brilliant, respectful academic past his breaking point—that he was pure sexual need, and nothing else.

"Delilah, are you sure?"

"Yes," I promised. "Yes, yes, yes."

"If you give me this, I'll take it all," he said, voice low. "I'll take everything."

I didn't give a single fucking thought to our jobs, Codex, or anything past fucking this godlike man who sat in front me.

I sat up, gripped his cock. Gave him a rough stroke that had him shuddering for breath. "Good," I said, voice silky. "Because I want it all."

His palm landed on my chest. He shoved me back, prowled up my body with obvious focus. His mouth captured mine in a hot, hungry kiss that had me arching off the bed. His lips moved down my jaw, licked along my throat. Henry kissed the edges of my collarbone, worshipped the valley between my breasts. With a strangled sigh, he took the entirety of my breast in his mouth, and covered the other with his palm, rolling the nipple around and around. His tongue flattened, sucking and pulling as I gripped the back of his head and held him in place.

The beginning of an orgasm was already fluttering deep inside of me—I could feel my internal walls clenching as Henry caressed and licked my nipples like we had all the time in the world. He tongued the swell of my breast, scraped his teeth along my ribcage.

Then his teeth traveled to my other breast, tugging the nipple gently.

"Oh, *fuck*," I said, hips thrusting brutally. The pinch of pain and swirl of pleasure had me half out of my mind.

"Do you like that, beautiful?" he murmured against my skin.

"I fucking love it."

He responded with a harder bite, using his teeth with devious intent, alternating with cooling breaths and gentle laps of his tongue. He took long, hard pulls of the greedy peaks, again and again, and I was grinding myself against his cock mindlessly, driven by friction and his talented mouth.

I caught him staring up at me as he fluttered his tongue against the tip, lapped at it.

I wasn't going to make it. Ten minutes in and Henry was destroying me. My moans were already bordering on a wail— it felt extra illicit not having to mute my obvious pleasure from security guards or bodyguards or limo drivers. Henry wasn't quiet either—his deep, rough groans were sending goose-bumps ricocheting up my spine.

When he began shifting his mouth down my body, my hips went wild. Henry's laugh was almost menacing—a dark tease. Wet, open-mouthed kisses moved down my stomach, my hips, my thighs. When he dragged my underwear down my legs, he growled so loudly he had to bite my inner thigh. Henry gripped my knees, thumbs stroking the sensitive skin there. He pushed them roughly to the bed, exposing me. Even Henry couldn't seem to tease any longer—his head descended between my legs and he inhaled me like a man consumed with lust.

Henry's head was between my thighs.

Every semi-coherent thought felt like it took three seconds to penetrate the rational part of my brain. And I'd been right. Having his focused intensity on my body evoked a deeply satisfying pleasure that seemed to only heighten by the minute. I felt deeply cherished by his thoughtful attention to my every desire.

I also felt deeply debauched. A panting, hungry woman who'd do anything to get fucked.

His rough palm scraped up my stomach until he reached my nipple, pinching it hard, a delicious cut of pain that had me arching again. His breath feathered over my clit in short bursts, then he rubbed just his lips, up and down. Mimicking the motion with his fingers at my nipple. I cupped my other breast, watched our hands working together to pinch and tweak as he caressed my clit with his closed mouth.

Henry's tongue landed on my clit.

Light exploded across my vision. But I kept my eyes open, locked on his. He held my gaze, dipped his finger inside my pussy and lapped his tongue against my clit like it was a dish he wanted to slowly, sweetly lick clean.

We were made for each other, primed to respond only to each other. Every time I neared the edge, he backed off, lightened his strokes. I'd never had a man stare so soulfully into my eyes as he licked me, never had a man beg me to come this way. But his tongue was a devil, never letting me get close, fluttering in light, intricate circles. I was a gasping, pleading mess of raw nerves—a writhing body, slick with sweat and arousal.

A second finger hooked inside me, and I wailed Henry's name. I needed *more*. More *pressure*, more *tongue*, more *everything*.

I reached down and wrapped my fingers around the back of his head, stilling him. And dragged my pussy against his tongue, fucking his face for one shameless second.

"You want harder, Delilah?" he said in that sinful voice.

I rotated my hips again, sliding his tongue up the length of my folds. Henry groaned and sat back on his knees and lifted the entire lower half of my body clear off the bed. My legs wrapped around his shoulders, arms thrown back over my head—and I was fucking floating. Floating through a sea of sensations that kept climbing...*climbing...climbing*. I was outright screaming now as he lashed my clit with deliberate movements, thrust his fingers with brutal efficiency. My eyes filled with tears, my core tightened, my pussy clenched and clenched and then...

Euphoria.

I soared somewhere I'd never been before—a place I never wanted to leave. Henry's talented, focused ministrations took me to a blinding climax that sent tears streaking down my cheeks.

And instead of letting me down gently, he curled his tongue against my clit and ignited a second orgasm that electrified my senses. It took me ages to come back into my body; ages before Henry lowered me down softly; ages before I realized Henry was holding me to his chest and stroking my hair.

I opened my eyes to find him staring at me with such a satisfying blend of carnal hunger and tenderness. I beamed up at him like a lovesick fool.

"You're beautiful when you come," he whispered.

I responded by sliding my hands up the hard ridges of his stomach. Dragged my tongue up the center of his body and his breathing hitched. Between my legs, his cock was hard as steel. When I reached his nipple, I flattened my tongue, and he fisted his fingers in my hair.

"I want you to feel what I just felt," I murmured.

Henry had a lean, beautiful musculature that looked carved, sculpted—like a statue in the museums he loved to study. I flipped him over, snagged the waistband of his sweatpants between my teeth, and pulled them all the way down. His cock jutted up and out like the filthiest dream. My mouth watered, fingers moving up his thighs. My tongue landed at the base, and I licked it all the way up.

His fingers tightened in my hair, yanking my mouth back before I could suck.

"Delilah." He was up on his elbows, abs flexing.

"Yes, Henry?" I teased, hand gliding up his shaft. So silky, so smooth, so big.

"Your mouth...it's too...too fucking good."

Henry Finch was coming undone, and it was the hottest thing I'd ever seen.

"Just a taste," I pleaded. "Just one."

I swirled my tongue at the tip, and his hips flexed off the bed, took him between my lips and lowered them as far as I could. Henry let out a strangled, desperate groan that had another orgasm calling my name from the sounds alone, the masculine taste of him, his fingers in my hair. He was out of control, head back, chanting, "*Delilah*." The syllables had never sounded so filthy and depraved. I let Henry fuck my mouth, let him use my wet tongue the way he needed. My movements grew more frantic, pace frenzied—the closer he crept toward climax, the closer I got to my own.

With a half-roar, Henry twisted my hair and pulled me up.

And had me facedown on the mattress, legs spread, eyes covered.

I felt his mouth dip to my ear. "I'm going to fuck you, Delilah."

My hands ripped at the sheets. I couldn't quite see Henry, not yet, which had my body primed in anticipation. His hands slid around my waist, over my ass cheeks, spreading them. His mouth was on the curve of my ass, drifting down my folds to lick his tongue inside me.

I cried out, bucked against his lips as he tongue-fucked me. One hand slid up my spine to land at the base of my neck, holding me in place. There was the tell-tale sound of a condom—and the head of his cock was pressing right at my entrance. I tilted my hips, allowing him greater access. He pushed inside me, inch by inch. I screamed into the mattress. Henry went deep.

And then deeper.

And then so fucking deep I had to bite my hand. He was completely still, letting me get used to his size. I was burning up, already on the edge. He slid all the way out. Then all the way back in.

Right over my G-spot.

"Oh my god," I moaned. "Henry, it's... Oh my god, do that again."

His weight dropped carefully on top of me—my back to his chest. His hands landed on either side of my head, muscles of his forearm bunching as he fucked into me again. A slow, steady rhythm that had me panting.

"More," I said. "Henry, more."

His mouth landed at my ear again.

"I'll give you everything you desire, Delilah," he rasped.

He speared his fingers in my hair and pulled. And thrust into me with force.

"It's a privilege to bring you pleasure." He clamped down on the spot between my neck and shoulder, pinning my hips down with his. The angle was deliciously deep as he twisted the strands of my hair.

Henry kissed my neck, licked along my jaw, and fucked me in all the dirty ways I'd always fantasized about. I turned my forehead to the bed, stretched my arms out farther—feeling that wonderful combination of cherished and debauched again. The sensations building inside of me layered, grew, heated my lower belly. Tears were rolling down my cheeks from the exquisite sensations, Henry's steady thrusts.

His arm banded around my waist, and he lifted, sitting me backward on his lap and driving his cock into me. I screamed his name, head lolling back on his chest so he could continue kissing my throat. He reached down and yanked my knees wide, flattening two fingers right against my clit. Our bodies were slick with sweat, our chests heaving.

"Ride me, Delilah," Henry commanded in my ear. "Chase it. Take what's yours."

I snapped my hips, taking his cock deep, placed my hand over his as he rubbed my clit. His other hand landed on my breast, where I entwined our fingers—holding Henry, holding me, giving us both what we needed. My final orgasm stole my breath with unabashed speed, blackened my vision, robbed my body of strength.

I let everything pour out of me—my fears, my anxiety, my nerves, my guilt. Nothing about Henry and me being together could possibly be wrong.

Henry came with a rough grunt, a grateful moan—tilting my face and kissing me until I was sighing. My tears landed on his fingers. He wiped them away. Kissed my temple, caressed my hair. Our hearts slowed, our breathing slowed. And the sudden realization I'd been avoiding came racing up through my sex-muddled thoughts.

Henry Finch—sexy librarian, newest coworker, partner, fake husband—was the man I was falling for.

47

HENRY

"Chocolate chip or blueberry?" I held up each ingredient to Delilah's inscrutable expression.

She rocked her head back and forth. Tapped her chin. "Chocolate chip."

I gave her a sloppy kiss on the cheek. "My kind of girl."

She giggled, swinging her legs on the island. After epic, life-changing sex, I'd dragged her to my kitchen for breakfast. We were starving and in desperate need of coffee. While she prepped the pot, I brought down batter, eggs, homemade maple syrup. Flicked on burners and greased skillets.

I was making Delilah Barrett breakfast in my warm, sunny kitchen. It felt so marvelous to enjoy each other in the light of day—not in some utility closet or in the shadows of a room. Not secret, hidden, or fake. It gave real credence to whatever was happening between us—the trust, the opening, the passion. We were barefoot in my kitchen, hair mussed, limbs loose and relaxed.

It wasn't hard for me to crave this as my reality.

Delilah had scrubbed her heavy makeup off and tossed on my white tee-shirt. She was naked underneath. I put the

329

skillet down, wrapped my fingers in the shirt, and pulled her toward me.

"I like you here," I said against her mouth, kissing her.

She kissed me back, laughing. "I like being here."

I let her go—reluctantly—and went back to work cooking us pancakes. She poured me a cup of coffee before wandering over to the wall of photos I'd framed and hung the first weekend I moved back.

"What are all of these places?" she asked.

Without looking, I said, "Oxford, various places in England. Ireland, France, Prague, Spain. There's a photo of Rome too."

"Henry the nomad?"

"That's pretty accurate," I said, dropping chocolate chips into the batter. "The McMasters Library was my longest placement for more than ten years. But before that, I bounced around libraries all through Europe and the United Kingdom. Traveled most weekends for a while."

"And this is your family?" I glanced at that one—it was taken at Christmas on one of my rare trips home for the holidays. My parents and I, with Joelle and Jeremiah, were posed in front of a lit-up City Hall.

"That's them."

Her eyes were scanning each picture with frank interest. "Your siblings look moments away from inciting mischief."

"I think after that shot was taken, they had all of us ice skating. We were a mess. But, as usual, they made it fun. I see them now every Sunday at Sabrina's Cafe for weekly brunch."

She hopped back up on the island. "It's funny the things we miss when we live far away from those we love. Some days, I seriously contemplate driving the five hours to my dads' house just for Sunday dinner."

"I understand that feeling," I replied. We cooked and

sipped in silence for a minute before I said, "Can I ask you something I've been wondering this whole time we've known each other?"

"Sure," she said. "Have at it."

"How did a rural tree-climber end up being a Philadelphia police officer?"

I slid a bowl of blueberries her way. She popped one in her mouth. Thought for a moment.

"I abhor missing things," she said. "Almost as much as I abhor the thieves who made them missing. When I was a kid, the few neighbors we had would stop by for local gossip. Toss out that they lost their cat or their keys or their wedding rings. The thought of it made me *itchy*. Unbalanced. So I started a detective agency when I was ten."

I turned at that. "You were like...the Nancy Drew of your small town?"

Her lips curved. "Yeah. I guess that's a good comparison. My dads helped me make a sign that had little slips of paper at the bottom with our phone number. It had my school picture in the middle and it said *You've lost it? I'll find it.*" She was laughing a little at the memory, hair blazing with the morning light from the window. It was like a halo of fire. "We put them up at church, the one diner, my school, the library. I had a decent list of customers until I went off to college."

The pancakes sizzled on the griddle as I flipped them. "Give me an example of a case."

"Well..." She thought for a second. "My first one was Betsy. She lived on a farm a half mile from the state park. She was constantly losing her keys, so on a whim, she called me. I think she thought it was cute, you know? She'd known me since my dads brought me home, used to babysit me and my siblings from time to time. But I fucking found them."

My brow lifted. "How?"

"I interviewed the whole family and did an assessment of Betsy's movements and daily activities. She had a Monday through Friday purse, but also a weekend purse. It was Wednesday, and she'd lost the keys on a Tuesday." Delilah shrugged. "She never thought to look in that weekend purse."

"Brilliant," I said.

"Why, thank you." She gave a mock bow before eating another blueberry. "It piqued my interest in criminal justice, and as soon as I started my classes at Temple, here in the city, I was hooked. Plus it fit very neatly into the way I viewed the world."

I held out my hands, mirroring her pose from that night we'd discussed justice at the VIP event. "Good and evil."

"Yes." She smiled. "And you look like you want to say something, husband."

I slid warm pancakes from the griddle, glanced over my shoulder at her. "I'm not your husband anymore, Delilah."

Her cheeks grew pink. "Oh, that's right."

"I'm teasing you," I said, giving her a plate of pancakes. "You know I like it."

I kissed her again. She tasted like dawn and fresh coffee. "And I was only going to ask if you'd shifted your opinion on that a little?"

Delilah carefully cut into her breakfast, ate a piece, gave a husky moan that sent my heart racing.

"Don't try and distract me."

She smirked, ate another piece. "These are delicious."

"Thank you."

"And, um..." She peered out the window. "Maybe. When we saw Victoria through that painting and Sven told her we were the ones who had broken in to the passageways, I felt *guilty*."

I nodded, drizzled syrup across my plate. "Bernard is probably the world's greatest book thief, but he was also a great academic. Victoria will buy anything just to buy it, even if it's stolen. And she's also donated millions of dollars to improve literacy."

"I dated my superior officer, even though I knew it was against the rules," she said, but without the sadness of last night.

"And I withheld evidence of Bernard's crimes because I was blinded by my admiration for him."

The weight of all of that *gray area* hung between us in the kitchen. Delilah sipped her coffee, narrowing her eyes at me over the rim.

"I'm still thinking about it," she said. "But—yes, I think...I might be. Did you feel a little guilty when we saw Victoria?"

I blew out a breath. "There was a moment when she was saying goodbye to us, flitting back into the crowd. I wondered if it was going to be the last time we'd ever see her, and the knowledge of that felt sad and anticlimactic. I realized how much I..."

"You what?"

"How much I like that kooky heiress."

"I feel that too," she admitted. "All of this is entirely new for me, by the way."

"Why did you feel guilty then?" I asked.

"We convinced her we were her friends. She shared confidences with me. We built a relationship, however quickly, on mutual trust, and we betrayed it. Even though she's a criminal. I've never felt that way before. I think you're making me soft."

"And I think you're making me more bloodthirsty," I admitted. "If we'd had the time, I would have taken those stolen books myself and marched right to the FBI."

This is why we make such great partners, I wanted to say. But that would mean bringing up work—the great unknown—and shattering our morning happiness seemed like a travesty.

"I've turned you into a real detective, Henry Finch." She wiped chocolate from her mouth. Before she could lick it away, I stepped across the floor, grabbed her wrist. Stepped between her spread legs and sucked her finger between my lips. Her eyes danced with mischief.

"Delicious," I repeated.

Delilah hooked her legs around my waist, tugging me close. "Did you want to be a librarian when you were a little kid?"

"I did," I said, settling my hands on her hips. "Without books, I would have been a real lonely kid. Joelle and Jeremiah had tons of friends, and you know my parents worked constantly because of their jobs. Books were my escape—to different worlds, different universes. I could be a Viking or an archer, go back in time or see a distant future. And libraries held the key to all of that." I marveled at the flecks of green shining in her eyes. "If libraries didn't exist, where would we go to discover all the worlds we haven't traveled to yet?"

Delilah fairly beamed at that, until a shadow crossed her face. "I'm sorry Bernard took that from you."

I gave her neck an open-mouthed kiss. She shivered. "The more time I spend at Codex, the more time I spend with *you*, Delilah—the more I realize he can only take what I allow him to take."

An understanding flooded her expression at that. She cupped my face and brought our mouths together in a sweet and silly kiss that still left me filled with longing.

She went to pull away, but I scooped her forward with a low growl, let our mouths open together, our tongues sweep, my fingers splay across her ass. It was a lazy, chocolate morning kiss; it was hot coffee and sunrise and the intimacy of bare feet.

Her legs tightened on my waist, and I dragged my palms up her back to gather in her hair. A breathy moan escaped her lips as I kissed along her jawline. Down her neck. Right along her collarbone...

Delilah's cell phone rang out in the silence. Without breaking the kiss, she reached across the island and flipped it over.

"Fuck, it's Abe," she said, touching her swollen lips.

I nodded with a grimace. "Put it on speaker."

She did, pulling her legs up and away from me.

"Hey," she answered, voice tentative. "Everything okay?"

"Good morning," Abe said crisply. "I've been trying to reach Henry all morning. Do you happen to know where he is?"

I rubbed a hand down my face. My phone was probably at the bottom of my bag, ignored since I'd brought Delilah home last night.

"Um... no," she said, brow furrowed. "But I can give him a ring. Maybe he's on a run or something. Is everything okay?"

I crossed my arms and leaned back against the counter.

"I need him to verify authenticity of the manuscript this morning. Francisco is so ecstatic about the recovery he's throwing an intimate VIP event tonight for special guests to get early eyes on the Copernicus."

"Oh," Delilah said. "That's good...I guess?"

"And he wants us all there, to celebrate." There was a long pause. "You'll be there?" It was more command than question.

"Of course," she said. "And I'll find Henry for you."

"Thank you," Abe said. Then he cut the call.

She placed the phone down. Cleared her throat awkwardly. "I should probably go so you can head to Codex."

Her cagey movements made me nervous. But she flashed me a flirtatious look. "Which is sad, since I had some ideas for that leftover chocolate." The kiss she gave me was much less sweet and much filthier. "I'll see you tonight, at this event?"

Was this how it was going to be now? Seeing Delilah in my kitchen—and then seeing her at work? Pretending we weren't falling for each other while still going undercover? Something wasn't sitting right, but Abe's orders to authenticate the Copernicus demanded my full attention.

"Of course," I said, squeezing our fingers together. "I'm already excited to see you there."

She blushed again—and it was so damn cute I wanted to press *pause* on this day, take her back to my bed, enjoy her luscious body for hours on end.

She slid off my counter.

"And what are you going to do?"

She threw a few jabs, bounced on her toes—blush disappearing as quickly as it appeared. "Off to spar at the gym."

"Do you need a fighting partner soon?" I asked.

"I don't know. I'm really looking for a partner that's *actually* a challenge?" She propped her fists on her hips with another smirk.

"Smart-ass," I said, nipping at her neck.

She squealed, danced away from me, as light on her feet as ever.

"Bring that fighting spirit tonight, newbie," she said, strolling up my stairs. My eyes lingered on her bare legs until they fully disappeared from view.

While my heart clamored against my ribcage like a tambourine—rattling around everything I once thought I knew.

48

DELILAH

*I*t'd been more than two weeks since the four of us had fled up these stairs, chasing a shared hunch that a book had been stolen. Now we stood in front of the Romanesque columns of the Franklin Museum and stared up at a banner that read: *Revolutions of Spheres: Copernicus and the Heliocentric Solar System.*

"The last time a first edition of this book was in the United States was more than thirty-five years ago," Henry told us. "This exhibit will be spoken of for a long time in the academic community."

"Good thing the book didn't disappear for good," Abe said briskly.

He'd been cooler than usual to Henry and me since we'd appeared in front of the steps. I knew his anger would blow over—it always did—but I couldn't help but feel those twinges of guilt over Victoria blossom into something more urgent when I looked at Abe and Freya. A desire to protect their trust in me at all cost.

And when I turned and caught Henry's eye, I knew where

that feeling stemmed from. But how could I keep that trust while falling for my partner?

We stepped into a museum teeming with people, the buzz of the audience high and excited. Henry and I were once again strolling through Philadelphia high society, but it was all different. *We* were different. And Henry seemed easily in his element as usual—I remembered that first night at the art gallery, watching him study each painting as if he wanted to decipher every one of its secrets. He was doing it now, examining each artifact, uncovering its hidden seams.

Freya already had two glasses of champagne and was pressing one into my hand. She'd grumbled about dressing up again—but cheered up considerably when I let her wear my garter belt of zip-ties.

"One hour," I teased, holding up my finger.

She rolled her eyes. "You know me so well." Freya nodded at the display shining in the middle of the room. "I still can't believe she really had it. Just like this, in her mansion, while 300 people milled about at a party."

"Victoria is the reason why Codex will never go out of business," Abe said pointedly. "There will always be people like Victoria who believe they deserve to steal a piece of history simply because they can."

"What's the word on her?" Henry asked. "Did she go underground, like Bernard?"

Abe shook his head. "The FBI scooped her up for questioning the morning after the party, thanks to some of the incriminating evidence you two uncovered. I submitted your photos to my contact at the Art Theft department as well as Francisco."

Henry gave me a small smile.

"All I know so far is she's hired the best criminal defense lawyer in the country."

I felt that twinge again, thinking of Victoria sitting in a prison cell. But my eyes landed on the book, and I remembered just how carelessly she'd gone about the whole ordeal —as Abe had said, how confidently she operated in the shadowy world of rare book theft. She appeared unconvinced that what she was doing was a crime, and people like that only ended up stealing and stealing until one day they were caught.

Good Victoria. Bad Victoria. She was effortlessly *both*.

"Can we go see it?" Henry asked.

Abe nodded, directing us toward the glass podium where a crowd was gathered around. A docent was quietly illuminating the audience with facts about the text, but I tuned him out, content to merely gaze at it. The gravity of the moment stunned all four of us into a shared silence. It was open to its seminal page—the science that posited the revolutionary theory that the planets of our solar system orbited the sun.

I studied the concentric circles, thought about all the tiny decisions and actions that set in motion the discovery of this theory; the hand printing of this specific book, the banning of it, the many people and hands who had owned it over the past 500 years.

Victoria stealing it.

And finally: Henry and I fleeing with it in the night, against all odds.

Henry couldn't contain the joy on his face. I watched him stand with Abe—he fit here, at Codex. He *belonged*.

"I know, in this field, it's easy to get caught up and captivated by people like Bernard or Victoria," Abe was saying softly, mostly to Henry. "They dominate the landscape with their privilege and their power. But at the end of the day, people will steal regardless of the legal implications. In the middle of it all, is the book."

"The book is the most important," Henry repeated, and I

could tell he really believed that. Even with his sudden interest in crime and punishment, he was a librarian at heart, would always be a librarian. That dedication would be the key to Codex's future success.

His eyes slid toward mine, and I wondered if he was thinking what I was—that in this vitally important moment, I wanted to hold his hand, kiss his wrist, lean against his body and have him caress my hair. I wanted us to celebrate as part-ners—professionally *and* romantically. The urge was so strong I had to plant my feet and lock my knees to keep from going to him.

"I don't like to repeat myself, as you know," Abe said. "But I think it goes without saying that you two pulled off our most successful recovery to date."

Henry nodded, hands in his pockets.

"Thank you," I said. "It was an honor. Henry's first case in the field."

"So what do you think?" Abe said. "Your three-month probationary period is up. Does Codex suit you?"

"Absolutely," he said, face brightening. "I'm not sure I can go back to being a librarian now."

"Yay!" Freya cheered. "Welcome to the team, Henry. Permanently."

I couldn't look at Henry now. I glanced back at the book, felt a surge of pride. And a surge of...what? What was it exactly?

"You kept the rings?" Abe said.

"Yep," I said, sounding nervous.

"Good." Abe studied the room, as if he could already sense our next case brewing in this room of high society and under-ground thieves. "I think the Thornhills might come in handy in the future. People love a married couple."

I gulped. I wasn't going to lie and say these weeks of dirty marital fantasies hadn't been part of the fun. But how was I supposed to *pretend* to be in love with Henry and then hide these feelings?

"You'll have to fight me for her, Henry," Freya said with mock ferocity.

"You'd win. Hands down," Henry said, chuckling into his drink. He seemed comfortable, relaxed.

Happy.

"I'm going to find a restroom," I said quickly. "Be right back."

I made my way through the crowd on shaky legs, leaning my back up against the wall that led to the bathrooms and taking a few rapid breaths. It was quiet and cool here, far from all the people.

"Delilah Barrett?"

I turned to find, of all people, Margaret Pierce. My former coworker who was going after Mark Davis.

"Margaret," I said, brow furrowed. "What are you...what on earth are you doing here?"

"I work security for the Franklin Museum now," she said, and I finally realized she was in uniform. "I can't believe you're *here*. I've been meaning to talk to you."

For a moment, I could only gape at her. Even after Freya had mentioned her website to me, I still felt like I was gazing at a unicorn—something magical that couldn't quite be believed.

"Freya told me about you," I finally said.

"I'm sorry?"

I shook my head. "My, um, my coworker. She found your website. You're looking for testimony. About Mark."

Margaret gave me a sweet smile, filled with the kind of understanding that exists between victims of the same crime. "I am. About a year after you left, Mark seduced me into a pretty intense relationship and fired me under the guise of—"

"Taking out the trash," I said, dazed.

Her lips pressed together. "Exactly. I was pretty important to the political campaign he was running at that time. 'Women like Margaret Pierce and Delilah Barrett have no right to hold the office of a public servant.'"

Anger boiled in my veins, white-hot and dangerous. "He said that?"

"In one of the many articles about me, yes." I could see pain in her expression, but also a purpose. A direction for all that fury.

"I know what he did to you," Margaret said gently. "And I think we have the potential for a case. That man shouldn't be allowed to hold public office. He is corrupt in every single way."

"I saw him at a party last week," I blurted out. "I threatened to stiletto him in the face."

Margaret glanced at my arms. "I have a feeling you could do that."

"How did he get to you?" I asked, suddenly desperate for details.

She leaned against the wall. "I was a rookie cadet. He wasn't my direct supervising officer, but we were in the same office building. I thought he was handsome, charismatic."

I nodded along, recognizing the beats of this story.

"There was another couple dating—in secret, technically, but also somewhat openly. It was causing a flurry of drama, people were worried about bad press again. I think he saw me as his next opportunity. He fired me and he fired the couple too, all three of us on the same day. All three of us were technically in violation of personnel policies...but in my instance, so was he."

"Margaret," I said, "he had me delete any evidence of our relationship, emails, text messages."

"I did the same." She tilted her head. "But I think we still have a chance. I know how hard it is to tell the story, over and over. How it takes a little piece of you every time."

I swallowed hard at that.

"But I want to at least try and fight him, even if it's painful. I need to at least *try*."

I finally returned her tentative smile. Remembered Henry's words from this morning: *he only takes what I allow him to take*. Hadn't I just proven that my instincts were intact? That I could reach out, trust, be vulnerable? Mark hadn't taken those things at all—he'd merely put them into hiding.

But I was a great detective. I'd recovered them. I'd raced through a dark hallway and taken out guards and protected my partner; had given myself up to hot limo-sex and beautiful intimacy and chocolate-chip pancakes with a man who made me happier than I'd ever thought possible. My instincts, my trust, my very *being* was still there, right where I'd left it.

"Will I be named in the paper, you think?"

"Not necessarily," she said. "But if you decide to use your name, then yes."

"Good," I said. "I want him to know it was me." I lifted my chin and Margaret squeezed my hand. "I'll do it."

"Thank you," she whispered. "You have no idea what this means to me."

"And to me," I said, squeezing back.

*F*reya found me in the hallway a few minutes after Margaret left.

"What happened?" she asked, noticing the look of shock on my face. But when I relayed what had happened—the strange, fateful meeting of two women who experienced the same crime—she merely took my hand and squeezed it, just like Margaret had.

She leaned against the wall and rested her shoulder against mine. Abe and Henry were perfectly framed for us in the distance—Henry talking animatedly over the glass case, Abe listening with mild bemusement.

"Are you upset?" she asked.

"No," I said. "No, I feel absolutely wonderful."

My heart was thudding against my chest the longer I watched Henry. I thought about all those tiny decisions that had led a five-hundred-year-old manuscript from its first printing, all the way back here.

Maybe there was another decision too—the real reason why I was standing here, watching Henry like a lovesick teenager.

"I have to tell you something," I started, "and I'm not quite sure what the solution is yet."

"You're falling for Henry."

I turned to her—she was looking at me with clever eyes. "Anyone ever tell you you're too smart?"

"All the time."

"You think Abe knows?"

"I doubt it," she said. "He's pretty dense when it comes to human relationships. And it's not like the two of you are *overly* obvious. But I did always think it was interesting that Victoria Whitney thought you were newlyweds that night at the art gallery."

I had forgotten all about that. What had she seen then that I was now discovering?

"I don't think...I don't think we can work together," I said. "Abe would never allow it."

Freya chewed on her bottom lip. "I think you're right."

I'd already come to this conclusion but hearing her confirm it still sent a bolt of disappointment through me.

"I'd do a lot of things for you, Delilah," she said, "but I can't keep this secret for you. And I can't protect you from Abe."

"I know. And I don't want to pursue this in secret. That makes it wrong, dirty, like what Mark did to me. I'd like to..." I trailed off, watched Henry staring at a handful of buttons beneath glass—some piece of clothing from the past. He saw their value, he understood the stories carried in on the dirt, the lives touched by each tiny bit of metal. "I'd like to fall in love with Henry out in the open."

Freya let out a long sigh at that. She looked...sad.

"I know," I said. "Things are going to change."

"I'm going to miss my partner," she said softly.

"I won't go far, promise," I said. "Still friends."

She beamed at that, tucking a strand of hair back into her bun. "I dig it. I guess I still need someone to eat donuts with every morning."

"I'm your girl," I winked.

But her eyes grew wider. "What are you going to do about it, though?"

"I have an idea," I admitted. A dozen lightbulbs were flaring to life in my brain the longer I admired my formerly fake husband. "But I need to be sure. By tomorrow, something will have happened. Can you keep a secret just for tonight?"

"Yes, I can," she said.

I watched her shove up her glasses with one finger. "Have you ever felt this strongly about another person before? Like it's all you can ever think about?"

"Strongly like you and Henry?"

I nodded.

Her smile was half-formed. "Once, back at Quantico, before I left."

Freya didn't speak much about that time in her life. I only knew the basics: she'd been a rising star at the FBI training academy, poised for greatness, until she'd left. Abe had apparently first met Freya while teaching at Quantico and had been so impressed with her natural skill set, he'd thought of her immediately when he founded Codex.

"Was this person...a boyfriend? Girlfriend?"

"Ugh, *worse*," she said. "He was my enemy."

Her nostrils flared, jaw clenched hard. Freya wasn't really the type of person who seemed to ever get angry—she was light-hearted, nerdy, funny. But as soon as she started speaking, her spine had gone rigid.

"Pushed your buttons that badly, huh?" I asked.

"In all kinds of ways." She shook her head. "So it was different, because I hated him. But there's a thin line between love and hate. I've been on the hate side, so I sort of get it. It changes you."

Henry's eyes caught mine easily in the crowd. I felt him calling to me, longing for me. Even in this crowded, public space, I could feel his *craving*.

I loved this job to the core of my being—but hadn't I loved eating chocolate-chip pancakes with Henry in his sunny kitchen just this morning? Or maybe it was okay that I loved both of these things equally. If I didn't, it wouldn't be a sacrifice.

"Whatever happens, we'll still have our taco stand," Freya said with mock seriousness.

I looped my arm through hers.

"Let's go mingle," I said, pulling us back toward the crowd.

Back toward my destiny.

50

HENRY

*D*elilah appeared serene and calm at the end of the evening—chatting with Freya, making small talk with the guests, peering at the exhibits. I had no idea what was going on behind those blue eyes of hers—and no idea if she'd ever tell me. According to Abe, we'd be fake married and on another case as soon the Thornhills were needed again.

I didn't know how the hell to feel about that. But I did know that standing around with my coworkers and pretending like I didn't want to kiss Delilah Barrett absolutely senseless felt *terrible.*

All four of us were leaving—standing at the top of the steps with the skyline glittering below—when Francisco found us, hands out in apology.

"Delilah," he said, grasping her hands. She arched her brow at him. "Please accept my deepest apologies for the things I said to you the other night. Completely unprofessional and highly unwarranted. Obviously, you knew what you were doing."

"She did," Abe said protectively. "Delilah is the reason we approached you that night."

"And the reason we got the book back at all," I inserted.

She flashed me a sly look. "I remember you having quite a hand in our success as well, Henry."

"*Both* of you," Francisco said, shaking his head. "I am embarrassed and ashamed. That's all I can say."

"Is payment being processed?" Abe asked.

"Of course."

"Then no more apologies are necessary."

I watched Delilah hide a smile behind her hand. But she shook Francisco's hand sincerely. "Tempers were high. We've all been there. It has been an honor being a part of this book's journey."

Francisco didn't look entirely convinced that he shouldn't *keep* apologizing. But then he startled us both by turning, clamping a hand on my elbow. "I didn't want to say this the other night. But I wanted to tell you how sorry I am about Bernard. He fooled us all."

My brow furrowed. "I'm sorry?"

The first time I'd met Francisco he'd indicated that he knew *of* me. *Because of Bernard Allerton.* But for what reason, he'd never said.

Francisco leaned in close to me and dropped his voice. "I know it's not entirely public knowledge, but word travels fast in the antiquarian community. You know that. I'm aware of what transpired between you and Bernard. Believe it or not, you were gaining quite the reputation yourself before you joined Codex."

My young successor. My heart broke—just slightly—at the reminder. And I wondered if I'd ever be able to think about that night without the deluge of guilt, regret, and utter sadness.

"I...had no idea," I said.

"He was a mastermind. The access I gave Bernard when

349

he'd come to visit the museum was extraordinary. He could have walked out of here with any number of things. I shudder now to think of how easily he manipulated me."

Delilah was staring at me with wide eyes.

"In my experience," Francisco said, "half the people in this room would do what Bernard did if they had the time and resources. Human beings are a covetous lot. Men like Bernard make a living out of fooling people."

"So do women like Victoria," Delilah added.

He took a step back at that. "Yes, well, now I need to live with my decisions. Because Victoria Whitney was given the same kind of access to that manuscript."

"Bernard will turn up," Abe said firmly. "And when he does, he will go to prison for a very long time."

"And in the meantime, Codex has restored a tiny amount of justice. We have world-renowned astronomers here this evening who have told me this book is the reason why they became interested in our galaxy. School children will be here later this month for private viewings, to learn about the power of the brightest star in our sky." He bade us farewell after that.

And as we walked down the stairs toward the curb, there was nothing I wanted more than to hold Delilah's hand.

"Freya and I will be in the office tomorrow," Abe said. "Come in if you'd like. If not, take a well-deserved day off."

Freya gave Delilah a hug and clapped me on the shoulder. "See you on Monday?" Her gaze was quizzical, like she was puzzling something out. And when she looked back at Delilah, there was resignation there.

"Of course," I said. Delilah and I both said good night to Abe and Freya, and I was grateful when they decided to share a cab home.

As soon as the taillights disappeared into traffic, Delilah turned to me and said, "My former coworker Margaret found me tonight. She's bringing a lawsuit against Mark for manipulating her and lying to human resources to gain promotions."

"You're serious?"

Delilah nodded. "I told her I'd provide testimony. Public testimony."

She stepped into me, and I wrapped my arms around her, filled with relief that I could touch her, hold her, caress her. Filled with happiness that she was fighting back in a way that made her proud. "The world is lucky to have you, Delilah Barrett."

She lifted her head up, chin pressed to my chest. "Even Francisco was fooled by Bernard. You weren't the only one."

I knew she'd get it. "I think I can finally let it go."

"Working at Codex, you mean?" Her eyebrows knotted together.

"No," I said. "No, I want to work here. I mean that I've allowed Bernard to control me long enough. He was controlling me for ten years without my knowledge. I took this job because of him. I went after Victoria because of him. Maybe it's time I do this job for me."

A kind of peace came over her. "Take me home."

My arm was raised to hail a taxi before she even finished the sentence. I knew we needed to talk. I *knew* whatever we were about to embark on couldn't exist within our current reality.

But maybe we could have one more night.

51

HENRY

*D*elilah didn't seem to want to talk—not on the ride to my house, not when we walked through the door, not as she took my hand and led me slowly up the stairs to my bedroom. She kept the lights dim, allowing the glimmering moonlight to shine through the windows, painting my room silver. With her back toward me, she turned over her shoulder—allowing me a glimpse of that classical profile.

"Sit," she instructed.

I sat.

Back still toward me, she reached behind and untied the knot holding her dress up. The material parted away from her spine, curving like the bow of a cello, revealing her skin in a slow, sensuous tease. With refined grace, Delilah hooked her fingers into the sides of her dress and slid the material over her hips, a private striptease, just for me.

With a sly grin, she dropped the material to the floor. She was left in sheer panties and black stilettos. I could barely swallow—my cock was so hard I could feel it pressing against my zipper.

When she turned all the way around, I was presented with

an almost nude Delilah, shining with moonlight, eyes honest and face open. Whatever had happened between us, whatever had been holding her back—even slightly—had vanished. Delilah came to me like a vision, and as I curved my fingers up the back of her thighs, I could only stare up at her in wonder.

This woman had taken out half of Victoria's guards without batting an eye. Had stared down an armed psychopath with nary a tremor. Was about to fight back against the man who had tried to steal her bravery.

But he hadn't succeeded. If there was one thing I was learning, it was to never, ever underestimate Delilah Barrett.

She stroked her fingers through my hair, caressing each curl.

"Any man that doesn't realize your love is a privilege is a goddamn fool," I said before I could stop myself.

I felt her shudder. Then her fingers, tugging off my tie gently. "I trust you, Henry." She lifted my head.

"I trust you too."

Her eyes searched mine. "Tonight, I want you bare. No barriers. No Thornhills."

"I'm clean," I said against her belly.

"Me too. And protected." Her fingers caressed my cheeks.

"Take what you want," I rasped. "You can have it all."

Delilah nodded and dropped the tie into my palm. Closed my fingers around it. "Didn't you once tell me you'd tie me to your bed and fuck me for days?"

I was stripped of speech. My palms on the back of her thighs slid up to her ass—yanked her hard into my body. She smirked.

"You want me to tie your beautiful wrists to this bed?" I asked in a rough voice.

"Please." In her eyes was an alluring combination of challenge and submission—and I was the luckiest man alive to tie this goddess to my bed. My head was between her legs, mouth covering her mound, tongue gliding along her slit through the wet fabric.

"Why do you smell so fucking good." It was no question—more a curse, an acceptance. I growled against her clit, gripping her waist, holding her still for my worship. I plucked the sides of her panties between my fingers and dragged the silky fabric down her thighs, exposing the glistening lips of her pussy. I licked my tongue inside her cunt.

"Oh, yes," she crooned. I explored deeper stroking my tongue until her legs shook. I scooped her up and threw her back onto the bed with more force than I meant, but she only spread her legs wide for me.

My belt hit the floor with a *thwap*. Then my pants, my vest. Down slid my white shirt—every item of clothing came off until I was naked and fisting myself in front of Delilah's hungry eyes.

I dropped to the bed and prowled up her body with deliberate intent. She backed all the way up and presented her wrists with an innocence I found wickedly deceitful. I took her panties, bound them around her wrists, secured the material to the bars on the bed.

"Okay?" I whispered against her lips.

"Perfect," she assured me.

I wrenched her knees open, pressing them as wide as they could go. "I'm going to fuck you until you know, beyond a shadow of a doubt, that you are mine."

I dragged the head of my dick through her folds, right against her clit—sliding, grinding, applying the right amount of pressure to have her head thrown back in submission. I palmed both of her breasts, rolling her nipples as she squirmed.

"Mine," I said.

I gripped her waist, lifted the entirety of her lower body off the bed. Wrapped her legs around my head and fluttered my tongue against her clit.

"Mine."

Suspended in the air, Delilah let out a series of wails that increased in volume as I lavished her clit with my tongue—bringing her right up to the edge before stopping.

I dropped her back to the bed. Kissed up every single inch of her body, from her ankles to her mouth, an exploration of details I didn't want to miss—details I couldn't believe I hadn't focused on before: the splash of freckles on her belly, the curve of her ribcage, the rounded softness of her shoulders, the rippling strength of her thighs. Fingers, tongue, lips, teeth —I cataloged this woman's body with the devotion of a scholar.

And by the time I reached her mouth, she was gasping with pleasure.

I entered her body with shallow strokes, gliding both hands to entwine with hers on the headboard. My hips moved between her legs with a luxury born of understanding—that we could have all the time in the world to discover the depths of our feelings.

Because in that moment, sharing a breath, hearts beating as one, I knew what I had to do tomorrow. Knew it and embraced it.

I gave her a kiss that had us both gasping, groaning when her heels dug into the small of my back with each thrust. She was softly chanting *"yours, yours, yours"* as I used my teeth to mark the spot between her throat and her shoulder, uniting us with the same sweet bite. Her chants became cries and her cries became loud, keening moans. Her internal muscles were squeezing my cock so tightly I knew she was close. Keeping one hand with hers, I let my other hand land on her clit, massaging her in tight circles as my thrusts grew frenzied, wild, out of control. The headboard smacked against the wall, the bed shook, and I poured every piece of myself into this moment, this time, this glimpse at paradise.

Delilah and I climaxed together, in a kind of erotic harmony I'd never experienced before in my life. I pressed our mouths together as I rode out our dual orgasms. When the aftershocks had finally abated—when we were nothing but a panting, sweating, tangled mess of limbs—I untied her bound wrists. Pulled her into my body, needing her as close as she could be. Her blue-green eyes shone in the darkness.

"We need to talk," I said.

"Mhmmm," she hummed, clinging to my chest.

I grinned against her neck, fully understanding the permanent shift that had occurred between us. The fact that I'd even briefly entertained the notion that Delilah and I could work together at Codex—and also have a romantic relationship—was ludicrous. They couldn't coexist.

I'd made a living out of cataloging the tiniest of details in the oldest of books—appreciating each mistake and flaw, each poetic line and brilliant page, because that was what told the story. Love could be expressed through these tiny details, through gestures, through actions.

It told the story. It *was* the story. I recognized the massive poignancy of Abe, bringing his staff donuts because he struggled to say *well done*. Of Freya, staying up all night, bringing Delilah tacos so she wouldn't get hungry on stakeouts. Francisco, admitting he'd been fooled by Bernard as easily as I: friendship, trust, connection.

I was falling in love with the woman I held in my arms. And I needed a way to show her.

"Delilah?" I whispered. She was snoring softly, already asleep.

Which was fine—she'd only try and talk me out of it anyway.

I slept deeply that night, Delilah wrapped around me, the sweet feel of her skin sliding against mine as she shifted and dreamed. When I woke, my decision felt hard—but also easy. Relieved, I turned over in the bed. Only to find it empty.

Delilah was gone.

52

DELILAH

*A*be glanced up from his computer with a look of concern. Freya had given me a comforting smile when I'd come in, noting the piece of paper in my hand. But I wasn't nervous or scared. Unlike that day two years ago, I wasn't walking into a room with a man who had manipulated me to do his bidding.

I was making my own decision. And I trusted how this story was going to end.

"I didn't expect to see you this morning," he said. "Especially so early."

I clicked his door shut. Sat primly in the chair across from his desk.

"I need to talk to you."

Brow furrowed, he sat up straighter. "Go ahead."

I searched my body for signs of uncertainty but found none. "When you hired Henry, I figured he'd be a research assistant, hidden away in an office somewhere. I didn't think he could do fieldwork. I *definitely* didn't think he could go undercover. And when we became partners, I was certain we were doomed."

Abe was silent, watching me with wary eyes.

"I know all of that to be untrue now. Henry Finch is a brilliant detective who took to undercover work like a natural. You won't find a lot of people like him. Or anyone, to be exact. I believe him to be one of a kind."

I placed the sheet of paper down on the desk.

"That night at Victoria's mansion, I instigated us going against your direct orders," I said, comfortable with the half-lie. Henry might have initially suggested it, but I hadn't stopped it. "I was the veteran, technically in charge, and I pushed us into a situation that was dangerous and out of control. I put Codex at risk and Henry at risk."

I slid the paper, faceup, toward him.

"For your consideration," I continued, "here is my letter of resignation from Codex. Effective immediately."

"Are you firing yourself?" His face was cold.

"I believe Henry is level-headed, calm, and can charm anyone in a room. He's a better fit here."

"All of those words are words I would use to describe you as well."

"Thank you," I said, chest starting to pinch. I hadn't fully allowed myself to imagine going about my days without seeing Abe and Freya. It almost threw me off course, but I soldiered on. "This job has been the best two years of my professional life. After what happened, I thought I'd never love a job again, believe in myself again. But you took a chance on me and gave me an opportunity I will always be grateful for. You taught me that the book is always the most important. Here, at Codex, Henry is the most important."

Abe picked up my letter and gave it a cursory glance. One eyebrow lifted, like the sight of it was personally offensive. "You still haven't told me why you believe you and Henry cannot work here, together."

"Because I have feelings for Henry," I blurted. "Romantic feelings." I clutched at the armchair, steadying myself. "I'm falling in love with Henry and I refuse to hide it. But I highly doubt you would approve of two of your employees dating, especially after your experiences in the FBI. That means, in order for Henry and me to be together, one of us can't be at Codex."

After a long, painful silence, he put the paper down onto his desk. "I see. You are sacrificing yourself for Henry?"

I exhaled, the answer filling me with complete and total happiness. "It's no sacrifice."

That had his eyes locking on mine in disbelief. He knew how much I craved this job.

"Do you...accept my resignation?"

"I have a phone call in one minute," he said brusquely. "I will be in touch with you later today." He turned back toward his computer, but I could see the muscles of his throat working.

"Oh," I said, standing up awkwardly. "Well, okay."

Abe didn't respond. So I stood and opened his door—regardless of what he said, at least I could walk out of here with steady legs and a clear conscience. The first thing I saw was Freya, staring wide-eyed at me like I'd suddenly grown a pair of wings and a horn. She was trying very hard not to laugh.

"What is it?" I said.

And that's when I saw Henry. He was dressed sharply in a navy-blue suit, yellow tie, glasses. And he was holding a piece of paper that looked suspiciously like my own.

Abe walked out. Saw Henry, staring at me. Freya, staring at us both. And the paper in Henry's hand.

"Oh, for fuck's sake," Abe sighed wearily. "What's in your hand, Henry?"

I could see Henry attempt to puzzle out the bizarre scene unfolding before him. "I'd really rather talk to you in your..."

"What is it?" Abe repeated.

"My resignation letter." Abe was standing between us, but our eyes were locked together.

My jaw dropped.

That was why Freya seemed like she was about to lose her shit.

"Am I being pranked?" Abe said this in a deadly, quiet tone.

"*What?*" Henry asked.

I leaned my back against the wall, trying to rein in my thoughts.

Abe glowered back and forth between the two of us. "Well? Am I?"

"Why would I prank you by resigning?" I asked. When Henry heard the words, his expression mirrored my own.

Abe pinched the bridge of his nose, muttering something beneath his breath. "Get in here," he barked.

I exchanged a crazed glance with Freya, who shrugged and mouthed *What do we do?*

But then Abe was slamming the door behind me.

"Sit. Both of you."

He picked up Henry's letter of resignation, picked up mine. Scanned them both quickly. I didn't dare look at Henry. Abe placed them down on the desk gingerly, like he was worried they'd shatter.

"Tell me why you think you need to resign, Henry," Abe said.

"I purposefully withheld information from you and Freya, the night of the party. I knew—or thought I knew—about the secret hallways and recognized that by bringing them to Delilah's attention, we'd likely go against your orders. Which I pushed her to do so, fairly emphatically. I believe all of those behaviors indicate that I'm not a fit, moving forward." Henry took a shaky breath. "As much as I'd love to stay."

Abe tap-tap-tapped his index finger on the letter. "And is there any other reason?"

Henry cleared his throat. "Yes, there is. The other reason is because of my feelings for Delilah."

I turned fully in my chair, chest rising and falling with rapid breaths. *Henry.*

Abe's nostrils flared with annoyance. He rapped his knuckles on the desk.

"And why you, and not her?" he asked.

"Because she's the most talented detective you've ever worked with," Henry said, as if it was blatantly obvious.

Another sharp *rap*.

"Did you plan this?"

"No," I promised. "I didn't tell him because I assumed he'd talk me out of it."

Henry's lips lifted into a smile. "I assumed the same."

And thankfully Henry didn't say what would have naturally come next: *I woke up this morning after a night of passionate sex and you were missing from my bed.*

Abe steepled his fingers together and leaned back in his chair, as if he was our tribunal. "Two of my talented agents are willing to leave their jobs because of your commitment both to each other but also to *Codex.*"

It was a statement, but Henry and I nodded just the same.

Abe was quiet again.

"I'm not sure what the issue is," I said. "I resigned first. Accept it. You, Henry and Freya will hire another detective."

"Don't do th—" Henry started.

Abe held up his palm and Henry stopped.

"What's interesting," Abe began cautiously, "is that the

mutual trust and respect you have for each other—plus your complementary skill sets—is one of the reasons why you make such great partners. If this hadn't come up, I would have paired you up again by the next case."

I felt an unexpected *thrill* at those words—to do this, I had to forcibly ignore how much I'd enjoyed working with Henry; that in the best of both worlds, we could be together *and* hunt down book thieves at the exact same time.

There was another long, excruciating pause. What was he *waiting* for?

"But even though that might be true, I still believe romantic entanglements are a dangerous distraction, and if the two of you are to continue working here, it is not something I take lightly."

"I'm sorry," Henry said. "What did you say?"

Abe picked up our letters, stacked them together. And tore them clean in half.

He looked down at the floor. "The fact that you were both willing to sacrifice your job for the other tells me that this relationship is very real." He appeared painfully awkward as he scooped the pieces of our letters into the trashcan. "But you'll be prohibited from working cases together until I can trust the two of you. Is that clear?"

I considered Henry—whose eyes were wide behind his glasses. When the words finally, truly, sunk in, the smile that spread across his face was magnificent.

"I also won't hesitate to ban eye contact between the two of you."

"Yes, sir," I said quickly.

"I'll never look at her again," Henry agreed.

"Moving forward," Abe said, "we need to be honest with each other. There will be no more chances."

Henry and I were nodding so vigorously I worried we'd fall off our chairs.

Abe let us stew for a minute longer...and then the ends of his lips curved up in an *almost*-smile. "We might as well have a staff meeting if we're all in." He opened the door. "Freya, get in here."

She strode in, fixing her bun with a pen between her teeth. "I'm guessing...we're a team of four again?"

"Yes," Abe said.

Freya arched an eyebrow at me, and I actually blushed.

"Well, good," she grinned. "I'd hate to see Henry go. It's nice to have another Ravenclaw on staff. And four is the perfect number to catch thieves."

"Speaking of," Abe said, "I have updates on Victoria."

And just like that, the universe balanced, my world righted, my mind was clear, and my heart was true. Henry. Me and *Henry*. Not only together but also *still here* at Codex. The feeling was momentous enough to have me giving Henry the *tiniest* smile—a smile brimming over with joy and hope and all that was good on this earth.

I leaned forward in my seat toward Abe, content to know my love for Henry was now out in the open for all to see.

"The FBI completed their interviews with her, and our kooky heiress sang like a canary."

"Smart move," I said, shaking my head. "Although I'm sure it must have hurt her ego to admit she wasn't the highest up on whatever chain of command exists in that world."

Abe was flipping through his files. "And no word from Victoria on Bernard."

"She didn't give up his whereabouts?" Henry asked. "She has to know where he is."

I felt a strange warmth in the center of my chest. Because I knew why not.

"She's in love with him still," I said, recalling our conversation in the cloisters.

"Interesting," he said. He slid a photo our way. "Victoria gave up Alistair."

"The man from the auction house?" I asked.

"Bernard's intern." Henry picked up the picture and rubbed his jaw. "Did Alistair give anyone up?"

"He's still in the process of being sentenced, but it's not looking likely." Abe tapped his fingers together. "This comes from my FBI contact and isn't public knowledge, so don't repeat it. Victoria paid Alistair a fantastical sum of money to steal it for her, relying on the access she could give him to the manuscript as the board president. The plan all along was for her to move it to her beach house in Santa Barbara, which holds a special significance to her because that's where her mother was born."

"So she wasn't going to, like, sell it to another collector? She stole it for herself?" Freya asked.

"For her mother," I said softly. "She stole it to feel closer to her mother."

Victoria Whitney was a wildly complicated philanthropist, a charming egomaniac, and a thief that believed she existed above all law. She was all those things—and probably more. Victoria *was* the gray area.

And I was okay with that.

"According to Alistair, they were supposed to move it the night *before* the party, but there was some massive bungling and it was delayed by twenty-four hours."

"Good thing or we'd never have gotten it," I said. "What about the guards?"

"There was trouble in paradise between the Victoria and Alistair partnership from the very beginning. I'm not sure the trust was ever really there, although money can certainly fake that. Alistair hired those guards for Victoria, I'm assuming because he recognized that her ego might get her in trouble, therefore possibly getting *him* in trouble."

"Which it did," Freya added.

"Victoria's very famous lawyer is working on a plea bargain. House arrest and a fine. According to Francisco, she's telling anyone who will listen that the Copernicus was 'just a bit of fun' and she didn't realize how serious it was."

I shook my head in disbelief, laughing a little at Victoria's sheer lunacy. Of *course* Victoria Whitney could get away with something like this—and probably come out of it smelling like a rose. "She'll do it again," I finally said. "I wouldn't be surprised if we bump into our kooky heiress a year from now at the auction house."

"A person like Victoria continues to believe she's above the law even while in prison," Freya said. "Whatever she takes again, we'll get it back."

"Where does someone like Bernard fit into this? Or Codex?" Henry asked.

Abe seemed thoughtful. "I still believe that what we're starting to see is an organization, or a ladder or a pyramid or some kind of cohesive group that is orchestrating these larger, more skillful thefts of rare books and antiques," he said. "With one person at the top, pulling all of the strings."

"Bernard?" Henry asked.

"Maybe he works closely with that person. Or maybe he *is* that person. The majority of our casework will still be going after quick, poorly planned thefts that are more sudden opportunities than well-planned heists. But an organized attack makes our job a lot harder. They can hide the books faster and better than what we've been seeing."

"It also makes our job more exciting," I said, feeling that

old, familiar *thrum* in my veins. Adrenaline, the hunt, justice... all of it making me feel completely alive.

After a minute, all three of my coworkers responded in kind.

"Also true," Abe smirked. "It's never boring, that's for sure."

"What happens next?" Henry asked.

"Easy," I said. "We wait for the next book to be stolen. And we get it back."

53

HENRY

I'd barely finished ringing her doorbell before Delilah was pulling it open and leaping into my arms, legs around my waist and face pressed to mine. I dropped the bouquet of lavender I'd brought her and held her tight, mouth in her hair. Time slowed to an ethereal crawl, and then I was kissing Delilah with a dizzying freedom; let our mouths meet in breathless wonder. It was a kiss of sweet new beginnings, of ardent passion. It felt like reading the first chapter of a book you already knew you loved.

"You resigned for me," she said, our lips still connected.

"You resigned for *me*."

I slowly set her down, stepped back to fully take in my warrior. It was an unusually warm spring night, and she was dressed in a pair of ripped, worn jeans and a white tank-top—barefoot, but still adorned with red lipstick. I brushed a strand of hair from her forehead, smiling as she took in my similar outfit. We'd shed our barriers; we weren't dressed up like undercover agents, or in office wear like private detectives. And we most certainly weren't the Thornhills.

We were just us.

"Not kissing you today was the hardest thing I've ever done in my entire life," I said.

"I think you'll have to get used to it," she grinned, biting her lower lip. "But after Abe told us we could keep our jobs, I almost dragged you into my office to have my way with you."

"I would have liked that very much," I admitted.

She gave me a playful kiss in response—but we both knew how important it was to guard Abe's trust right now. Especially since it appeared that we'd both be working at Codex for a long time. But as we'd left the office, I'd grabbed her hand, kissed her wrist, and asked her on our first date. And she'd told me to come here.

"I set something up for you, for our date," she said, almost shy.

I remembered the crushed lavender and scooped it from the ground, presenting it to her with a flourish.

Delilah inhaled the purple petals. "My favorite scent. How did you know?" she asked.

"I notice a lot of things about you, beautiful," I replied.

She took my hand at that, leading me up the narrow stairs inside her row home. My first recognition was *green*. Delilah lived in a veritable greenhouse, with house plants and succulents springing from every surface and shelf.

"Delilah, your house is—"

She turned around, squeezed my hand.

"It's gorgeous."

"It makes me feel less homesick," she said. We passed her kitchen, her living room, and were climbing the third story to her loft-style bedroom, which had the same abundance of plant life. "One of the first weekends I moved back here, my dads and my siblings helped me do this. Spent the weekend making my city house look more like our favorite woods."

I spied a framed picture on the wall— her dads, smiling on

their wedding day. They wore matching suits and the kind of obvious love I recognized on the faces of my parents, my grandparents.

Delilah.

Next to it was Delilah and two other people, arms around each other and laughing at a lake surrounded by trees. "Elizabeth and Max," she said, "my brother and sister. We spent every day at this lake during the summer until we were sun-drunk and exhausted and the fireflies had come out."

And next to that, a picture of her dads laughing as they held a smiling baby. "Is that you?"

"That's the day I was adopted." Delilah touched the frame lovingly.

There was a punching bag in the corner of her room, hot-pink boxing gloves laying over a chair, and a spiral staircase in the far corner. "Come on up to the roof."

I followed this woman—my partner, my fake wife, this brave and courageous woman who I would protect at any cost. Delilah was the strongest woman I'd ever met—charging down dark hallways unafraid of what lurked in the corners, only understanding the human desire to *keep going.*

When we surfaced, it was onto a rooftop garden. Small, but packed with plants and flowering vines and even a tiny tree, growing from a barrel. Delilah had hung string lights from one side to the other, and a small speaker played Etta James. I cocked my head, smile widening when I took in the make-shift dance floor she'd created.

"Delilah Barrett," I started.

She was standing there, barefoot and beautiful, beckoning me forward. The night air was warm and perfumed with plants, and she was very much at home against a backdrop of leaves.

"I kept thinking about what you said, the night at the

museum," she said. I clasped her to me, cradled her hand at my chest, and our bodies began to sway naturally in time with the languid music. "About your grandparents being devoted to each other, still dancing. About the Thornhills and the romance of a slow dance in their kitchen. I know it's not the most exciting first date, but I figured we've had our fair share of excitement." She smiled ruefully. "For a few days, at least."

"I'd like to be the man that wants to dance with you every night," I said, remembering her admission that none of her romantic partners had ever wanted to in the past.

"I'd like that very, very much." Delilah ghosted our lips together, staring up at me with wide blue eyes. We swayed like that, content in our silence, our toes brushing together on the dance floor.

"I can't believe you were going to resign for me," I said. "Even after everything with—"

But she shook her head. "It's like you said yesterday morning—Mark can't take anything from me any longer. And my choices and decisions are free to be mine and mine alone. I wasn't scared at all. I didn't know what would come next or where I would work but isn't that what love is? Excited for whatever comes next?"

"Love?" I whispered. I needed to make sure I heard her correctly.

Delilah kissed me then said, "I love you, Henry Finch. If there had been a hundred guards in that mansion, I would have taken each one of them down to protect you. And if we *hadn't* found the Copernicus there, I would have begged Abe to send me out again and again until I found it for you. When I woke up this morning, there was no room for doubt in my heart, only elation."

The book we'd spent weeks chasing down had only existed because a scientist had stared up into the heart of the big, brilliant Milky Way and wondered if all the theories he'd once held true about the sun were false. Delilah dazzled like the sun now—pulling me toward her brazen trust, her beautiful faith in who we would become. Together.

"I love you, Delilah Barrett." My voice was rough with emotion. "And I want to be clear about my intentions before we go on our first *real* date." She kissed my fingers. "I want to court you. I want to take you on *real* dates, starting with tonight." I tucked a wild, raven curl behind her ear. "I want to meet your dads and learn how to climb trees in the woods where you grew up. I want you to come to Sabrina's Cafe for Sunday brunch with my siblings and argue with my parents about philosophy."

Delilah radiated a quiet joy.

"I want to shower you with gifts and surprise you with holidays and fall asleep in the warm grass on a summer's day with you. Because of all the things I have seen in this life—the paintings, the manuscripts, the gilded edges, the rare drawings and ancient tomes and crumbling ruins—*all of it*, all of it, dims before the light of *you*, Delilah."

We danced like that—beneath city stars and twinkle lights —for the rest of the night, content to hold each other, to laugh, to kiss, to make plans for our next adventure, to embrace our future as partners, in every single way.

I understood, then, the parallel narratives of our lives becoming one story—the wings of our destiny open like a book without a written ending. The joy of that, the mystery, the sorrow, the surprise—the hundreds of thousands of words that would grow between us over the years. It could never be stolen, only recovered, cherished, adored.

It was our love story, the rarest of books, meant to be read over and over and over.

EPILOGUE

DELILAH

One year later

*E*verybody loved a married couple.

And tonight was no exception.

The Walt Whitman Bridge had been cleared of cars, walled off and dressed with tables and barstools for Philadelphia's annual *Bridge To The Stars* dinner. Henry and I were perched on stools facing a dazzling skyline, sipping martinis as a jazz band set the mood.

Thieves were everywhere. I could *feel* it.

The *Bridge* dinner raised funds for Philadelphia's Archaeological Society—a cause which antiquarian lovers and rare-book collectors tended to flock to. Our source had directed us here, said they'd be all too happy to cut a deal involving something tiny and gorgeous they'd recently come into. *Legally*, they were sure to clarify.

Codex knew that to be highly inaccurate. It was a third edition of Lewis Carrol's *Alice's Adventures in Wonderland*, and a trio of thieves had stolen it from the Central Park Rare Manuscript Library just last week.

Bring one hundred grand in a paper bag tonight and it's yours were the instructions that Freya had received. Abe had smirked, sensing an easy win and a *lot* of cash. Because it meant the trio of thieves were more likely opportunistic college students who had seen *Ocean's Eleven* one too many times.

And after a night of dancing and drinks as the Thornhills, we'd finally snagged our guy.

And he was, clearly, a college student in his early twenties named Carl.

"So how often do you visit Reichenbach Falls, Carl?" I asked, sipping my drink.

Henry was stroking his fingers in a circular pattern around my knee.

"Oh, uh...all the fucking time," Carl drawled. He looked briefly flustered, but then recovered. "Basically every day."

"Interesting," Henry said. His thumb roamed the back of my thigh. "My wife and I don't visit as much as you, but we're always happy to meet fellow travelers."

"Oh, that's right, you're married," Carl said—although he said *married* as one might say *aliens from outer space*. "Gnarly."

Henry chuckled into his drink, and it wasn't feigned at all. "That's what I said during our vows."

Carl narrowed his eyes, as if trying to figure out if we were making fun of him. But then he grinned, flagged down another beer. I covertly checked Henry's watch and knew Dorran was probably waiting for us.

"Speaking of," I said, leaning in close, "we have to leave in a few minutes. Was there something you wanted to show us?"

"Yeah." He slid his hands into his pockets, rocking back on

his heels. "Lemme go get it. Meet me on the other side of the bridge?"

We both nodded, and I breathed a sigh of relief when he wandered off. Henry went back to slipping his fingers beneath my skirt.

"Dirty husband, Mr. Thornhill," I said, eyes on his over my martini glass.

"Our orders were to convince everyone here that we're madly in love." He leaned in, parting my legs on the stool so his hand could slip higher. "I'm just doing my job."

I made sure I had one eye on our young, bumbling target, then purred a little as Henry's mouth teased at my ear. "Do you think we're convincing enough?"

"I'm not sure, wife," he rasped. "Maybe we could find a utility closet and make things more realistic?"

I laughed at that, and Henry pulled back with a charming grin and a wink. After the past year we'd all had at Codex, it was nice to have an easy case with few complications. And it had taken a while for Abe to put Henry and me on cases together—although he'd been right. The Thornhills moved easily in this world; between Henry's natural charm and our fake marriage, trust built quickly. We still operated in a tiny community of antiquities lovers, so we're constantly aware of keeping our story straight, of being recognized. But it appeared as if embarrassment had sealed Victoria's lips—we'd never been called out by any of her former friends.

It was safe to say that Henry and I never had a dull day at the office.

And our nights in bed were anything *but* dull.

"I think he's waiting for us," Henry said, seriously this time.

I straightened my spine, brushed a strand of hair behind my ear.

"Let's go get that book back," I said.

With our hands clasped, Henry led me through the crowd of Philadelphia high society and academics and philanthropists. As usual, various people openly admired my husband as we walked past, and I flashed them all a mysterious smile. It never ceased to amaze how deliriously happy it made me to declare Henry as *mine*.

Carl was standing all the way at the end, off on a side road full of patrons and valets milling around. I spotted Dorran parked nearby. He flashed his headlights just once. Henry squeezed my hand. Being so exposed would have been an issue for most of the book thieves we hunted down, but Carl was proving to be a special case indeed.

But I'd need to get him to do my bidding without causing a scene.

"I see it now," he said, shifting back and forth on his feet, "the married thing."

I glanced around, shocked that he wasn't more worried. "Is that it? Our Alice?"

He was holding a small lockbox with a devious smile. "Check this shit out."

The box popped open and I allowed Henry the honor of peering in first. I knew, now, when my husband was staring at a book—his expression was always filled with wonder.

"There she is," Henry said softly. He flicked his eyes up at me, gave a nod.

"Carl," I said, directing his attention to me, "we are very pleased with what you've brought us."

Henry was gripping the box, prepared to bolt with it if need be. Carl seemed vaguely distracted by that, brow furrowed. But then he stared at me when I reached into my purse. I pulled out a brown paper bag stuffed with blank slips of white paper. His eyes boggled as I handed it over.

"Now I don't want to get you into too much trouble." I dropped my voice. "But Henry and I are going to take this book now. *Illegally*," I clarified.

Carl cursed as the white slips of paper flew up in the air. He went to yank the box back. But Henry moved swiftly, leaving me room to step in between. Carl's hands shot up in my direction, but I caught them easily, adding force to a pressure point at his wrist that had him wincing in pain.

"Don't come at my husband," I warned. "Or I will flag down the two police officers right over there who are strolling toward us. I'm sure they'd love to learn how you and two accomplices stole this book from the Central Park Library."

He scrubbed a hand down his reddening face. "What the *fuck*?"

Henry closed the box. "Let's go. Carl, it's been swell. Darling?"

He extended his arm and I took it.

Carl took another step toward us.

"Now what did I just say?" I crushed my heel into his toe. He yelped, bent over, and I took that as our cue to leave as discreetly as possible.

My long skirt dragged on the ground behind me as we strode confidently toward the limo, book in hand. Once in the limo, I texted Freya the good news, and she sent back a string of silly messages in response. And I called Abe but left a voicemail. Something that had been happening more recently—he was no longer working as late, and no longer as available, in the best way possible.

Everything had been changing at Codex—all of us were happier than ever.

"Well done, wife," Henry said.

I crossed my legs, winked flirtatiously. "Same to you."

"I've brought my earplugs tonight, Ms. Barrett," Dorran

called through the privacy glass. Henry laughed as I blushed, slapping a hand over my mouth.

"That's not necessary," Henry said through the window. "But thank you for letting us know."

Dorran knew there was *one specific thing* my husband and I liked to do after we closed an exciting case. And as the limo neared our row home in Rittenhouse Square, I was already breathless with anticipation, dizzy with longing. We were completely silent as we crept through the narrow streets. Henry held my gaze with his dark, teasing one, slowly palming his hardening cock through his suit pants.

Fuck, I mouthed. His expression told me it was just what he had in mind. With a dominant grin, he waved his finger through the air.

Open, he mouthed back.

I bit my lip. Lifted my skirt just like I'd done a year ago, as we'd been speeding toward Victoria's mansion. I kept lifting until I was exposed to him. Another flick of his finger and I spread my legs obediently.

His nostrils flared, palm moving more quickly. I cupped my breasts through my dress, arching a little when my nipples hardened.

Henry could only shake his head at me. And as the limo rolled to a stop, he caught my wrist and yanked me forward.

"You are exquisite." And then he kissed my cheek.

Cherished and debauched. Filth and tenderness. That was my husband. It never changed between the two of us—this adrenaline-fueled electricity that spurned on some of the hottest sex I'd ever had in my life. Made only more beautiful by our *love*.

We bade farewell to Dorran, and Henry cradled the recovered book as I led us inside. We'd moved in here barely a month ago; a historic, brick row home with as many stories embedded in the stones as there are stars in the sky. We filled it with books and flowers, novels and plants, and our kitchen was big enough for us to slow dance in it most nights. Framed on the walls were pictures of Henry with my dads, climbing trees with my siblings (not well, but very sincerely), trips I'd taken with Jeremiah and Joelle, lectures with Henry's parents. During one spur-of-the-moment trip, Henry had taken me to all of his favorite places in Europe, and we'd spent it on cobblestone streets, drunk on wine, kissing in bookstores.

In a single year, our love story was already shaping up to be quite the adventure.

Dimly, I heard Henry secure the book, but I was already waiting for him in our bedroom. Wall-to-wall bookshelves held his favorite novels, and fresh lavender grew in our windowsills. Henry was striding into the room; passion, lust, yearning, craving. He spun me around, lifting me up onto our table and stepping between my spread legs.

"Rings, please," he said, pressing an open-mouthed kiss to my neck. I held my left hand up, and just like every night, he slowly removed the gaudy ring with four diamonds. And I removed his thick gold band. They went in a small glass near the other ones. Behind it was a framed picture from our wedding day—Abe, Freya, our families, all were cheering wildly as they showered us with rose petals. Henry was smiling like he was positive he was the luckiest man alive. I was beaming in my white wedding dress, short veil. Red heels.

Behind us was the grand, awe-inspiring Long Room at the Trinity Library.

Only Abe and Freya knew the significance of the Trinity Library, the whimsical, spur-of-the-moment tale Henry and I had stumbled through for Victoria one year ago. It felt right to have it at a place that had brought us together—from fake elopement to real wedding. I'd *almost* sent a copy to Victoria but thought better of it.

Some books were better left closed.

With absolute reverence, Henry replaced my fake wedding ring with my real one—a rose-gold band with an opal. His wedding band was silver titanium. They fit us, the real us; two people whose ultimate trust in each other had paved the way for this very moment. Engraved on the inside of each ring was the phrase *thank you for catching me.*

The kiss Henry gave me promised a lot of things, and as I tightened my legs around his waist, he tilted my chin back. The only thing that existed in my world was Henry. The sun was the center of our universe, but Henry would always be the center of mine.

Henry gave me that slow, crooked smile that never ceased to make my toes curl.

"I love you, Delilah," he said, caressing my temple. "You are the only star in my sky."

"I love you," I repeated, pulling him close. "Now will you please make me the happiest woman on this earth and have your way with me in a utility closet somewhere? Preferably a crowded gala?"

That laugh—Henry's *laugh.* Every time I heard the sound, it imprinted on my heart.

"I'll do anything for you, wife." His kiss was sweet, then firm, and then he was biting my bottom lip. My sexy librarian husband. My partner, my soul mate, my *everything.*

Our love was rare and singularly beautiful—and all our own.

I was never letting go.

THE END

Don't you worry. The Codex Team will be back in 2020 when you get Freya and her Mystery Man's story.

#GetTheDamnBookBack

A NOTE FROM THE AUTHOR

Dear Reader,

What a journey this book has been. I first conceived of the idea of a team of professionals that hunt down stolen rare books back in early 2018 – back then Henry and Delilah were mere concepts, and I wasn't entirely sure what their world would look like. After more than nine months of research, writing, massive rewriting and months of intensive edits, BEHIND THE VEIL finally revealed itself in all its sexy, glamorous, mysterious glory.

When I was first thinking about Henry and Delilah, I'd written a short story for them for the KU Korner on Facebook. The first line had been "I was here for an extraction." I'd become obsessed with characters who were sent to infiltrate a world they didn't belong in to extract an object we wouldn't normally think of – not a rescue, not a kidnapping, not money or jewels. Books. *Rare* books.

And that was how the Codex team was born.

The research I did took me on a journey that was strange and bizarre. Unfortunately, theft of rare books is alive and well in the antiquity's community, and it is as hushed and underground as I convey in BEHIND THE VEIL. It truly is a world composed of secret handshakes and implicit trust, which is why these thefts are so devastating – they often are perpetrated by academics and researchers, professors and librarians. What piqued my interest was a news article in The Guardian about a wide-scale theft of rare books that had occurred in a hangar – the thieves had literally rappelled down from the ceiling, *Mission Impossible* style, and made off with $5 million in rare books. As soon as I'd read that article, I knew this was the world I wanted to create.

Henry and Delilah were originally an elusive pair – over the course of many, many drafts they shifted, changed, showed me hidden motivations and revealed their deepest vulnerabilities. Fake marriage is my favorite trope, and writing it against the backdrop of Philadelphia high society was so fun I never wanted it to end. Having recently moved back to my hometown, I loved setting this story in historic Old City in Philadelphia – a place filled with secrets and stories. As Victoria Whitney would say: "Secrets are what make life interesting, darling."

The Codex team will be back in 2020 with Freya's story, followed by Abe's. I can't wait to bring you along as they work together, eat Federal Donuts, fall in love and always, always, get the damn book back.

-Kathryn

ACKNOWLEDGMENTS

Like every book, BEHIND THE VEIL is a combination of the time, talents, passion and energy of many, many people in my life. No book is created in a vacuum and that is absolutely the case with this one.

To Faith, who played a major role in the reconstruction of this book right when I needed it. We worked and sweated and edited and brainstormed and slowly, slowly Henry and Delilah revealed themselves in their full glory. Thanks for being my best friend.

To Jodi and Julia, my incredible beta readers, who made sure every line, remark and detail matched up just right, which is vital for a book of romantic suspense. They found the flaws, the missing details, the tiny key-holes that needed extra information – all the building blocks that made the Codex world complete. I couldn't have done it without you!

To Joyce, Tammy, Bronwyn, Beth, Steph, Jessica, Lucy, Pippa, Claire, Mika and all the kind authors, friends and readers who listened to me flail around dramatically about the pitfalls of this book – and then cheered me on when I finally loved it. Thank you for your support – it is absolutely vital!

To the Hippie Chicks – you rock. Every last one of you! From cheerleading to spreading the word to reviewing and shouting about my books, everything you do is amazing and helps so much. Your positivity is a bright light in a community. Thank you.

To my pal and college-class-buddy Bob Jones – your private detective knowledge was everything I ever needed! Thank you thank you!

Finally, for Rob and Walter, my little adventurous family – I can't imagine going through this life without you by my side. Mostly because you know Walter hates when the pack gets split up. And also because I love you so much I can't stand it.

ABOUT KATHRYN

I'm an adventurous hippie chick that loves to write steamy romance. My specialty is slow-burn sexual tension with plenty of witty dialogue and tons of heart.

I started my writing career in elementary school, writing about *Star Wars* and *Harry Potter* and inventing love stories in my journals. And I blame my obsession with slow-burn on my similar obsession for The *X-Files*.

I'm a born-and-raised Philly girl, but left for Northern California right after college, where I met my adorably-bearded husband. After living there for eight years, we decided to embark on an epic, six-month road trip, traveling across the country with our little van, Van Morrison. Eighteen states and 17,000 miles later, we're back in my hometown of Philadelphia for a bit... but I know the next adventure is just around the corner.

When I'm not spending the (early) mornings writing steamy love scenes with a strong cup of coffee, you can find me outdoors -- hiking, camping, traveling, yoga-ing.

HANG OUT WITH KATHRYN!

Sign up for my newsletter and receive exclusive content, bonus scenes and more!
I've got a reader group on Facebook called **Kathryn Nolan's Hippie Chicks**. We're all about motivation, girl power, sexy short stories and empowerment! Come join us.

Let's be friends on
Website: authorkathrynnolan.com
Instagram at: kathrynnolanromance
Facebook at: KatNolanRomance
Follow me on BookBub
Follow me on Amazon

BOOKS BY KATHRYN

BOHEMIAN

LANDSLIDE

RIPTIDE

STRICTLY PROFESSIONAL

SEXY SHORTS

BEHIND THE VEIL

Made in the USA
San Bernardino, CA
10 August 2020

76839297R00244